BACKSTREET CHILD

Also by Harry Bowling

The Girl From Cotton Lane
Gaslight In Page Street
Paragon Place
Ironmonger's Daughter
Tuppence To Tooley Street
Conner Street's War

BACKSTREET CHILD

Harry Bowling

LONDON   NEW YORK   SYDNEY   TORONTO

This edition published 1993
by BCA
by arrangement with Headline Books Ltd.

CN 3424

Printed in England by Clays Ltd, St Ives plc

To my brother Ron,
in loving memory.

1938 – 9

Chapter One

Rain had been falling heavily all day, but as darkness set in, it finally ceased. In the empty Bermondsey backstreet the rain-sodden brickwork of the little houses glistened in the flickering light of the two gaslights, and overhead, pungent smoke from coke fires poured out of rickety chimneys towards the night sky. Rainwater ran along the gullies and down the drains with a gurgling, sucking noise, carrying with it soot and industrial dirt from the cobblestoned roadway.

In the chill night air of the deserted street two middle-aged men walked along together, their hands thrust deep into their trouser pockets. They were of the same height, though one walked with a pronounced stoop and a rolling motion of his shoulders, betraying the fact that he had spent some time in the boxing ring. His companion walked straight-backed, his cap pulled down over his forehead and his red neckerchief tied loosely round his throat. They remained silent as they rounded the elbow of Page Street and caught sight of the light from the Kings Arms public house up ahead. At the bend stood a derelict yard, its entrance barred by high wooden gates that were peeling paint, sealed with a rusting padlock. Above the heavy gates was an arched signboard which had once announced in gold lettering that George Galloway & Sons, Cartage Contractors, operated from the premises. The words had been painted over when the firm moved to a larger site and a rag sorter moved in, but he too had gone, and now the yard was left to the mice and rats.

The straight-backed man glanced quickly at the first house on his right as they turned the corner. It was the house where he had been born, where he had grown up, until his family were forced out and had ended up stuck in the notorious Bacon Buildings nearby.

The two rows of little houses, all with their front doors bolted against the night, led up towards the corner pub and the Jamaica Road, and as the two men walked along to the end of the turning, a lone tram rattled by, shattering the quietness of the night.

Sounds from the bar piano reached the men's ears, and as they entered they were greeted by the florid-faced, heavily built landlord Alec Crossley, who stood with his arms folded and his bulk pressing against the counter.

3

'What'll it be, gents?' he asked.

Before they could answer him an elderly man staggered up to the new arrivals and pushed between them, looking up at the round-shouldered one.

'Bloody 'ell, if it ain't young Billy Sullivan,' he slurred. ' 'Ow's the ole man? I ain't seen 'ide nor 'air of 'im since 'e left the docks.'

Alec leaned forward over the counter and glared at the inebriate. 'Now I told yer before ter sit down an' be'ave yerself, Nobby,' he scolded him. 'I ain't gonna tell yer again. I can't 'ave yer annoyin' me customers. If yer don't sit down I'll chuck yer out meself. Is that understood?'

The elderly drunk grinned lopsidedly at Billy, ignoring the landlord. 'It's that silly ole mare Axford. That's who's upset 'im,' he explained, jerking his thumb in Alec's direction. 'I wouldn't care, I was only jokin' wi' the scatty cow. I dunno why 'e wantsa get so upset.'

Alec prodded the elderly man's bony shoulder. 'This is the last time I'm gonna tell yer, Nobby. Sit down an' be'ave yerself,' he growled.

'All right, all right,' the ex-docker growled back. 'I only 'ope the new lan'lord is a bit more cheerful than you, yer miserable ole sod.'

The angry pub owner raised his eyes to the ceiling and watched as the old man returned unsteadily to his seat in a corner, then he turned to the two men. ' 'E 'ad the cheek to ask ole Florrie Axford of all people what colour drawers she was wearin',' he said, shaking his head and hiding a grin. 'If it wasn't fer Maisie grabbin' 'old of 'er, Florrie would 'ave floored 'im − old as she is. Anyway, the first drink's on the 'ouse ternight. What's yer pleasure, lads?'

Billy Sullivan grinned at his companion and leaned an elbow on the polished counter. 'I'll 'ave a mild an' bitter, Alec,' he replied.

The landlord turned to the straight-backed man. 'What's yours, Danny?'

'I'll 'ave the same,' Danny Tanner told him, pushing his cap onto the back of his head and revealing a mop of fair wavy hair.

While he was pulling down on the beer pump, Alec Crossley cast his eyes around the bar. There were the usual familiar faces, folk he had come to know very well over the years, and there were one or two strangers as well. Barflies, he thought. The sort who had heard that the pub was changing hands and had come along partly out of curiosity, and partly to see if there were any free drinks going. Well, they had been unlucky. Free drinks were for the likes of Danny Tanner and Billy Sullivan, men who had patronised the pub since they were young striplings.

The portly landlord passed over the two pints with a wide grin. It did not seem all that long ago that the two men had stood there at the counter looking smart and proud in their army uniforms before they went off to the bloody fighting in France. How quickly the years had rolled by, Alec thought with a sudden twinge of sadness. Now it looked as though history was going to repeat itself. Another war was looming, he felt sure, despite the views of certain politicians and some newspaper editors.

The two younger men picked up the frothing pints and raised them to the landlord in salute.

'Well, 'ere's ter you an' yer missus, Alec,' Danny said with a smile. 'May yer retirement be an 'appy one.'

'I'll drink ter that,' Billy said, taking a large gulp and rubbing the back of his hand across his lips. 'I bet yet yer gonna miss this place.'

Alec shook his head. 'Me an' Grace 'ave 'ad this place fer nigh on fifty-five years an' we've made a lot o' good friends,' he said quietly. 'It's gonna be sad when we leave 'ere termorrer, but we made our decision an' there's no goin' back.'

'Yeah, it's a long time ter be in one pub,' Danny remarked.

Alec leaned forward on the counter and stroked his chin thoughtfully. 'D'yer know, lads, I was only finkin' about it last night. I'll be seventy in December. Grace is sixty-five. I fink we've earned our retirement.'

'Yer certainly 'ave,' Danny replied. 'Anyway, yer might be well out of it, if the curtain does go up.'

'D'yer reckon it will be war?' Billy asked, concern showing on his broad, ring-scarred face.

'I'm certain of it,' Alec told him. 'All right, I know people was linin' up ter cheer ole Chamberlain when 'e drove back ter Downin' Street a few weeks ago, but yer've got ter look at the facts. Read yer papers an' see what's goin' on in the world. Look at the air-raid shelters they're puttin' up everywhere, look at the amount o' gas masks they're dishin' out. It stan's out a bleedin' mile what's gonna 'appen. It'll come sooner than later, if yer want my opinion.'

The piano player was taking a well-earned rest, and among the voices raised in earnest conversation at least one was holding forth with authority about the dangers of war. Nobby Smith was beginning to irritate another customer with his expert declamations.

'What's the good o' dishin' out gas masks?' he remarked to Granny Phillips. 'That there mustard gas can burn the boots orf yer feet.'

'Well, I ain't gonna put the gas masks on me bleedin' feet,' Granny Phillips told him in no uncertain terms.

'What I'm sayin' is, one sniff o' mustard gas an' yer done for,' Nobby persisted. 'Yer ain't gonna 'ave time ter put the bloody mask on.'

'Oi, you,' a voice piped up. 'Why don't yer stop frightenin' 'er. Piss orf an' frighten somebody else.'

Nobby turned to the wizened figure of Jack Whitmore, a pensioner who had been making eyes at Granny Phillips for the past hour. 'Shut yer noise, you,' he countered. 'What d'you know about such fings? What I'm sayin' to 'er is, that there mustard gas is terrible stuff. A lot o' people don't know anyfing about it.'

'Well, I was in the trenches an' I do,' Jack replied, his eyes bulging with temper.

'Yeah, but she's never bin in the trenches,' Nobby went on, slurring and blinking in an effort to keep his eyes focused on his adversary. 'The silly ole cow ain't bin nowhere.'

The diminutive pensioner had heard enough and he staggered to his feet. 'I've a good mind ter smack yer in the chops,' he said, his voice rising.

'Yeah? You an' whose army?' Nobby goaded him.

Alec had been watching the confrontation. He lifted the counter flap with a sigh and walked over to the tables. 'Look, Nobby, I've 'ad me fill o' you. Now c'mon, out yer go,' he said firmly, hands on hips as he jerked his head in the direction of the door.

Nobby could see that it was useless to argue and as he attempted to reach for the dregs of his ale, Alec took hold of his arm and propelled him to the door. Jack Whitmore meanwhile had taken his seat once more and he smiled in Granny Phillips' direction, only to be given a blinding look.

The pianist had returned and as his hands moved quickly over the keys some of the customers began singing loudly. Billy Sullivan finished his pint and turned to Danny. 'I'll get this one,' he said. 'Same again?'

With their glasses refilled, the two men spoke of their own fears of a likely war, raising their voices to be heard against the din.

'Me an' Annie 'ave bin talkin' about what we're gonna do wiv the kids if the worst should come,' Billy said. 'She reckons we should get 'em evacuated.'

Danny stared down at his drink. 'I dunno what we're gonna do,' he replied. 'Ter be 'onest I'd sooner keep 'em 'ere. Iris feels the same way, though we ain't decided fer sure yet. Trouble is, Billy, if war breaks out, this area's gonna be a target, make no mistake about it. They're bound ter go fer the docks an' wharves, as well as the railways an' factories. It could get really nasty. We'll just 'ave ter wait an' see.'

Billy nodded and took a swig from his glass. ' 'Ow's your Carrie doin'?' he asked after a while. 'I ain't seen much of 'er lately.'

'She's a different woman now,' Danny replied. 'Joe's 'elpin 'er wiv the business an' she told me 'e ain't touched a drop since 'e's bin back. Young Rachel's pleased as punch. After all, it was 'er doin' they got back tergevver.'

'Yeah, she's a smart kid,' Billy remarked. 'She's growin' up fast too. I see 'er the ovver day, spittin' image of 'er muvver when she was 'er age.'

Danny afforded himself a smile. 'Rachel's talkin' about joinin' up if there is a war,' he said. 'Carrie's worried over 'er. She knows very well she wouldn't be able ter put 'er off. The girl's too strong-willed. Like the rest o' the family I s'pose.'

'Ain't you gonna try an' talk 'er out of it, Danny?' Billy asked. 'After all, you are 'er favourite uncle.'

'Not me,' Danny replied. 'Young Rachel wouldn't listen ter me or anybody else fer that matter if 'er mind's made up.'

The singing grew steadily louder as the evening wore on and the fears of a probable war were forgotten for a little while by the Kings Arms' customers as the pints of ale flowed. The fact that Alec Crossley was remaining quite sober on their last night in the pub did not go unnoticed by his wife Grace, and she could see that, like her, he was saddened about leaving the noisy metropolis for the comparative peace and quiet of the country. Grace had been flitting between the two bars talking to old friends and exchanging reminiscences, and she knew how sorely they would miss all the old locals.

'Are you all right, luv?' she asked Alec during a brief lull in the busy evening.

'Yeah, I can't fancy a drink ternight,' Alec replied quietly. 'I know it sounds stupid, but I feel sort o' guilty.'

'Whatever for?' Grace asked, her eyebrows raised in puzzlement.

'I dunno, really,' he answered. 'I feel like we're runnin' away at a bad time. I can foresee a terrible time fer this area an' the poor sods who live around 'ere. I keep gettin' this feelin' we're desertin' 'em.'

Grace squeezed his hand fondly. 'Now listen ter me, Alec,' she began. 'Ever since we've bin in this pub both of us 'ave tried ter be good listeners when it's bin required of us. We've 'elped people when an' where we could, an' we've earned respect from the folk round 'ere. We can leave this pub termorrer mornin' wiv our 'eads 'eld 'igh. Now pour yerself a stiff drink. Yer know yer get all mean an' 'orrible when yer go wivout one.'

Sunday evening was quiet for Carrie Bradley. She had finished going over the weekly accounts of her transport business and she leaned back in her comfortable armchair. The fire was burning brightly and the warmth had spread throughout the small parlour. Opposite her, Joe Maitland dozed, his head to one side and his arms folded over his broad chest. The wireless was turned off and only the sound of Joe's light snoring broke the silence. Her mother would be back from evening service at St James's Church soon and then she would get Joe to lock the front gate for the night.

The Tanner family's house in Salmon Lane was situated inside the transport yard which stood halfway along the street, wedged between a row of little houses on the left-hand side when looking down from the Jamaica Road. The houses leading on from the yard ended at a pickle factory, and facing them was an unbroken row of identical houses which reached along to a large warehouse. At the end of the turning a narrow walkway, bounded by a four-foot-high wall, ran past between the factory and warehouse and the swift-flowing River Thames. At high tide the water rose over the old banking and thick stanchions and lapped against the base of the wall, and when there was an exceptionally high tide the river threatened to flow over into the street.

Salmon Lane was one of the many little turnings which led off from the wide, busy Jamaica Road, and there had been a transport business sited there as long as anyone cared to remember. Carrie had bought the horse transport firm from a George Buckman after selling her transport cafe in Cotton Lane. With the business had come a couple of lucrative contracts with local firms, and Carrie had worked hard and successfully to build up the concern and win further contracts, despite the general opinion that a woman would never succeed in the fiercely competitive transport business. She was now held in high regard by all who knew her and she had earned the grudging respect of her business rivals, including the Galloways, father and son, who had played such a fateful role in the Tanner family's fortunes over the years.

Carrie had called the business 'Bradley's Cartage Contractors'. It was her married name, and she had purchased the firm at a time when her husband Fred was very ill. He had known that he was not going to get better and he had given her his blessing in his own way, hoping that it would provide for her future in a way that their cafe business never could. Fred had been ten years older than she was and although she had never loved him in the way she now loved Joe Maitland, she had been a dutiful and caring wife until the day he passed away.

Inside the yard, the Tanners' house stood on the right, and opposite was a small office and a stable for twelve horses. The carts were stored in a large shed adjoining the house and the four Leyland lorries that Carrie had recently acquired were parked in the yard itself. The house was well maintained and neatly furnished. The upstairs bedrooms were occupied by Carrie's mother Nellie, who slept in the back bedroom, and Carrie's daughter Rachel, who had the bedroom overlooking the yard. Carrie and Joe slept in the downstairs bedroom which led off from the end of the passageway. Since her father had died, Carrie had seen the gradual change in her mother and she worried for her. Nellie Tanner had lately become a regular attender at the local church, and in her daylight hours, if she was not visiting her old friends in nearby Page Street, she tended to spend much time shut away in her bedroom, usually sitting by the window which looked down onto the back yards of neighbouring houses and the pickle factory yard.

The years had been kind to Carrie. Her face was unlined and her pale blue eyes were bright and clear. Her fair hair reached down to the middle of her slim back, when it was not piled high on her head like it was now, and her figure was still shapely and slim. As she sat in front of the glowing fire, Carrie watched Joe's handsome face twitching as he slept and she sighed contentedly. He had been her lover since the physical side of her marriage had ended.

Joe Maitland had once owned a thriving buying and selling business, until he fell foul of a powerful enterprise that not only put him out of business but got him sent to prison as well, where he spent five years. As she gazed at the sleeping figure facing her, Carrie remembered the time when he stood at the front door, looking gaunt and tired on his return from prison. He had stayed with her at first as a paying lodger, but there had been too much darkness inside him, and she remembered with a shudder the day he walked out of the house and out of her life.

Joe was stirring now, baring his even white teeth as he yawned, his dark, greying hair tousled. Carrie got up quickly and went to the scullery. She found it hard not to be a little frightened every time Joe woke up from an evening or afternoon nap. When he had been drinking to excess, those moments of waking had filled her with dread. He would be snappy and hard to talk to, and one day, when the drink had almost pickled his liver, he had raised his hand to her. That was when he had walked out on her.

As she waited for the kettle to boil, Carrie bit on her lip. How close she had come to losing him for ever, she thought. He was the only man she had really loved, and who had loved her with an all-consuming passion. She loved him still, and he loved her, but now their love was different. It had grown from the desolate wreck of their earlier relationship, and they were each determined to hold on to what they now had together.

Joe grinned drowsily as he took the cup of tea from Carrie. 'What's the time, luv? 'Ave I bin asleep long?' he asked.

'Not long,' she replied, glancing up at the clock.

Joe followed her eyes. 'Christ! I've slept fer hours,' he said, stifling a yawn.

Carrie sipped her tea. 'I've just finished the books,' she told him. 'You was in a good sleep so I left yer.'

'Is yer mum back yet?' he asked.

She shook her head. 'I'm gettin' a bit worried. She should've bin 'ome by now,' she replied.

'Shall I slip out an' see if I can see 'er?' he asked.

Carrie looked up at the mantelshelf clock once more. 'Let's give it a few more minutes,' she said. 'She might've called in ter see one of 'er ole friends. She's done it before.'

Joe went out to the scullery where he splashed cold water over his face, dabbing it dry on a clean white towel. The desire to take a drink tormented him only rarely now but occasionally he found a sudden urge assailing him, and he threw icy water on his face and neck in an effort to shock it out of him. He stood in the cold, stone-floored room at the back of the house and looked through the window at the rising moon, half hidden behind a chimneypot. He wondered whether he would ever be totally free of the urge to swallow a strong drink and let it ease the feeling of want which had invaded his stomach. He dare not succumb to the desire, he knew that only too well. He owed it to Carrie, who had taken him back and given him her love once more, and to young Rachel, who had sought him out from the dark debris of humanity and led him unashamedly into the light once more.

Joe gritted his teeth as he recalled those terrible days and nights he had shared with the tragic figures who lived and worked in the fish market beside the river. Drink-sodden, cold and hungry, he had wandered aimlessly through the dark cobbled lane one evening and found himself on Tower Hill, and there he stood listening to a preacher who was addressing a small gathering. Joe remembered how he had looked down at his raw, shaking hand when the preacher ranted, 'If thy right hand offends thee cut it off.' He had wanted to do just that, but he had known full well that he would cheerfully sip from the gutter, had the liquid he craved flowed there – anything to sate the agonising pain he felt then in his stomach. Now, as he stood alone in the scullery, Joe looked down at his hand and turned it over slowly. He still carried the corns and scars from pulling the fish barrows up the steep lanes but his hand did not shake any more. He could remember well the rasping pain in his chest as his breath came in gasps at the top of the wet and slimy cobbled hill, and how the drivers of the horse-carts and lorries shouted abuse at him and the rest of the up-the-hill men as they struggled with the laden barrows.

Joe smiled to himself and took comfort. Just a few short months ago the shake had been marked. He knew that he was winning the long fight and nothing would make him slip back into that dark abyss of degradation and despair.

'Joe?'

He turned quickly, startled by Carrie's voice, and saw her framed in the doorway. She moved towards him and he encircled her with his strong arms.

'D'yer still feel it?' she asked fearfully, her head against his chest.

'It's there at times,' he said truthfully, 'but it's easy ter manage now. After all, it's bin over eighteen months since I took a drink.'

Carrie could feel his heart beating strongly as he held her to him. 'Never shut me out, Joe,' she said softly. 'I'll always be 'ere for yer.'

Joe eased her away gently and looked down into her anxious face. He could see the pleading look in her blue eyes as he gazed appraisingly at her. He saw her firm full lips, the line of her fair hair and her tiny ears. 'Yer still a beautiful woman,' he said, a smile showing on his face. 'D'yer remember that time at my place in Tower Bridge Road when we first made love?'

Carrie nodded. 'I've never stopped lovin' yer, Joe,' she whispered. 'I'll always love yer. That's why yer must never shut me out.'

He put his arm round her shoulder and led her back into the warm parlour. 'I s'pose I'd better go look fer that muvver o' yours,' he sighed.

Chapter Two

Nellie Tanner had enjoyed the service, and when it was over she took a roundabout route back home via Page Street. The night air felt cold on her face but the thick coat with the fur collar which Carrie had bought her last winter kept her body warm, and she felt that the extended walk would do her good. The little backstreet was quiet as she turned into it from Jamaica Road. Ahead she could see the gates shining under the corner gaslight and the little house where her children had all been born. At the elbow of the turning, Nellie stopped and stared along both stretches of road. Apart from a couple up ahead, caught in the glare of the far gaslight and walking arm in arm away from her, the street seemed uncannily devoid of life.

Nellie puckered her thin lips as she stared over at the house next to the padlocked gates, and as though from far away, getting gradually louder, she heard the clatter of horses' hooves. She could see children swinging from a rope hanging from the gaslamp and she heard their laughter. William was standing by the gate beckoning to her. How handsome he looked. Behind him she could see George Galloway. He was half smiling, half leering at her and Nellie's eyes narrowed. Hatred for the man who had almost ruined her and William burned fiercely in her breast and she gritted her teeth. She looked away and fixed her gaze on the little house with its whitened front doorstep. Was that Charlie standing there by the front door? Yes, it was. He looked smart in his uniform, and there was James too, his arm round his younger brother. William was pointing to the boys, trying to draw her attention to them. 'It's all right, Will, I've seen 'em,' Nellie called out to him. Her husband had vanished among the shadows now but Nellie's eyes were on the two young men. 'Where's young Danny?' she called out to them. 'Yer know yer promised me yer was gonna keep an eye on 'im. I'll give yer what for if yer disobey me.'

James was moving off, away from his brother, and there was a smile on his pale face. Charles was beckoning him back but James raised an arm and with a fleeting wave disappeared from his mother's sight.

'Danny, Danny,' Nellie called out. 'C'mon in, it's gettin' late.'

'It's all right, Ma. Danny's at the gym,' Charles said reassuringly.

'Go an' get 'im this very minute, d'yer 'ear me, Charlie?' she called out. 'Yer know I can't abide the boy fightin'.'

'But, Ma.'

'If yer stand there arguin' I'll take the strap ter yer. Now get 'im this minute.'

The night mist was beginning to drift in from the river and it was turning colder. Nellie shivered and pulled the fur collar of her coat up round her ears. The street was empty again but she could hear noises. Everyone was coming out from the houses. Sadie Sullivan was carrying a rolling pin and Maisie Dougal had her knitting with her. Florrie Axford was there too, her gaunt face set firmly. Nellie could see the women lining up across the street. They had brought their own chairs out and Maudie was singing 'Onward Christian Soldiers'. 'It's all right, Nellie, jus' leave it ter yer ole friends,' someone called to her.

The mist was thickening and Nellie strained her eyes. They had gone now, all except Aggie Temple. She was bent double, a brush and pan held in her hands as she swept the dust from her doorstep. It was deathly quiet, and Nellie leaned against the corner lamppost, her heart beginning to pound and her breath coming in short gasps. For a while she stayed there until the pounding of her heart grew calmer. As she started to walk on, a lorry thundered along the turning and she saw Aggie Temple get up from her knees at her front door and curse after it, shaking her clenched fist at the trail of dust. 'Yer can't keep yer step clean fer five minutes wiv those bleedin' lorries,' she grumbled.

' 'Ow's the ole man?' Nellie called out to her.

Aggie shook her head. 'It's 'is back. Bin out fer weeks wiv it,' she replied.

'It's the cold,' Nellie told her, but Aggie had gone.

She felt the pressure of a hand on her arm. 'Well, yer better get indoors an' get yer feet in front o' the fire,' Joe Maitland told her.

' 'Ello, Joe. What yer doin' out on a night like this?' Nellie asked him.

'I've come lookin' fer you, Mum. Carrie's bin worried about yer. D'yer know it's nearly nine o' clock?'

Nellie slipped her arm through his. 'It's all right, Joe. I was just takin' a stroll down the old street. Yer know somefink? There was a time when I could tell yer the name of everybody in this turnin'. I knew all the people an' all their troubles. I've seen 'em come an' I've seen 'em go. D'yer know somefink else? I knew the names of all the kids in this street once upon a time.'

'I know, Ma,' Joe said in a kind voice. 'Now let's get yer 'ome before yer catch cold.'

Nellie blinked once or twice as though trying to compose herself and suddenly she swayed forward. Joe quickly put his arm round her waist to steady her and after a moment she looked up into his eyes. 'I must

13

'ave lost meself fer a while,' she said slowly. 'Where are we, Joe?'

'Memory Lane, luv. C'mon now, 'old on tight ter me arm,' he told her.

In the small front bedroom overlooking the yard, Rachel stood peeping through the drawn curtains. She had heard the wicket gate creak open and she frowned as she watched Joe help her grandmother through the opening and escort her to the front door. She heard her mother's enquiring voice and mumbled words from Joe, then the door banged shut and it was quiet again.

Rachel resumed her position in front of the dressing table and studied her face. The spot just to the side of her full lips irritated her and she put a dab of foundation cream on it in an effort to hide it. Every month the spot seemed to flare up. Rachel pulled a face at herself. 'Tonight of all nights I wanted to look my best when Derek comes round and instead I look terrible,' she groaned to herself as she picked up the hairbrush and proceeded to run it through her long flaxen hair. It was important that she looked her best for her special date with the young man who had attracted the attention of most of the young women at the Methodist youth club at Dockhead. Derek worked in a shipping office in the City and all the young girls thought he was very handsome. His quiet way and good manners were in contrast to most of the other young lads who frequented the place, and his sense of humour often had the young ladies giggling as they sat together in the club's canteen. Rachel had tended to avoid him at first due to her natural reserve, and Derek had been prompted to get to know the one young woman in the club who showed little interest in him. They had been dating for some time now and he had approached her earlier that week and asked her to go to the jazz club with him on Sunday evening.

Rachel was not too keen on jazz, from what she had heard on the wireless, but she was excited to be asked out to the club by the young man and felt that it could be an exciting evening. Derek had mentioned some of the more famous jazz musicians and he seemed to know a lot about the music, although he told her he did not play an instrument himself. She was worried about what her mother might have to say, however. Derek laughed when she told him of her fears. 'It's a pub off the Old Kent Road where jazz musicians get tergevver on Sunday evenin's. The music's really good an' lots o' young people go. Everybody enjoys 'emselves,' he told her enthusiastically.

At first Carrie had been worried about her daughter going to a pub with the young man but Rachel had found an ally in Joe, who said that he used to go to certain pubs where jazz was played and it was all very civilised.

Finally, when her hair was shining and secured in front of both ears with small bone clips, she studied her face once more, turning her head

14

first one way and then the other. With a sigh she tucked her tight-fitting white blouse further into her black woollen skirt and reached for her coat.

Carrie glanced up and smiled at her daughter as she came into the parlour. 'You look really nice. I told yer that blouse o' mine would go wiv that skirt,' she said, leaning back in her chair as she appraised her.

Joe grinned at Rachel and nodded in agreement as Carrie glanced at him, but Nellie continued to stare into the fire as she sipped her tea. Rachel gave her mother a quick puzzled look but Carrie shook her head quickly to stop her saying anything. 'Now I don't want yer out too late, young lady,' she said firmly as Rachel reached down to slip on her shoes.

Joe and Rachel exchanged a furtive grin, and suddenly Nellie lost her grip on the cup and saucer and it clattered into the hearth. Joe got up instantly to go to her but Nellie waved him away.

'I'm all right,' she said quickly. 'I jus' lost meself fer a second.'

Carrie's face was lined with concern. 'Why don't yer get an early night, Mum?' she suggested as she bent into the hearth to pick up the pieces. 'You go up, an' when yer settled I'll bring yer up a fresh cuppa an' a couple o' those biscuits yer like.'

Nellie glared at her daughter. 'Why? D'yer want me out o' the way before Rachel's young man calls?'

'No, Mum,' Carrie replied with a sigh. 'I'm jus' worried about yer, that's all.'

'I'm all right. I'm not plannin' on snuffin' it yet,' the older woman said sharply. 'Anyway, I'm goin' up now,' she added and abruptly left the room without saying any more.

Rachel turned to her mother. 'I saw Joe bringin' Nan in. 'As she bin wanderin' again?' she asked.

Carrie nodded. 'Joe went out ter look fer 'er when she was late gettin' back from church an' 'e found 'er in Page Street. She was standin' by the lamppost talkin' to 'erself.'

'Poor Nan,' Rachel said quietly.

Joe slumped down in the armchair facing Carrie and shook his head sadly. 'The ole gel's bin like this on an' off fer a few weeks now,' he remarked. 'I don't want ter worry yer, Carrie, but I fink yer mum's in fer an illness. I noticed 'ow 'er arm seemed ter slump when she dropped that cup. I fink yer should 'ave a word wiv the doctor. 'E could give 'er a check-up an' maybe give 'er somefink.'

The gate bell sounded and Joe took hold of Rachel's arm as she made for the door. 'I'd better answer it,' he said, 'just in case it's not Derek.'

Rachel slipped on her coat quickly and cast a glance at her mother as she sat by the fire watching her.

'Now remember what I said,' Carrie reminded her.

Rachel's face flushed slightly as Derek came into the room followed

15

by Joe. The young man was tall and slim, with a thick mop of dark brown hair and he smiled shyly at the young woman. 'Sorry I'm a bit late. I fink the fog's slowin' the trams up,' he said, concern showing in his eyes.

Rachel glanced at the mantelshelf clock as though somewhat peeved, but really she had been glad for the few extra minutes to get ready. As the two young people prepared to leave, Carrie had a parting word for Derek. 'Don't keep her out too late, young man,' she said with a searching look.

Later, when the house had become quiet, Carrie turned on the wireless in time to hear the solemn chimes of Big Ben heralding the nine o' clock news. During the broadcast Carrie noticed the serious expression on Joe's face and when the news had finished she stood up and turned the volume of the radio set down.

'It's worryin',' she said with a sigh.

Joe attempted an encouraging smile. 'I don't fink it'll come to it,' he said shaking his head, but Carrie was not fooled.

'I wish I could believe yer, Joe,' she said, leaning back in her chair and glancing towards the ceiling. 'I fink it's gotta come. Gawd 'elp us if it is war. Look at last time. What a terrible waste o' life.'

Joe leaned forward in his chair and reached out, taking Carrie's hands in his. 'We should get married,' he said, looking intently into her eyes.

Carrie gave him a brief smile and gazed down at the fire. 'We've agreed to wait, Joe,' she reminded him in a soft voice. 'Yer know I'm not worried about what people might fink, an' what they say, outside the family that is, but I need ter be careful about Mum's feelin's, especially the way she is lately.'

Joe released her hands and slumped back in his armchair. 'I realise that. It's just that the way fings are goin' it might be better not to wait. It's just a feelin' I've got, but don't ask me why. Anyway, yer know the way I feel about yer. I've not touched a drop an' there's no way I'm gonna slip back. Yer'd 'ave no regrets, Carrie.'

Carrie gave him a warm smile and stared back into the flames without replying, remembering the discussion they had had soon after Joe returned to her. 'I want ter marry yer, Carrie,' he had said. 'I want yer ter know that I'm off the booze fer good an' I'll make yer a good 'usband. I realise that we both need time an' I'm prepared ter wait as long as it takes fer yer ter say yes.'

Carrie could remember how she had felt on that evening when she was nestled in his arms before the fire. She loved him dearly and needed him desperately, but there was a lingering fear between them that made her wary. He was sleeping in his own room then and would come to her occasionally very late at night. She wanted time, they both did. She needed to know for sure that he was going to be as good as his word over leaving the drink alone before committing herself to marriage. Since then, during the past few months, Joe had proved to her that he really had beaten his addiction, and he had worked hard alongside her in the business. He had made her very happy by leaving his room for hers and now they were living as man and wife. They had planned to wait until the spring of '39 to get married properly. Carrie felt that by then enough time would have elapsed since Fred's death. She knew that her mother did not want her to marry too soon after her husband's death, though her daughter Rachel seemed to think it did not matter. But then Rachel was different in outlook to the matriarch of the family, that was plain. The old lady was concerned about wagging tongues and had said as much to her daughter, while Rachel laughed contemptuously at what folk might think. 'Yer've got one life, Mum,' she had said on more than one occasion. 'Yer can't mourn ferever. Just be 'appy.'

The sound of her mother's voice carried into the room and Carrie hurried up the stairs to the back bedroom. Nellie was sitting up in bed with a shawl round her shoulders, holding a photograph of her late husband William in her hands.

'Could I 'ave anuvver cuppa before I go ter sleep, Carrie?' she asked, looking somewhat sorry for herself.

Carrie nodded as she sat down on the edge of the bed. 'That's a nice picture o' Dad,' she said softly.

Nellie brought the photo nearer to her face. ' 'E was very young then,' she replied. 'That was taken just after he started work fer ole Galloway. We was 'appy then. I was expectin' you at the time an' yer dad was gettin' all excited. Little did I know what was in store fer us.'

Carrie nodded her head slowly. She knew what her mother was thinking about. 'Yer shouldn't dwell too much on the bad fings,' she told her. 'There was a lot of 'appiness in our family. I was very 'appy as a child, especially when Dad let me near the 'orses.'

Nellie gave a brief smile and then her face became sad again. 'Young James took after yer dad,' she said, nodding her head slowly. ' 'E was the one most like 'im. I can picture the lot o' yer sittin' roun' the table at mealtimes when we lived next ter the stable. James 'as gorn, an' Charlie too. There's only you an' Danny left now.'

'I'm sure we'll see Charlie again one day, Mum,' Carrie told her.

Nellie shook her head sadly. 'I won't,' she said almost in a whisper. 'India's the ovver side o' the world. My Charlie made a new life fer 'imself out there an' 'e won't ever come back now. George Galloway's got a lot to answer for, an' I'm not altergevver free from blame when yer come ter weigh it all up.'

Carrie gently took the photograph from her mother's limp hand and stood up. 'I'm gonna bring yer up a nice cuppa an' I want yer ter try an' get some sleep,' she said soothingly. 'P'raps we'll pop roun' an' see ole Dr Baker termorrer. 'E might be able ter give yer a tonic.'

Nellie's face stiffened. 'I ain't goin' ter see no doctor,' she said quickly. 'There's nuffing wrong wiv me that a good milk stout won't put right. As a matter o' fact I'm goin' round ter see me friends termorrer night. We're goin' up the Kings Arms ter see what the new landlord's like.'

Carrie shrugged her shoulders in resignation and left the room. As she went down the stairs, her mother called after her. 'Make this one a bit stronger, gel. The last one tasted like gnat's piss.'

The evening had gone well and Rachel felt happy, chatting easily with Derek as they walked to the Bricklayer's Arms junction to catch the tram home. She had sipped her port and lemon and enjoyed the music; everyone seemed friendly in the pub and the jazz had been a series of impromptu renderings, with musicians getting up on the stage and joining in at will. The final piece of music had had the whole place buzzing and all the musicians taking part. Rachel had found her feet tapping, and when she glanced across the table at Derek he seemed enraptured by the music and his eyes were closed as he tapped his fingers on the table-top in time to the finale.

Now as they strolled to the tram stop, Derek suddenly took her arm. 'We'd better cross here,' he said.

Rachel felt a familiar little shiver at his hand on her upper arm, and when they reached the other side of the road she slipped her arm through his. Derek looked pleased and he smiled briefly at her, then gazed steadily ahead until they reached the tram stop and joined the people already waiting there.

'That there bloody Adolf 'Itler's gotta be stopped, that's what I say,' the large woman in front of them declared loudly to her friend.

'Too bloody right,' her equally large friend agreed. 'My ole man finks it won't be long before we're all in it.'

Rachel grimaced to her escort and Derek merely smiled.

'I don't know, I'm sure,' the first woman said. 'It was bad enough the last time. It'll be ten times worse this time. I was only talkin' ter Mrs Allen the ovver day. She reckons they're buildin' a great big shelter under Weston Street. They say it's the sewers they're doin', but they would say that, wouldn't they? Anyfing ter stop people gettin' worried.'

When the tram arrived and everyone climbed aboard, the two large women sat together on the bottom deck and continued their conversation in loud voices, to the consternation of those around them. Rachel turned to Derek with a worried look on her face. 'Everybody seems ter be talkin' about a war,' she said in a whisper.

Derek's face looked serious as he turned his head to her. 'I'm goin' in the navy if there is a war,' he said without emotion.

Rachel looked out of the window at the shuttered shops for a few moments and then she turned to Derek again. 'You don't really fink it'll come to it, do yer, Derek?' she asked him.

He saw how concerned she was and smiled. 'Course not,' he said, and then paused for a moment. 'Would yer like ter come ter the pictures on Wednesday?' he asked.

Rachel nodded and snuggled close to him. 'Yes, if yer like.'

'Shall I call fer yer at seven?' he asked.

'Yeah, all right.'

The conductor had been collecting fares up top and when he hurried down the stairs and started issuing tickets on the lower deck he became aware of the loud discussion going on, which by now had spread to other passengers. 'No war talk on this tram,' he announced in a loud voice, winking cheekily to Rachel.

'The trufe will out,' the large woman told him in an even louder voice.

'What trufe? It's all rumours,' the conductor told her, feeling pleased with the smile Rachel gave him.

'Oh, I see,' the large woman's large friend cut in sarcastically. 'So all the gas masks they're dishin' out ain't really 'appenin'. It's jus' rumours.'

'An' that bloody great shelter they're diggin' in Weston Street ain't really a shelter.'

'Yer know somefink, missus. I used ter like my job,' the conductor said, trying not to laugh.

'Well, if the war does start, yer can 'ave a change, can't yer?' the first woman told him.

'They won't take me, luv. They ain't got no trams in the army,' he replied, grinning broadly now.

'Yer'll be laughin' the ovver side o' yer face when they put yer in uniform an' give yer a rifle an' bayonet,' the second large woman said sharply. 'Yer won't 'ave it so cushy then.'

For a moment the conductor's face showed a glimmer of anger, then he chuckled. 'They wouldn't trust me wiv one, missus.'

As the tram reached the corner of Tooley Street, the conductor stepped down painfully into the roadway and hobbled over to switch the points. His war wound had been playing him up all day and he was thankful that his shift would end a mile or so along the road at Rotherhithe Tunnel.

At Dockhead, Derek helped Rachel from the tramcar and together the two walked through the foggy night to Salmon Lane. At the entrance to the yard they halted and the young man turned to his partner. 'I'll call on Wednesday, then?'

Rachel agreed with a smile but made no attempt to press on the yard bell. She was waiting for his arms to go around her, impatient to feel his lips on hers.

'I'm glad yer liked the jazz,' he said, moving close.

'Yeah, I did,' she replied.

'P'raps we could go again, if yer really enjoyed it,' he went on.

'I said I did,' Rachel said quickly, her eyes flitting briefly along the quiet street.

Derek detected a note of impatience in her reply and suddenly he slipped his arms round her waist and pulled her to him, his head tilted as he pressed his lips to hers. The touch of his body as she slipped her arms round his neck made Rachel shiver with pleasure and she moulded herself to him. She could feel the warmth of his body and she closed her eyes to savour the kiss as his arms tightened around her slim waist.

They stood in the shadow of the yard gate for some minutes, locked in a warm embrace, until the sound of revelry drifted down the turning.

'Well, good night then,' Derek said as they moved apart reluctantly.

'Well, good night, Derek,' she answered, reaching for the bellpush.

Suddenly, they could hear the strains of, 'There's an old mill by the stream, Nellie Dean', and they saw two lurching figures coming toward them.

'I'll see yer then,' Derek said with a sigh of resignation as he turned to walk away.

Rachel watched him until he passed by the drunken revellers and then she returned his wave before stepping into the cobbled yard.

Chapter Three

At number 22 Tyburn Square, George Galloway sat with his son in his large front room. The houses in the quiet Bermondsey backwater had all been electrified recently and behind the curtains bright lights shone, but at the Galloway residence the front room was only dimly lit by a low-wattage table lamp standing in a corner. George sat in a large leather armchair beside the fire, with his son Frank facing him. Both men were heavy of build with florid complexions. Frank's thick wavy hair was grey at the sides, while his father's was now snowy-white and thinning. George Galloway was in his eighty-second year and still very much the man in charge of the thriving transport concern. He had taken to drink many years ago after the death of his wife in childbirth, and some people were convinced that he would end up killing himself unless he eased up on the Scotch whisky. Nevertheless, as the two men sat together in the gloomy room, the old man had hold of a glass containing his favourite tipple, and for his age he looked hale and hearty.

Frank was George Galloway's younger son and the sole survivor of the three children born to George and Martha Galloway. He ran the cartage business and was given a free rein in the everyday matters of management, but the overall direction of policy and major decisions required the old man's say-so. Frank was resigned to the situation, knowing that in a few years he would inherit the business and the properties that his father had amassed over the years.

Frank Galloway was married to Bella Ford, once a popular music-hall star who was now reduced to pleading for minor roles in musicals and revues. They had one child, a daugher named Caroline, who at twenty-one was as spoilt and inconsiderate as her mother. Frank knew full well that his marriage had been a disaster from the beginning, and that Bella had taken lovers throughout their miserable union. He too had had his share of available women over the years, and now in his middle age he was a very unhappy man.

Tonight the two men were discussing the possibility of their transport concern being taken over by the Government if war broke out. 'The Road Haulage Association don't seem to know exactly what will happen,' Frank was saying. 'It seems that the railways have told the

Government they can handle all the extra freight but the road hauliers have contested it. From what I can gather, as long as we've got regular contracts that don't rely on dock collections solely, we'll be all right. They seem to feel that a lot of shipping will be re-routed to West Country ports in the event of war. As it happens, that brewery contract we've managed to acquire could be our get-out. Then there's the food contract with Murray's. The main problem is likely to be petrol rationing, but there again it depends on the sort of goods we're hauling.'

George downed his Scotch and pulled a face. 'It seems ter me that the 'ole bloody lot don't know their arse from their elbow,' he growled. 'We'll jus' 'ave ter wait an' see.'

Frank stared at his father as the old man toyed with the small gold medallion that hung from his watch-chain. 'I've heard that Carrie Tanner has got rid of her horses and she's getting two new lorries,' he remarked.

George snorted as he stared at the flickering flames of the dying fire. 'I should fink she's takin' a chance, the way fings are,' he said coldly.

Frank had come to respect the business acumen of Will Tanner's daughter even though he disliked her intensely. She would know what she was doing, and must have the necessary cartage contracts to warrant the purchase of two more lorries. They were not cheap by any means, he knew, and the sale of her horses would not have raised enough capital to buy the vehicles. 'I don't think we should underestimate her, Father,' he remarked. 'She's caused us enough problems over the years and well we know it.'

The old man leaned down and took up the poker. 'I'm well aware of that,' he grunted as he disturbed the low fire. 'It's up ter you ter see that she don't give us any more problems. In fact I'd be much 'appier if I thought we could pinch a couple of 'er contracts when they come up fer renewal. See 'ow she copes then, wiv the bank breavin' down 'er neck.'

'That's not going to be so easy,' Frank told him. 'Carrie's got a good reputation. Besides, the businesses around this area are not likely to change their cartage contractor with the danger of war looming.'

'Well, that's your worry,' George said, eyeing his son sharply. 'You run our business now, get yer finkin' cap on. Who knows, we might buy 'er out yet.'

On the wintery Monday morning in nearby Page Street at eight thirty a car pulled up outside the gates of the derelict yard and three men got out, each carrying papers and clipboards. The eldest of the trio seemed to be in charge and he walked up to the rusting padlock and gave it a tug.

'It's locked. Yer can't get in there,' a voice called out to him.

The men looked over and saw the buxom figure of Maisie Dougall standing on the corner clutching an empty shopping bag.

22

The leader nodded and proceeded to push on the gate as though testing its strength.

'I told yer it's shut. Nobody's there,' Maisie informed them.

'Yes, I can see that,' the man said testily.

'It used ter be a transport yard, Galloway's as a matter o' fact. After that some ole rag sorters took it over. They've bin gorn fer some time too,' Maisie went on.

'Really,' the man replied, turning his attention to the gates once more.

'I dunno who's got the key,' Maisie said, trying to be helpful.

'It's not important.'

'Well, yer gonna need the key ter get in, ain't yer?'

'I don't need to get in, I just want to have a look,' the man said with a condescending smirk in her direction.

His two companions were grinning as the helpful lady from Page Street sauntered over.

' 'Ere. Yer not bin sent by Kate Karney, 'ave yer?' Maisie asked.

The two subordinates turned away to hide their amusement while the older man gave Maisie a scornful look. 'Kate Karney?' he almost shouted.

'We 'eard that Kate Karney was gonna take this yard over fer a new music 'all,' she explained, scratching the side of her head through a tattered hairnet. 'Ter tell yer the trufe though, I fer one never believed it. Who the bleedin' 'ell in their right minds would open a music 'all in this turnin'? They wouldn't, would they?' she asked.

'Look, if you don't mind, I've a lot to do. Thanks for your help,' the man told her.

'Well, yer can't do much if yer can't get in there,' Maisie went on. 'Why don't yer send one o' yer lads ter see if ole Galloway's got the key? I should be careful though.'

'Oh, and why's that?'

'I bet there's rats in there big as our moggie.'

The official turned to his two subordinates, who were by now wearing even bigger grins. 'Let's get started then,' he said irritably, and in a lower voice he added, 'I hope she's not going to stand over us.'

Maisie had other plans. She had glimpsed the wording on the paper pinned to the clipboard and felt that her old friend Florrie would be interested in her little discovery. She was planning to visit her anyway that morning.

'Well, I'd better be off,' she told the men.

'Hurry up then,' the leader growled under his breath.

As soon as Maisie left, the men proceeded to take measurements, pavement to wall and across the gates; then they stood back and studied the site, scribbling on the clipboards and conferring with each other, unaware that they were being observed from behind more than one pair of lace curtains.

It was bright but still cold, and the early morning frost had left the cobbled transport yard wet and slippery. The last of the horse-carts had left and Joe was busying himself in the end shed repairing the splintered side panel of the spare wagon. Across the yard Carrie was sitting in the office going over the work schedules with Jamie Robins, her clerk and book-keeper.

Jamie was a quiet, slim young man who, having once worked for George Galloway, enjoyed the more congenial working atmosphere at Bradley's Cartage Contractors. Carrie had been lucky to find Jamie, for not only was he a sensible, reliable clerk and book-keeper, he was a mine of information. He had been able to give his new employer a good deal of advice on contracts and charges, as well as having contacts with many of the local firms' transport and dispatch managers. He had settled in very happily with the Bradley firm and was well thought of by the young owner.

'What'll 'appen ter the contracts if war breaks out, Mrs Bradley?' he asked, looking up from the ledger.

Carrie shook her head. 'I really don't know, Jamie,' she replied. 'As far as food goes, we'll prob'ly carry on as normal. As fer the rum an' leavver contracts, we might lose 'em. It all depends. Anyway, I'm not worryin' over somefing which might never 'appen.'

'I read in the Sunday paper that they might call up twenty-year-olds soon,' Jamie informed her.

'You're twenty-four, aren't yer?' Carrie said.

'Yes, but they'll soon get round ter the older ones,' Jamie replied, looking a trifle worried.

'Well, if that's the case I'll ask fer a deferment for yer, Jamie. I can't manage this business efficiently wivvout yer, an' I'll tell 'em so too,' Carrie told him forthrightly.

Jamie's face brightened. 'That would be really good if yer could,' he said. 'Me mum's worried about me gettin' called up now me dad can't work.'

Carrie knew the problems his family faced since his father had been badly injured in a factory accident and she gave him a sympathetic smile. 'Yer might be able ter get off by claimin' yer the sole breadwinner,' she suggested.

'I 'ope so,' Jamie replied, dropping his head once more to the sea of figures in the ledger.

Carrie left him to cope while she went across the yard to make their morning tea. She felt sorry for the young man. He was painfully shy and did not have a girl friend, and he had been quick to point out to her when she had asked him if he was courting that he could not think about marriage while things were difficult at home. Carrie knew, however, that it had not stopped Jamie being attracted to Rachel; she had seen the

24

young man's reaction whenever her daughter walked into the office. His eyes would light up and he would become flustered when she spoke to him. Rachel had mentioned Jamie's shyness and how nervous he appeared when she helped him prepare the men's wages every Thursday. Carrie hoped that the young man would gain in confidence, but she had to admit to herself that things did not augur well for him at the moment.

Maisie Dougall had been to the market to get her groceries, and once back in Page Street she pulled on the doorstring of number 10 and stepped into the dark passageway, wiping her feet carefully on the coconut mat as she called out.

'I'm in 'ere,' the old lady answered in a weak voice.

Maisie walked into the tidy parlour and found Florrie huddled over a low fire with a black shawl wrapped round her, the tasselled ends resting in her lap. Her face looked ashen and she raised her head slowly. 'What's bin goin' on over there then?' she asked, nodding towards the window.

Maisie knew very well that ill as Florrie was, any unusual happenings in the street would not go unnoticed by her, unless she was confined to her bed. 'Did yer see those blokes pull up in that car this mornin'?' she asked her.

'I saw 'em from the winder,' Florrie replied. 'Who were they?'

Maisie sat herself down in the vacant chair facing the old lady and put her shopping bag down by her side. 'Well, I was just orf ter the market when I saw the motor draw up. Aye, aye, I ses ter meself, who's this then? They looked a bit posh ter me an' I see the old bloke tryin' the padlock, so I asked 'em what they wanted.'

'An' what did they say?' Florrie asked, taking her eyes from the fire.

'Well, I couldn't get much out of 'em,' Maisie said, 'but I saw what was written on the piece o' paper this bloke was 'oldin'. "Bermon'sey Borough Council" it said.'

'I reckon they're gonna pull the place down,' Florrie offered.

Maisie shifted her position in the chair and folded her arms. 'I was finkin' it might be somefing ter do wiv what Maudie was sayin'. She 'eard at 'er muvvers' meetin' that Kate Karney was finkin' o' buyin' it fer a music 'all.'

Florrie pulled a face. 'I've told yer not ter take any notice o' that there Maudie Mycroft,' she growled. 'She's as silly as a box o' lights, an' I fink that crowd she gets wiv lead 'er on, I do really.'

Maisie had been watching the older lady while she was speaking and there seemed to be something different about her, something that was beginning to puzzle her. There had been a note of irritation in her voice as she sat there huddled up.

That was it. Florrie had not reached for her usual pinch of snuff from her tin, and Maisie realised that the difference was apparent on the old lady's face. The brown snuff mark was missing from around her nose. ' 'Ere, Flo, ain't yer takin' yer snuff?' she asked her.

Florrie shook her head slowly. 'Ole Dr Baker come in yesterday,' she said. 'I was feelin' bad an' I knocked on the wall fer Mrs Wallis next door. 'Er boy went fer 'im. Anyway, 'e examined me an' then 'e stood there scratchin' 'is 'ead. " 'Ow old are yer?" 'e asked. "Eighty next birthday," I told 'im. "Well, it's yer blood pressure," 'e said. "Leave the snuff alone till yer feelin' better. Snuff makes yer blood pressure go up." "Gawd 'elp us, doctor, I've bin takin' it fer years ter keep it down," I told 'im. 'E got a bit shirty but 'e give me some tonic an' some pills fer me back, so I thought I'd better leave the snuff orf fer a few days.'

'D'yer feel any better fer it?' Maisie asked.

Florrie shook her head. 'I feel worser terday,' she replied.

'Well, why don't yer try a pinch then?' Maisie suggested.

'As a matter o' fact I was just out of it when I was taken bad,' Florrie said.

Maisie stood up and buttoned her coat. 'I'll run up the shop an' get yer some. I'll leave me bag 'ere.'

As the good Samaritan hurried to the shop in Jamaica Road she wondered and worried about Florrie. She shouldn't be on her own, Maisie thought. Not at her age. As far as she knew, Florrie had no relatives to look after her and, apart from Mrs Wallis, no one was on hand should she have another bad turn. Maybe she could come and live with me and Fred, Maisie considered. I'll have a word with Fred soon as I get in.

At eleven o'clock that Monday morning a removal van pulled up at the end of Page Street. Watched by one or two sad faces, the removal porters started to load up the possessions of Alec and Grace Crossley. Their work was soon done and the van drove off. A little later the publican and his wife emerged from the pub and stepped into a waiting taxi. The few bystanders shouted their good luck messages and waved to the sad couple. Grace dabbed at her eyes and Alec blew hard into a handkerchief as the cab slowly drew out into Jamaica Road.

'I'm gonna miss their moanin' an' their miserable faces,' Grace said quietly.

Alec nodded. 'When yer come ter think of it, they ain't got much ter be 'appy about,' he replied. 'Still, never mind, luv. We'll come back an' see 'em all before long.'

Grace stared out of the cab as it swung round the bend in the road and accelerated towards Tower Bridge. She felt in her heart that they would never return to the riverside borough and to the folk they had grown to love over the years.

It was as the taxi turned towards the high twin towers of Tower Bridge that she saw the placard at a newspaper stand: 'New German visit planned for Premier'.

'Gawd 'elp us all,' she said aloud.

Word had spread about the Council officials' visit to Page Street, and by the time Nellie Tanner was feeling fit enough to look up her old friends it was commonly accepted that work was to start soon on a new block of flats to replace the old houses.

'They're all comin' down soon as the flats are ready,' Maudie told Nellie when the ladies had gathered at Maisie's house.

'We're all goin' in there. There's gonna be barfs an' 'ot water,' Maggie Jones added.

Sadie Sullivan snorted. 'I don't see as 'ow any of us are gonna be able to afford the rents.'

Maisie was ever the optimist. 'I think they'll charge us the same as we're payin' now. They know we can't afford ter pay any extra.'

Florrie was feeling better and had regained a little of her perspicacity since resuming her lifetime habit. 'Well, I fink yer all barkin' up the wrong tree,' she told them. 'If yer wanna know what I think, I'll tell yer. They're gonna build a great big air-raid shelter there, mark my words.'

Maudie bit on her lip and Maisie chanced a grin. Sadie shook her head, but Florrie was undaunted by her friends' reaction. 'Don't you lot ever read the papers?' she went on. 'I tell yer somefink, fer what it's werf. I bet yer there's a war before the year's out, an' I bet yer that shelter's gonna be needed.'

Maudie Mycroft was by now feeling more than a little sick with worry. 'My Ernest said there's not gonna be any war. 'E said we've signed a treaty wiv 'Itler an' Mussolini.'

'Well, all I can say is, your Ernest is talkin' out of 'is arse,' Florrie said quickly.

Maudie turned her head away from Florrie's icy stare and fiddled with the straps of her handbag while Maisie set about collecting the empty teacups.

'I'll give yer an 'and,' Nellie offered as she followed Maisie into the scullery, glad to stretch her legs.

'I 'ad a word wiv my Fred about lettin' Florrie live wiv us,' Maisie told her as she put the kettle on, 'but 'e wasn't too keen on it. My Fred reckons the old lady would be more than we could manage. After all, we're gettin' on ourselves. I'm seventy-two this year an' Fred's nearly seventy-five. 'E reckons she wouldn't come anyway, so what I'm gonna suggest is that we all take turns ter keep an eye on 'er. I can't say anyfing while she's 'ere though.'

Nellie nodded. 'I fink it's a good idea. After all, we've all bin friends fer more years than I care ter remember.'

Maisie proceeded to swill the cups under the running tap and line them up on the draining board. 'I know Florrie talks a lot o' sense at times but I fink she's got it wrong about the yard bein' turned into a shelter,' she remarked.

'Well, I fink Sadie's right about one fing,' Nellie said. 'I reckon that if they build flats there we won't be able to afford the rents.'

Maisie looked a little downcast as she spooned tea into the large teapot and Nellie decided to change the subject. 'My Carrie's gel 'as got 'erself a young man,' she said. 'Nice lad, 'e is. Ever so polite. 'E's got a good job too, so Carrie told me. 'E works in a shippin' office in the City.'

' 'Ow old is Rachel?' Maisie asked.

'She'll be nineteen soon,' Nellie replied. 'She's a good gel. There's not many who'd 'ave done what she done when my Will was ill. She 'elped Carrie an' me no end. Proper little nurse she was. It was 'er who found Joe when 'e was on the piss an' run orf.'

Maisie had heard the story before but she feigned surprise. Nellie seemed prone to repeating herself lately and it made Maisie feel sad. They were all showing the ravages of time now, but it seemed to Maisie that she herself was the only one of the old group who still looked fairly well and younger than her seventy-one years. Had she known what was going through Nellie Tanner's mind at that moment she would have been very upset. For some time Nellie had considered her to be a scatterbrain, and as she watched Maisie pick up the tea caddy again and open the lid she sighed. I'm sure the woman's beginning to lose her mind, she thought as she gripped Maisie's arm. 'Yer've already put the tea in,' she said.

A week later a lorry pulled into Page Street and workmen jumped down. One attacked the padlock with a crowbar and other workmen put up a rope on iron stands across the pavement on both sides of the yard. Maisie had seen the lorry arrive, as had Florrie, who went to her front door to watch. They saw the gates being quickly removed and loaded onto the back of the lorry, and then as the lorry disappeared from the turning a high-sided vehicle took its place. It reversed into the yard and it was not long before the noise of demolition carried along the turning. Dust rose into the air and black smoke climbed up into the sky from a huge bonfire the men had lit. All day the noise went on, and by early evening when work ceased the yard buildings had been reduced almost to a pile of rubble. Only the main stable remained, without its roof.

That night a watchman sat in the yard in front of a burning brazier guarding the workmen's equipment and Maisie in her infinite wisdom decided to take the man a mug of tea in the hope of gleaning some information from him.

' 'Ere we are, luv, get that down yer,' she urged him. 'Yer must be fed up o' sittin' all on yer own.'

The man gave her a toothless smile and sipped the hot tea gratefully. 'I used ter be on the demolition but I got an injury, yer see,' he told her. 'Can't do no 'eavy work now, so they gave me this job. I gotta be fankful, I s'pose.'

'I reckon yer still know what's goin' on though,' Maisie said with a crafty grin.

The elderly man nodded vigorously. 'Oh yeah. Me an' the guv'nor's quite friendly. 'E keeps me in the know.'

'What they gonna build 'ere then?' Maisie asked him.

Albert Twist was ready for it. He had been warned only that day that should anyone ask him such a question he must say simply that he did not know, and he had been made to understand that his job depended on it. But he felt that giving out a little information, wrong though it was, would be better than saying he did not know what was going on, especially after what he had just told the woman.

'As a matter o' fact it's a church they're buildin' 'ere,' he told her in a low voice.

'A church?'

' 'S'right, missus. Though yer mustn't let on to anybody, or I'll get the sack,' he warned her.

'I can't believe it. We've got plenty o' churches round 'ere already,' Maisie told him.

Albert was enjoying her consternation. 'Well, it's not yer usual sort o' church,' he went on, sipping his tea while Maisie scratched her head through her hairnet. 'It's more like one o' them there monastery churches. It ain't gonna be fer everybody.'

'Yer mean ter tell me monks are gonna live 'ere, in Page Street?' Maisie asked incredulously.

' 'S'right.'

'I don't believe it.'

'Well, yer can believe what yer like, but I'm tellin' yer what I know,' Albert said, staring down into his tea so as not to laugh at the look on Maisie's face. 'Yer see, there's a problem wiv overcrowdin'.'

'Overcrowdin'?'

''S'right.'

'What d'yer mean?' Maisie asked, furrowing her brow.

'Well, yer see,' Albert went on, 'there's a lot o' blokes who won't sign on fer the army an' what 'ave yer, an' quite a lot of 'em are joinin' the monks. That way they can't be touched. I 'eard there's fousands signin' up ter be monks.'

'Well, I fink it's downright disgustin',' Maisie stormed.

'Yer will do when they come knockin' at yer front doors scroungin' food an' money,' Albert told her.

'I didn't know monks scrounged fer food an' money,' she said.

'This lot will,' he told her.

29

'Who's buildin' the place?' she almost shouted.

'It's the borough council,' he replied, still not looking at her.

Maisie felt her temper rising to screaming point. The houses in the street were almost falling down and the council were more concerned about building a monastery. It's about time we all woke up round here, she thought as the nightwatchman noisily sipped his tea. Wait till Florrie and Sadie know.

' 'Ere, yer ain't gonna let on to anybody about what I just told yer, are yer?' he asked, eyeing her with a worried look on his angular face. 'I don't wanna end up on the dole.'

'Well, somefink should be done about it,' Maisie said angrily. 'Jus' look around at these bleedin' 'ouses we all live in.'

'They look all right ter me,' he replied.

'All right?' she spluttered. 'They're leaky, cold bug 'utches, an' the lan'lord won't pay out a penny on repairs till 'e's forced to.'

'Well, it ain't fer me ter say,' he told her, scratching his head, 'but if I was you lot I'd get tergevver and go roun' the council offices wiv a petition, but fer Gawd's sake don't tell 'em where yer got the information, 'cos I'd just 'ave ter deny I said anyfing to yer if I'm asked.'

Maisie took the empty cup he was holding and smiled at him. 'Don't worry, mate. I won't drop yer in it, I promise. I'll jus' say somebody over'eard the council people talkin' in a pub.'

When Maisie had left, Albert settled back in his seat facing the warm fire with a satisfied smirk on his lean face. If the women did go to the council with a petition, the proverbial sprat might catch a mackerel, he thought. If they find out what's really going to be built on the site, they'll be more than a little worried.

Wilson Street, just a few turnings away from Page Street, was where the Galloways operated their transport firm. It was also the site of Murphy's Gymnasium, named after a much-loved priest, Seamus Murphy, who had spent a lifetime in the borough and had organised money-raising for the boxing club. Murphy's was the brainchild of Billy Sullivan, once a leading contender for the championship before the war put an end to his ambitions. Billy now laboured for a local building contractor, and on two nights a week, along with his friend Danny Tanner, he taught the young lads of the area to box at the club.

Murphy's Gym was administered by St Joseph's Church, which had appointed Father Kerrigan to take charge. Patrick Kerrigan was a huge, genial Irishman who allowed Billy and Danny a free hand at their coaching sessions, but change was threatening. The church committee had agreed to the use of the gym as a gas-mask fitting station and for civil defence training. They had also discussed plans to turn the club into an air-raid shelter in the event of war. The committee had informed the two coaches of their plans and it was the subject of discussion at the Sullivan household that Monday evening.

'I s'pose we can't argue, Billy,' Danny said, spinning the wheels of a wooden toy belonging to Billy's son Brendan. 'If the worst came, most o' the youngsters would be evacuated anyway. There wouldn't be enough lads left ter teach.'

Billy picked up his five-year-old daughter Mary Jane who was standing by his knee and sat her on his lap. His face looked troubled as he glanced at the room door and then back at Danny. 'The church 'as bin on to Annie about movin' out o' London if the worst comes ter the worst,' he said in a low voice.

Danny's face dropped. 'Where would yer go?' he asked, puzzled.

'Not me,' Billy replied. 'Only Annie an' the kids. Apparently there's a Catholic 'ome in Gloucester fer young gels who 'ave babies wivout bein' married. Farvver Kerrigan was tellin' us they might need some more workers down there. Wiv Annie's nursin' experience wiv babies she could work there an' the kids could stay in the 'ome wiv 'er.'

'What does Annie fink o' the idea?' Danny asked.

'Well, she don't wanna leave me 'ere on me own but there's the kids ter fink about. I could go down ter Gloucester some weekends ter see 'em. At least they'd be more safe there than in London.'

'Yer could always come round ter me an' Iris. She'd cook yer meals,' Danny offered.

Annie entered the room with cups of tea. Her dark hair was piled onto the top of her head and her deep blue eyes had dark circles round them. Her pretty, angular face was pale and she had a worried expression. 'Has Billy told you about Gloucester, Danny?' she asked.

Danny nodded as he took the cup of tea. 'Let's 'ope it don't come to it,' he said quietly.

Annie sat down in the only vacant chair and smiled at Billy. 'I'll be worried about him if we have to leave him here on his own,' she said to Danny with a sigh. 'Billy can't even boil a kettle and I'm sure he'd starve.'

'I'll go back ter me muvver,' Billy said, grinning.

'I've already told 'im Iris'll cook fer 'im,' Danny reassured her.

The children were seeking attention and Annie took Mary Jane from Billy's lap. 'Come on, chicken, it's past your bedtime,' she said hugging the child to her.

Eleven-year-old Patrick was getting the better of his younger brother Brendan in a tussle and Billy got up to pull them apart. ' 'Ow would yer know these two were Sullivans?' he grinned.

Danny stood up and ruffled Brendan's hair. 'Well, I'd better be off,' he said stretching and reaching for his padded coat. 'It's gonna be a long night. We've got a union meetin' before we start work an' we can't afford ter miss the tide. We've got a line o' barges ter moor.'

31

Billy collected the empty cups as his lighterman friend left for his night shift and he sighed deeply. He could not help thinking how terribly he would miss Annie and the kids if they did leave London.

Chapter Four

Christmas was over, the New Year church bells rang out through the little backstreets of Bermondsey, and worried folk raised their glasses to peace. But as 1939 got under way, at workplaces, on doorsteps and in the pubs everyone was talking about the preparations for war. People read of massive rearmament and the dwindling unemployment queues, and in March the headlines announced that Germany had swallowed up Czechoslovakia. Men hurried to join the Territorial Army, and everyone was talking about the news that Britain had signed a pact with Poland.

'Well, that's it as far as I'm concerned,' Nobby Smith said to a frightened Granny Phillips as they sat round an iron table in the Kings Arms one Friday evening. 'That git 'Itler ain't gonna pay no 'eed ter no pacts. 'E's already marched inter Czechoslovakia. Poland's next, an' where does that leave us, I ask yer?'

'Don't ask me,' Granny Phillips told him with a worried look on her face.

'I'll tell yer where,' Nobby went on. 'Right up the Swannee.'

Jack Whitmore, Nobby's arch enemy for the attentions of Granny Phillips, puffed loudly as he leaned forward on the table. 'Them Germans won't start war wiv Poland,' he said emphatically. 'Not now we're signed up wiv the Poles. Those Germans 'ad enough of us last time.'

Nobby gave Jack a withering stare. 'Don't talk such rot,' he growled. 'The Germans 'ave bin itchin' ter take us on again. They've bin rearmin' fer years now.'

Jack was not to be put off. 'Yeah, but what you don't seem to understand is, we wasn't rearmin' then an' the Germans knew it. Now we've let 'em know we're gettin' ready, they'll back down,' he said, smiling at Granny Phillips.

Nobby looked over towards the counter where the new landlord was busy talking to a couple of dockers. He was well aware how his views often caused his rival to take offence, and in the past the raising of voices had always upset the landlord. The new tenant of the Kings Arms looked a mean character to Nobby, not someone who would tolerate their little discussions so easily, he thought.

'Look, me ole mate,' the ex-docker went on in a conciliatory voice. 'I ain't sayin' that it's definitely gonna be a war, but yer gotta realise that once yer go too far, there ain't no goin' back. That's all I'm tryin' ter say.'

Jack leaned forward, a wicked glint in his rheumy eyes. 'In the first place, I ain't yer ole mate,' he growled. 'In the second place, I ain't interested in yer views, an' nor is Mrs Phillips fer that matter, are yer, luv?'

The elderly lady was upset at having to endure the constant bickering of the two men; she felt they were old enough to know better, and she decided that a change of seating was the answer. With a huge puff of indignation she got up and took her empty glass to the counter, and when it had been refilled she walked over to another table and sat down beside Florrie Axford who had just come in on the arm of Maisie Dougall.

'Yer don't mind me sittin' 'ere, do yer, Flo?' she asked. 'Those two are drivin' me roun' the bleedin' twist wiv their talk.'

Florrie shook her head. 'Them two caused enough trouble when Alec Crossley was runnin' the pub,' she said. 'This one don't look like 'e'll put up wiv it. 'E looks a bit of a cowson ter me.'

Nobby had been expounding the international situation and had not noticed Granny Phillips move places. Jack had, however, and he knew then that he had lost his chances of encouraging her to accompany him home when the pub closed, for a cup of tea and a little canoodling. He looked at Nobby with venom.

'Look what yer bin an' gorn an' done now,' he grated. 'I was gettin' on all right wiv 'er, till you opened yer big trap.'

Nobby looked over to where Maria Phillips was seated and then back to the angry suitor. 'Don't worry, mate,' he said, trying to mollify him. 'They're all the same. Fickle, that's what they are. Take my first ole woman.'

'I don't want 'er,' Jack cut in quickly. 'What's more, I don't wanna listen ter you spoutin' orf about fings yer know nuffing about. Now why don't yer piss orf an' leave me alone.'

Nobby felt he had tried hard to be friendly but there was a limit to what a man could stand. 'Right, that does it,' he said, getting up as quick as his legs could manage it. 'I know where I'm not wanted.'

' 'Ave yer only jus' found out?' Jack growled, picking up his pint and taking a large swig.

'Yer askin' fer a smack on the 'ooter,' Nobby replied, leaning forward menacingly.

'Oh, an' who's gonna do it?'

'I am.'

'You an' whose army?'

'Me an' meself.'

Jack put his glass down heavily on the table. 'Why, yer silly ole sod, yer couldn't punch yer way out of a paper bag.'

Nobby forgot his promise to himself and raised his fists. 'C'mon then, on yer feet,' he snarled.

Terry Gordon, the new landlord, had been warned about Nobby and he knew from hard experience learned in various other pubs that trouble of this sort had to be nipped in the bud. He had already decided, however, that on this occasion it would be more prudent to use a bit of guile rather than brute force. He quickly slipped through the counter and confronted the sparring ex-docker.

'Now look, Nobby, I've 'eard all about you from Alec Crossley,' he said in a quiet voice. 'Alec told me yer've done a bit o' boxin' in yer time, is that right?'

Jack snorted contemptuously and was rewarded with a brief warning glance from the landlord, but Nobby's face relaxed somewhat and he rolled his shoulders. 'Yeah, yer could say that,' he said proudly.

'Well then yer know yer mustn't get yerself inter scrapes outside the ring, or you'll get it in the neck if yer get taken ter court,' the landlord reminded him.

Jack was still fuming over his spoilt evening with Maria Phillips. 'I wouldn't waste me time takin' 'im ter court,' he growled. 'I'd knock the silly bleeder right out.'

Terry had succeeded in getting Nobby seated once more by pressing down on the man's bony shoulder with his large hand, and he turned to Jack. 'I should 'ave thought yer'd seen enough fightin' in yer time, you bein' an ole soldier,' he said, shaking his head sadly. 'Now look, why don't yer call a truce an' I'll send yer over a pint each?'

'Suits me,' Nobby said grinning.

'Righto, guv'nor,' Jack said grudgingly. 'Long as 'e don't start up again.'

Terry walked back behind the counter with a satisfied grin on his face. He wanted to start off on the right foot in his new pub, and he considered that banning two harmless pensioners from the place before he had established himself with the locals would not make for very good business.

One sunny morning in April Jamie Robins walked into the office carrying the *Daily Mirror* and sat down heavily in his seat. He had read that young men of twenty and twenty-one were being conscripted and he was worried. It would be his turn to go soon and how would his hard-up family manage then? As he set about his tasks he could not get the problem out of his mind and he hoped his employer would remember her promise to help him get an exemption.

When Carrie came into the office Jamie showed her the paper. 'I don't s'pose it'll be long now before I'm called up, Mrs Bradley,' he said, hoping for a positive response, but Carrie was preoccupied at that moment and she merely gave him a sympathetic smile.

Later that morning Rachel made an appearance and Jamie's eyes lit up. 'I'd better keep these books up ter the minute, Rachel,' he said, giving her a smile. 'I'll be gettin' called up soon.'

Rachel, too, was preoccupied, and his mentioning the call-up only served to remind her of what Derek had told her only last evening. She merely nodded with a smile and busied herself at the other desk, much to Jamie's disappointment. He had wanted to attract her interest and sympathy, and he went back to his book-keeping feeling suddenly very depressed.

Rachel tried to sort out a pile of tax forms, aware that Jamie kept sending furtive glances in her direction, but her mind was on Derek. He had decided not to wait for his call-up and had volunteered for the Royal Navy. He had told her that if he waited until he was called up he might be drafted into the army instead. It was the navy for him and on that he was adamant. Derek was a determined young man, and he had argued away her objections.

'If I get called up in the army I might be sent abroad and not see yer fer years,' he had told her. 'At least wiv the navy yer get back ter port now an' then.'

'But yer signed on fer five years,' Rachel had reminded him.

'If war does break out it could last a lot longer than five years,' was his reply.

She had been going out with Derek for almost a year now and their relationship was getting more and more passionate. Now he had surprised her with his announcement Rachel felt vulnerable to his advances. He would be away for some time before his first leave and if war broke out he might be sent away to fight and maybe get killed or maimed before they had experienced full love together.

Jamie watched Rachel nibbling away at her bottom lip as she sat deep in thought. When he had mustered up enough courage, he put down his pen and turned towards her. 'Is there anyfink wrong?' he asked, a nervous tone to his voice.

Rachel was shaken from her reverie. 'No, I was jus' finkin',' she said quickly, giving him a smile.

Jamie tried to appear fatherly. 'It's an uncertain time, but I'm not worryin' unduly,' he said, leaning back in his chair. 'There's nuffink we can do about it anyway.'

Rachel nodded. 'My boy friend's volunteered fer the navy,' she said turning to face him. ' 'E felt it was better than waitin' ter be called up.'

Jamie's heart dropped. He had cherished the thought that one day he would pluck up enough courage to ask her out and now she had a boy friend it was no use. Maybe there was hope, though, he told himself quickly. 'If yer ever need somebody ter talk to, I'm 'ere,' he said suddenly, feeling his face going red.

Rachel smiled kindly. 'Fanks, Jamie. I'll remember what yer said,' she replied.

The young man lowered his head over the ledger once more. He was pleased with himself for planting the seed there in Rachel's mind but he felt he should have been more bold. Maybe she secretly liked him, enough to go out with him. Perhaps she was only waiting for him to ask her, despite the fact that she had a boy friend at the moment. He would be very proper if she did agree to a date with him, Jamie dreamed to himself. He would shake her hand when he said goodnight on the first date and then he would give her a gentle kiss the next time. Later of course she would become passionate towards him and he would be the gentleman and not take advantage of her maidenly desires. There would come a time, however, when she would expect him to make love to her and Jamie started to sweat as he thought about it. He would be very gentle and try not to hurt her. She would lie in his arms and sigh contentedly, then vow her undying love. God, the thoughts were making him feel shaky.

Rachel, too, was dreaming of love as she sat a few yards away from Jamie Robins watching the young man's Adam's apple moving up and down his neck. Derek was going to be very pleasantly surprised on their next date, when she would not attempt to remove his hand when they were in a passionate embrace. God, she thought, he had better not let her down or, worse still, ger her pregnant . . .

Across the quiet, sunny yard Carrie was sitting in the parlour with Joe and her mother. Her face was set hard. 'Yer know 'ow much I love those 'orses, Mum, that's the reason I've decided ter let 'em go,' she said forcibly.

'Is it?' Nellie responded with a disbelieving look. 'I fink it's the old feelin's showin'. It's yer 'atred fer Galloway what's swayed yer finkin'. I know you, gel. Yer won't rest until yer put that man out o' business. It's bin yer aim ever since yer went inter the transport game. Galloway's got rid of 'is 'orses an' now yer followin' 'im. It'll turn yer, Carrie. It'll make yer bitter an' 'ard if yer don't ease orf. Let it be, there's bin enough grief over the years an' nobody's got reason ter detest the man more than me, but I've come ter terms wiv it. There's little room fer revenge inside me any more.'

Carrie felt the emotion in her mother's voice and she went to her and sat on the edge of her armchair, putting her arm round her shoulders. 'I can't 'elp the way I'm made, Mum,' she said softly, 'but I promised that one day I'd see George Galloway out o' business. I can never change where 'e's concerned.'

'Galloway is an old man now, Carrie,' Nellie said, looking up at her. ' 'E knows the wrongs 'e's done ter people all frew 'is life. 'E knows that one day there'll be a judgment.'

Carrie caught Joe's eye and he shrugged his shoulders, not wanting to get involved in the discussion.

'Galloway might not be the force 'e was,' Carrie went on angrily, 'but 'e's still the guv'nor. All right, Frank Galloway's in control but the ole man's still pullin' the strings. Don't ask me ter ferget all what's 'appened, Mum, 'cos I can't. 'E got rid o' Dad after all those years o' loyal service an' we were chucked out on the street. It was the Galloway firm, too, that was be'ind that trouble wiv our transport. An' what about Charlie, Mum?'

Nellie suddenly dropped her head and Carrie could have bitten her tongue off. 'I'm sorry, Mum, I shouldn't 'ave said that,' she whispered, squeezing her mother's shoulders. 'It was stupid.'

Joe got up and left the room, and as the door closed Nellie raised her tear-filled eyes. 'It's all right, luv, I know yer didn't mean anyfing by it,' she said in a cracked voice, 'but yer see I've never got rid o' me own feelin' o' guilt, an' Gawd knows I've suffered over the years, knowin' what a good man yer farvver was an' 'ow I deceived 'im. It takes two ter make a baby an' Charlie was the result o' my weakness. I can't put the blame solely on George Galloway. What transpired was fate. What makes two people come tergevver in the first place? Of all the young ladies around, what made our Charlie fall fer young Josephine, the one gel wiv the same blood? Gawd knows, I dunno.'

Carrie slipped down on her knees in front of her mother and took both her hands. 'Dad can't be 'urt now, Mum,' she said quietly. 'An' yer mustn't keep blamin' yerself. Galloway took advantage of yer an' if 'e'd 'ave bin closer ter 'is poor daughter she'd still be 'ere now. Josephine 'ad nobody ter turn to. She killed 'erself out o' despair. There's only one person ter blame, an' that's George Galloway.'

Nellie forced a smile. 'Anyway, don't let it turn yer mind, gel,' she said, patting her daughter's hand. 'If yer really gonna let the 'orses go, make sure it's fer the right reasons.'

Carrie kissed her mother's forehead and sat down once again on the arm of her chair. 'There's only one reason, Mum,' she replied. 'I don't want ter frighten yer but as far as I can see there's gonna be a war before long, an' this area's likely ter get bombed. At the meetin' last week some o' the transporters were discussin' their 'orse transport an' quite a few of 'em 'ave decided ter send the 'orses out o' London if war starts. I'm not waitin'. I've already ordered two more lorries wiv the 'elp o' the bank, an' I'm seein' somebody about the 'orses next week. I've got all the work I can 'andle an' they're regular contracts, so I can pay off the loan easily.'

'What about the carmen?' Nellie asked.

'I've got ter talk to 'em this Friday,' Carrie replied. 'I don't see any trouble.'

Nellie stared down thoughtfully for a few moments and then her eyes met Carrie's. 'D'yer remember when yer was little?' she asked. 'Yer wouldn't go ter school if there was a chance of a ride out in the country. Remember the time the stable in Page Street caught light an' yer grabbed that Cleveland that Galloway used ter use? I thought it was gonna trample yer farvver's 'ead in that night. You got it out safely though. I don't fink anybody else could 'ave managed that 'orse. Remember Titch, an' the big Clydesdales? Yer cried all night when Titch died. I 'ope yer not gonna miss the 'orses too much, gel, that's all I 'ope.'

Later that morning heavy mechanical diggers and noisy tracked vehicles roared into Page Street. Maisie hurried over to Florrie to find the old lady standing at her front door.

'Well, there's the start o' yer monastery,' Florrie said sarcastically.

Maisie winced. Ever since the day she carried the false story to Florrie she had been reminded constantly not to be taken in by people. Fred, too, had been quick to give his gullible wife the edge of his tongue. 'Bloody monastery?' he shouted. 'Yer gotta be dafter than 'e is ter believe 'im in the first place. I 'ope yer ain't bin spreadin' the news about. If ole Florrie an' Sadie get 'old o' this they'll bloody crucify yer fer the silly cow you are.'

Maisie had felt sick. She had been to tell Florrie and Sadie the news before she went home. 'I'm gonna go round the council an' see about this,' she had raved to them.

Florrie had been convinced that her old friend had been duped and she said as much to Sadie after Maisie had left. 'Let 'er go if she wants to, but I ain't gettin' involved. Besides, me legs won't stand up ter that bleedin' walk.'

Sadie had never been one to pass up a fight, even if it was the borough council, but she had to admit the whole thing sounded fishy. 'Where did Maisie get the information?' she asked.

'Well, yer know what she's like,' Florrie said, reaching for her silver snuffbox. 'She felt sorry for the ole nightwatchman an' she took 'im over a mug o' tea. It was 'im what told 'er. The scatty ole sod was 'avin' a game wiv 'er. The trouble wiv Maisie is yer can tell 'er anyfing an' she'll believe it.'

As she stood at Florrie's front door and watched the activity taking place at the yard, Maisie thanked her lucky stars that her husband Fred had dissuaded her from making a fool of herself at the council offices.

It was not long before Maudie Mycroft came by. She was carrying a shopping bag and looking more worried than usual.

'Can yer see what's goin' on?' she said, putting her bag down and leaning against the wall for support.

'I might be bad on me legs, Maud, but I ain't blind,' Florrie replied sharply.

Normally the timid Maudie would have retired into her shell at Florrie's sarcastic reply but on this occasion she moved nearer her and whispered, 'They're buildin' a shelter.'

'Who told yer?' Maisie asked.

'My younger sister's 'usband's workin' on it. 'E's a foreman, so 'e should know,' Maudie said with satisfaction.

'I knew it all along,' Florrie declared, taking a pinch of snuff. 'What did I say? Didn't I say it was gonna be a shelter?'

Maudie picked up her shopping bag. 'Well, I best be orf 'ome,' she announced. 'My 'Arold ain't none too good.'

Maisie left soon after and Florrie went into her parlour and threw a small knob of coal onto the fire, although the day was mild. Standing at the front door had become tiresome lately, she sighed, and there were things to do. She sat down in the fireside chair and reached for a tin box at her elbow. From the bottom of a pile of old photographs and dog-eared papers she removed a large green document and put the rest of the bits and pieces back in the box. With a groan she stood up and placed the document against the side of the mantelshelf clock. For a moment or two she stood staring down at the smoking coals, then she reached up to the mantelshelf again for her purse and took out a florin which she slipped into her apron pocket. 'I mustn't ferget,' she said aloud as she settled herself down in the chair once more.

On Friday Carrie held a meeting with her four carmen and told them that she intended to replace the horses with two new lorries. The news was greeted with a stony silence at first and then Paddy Byrne cleared his throat.

'Well, ter tell yer the trufe, Mrs Bradley, we're not surprised,' he said, looking round at the other men. 'We've 'eard that some o' the ovver firms are doin' the same, but if yer don't mind me sayin' so, ain't yer bein' a bit 'asty? After all, nobody knows if there is gonna be a war fer sure. It might all come ter nuffink.'

Carrie gave Paddy a brief smile. He was always the optimist, the most happy-go-lucky of her men. 'Look, Paddy,' she began. 'I'm sure in my mind that before long war's gonna be declared. I 'ope ter God I'm wrong, but I'm convinced it's gonna come to it. I can't keep those 'orses in a place like Bermon'sey. It'd be cruel wiv the bombin' that's sure ter come. Yer can see fer yerself all the air-raid shelters that's goin' up round 'ere. All right, I could wait fer a while, but once war is declared it'll be too late. A lot o' transport's certain ter be commandeered an' then it's unlikely I'll be able ter move the animals.'

Jack Simpson, the eldest of the carmen, shuffled his feet and looked up at his solemn-faced employer. 'So we're bein' laid orf?' he said.

Carrie folded her arms and looked round at the men one by one. 'There'll be a job fer two of yer, if yer want ter learn ter drive,' she told them. 'I've spoken ter Tubby Walsh an' Tom Armfield an' they both said they don't mind teachin' yer.'

Jack shook his head vigorously. 'Yer wouldn't get me in those lorries, missus, not fer anyfing,' he said emphatically.

Percy Harmer, the youngest member of the group, grinned. 'Well, that settles it fer me,' he said. 'I'm not married an' I ain't got any ties so I bin givin' it some thought about volunteerin' fer the army. That's what I'm gonna do now.'

Paddy looked at the others, then he turned to Carrie. 'All right, I'll give it a try,' he said cheerfully. 'I've always fancied meself as a lorry driver.'

Carrie looked at the remaining carman. 'What about you, Lofty?'

Lofty Bamford shook his head slowly. 'I ain't cut out fer lorry drivin', Mrs Bradley,' he replied. 'I'll stick wiv 'orses. I 'eard the railways are keepin' their 'orses, so I'll try there.'

Carrie nodded. The meeting had been better than she had anticipated. Only Jack showed any sign of ill feeling. The rest seemed to understand the position, she felt.

While the meeting was taking place in the office, Jamie Robins had gone over to the house to help Rachel and Joe plough through the mass of forms that had recently arrived. Along with the applications for road licences, there were government forms which required information on the number of vehicles owned and the current contracts, as well as applications for petrol supplies should rationing be necessary. Jamie was very relieved when he saw an exemption form that was among the pile of incoming mail. He knew that Carrie would do her best to keep him and he settled down to work happier in the knowledge.

Chapter Five

During the early summer the Dawsons moved into Page Street, and their neighbours the Smiths got to know them much quicker than they might have expected. It started innocently enough when Mrs Dawson finished unpacking her bits and pieces and then went next door to ask Alice Smith for change for the gas meter. Being an inquisitive person by nature, Alice was keen to find out a little about her new neighbour and she invited her in.

'I've got a tanner 'ere somewhere,' she said, going through her various hiding places before eventually finding it. 'Would yer care fer a cuppa while yer 'ere?'

'That's good of yer,' the buxom Dolly Dawson replied, her large green eyes widening. 'I've just about got straight before the tribe comes 'ome from school. I'm just 'opin' they find their way 'ere.'

' 'Ow many kids yer got?' Alice enquired, hoping it wasn't going to be too many. Her husband Bill would not be too happy if his afternoon naps were interrupted by screaming and shouting.

'Four,' Dolly replied, touching the back of her piled-up red hair. 'Two boys, one gel, an' Wallace.'

Alice had a puzzled frown on her face as she poured the steaming water into the teapot. 'That's nice for yer,' she said.

'My eldest boy Dennis is ten,' Dolly answered slowly, as if trying to remember who was who, 'the next one Leslie, 'e's eight, then there's the baby o' the family, Joyce, who's five.'

'What about Wallace?' Alice asked.

'My Wallace is a lovely boy, such a shame. 'E's so good-natured,' Dolly went on. ' 'E ain't much trouble really.'

Alice felt her head start to spin. 'Wait a minute. Yer said yer 'ad two boys, a gel an' Wallace. Is Wallace a boy or gel?'

Dolly waved her hand. 'I'm sorry, I'm always sayin' that. Wallace is me eldest son, but 'e's different, yer see,' she explained. 'Wallace was got just after me ole man came back from the war. Josiah was shell-shocked, or at least some o' the neighbours said that's what it was. Anyway, Wallace was born retarded. Lovely-lookin' kid 'e was too. The 'orspital said it was one o' those fings. Part of 'is brain was affected.

42

Mind you, 'e's no trouble, provided yer watch 'e don't get 'old o' matches. 'E's got this fascination wiv fires, yer see. Always playin' wiv matches, 'e is. 'E almost burnt me last place down. Wallace 'as settled down a lot since then though. I couldn't leave 'im at one time. I've left 'im next door wiv 'is colourin' books. 'E loves colourin', does Wallace.'

Alice was horrified. Of all the people who could have moved next door, it had to be a hair-brained woman with a son who was not only a half-wit, but a budding arsonist in the bargain. Whatever's Bill going to say, she wondered gloomily.

Dolly took the proffered cup of tea and crossed her thick legs. 'I 'ope I ain't put yer ter no trouble,' she said. 'It seems a nice turnin'. Better than where I come from.'

'Oh, an' where was that?' Alice asked.

'Bellamy Street, just orf the Drummond Road,' Dolly told her. 'They're pullin' the places down, that's why we 'ad ter move. Wallace is gonna miss the place though. 'E got used to it there, yer see.'

'Is yer ole man workin'?' Alice asked.

Dolly stared down at her teacup before answering. 'Josiah's away,' she replied.

'Away?'

' 'E's on the Moor.'

'The Moor?' Alice asked.

'Dartmoor. 'E's doin' five years.'

'I am sorry,' Alice said quickly. 'I shouldn't 'ave asked.'

'Oh, it's no secret,' Dolly told her. 'My Josiah's well known in Bermon'sey. It's the drink, yer see. Wivout a drink 'e's the nicest man yer could meet, but when 'e's got a skinful inside of 'im 'e gets violent. 'E's got previous, yer see.'

'Previous what?' Alice asked.

'Previous convictions. That's why 'e's on the Moor. Mind you, though, I don't fink it was all Josiah's fault the last time.'

'Oh, an' why was that?'

'Well, yer see, 'e was 'avin' a quiet drink in a pub one night when this big feller comes in, an' as 'e goes ter the counter 'e knocks Josiah's arm an' spills the beer all down 'is nice clean shirt,' Dolly told her. 'Well, my feller tells 'im ter be careful, or words ter that effect, an' this feller takes a swing at 'im. My Josiah does no more than chucks 'im out the pub. 'E didn't 'it 'im.'

'That seems a bit 'ard, puttin' 'im in prison jus' fer chuckin' a troublemaker out the pub,' Alice remarked.

'Yeah, but it wasn't frew the door, yer see,' Dolly explained. 'It was frew the winder.'

Alice was beginning to get worried. Her new neighbour's husband sounded like a lunatic. What was more, her crazy son Wallace had been left alone next door for some time now. If he got a little restless he might well start playing with matches again. All the turning could go up in flames.

' 'Ere, do yer believe in readin' the tea leaves?' Dolly said.

'D'yer do it?' Alice asked.

'Yeah, give us yer cup over.' Dolly straightened her tight dress.

Alice sat down facing her neighbour. 'I 'ope it's good news,' she said quickly, holding out her cup. 'I fink I'm due fer a change o' luck.'

Dolly took the cup and moved it round slowly in her hand, her forehead furrowing as she concentrated. 'Yeah, yer seem ter be due fer some good news o' sorts,' she said in a low voice. 'I can see some money too. It looks like a lot o' money. 'Ave yer bin worried lately?'

Alice nodded. 'I bin worried over my Bill.'

'What exactly? Yer must tell me the trufe, mind,' Dolly said searchingly.

'Well, yer see, my Bill's always bin in the buyin' an' sellin' game. 'E was known as Broom'ead Smith. Yer might 'ave 'eard of 'im. Well respected, 'e's retired now an' all 'e does is sit round the 'ouse an' get under me feet all the time.'

'It must be nice to 'ave 'im wiv yer all the time,' Dolly said. 'I wish my Josiah was sittin' under my feet all day instead o' that 'orrible place 'e's in.'

'Yeah, but it's the mumblin',' Alice went on. ' 'E jus' sits there mumblin' all the time, unless 'e's in the back yard wiv 'is chickens an' the rabbits. The only time my Bill's 'appy is when 'e's out the back.'

'Where's 'e now?' Dolly asked.

' 'E's gone ter see 'is youngest sister in the country,' Alice told her. 'I'm expectin' 'im in soon.'

'Well, I shouldn't worry no more,' Dolly said, smiling. 'Fings are gonna look up for yer. It all looks bright an' there's a warm feelin', but I can't quite get a clear picture in the leaves so I can't say no more.'

Alice suddenly raised her head and sniffed loudly. 'Can yer smell anyfing?' she asked anxiously.

Dolly sniffed the air and suddenly panic showed in her eyes. 'It's Wallace!' she blurted out. ' 'E's found the matches!'

Dolly rushed out back to her house and Alice hurried after her, standing on her doorstep waiting anxiously. She could hear screaming and shouting coming from next door, then Dolly reappeared, her eyes wide with fright. 'It's your yard!' she yelled.

Alice ran down the passage into the scullery and as she opened the yard door, smoke billowed in. She could see the pile of old sacking glowing and she heard a loud clucking coming from the small hen coop. The rabbits too were scratching and rushing around in panic in their cages. She grabbed a pail and quickly filled it, cursing loudly as she doused the smouldering bundle.

'I'm ever so sorry, luv,' Dolly said, her head peering over the yard wall.

Alice saw the idiotic expression on the flat face of a boy next to her before he quickly disappeared. She took a freshly washed towel from the clothesline and waved it about to disperse the smoke while Dolly watched anxiously.

'I do 'ope it ain't 'urt yer pets,' she said.

'So do I,' Alice growled, fearing the aftermath of this little episode when her husband got home. 'So do I.'

Rachel had mixed feelings as she waited at the tram stop for Derek. She was excited at the prospect of spending the night with him but there was also an angry feeling simmering inside her at his decision to volunteer for the navy. She understood his reasons but still she wished he hadn't been quite so eager.

She adjusted her silk scarf and smoothed down the lapels of her green costume coat which she wore over a matching pleated skirt. Her blond hair hung loose, apart from a marcasite hair slide which she wore on the left side of her forehead; her eyes were bright with good health and her complexion was clear, with two small flushes of colour on her cheeks. She carried a small suitcase, shoulder bag and white cotton gloves and she stood upright with her shoulders thrown back. Her figure was shapely beneath her loose-fitting clothes, and the high heels she was wearing accentuated the firm, round muscles of her calves.

Rachel's heart beat faster as the tram approached and then he was there beside her, looking smart in his blue serge, single-breasted suit and white shirt with a grey striped tie. His shoes were brightly polished and his dark hair was brushed back from his forehead. He looked very tall in his well-cut suit and as he leaned down to give Rachel a quick peck of a kiss he smiled widely, showing his white even teeth.

It had been difficult for Rachel to arrange this night together without arousing her mother's suspicions. She hated to be deceitful, but she had had no choice. Derek was leaving for the Chatham Naval Depot on Thursday morning, which gave them only two more days together.

'Yer don't fink yer mum suspects, do yer?' Derek asked as he fell into step beside her.

'I don't fink so,' she replied smiling, 'but she gave me a funny look as I left.'

The two young lovers climbed the long flight of steps that led up onto London Bridge Station and made their way to the platform. Rachel remembered how she had crossed her fingers behind her back when she casually mentioned that Derek was going down to Brighton for a couple of days to see his favourite aunt before he joined up and he wanted to take her with him to meet the old lady. She smiled to herself as she recalled her mother's raised eyebrows and her sharp enquiry about sleeping arrangements. The fictitious aunt was promptly described as a regular church-goer, who would not condone any impropriety. That, and a feigned look of horror at what her mother might be thinking, was good enough to get the permission needed.

'Yer still only nineteen, remember,' Carrie had told her. 'I don't want yer gettin' in trouble an' ruinin' yer life.'

The train was standing ready and the two lovers found a compartment to themselves. Derek stowed the luggage on the rack above their heads and then slipped down beside Rachel and slid his arm round her waist.

'Derek, somebody might see us,' she protested as he pulled her to him.

'I don't care, I love you,' he said in his Charles Boyer voice.

Rachel giggled and snuggled against him, feeling his strong arm round her. What would her mother say, she wondered, if she knew that they were lovers, and had been since that delicious night at Derek's home. She had needed him, desired him so much, and he had been almost overwhelmed by her passionate demonstration of love for him. Derek had tried hard to control his natural urge but she had not let him. She had climbed on top of him and borne her weight down upon him, her long fair hair brushing his face, her small firm breasts jutting forward as she arched herself and threw her head back, her hair flying round her. She had surprised herself by her lack of maidenly reserve and her determination to reach fulfilment at the first attempt. The pain and discomfort had quickly disappeared as she felt the torrent rising and Derek was sweating, his eyes wide and his mouth set firm as he desperately sought time. It was soon over, but every tiny moment was etched in Rachel's mind as she nestled her head on his shoulder.

Joe Maitland walked into the scullery and peeled off his sweaty shirt, cupping his hands under the running tap. He had been hard at it all day in the stables. He reached for the towel and rubbed his stubbled face, feeling fit and content. The urge for a drink was very rarely with him now, and on the odd occasions he found himself licking his lips he was able to sate his thirst with cold, sparkling water. He sensed, too, that Carrie was coming round to the idea of getting married sooner rather than later, and he had been happy to hear Nellie speak to her daughter about their delayed marriage only a day or two ago.

'Maybe yer should get it over an' done wiv,' she had said in her matter-of-fact voice. 'What wiv yer change-over an' the work yer've got ter do, yer won't find the time. Don't ferget yer gonna need a few days ter yerselves.'

Joe whistled noisily as he put on a clean cotton shirt and tucked the ends into his trousers. He could hear the strains of a brass band coming from the wireless in the parlour and the sounds of the table being laid. As he walked into the small room Carrie gave him a warm smile. He

46

looked handsome in a rugged way, she thought. His dark hair was greying at the sides and his stubbled jaw was square and firm-set. His eyes were bright as they appraised her and a little ripple travelled down her spine. She always got that feeling when Joe looked at her in that way. It was the unspoken word, the sign of his need, and she looked away, pretending to concentrate on a chore she could have performed with her eyes shut.

Three places were laid for tea, which was always the main meal of the day for them. The evening was chilly for the time of year and a low fire was burning in the grate. Nellie was sitting in her favourite chair and looking down through her iron-rimmed glasses which were perched on the end of her nose as she patiently set about unpicking an old cardigan and rolling the frizzy wool round her first two fingers.

'What's fer tea, Nellie?' Joe asked in an exaggerated whisper.

'It's plaice an' new potaters,' Nellie told him. 'I got the fish meself at Israel's. 'E always does a nice bit o' plaice, does Sammy.'

Carrie gave Joe a quick glance. 'Mum made the parsley sauce. She knows yer like 'er sauce.'

Joe took down a packet of cigarettes and then reached down into the fire with a taper. 'I was lookin' at that stable terday,' he said, puffing a cloud of smoke towards the ceiling. 'It's gonna be a job fer a demolition firm. It's a double fickness o' solid stone.'

'We'll need ter make some enquiries this week,' Carrie replied. 'Once the 'orses 'ave gone I want that stable pulled down.'

'I wonder what yer farvver would 'ave made of it all?' Nellie remarked without looking up from her unravelling.

' 'E would 'ave understood, Mum,' Carrie said softly. 'Yer know 'ow much 'e loved the 'orses.'

Joe eased himself back in his fireside chair facing Nellie and watched her deft fingers working away at the wool. As soon as Carrie left the room to get the food, he leaned forward. 'I'm gonna ask Carrie to agree ter bring the marriage forward, Nell. Would yer mind?' he asked in an attempt to make her feel fully involved.

The ageing woman looked up at him without stopping what she was doing. 'I fink it's the right fing ter do, as I've already told Carrie,' she replied. 'After all, yer man an' wife in every respect now, 'cept in the eyes of the Lord. Yer should get the blessin'.'

Carrie came into the parlour at that moment carrying a steaming dish which she set down on the chintz tablecoth. 'Come on, sit yerselves down,' she ordered. 'It'll soon get cold.'

The meal was eaten with little conversation and when Nellie was finished she pushed her plate back and folded her arms. 'I 'ope that daughter o' yours is all right,' she said, looking at Carrie reprovingly.

'She'll be fine, Mum,' Carrie replied. 'Derek's a very nice young man an' 'e'll look after 'er.'

'I wouldn't 'ave let you go at that age,' Nellie said firmly. 'Not all the way ter Brighton on a train, an' certainly not wiv a young man.'

Carrie gave her mother a patient smile. 'Times are different now. Besides, Rachel's a sensible gel. She wouldn't let any boy take advantage of 'er. They're stayin' wiv Derek's aunt an' Rachel said she's very proper. She wouldn't stand any nonsense.'

Nellie sniffed contemptuously and Joe and Carrie exchanged brief glances. They had both talked about it the previous night and Carrie had told him that she was convinced the two young people had become lovers. 'She's my daughter, remember, Joe,' she had said. 'I know 'ow I felt when I first came ter you. It was as though I was walkin' on air. I've sensed a change in Rachel this past few weeks. I can't explain it, it's jus' somefing I can feel.'

Joe nodded. He had been certain, too, by the change in Rachel's attitude towards him. She had always shown him her affection in an innocent, childish way, her eyes eagerly seeking his praise or approval. Lately, however, she had kept a distance, becoming almost shy on meeting his gaze. Joe knew that her love for him had not lessened in any way, but her manner was different now that she had experienced an all-embracing love with her handsome young man.

The meal had been delicious and the pleasant feeling of tiredness played at his eyelids as Joe resumed his place beside the fire. He felt happier now than he had felt for a long time. He had the love of a very attractive woman in his middle age, a home, and a life that was beginning to mean something again. The only cloud on the horizon was the dark threat of war, and at that particular moment he did not have the inclination to dwell on his fears.

Carrie came into the room and switched on the wireless. As he let his tired eyes close, Joe heard the chimes of Big Ben and then the deep voice of the news announcer. 'This is the nine o' clock news and this is Frank Phillips reading it. In Parliament today the Government announced a trial run of the blackout. It will take place some time in August . . .'

Sleep overtook Joe and he slipped into a troubled slumber.

Chapter Six

During the summer of '39 Page Street said goodbye to some of its long-time dwellers. First to leave were the Smiths. Bill 'Broomhead' Smith and his wife Alice did not bother to say farewell to their next-door neighbours when they left in June to go to live near Broomhead's sister in Kent. The ex-totter had effectively heightened his yard wall with corrugated sheeting after Wallace's attempt to burn the house down and from that day on no word was exchanged by the two families. Whenever they saw each other on the street they would cross over, or walk on by without a glimmer of recognition. Now, as Dolly Dawson watched the removal van leaving from next door, she prayed that her next neighbours would be a little more sympathetic towards her problems than the Smiths had been. Broomhead had often growled and pulled faces at Wallace over the yard wall, and on one occasion he had so terrified the backward young man by waving a hammer at him that he would not venture into the yard if he knew Broomhead was at home, which was exactly what the ex-totter had intended to happen.

In July there were more departures. Granny Phillips left, followed soon after by her long-time suitor, the elderly widower Jack Whitmore. Nobby Smith and his long-suffering wife were next to go, leaving a quieter and less volatile atmosphere in the Kings Arms, and in August, as the war clouds were gathering, Page Street lost one of its most loved characters.

Maisie Dougall had finished her shopping on Friday morning and called in at the tobacconist shop on the corner of Page Street on her way home. The proprietor Albert Lockwood had recently bought the shop and was eager to build up his trade. Albert had realised early on in his retailing career that like it or not he was obliged to spend time chatting with his customers to get their confidence, and thus their regular custom. Maisie was a thorn in his side, for she spent many hours of each day chatting to all and sundry, and when she walked into the little corner shop Albert Lockwood groaned to himself. He need not have worried on that particular morning, however, because Maisie was preoccupied.

'Two *Mirror*s an' six pennerf o' snuff, Albert,' she said sighing loudly.

Albert weighed up the snuff on his brass scales and gingerly tipped it into the greaseproof paper cone, folding in the ends of the paper before handing it over. Now for the daily bulletin, he thought.

'Tata,' Maisie said as she turned to leave.

Albert wondered if he had upset the chatterbox in any way and he gave her a big smile. 'Everyfing all right, Mrs Dougall?' he said tentatively.

Maisie stopped in her tracks and shook her head. 'Florrie ain't too good,' she replied. 'She's 'ad a fall.'

Albert winced. 'It's bad at 'er age. What 'appened?'

Maisie put down her shopping bag. 'She's bin pretty queer fer a few days,' she began, 'an' yesterday she got out o' bed ter make 'erself a drink an' she fell against the chest o' drawers. It must o' stunned 'er 'cos when I called in last night fer a chat she was propped up against the edge o' the bed. She remembers fallin' but she couldn't remember much else. I'd say she must 'ave bin sittin' there fer hours. She looked perished.'

'I'm sorry to 'ear it,' Albert said. 'Did yer send fer the doctor?'

Maisie nodded. ' 'E was round in ten minutes. There was nuffink broken but 'e was worried about the shock. After all, Florrie's no spring chicken.'

'Well, give the ole lady my best regards,' Albert said as another customer walked into his shop.

Maisie had not finished, however. 'Yer know, I blame meself,' she said. 'I should 'ave gone in an' made 'er a cuppa. Mind you, I did ask 'er but she said she'd be all right. I should 'ave gone in anyway.'

'Yer shouldn't blame yerself,' Albert told her. 'It could 'appen anytime. Yer can't be there on call all the time.'

Maisie shrugged her shoulders. 'No, I s'pose not. Ah well, better be orf.'

She left the shop and walked quickly down Page Street. She could see clearly the progress being made at the yard site. Lorries had been constantly going in and out of the little turning for weeks now and the unending rumble of the cement-mixing plant added to the sense of urgency. Wooden shuttering and reinforced bars of steel had grown upwards and the whole scene looked like a shipbuilding works. Maudie Mycroft seemed to have the most up-to-date news about the place and she said that when finished the shelter roof would be at ground level with a sloping path leading down to twin caverns. It was meant to hold two hundred and forty people in all, with priority being given to Page Street, Bacon Street and the adjacent backstreets. Maudie had also said that according to her sister's husband, the shelter would stand up to anything short of a direct hit.

Maisie was serious-faced as she let herself into Florrie's house. When she looked into the back bedroom she saw her old friend propped up in bed with her favourite black shawl round her frail shoulders. Her face was ashen, which accentuated the large circular patch of bruising on her right temple. She seemed to find it difficult to talk and Maisie patted her limp hand tenderly as she picked up the tiny snuffbox from the chair beside her bed and proceeded to fill it. The task done, Maisie adjusted the shawl round Florrie's shoulders and straightened the bedclothes. 'Right now, I'll get yer a nice cuppa before I go,' she said smiling at her.

Florrie nodded weakly and closed her eyes. Maisie hurried to the scullery and lit the gas jet under the iron kettle. It would take a few minutes, she reasoned, just time enough to hang out the bits and pieces of washing on the yard clothesline. At that moment she heard Florrie cry out in a high-pitched wail that filled her with dread. She turned out the gas instinctively before hurrying into the bedroom. She gasped as she saw Florrie lying forward on her side, her head hanging over the edge of the bed.

Maisie eased her onto her back and pulled the bedclothes up round her chin. Florrie's eyes were closed and her breathing was coming in gasps now.

'Oh my Gawd,' Maisie groaned, rubbing her fingers gently over Florrie's cold brow.

Suddenly the old lady's eyes flickered open and her breathing quietened. 'That you, Maisie?' she said in little more than a murmur.

'It's me, gel,' Maisie whispered, tears starting to fall down her face.

'The clock. It's be'ind the clock,' Florrie mumbled. 'They're comin' down the street. I can see 'em in their scarlet uniforms. 'Elp me up, Mais, I wanna see the band.'

Maisie felt the old lady's body stiffen as she made one last effort to rise, and then her shoulders dropped back against the bed.

For a time Maisie sat with her head held low, hardly able to believe that Florrie had died. Finally she stood up and leaned over the still form, brushing her forehead with a soft kiss before pulling the sheet up over her face.

The house was uncannily quiet as Maisie walked out of the bedroom and closed the door quietly. What was it Florrie said? she thought. 'Behind the clock', those were her words. She walked into the parlour and immediately saw the large green document resting beside the chimer in the centre of the mantelshelf. Feeling like an intruder she took it down and opened it. The document was a penny policy, and tucked in the folds was a sealed envelope addressed to 'Mrs M. Dougall' in Florrie's spidery handwriting. Maisie replaced the insurance policy beside the clock and opened the envelope.

Dear Mais,
I've always paid my way and that's how I want to go out, the same.

There's a few bob in the toffee tin next to the fireplace. What with the policy, that should be enough to give me a good send-off. Any money left is to be put behind the bar at the Kings Arms. Make sure that new bloke gives you full measure. Alec Crossley always did, after I told him of it that time.

Be a dear and put my snuffbox in with me.

Love to you, Mais, and the rest of the gels.

Florence Axford.

Tears fell onto the letter as Maisie stood there looking down at it. That was just like Florrie, she thought sadly. Always looking out for them all. Well, she shall have her last wish, she vowed, as she went back into the bedroom and picked up the tiny silver casket.

The day before Florrie Axford's funeral, London was put into darkness by a trial black-out. In the little backstreets that ran down to the dark river no light led the way. Gaslights were extinguished and the new electric lights along Jamaica Road went out. Blackout blinds went up and everywhere police and the newly mobilised ARP wardens toured the streets and knocked on doors if any light was showing.

Thunder rolled, and streaks of lightning flashed across the dark night sky, as though some entity were demonstrating to mere mortals the awesome power that would very soon be unleashed upon them.

In the Kings Arms it was very quiet. Danny Tanner sat with Billy and they drank their first pint without talking. Neither felt able to encroach on the other's private thoughts, and it was not until his glass was empty that Danny broke the silence. 'Same again?' he said.

The glasses were refilled and Billy leaned his elbows on the table-top as he studied his pint. 'Is yer muvver up ter goin' ter Florrie's send-orf?' he asked after a while.

Danny nodded. 'Yer couldn't keep 'er away.'

'My muvver's goin',' Billy said. 'She's gonna be missed, is ole Florrie. What a character she was.'

Danny smiled sadly as he gazed at his glass. ' 'Ere, d'yer remember that time you an' me 'ad the barney wiv that copper? Florrie got us out o' trouble that time, Billy.'

The ex-boxer stroked his chin thoughtfully. 'Yeah, not 'alf. She was a good 'un all right,' he said quietly.

The two lapsed into silence for a while and then Billy sat up straight in his chair. 'I see Parliament's bin called back then,' he said.

Danny nodded. 'They've called the reservists up too.'

Billy stared moodily into his beer and Danny searched for something to say. He knew the reason for his old friend's glumness: Billy worshipped Annie and the children, and tomorrow they were leaving for Gloucester. Annie had managed to have a few hurried words with

Danny that evening as he waited for his friend to get his coat. 'Watch out for him, Danny,' she had asked. 'My Billy loves you like a brother. He'll listen to you. Just watch out for him, you know how scatterbrained he can be at times.'

'I'm gonna go round the estate office termorrer,' Danny said, trying to get a conversation going. 'I'm gonna try an' move back ter Page Street. That 'ouse of ours in Wilson Street is fallin' down round our ears. There's a few 'ouses empty now, so there shouldn't be any trouble.'

Billy looked up, roused for a moment from his torpor. 'Yer don't fink ole Galloway'll put the block on yer gettin' a place, do yer?' he asked.

Danny shrugged his shoulders. 'I dunno really, but I shouldn't 'ave thought so. The estate office manages the properties fer 'im an' I'd 'ave thought 'e'd leave it ter them. Besides, they can't be too fussy now.'

Billy cast his eyes down to his drink once more and Danny studied him. His friend had been prone to bouts of depression in the past, after returning badly wounded from the war, and it was only when he became involved in the setting-up of the gymnasium in Wilson Street that he began to change. His subsequent marriage to Annie, whom he adored, and the birth of his children had made a new man of him. He had made a success as a boxing coach, too, and he was highly thought of in the area. What was happening to him now, though, was a cruel reminder of the past, Danny felt. The club had suspended its activities when the recent evacuation scheme began in earnest, and now he was to be parted from Annie and the children and left to his own devices.

As though aware of Danny's eyes on him, Billy suddenly picked up his pint and drained the glass. 'Let's get one more, then I'd better get back 'ome,' he said with a frown. 'Annie an' the kids are leavin' early in the mornin'.'

In the quiet of her parlour, Carrie was sitting with Joe and she was feeling excited. 'It's all fixed then?' she asked him.

Joe smiled as he leaned back in the armchair. 'Unless yer've changed yer mind?' he said with a crafty look.

Carrie feigned a look of indecision. 'Well, er, I . . .'

Joe got out of his chair quickly and reached down to her, taking her hands in his. 'I've waited long enough, young woman, an' there's no way yer backin' out now.'

Carrie yielded to him and slipped into his arms. 'I love yer madly, Joe,' she gasped as he squeezed her tightly. 'We're gonna be very happy, I jus' know it.'

'We are now,' he said to her.

Carrie ran her hand down his arm as she nestled against him. 'I know we are,' she whispered, 'but bein' yer wife is gonna make it seem even better.'

Footsteps on the stairs made them move apart and after a few moments Nellie came into the room. 'I've found me black bonnet in the back o' the wardrobe,' she said, 'but that black coat needs an ironin'.'

'All right, Mum, I'll do it right away,' Carrie assured her. 'They're deliverin' the flowers at a quarter to eleven.'

Nellie nodded sadly. 'It's gonna be a big turn-out. I'm in the first coach wiv Sadie, Maisie an' Maudie. We're wiv Florrie's relations. You'll be in the second coach, Joe. I dunno who'll be wiv yer.' A sudden loud crack of thunder made them all jump. 'I 'ope it doesn't do this termorrer.' Nellie shook her head. 'Florrie never liked thunder.'

Joe nodded. 'She's gonna be missed,' he said. 'I remember when I first come ter Bermon'sey. She looked proper stern when I knocked on 'er door fer lodgin's. She turned out ter be a diamond.'

'She always 'ad a soft spot fer you, Joe,' Nellie told him. 'She loved ter fink everybody was talkin' about 'er 'avin' a young man. That was Florrie all over. They broke the mould when they made 'er.'

Carrie noticed a look of distraction appear on her mother's face and she became concerned. 'Look, Mum, yer've got a long day in front of yer termorrer. Why don't yer go up an' get inter bed,' she urged her. 'I'll bring yer cocoa up in a few minutes.'

As the evening wore on, the storm gradually lessened. Soft music was playing on the wireless as Carrie ironed Nellie's coat in the scullery. Rachel sat at the parlour table writing a letter to Derek. Joe was lying back in his chair with his eyes closed, his feet resting on the iron fender. Suddenly Rachel looked over to him. 'Is it one or two g's in conflagration?' she asked him.

Joe opened his eyes and scratched at his head. 'Two, I fink. No, 'ang on, it's one,' he replied.

'Never mind, I'll put war,' Rachel said smiling.

'Is that to young Derek?' Joe asked.

'Who else?' Rachel replied, giving him a coy grin.

'Don't ferget ter tell 'im yer love 'im,' Joe said jokingly.

Rachel put down her pen and wiped ink from between her fingers. 'Derek's finishin' 'is trainin' soon. 'E'll be gettin' a ship then,' she told him.

' 'E's a nice young lad,' Joe remarked. 'I 'ope 'is intentions are honourable.'

'I wanted us ter get engaged,' Rachel said softly, eyeing the door in case her mother overheard her, 'but Derek feels we should wait.'

'Well, I fink the lad's talkin' a lot o' sense,' Joe told her. 'Yer both still young an' there's a lifetime in front of yer. Jus' take it easy.'

'Yeah, but if war does start, Derek could be away fer ages,' Rachel said, her face flushing slightly. ' 'E might be killed or badly wounded. I want 'im ter know I'm waitin' fer 'im, so 'e'll be more careful.'

Joe smiled fondly at her. 'Look, luv, Derek's gonna be all right, an' in any case it might not come ter war.'

Rachel stared down at her ink-stained fingers for a few moments. 'Yer love Mum, don't yer, Joe?' she asked quietly.

'More than anyfing,' he replied.

'Well, if it was you in Derek's place would you be sure that Mum would wait fer yer, as long as it took?'

'As long as it took,' he said.

'Well, that's 'ow I want Derek ter feel, that I'd be waitin' fer 'im, no matter 'ow long it took,' Rachel said with feeling.

'I'm sure 'e does. I could see that look in 'is eyes when yer came back from Brighton,' Joe told her, a ghost of a smile playing around his lips.

Rachel let her shoulders sag as she sat at the table. She felt at ease with Joe, she always had done, and she knew she could confide in him, tell him that she and Derek were lovers, but she knew by the look on his face that there was no need. He already knew. Did her mother know? she wondered. She and Joe would have talked about the trip to Brighton, and after all, they were lovers themselves. They would know the signs, see the looks she and Derek exchanged constantly.

Rachel picked up the pen once more. Joe closed his eyes and grunted as he stretched out in the armchair. Soon Derek would be home on end-of-training leave, and then maybe there would be a long separation. She would need him to love her, and not just during stolen moments alone with him. She would want to spend the nights with him, but she could not expect her mother to allow them that sort of freedom, however understanding she was. Being in love was so complicated, she sighed.

At eleven o' clock precisely the following morning, 24 August 1939, the funeral cortège left Page Street. Three horse-drawn coaches followed the hearse and almost everyone in the street saw it leave. Nellie and Maisie walked arm in arm to their carriage, closely followed by Sadie who was holding on to a very distressed Maudie. Old men stood silent at their doorsteps, their caps held reverently in their hands, and women wept into handkerchiefs. As the cortège turned into the Jamaica Road, Albert Lockwood emerged from his corner shop, cap in hand. Terry Gordon and his wife Patricia stood together at the entrance to the public bar, like the shopkeeper paying their respects to someone they had hardly known but nevertheless mindful of the respect and love Florrie Axford had gained during her long lifetime from the people of Page Street and many other parts of the riverside borough.

Billy Sullivan's ring-scarred face was set hard as he watched Florrie's body leave the street and tears welled up in his eyes as he stood alone at his doorstep. Sadness weighed heavily on him. He had returned from Paddington Station less than half an hour ago after seeing Annie and the children onto the Gloucester-bound train. Annie had shed a few tears as she clung to him, while the children stood subdued, not understanding the reasons for leaving their father. The station had been packed with women and children, many with labels pinned to their coats and all looking serious-faced as they boarded the trains for the West Country. Billy had stood sad-eyed as he waved Annie and the children off, and now his loneliness and sorrow threatened to overwhelm him.

Chapter Seven

On Saturday, 2 September, Joe and Carrie were married at the registry office in the Town Hall. They had decided to delay their honeymoon because of the exodus of evacuees and the transit of military personnel through the main stations, but they entertained their friends with food and drink at the house throughout the sunny Saturday. Nellie sat with her old friends in the parlour, while outside in the freshly washed cobbled yard a trestle table was set out with plentiful sandwiches and bottles of beer.

Sharkey Morris, Carrie's yard man, had been in early that morning to hose the yard down, and he now sat in the parlour with a pint of ale in his gnarled hand. He was nearing eighty and still sprightly for his age, although his eyesight was failing. He sat talking to Rachel, who had become very attached to the old man since he first came to work for her mother.

'I remember when yer mum was only a slip of a gel,' he told her. 'She used ter wear an apron that touched the ground when she worked in yer farvver's cafe. Good ter me, she was. She knew I was watchin' out fer 'er an' she used ter give me free cups o' tea. I wouldn't let none o' the customers take liberties wiv 'er, not while I was in the cafe. They all knew it too. They knew better than ter mess about wiv ole Sharkey.'

'You an' my gran'farvver were good friends, wasn't yer, Sharkey?' Rachel said.

Sharkey nodded his head vigorously. 'Me an' ole Will Tanner were the best o' mates,' he told her. 'What I liked about yer gran'farvver was the way 'e stood up ter that ole goat Galloway. Will wasn't frightened of 'im, not Will Tanner.'

Rachel sat listening for some time to Sharkey's reminiscences and then, when the Page Street women drew Sharkey into their conversation, she made her exit. Outside in the yard, its cobblestones warmed by the sun, she sat with Danny and his pretty wife Iris on a wooden bench and watched the children running around and squealing happily. Danny was looking worried though, and once or twice he left the yard to seek out Billy.

'I'm worried about that bloke,' he told Iris when he returned for the second time. ' 'E told me 'e was gonna be 'ere fer sure, but there's no sign of 'im.'

Carrie came out into the yard and looked around. 'No Billy?' she asked her brother.

Danny shrugged his shoulders. ' 'E's missin' Annie an' the kids. I bet 'e's proppin' the bar up at the Kings Arms,' he replied, looking at Iris for her sanction to go and look for him.

Iris gave Rachel a wry smile. 'Yer'd fink the two of 'em were 'usband an' wife the way they worry over each over, wouldn't yer?' she remarked.

Danny leaned his back against the wall. 'Billy can look after 'imself,' he said with feigned indifference. 'It's just that when 'e's 'ad a drink too much 'e's inclined ter get a bit stroppy. I wouldn't like 'im gettin' inter trouble. Since that new guvnor's took over the Kings Arms there's a few strange faces in there. Some of 'em look a bit evil.'

Iris knew that her husband would be like a cat on hot bricks until Billy Sullivan showed up, especially after promising Annie that he would keep an eye on him. They were like two boys rather than grown men in their forties, she thought. 'P'raps yer'd better go an' see if 'e's all right,' she said with another wry smile.

Danny acted as though he was making up his mind. 'Er, yeah, all right. I'd better go,' he said, getting up as if it was a chore.

He let himself out through the wicket gate into the quiet street. A few women stood at their front doors chatting to neighbours and two small boys were playing marbles in the gutter. Above, the sky was cloudless and a hot sun blazed down on the dusty backstreet. Salmon Lane was a few streets along from Page Street and it took Danny barely five minutes to get to the Kings Arms. It was nearing two o' clock when he pushed open the door of the corner pub and saw the damage. The customers were all at the far end of the bar, standing away from the broken glass and sopping wet floor. The barman and a couple of helpers were busy clearing up the mess.

Danny groaned aloud. 'What 'appened?' he asked, dreading the reply.

The barman pointed to the shattered ornamental mirror behind the counter. 'The dopey git chucked a bar stool at it,' he growled. 'Then it turned into a right free-for-all. Terry called the police an' then 'e copped a bottle on 'is crust. I don't think 'e was 'urt too bad but 'e's gone ter Guy's ter be stitched up. Mind you, it could 'ave bin a lot worse.'

'Billy?' Danny asked, knowing what he was going to hear.

' 'E's at Dock'ead nick. 'E's . . .'

Danny did not wait for the barman to finish. He rushed out of the pub, his heart sinking. 'What a stupid idiot,' he groaned to himself. What would Annie say? She's only been away for less than two weeks and already her husband's in trouble with the police and most likely

58

facing a jail sentence for assaulting a publican.

At Dockhead he hurried up the steps of the police station and pushed open the swing door. 'I've come to enquire about a Billy Sullivan,' he said, looking anxiously at the station sergeant.

The officer carried on scribbling in a book for a few moments then he looked up with doleful eyes. 'Billy Sullivan? Just 'ang on a minute. Fred, 'ave we got a Billy Sullivan 'ere?'

The police constable sitting at the back of the office pointed to a side door. ' 'E's in there wiv the chief inspector.'

The sergeant turned back to Danny. 'Jus' take a seat, 'e shouldn't be too long,' he said with a wave of his hand.

Danny sat down on a long wooden bench beside the counter and stared down at his shoes. 'Of all the stupid, inconsiderate, drunken idiots,' he groaned to himself.

Suddenly he heard voices and he looked up to see Billy emerge from the side room followed by a familiar figure. Billy had what looked like the makings of a black eye and he was grinning widely as he shook hands with the detective. Danny stood up quickly, surprise and relief showing on his face as Billy walked over to him. 'What's goin' on?' he asked.

Billy slipped through the counter and put his arm round his confused friend. 'Yer remember the inspector, don't yer, Danny?' he said, nodding over to the hefty figure of Chief Inspector Green. ' 'E was the one we saw over the business at the gym.'

The detective waved to Danny as he walked back into his office and Billy led the way from the station. 'I'm glad that's over,' he said.

Danny stopped and turned to face his friend. 'Well?' he asked in an impatient voice.

The ex-boxer shrugged his broad shoulders. 'It was like this, yer see,' he began. 'Yer remember after we got back from the weddin' I told yer I 'ad ter pop 'ome fer a few minutes an' I'd see yer later? Well, when I did what I 'ad ter do I decided to 'ave a couple o' drinks in the Kings Arms before comin' round ter the reception. Anyway, there I was 'avin' a comfortable chat wiv Terry Gordon an' that missus of 'is when these two blokes come in. They was total strangers ter me. Terry didn't know 'em eivver. They both looked like they'd already 'ad a skinful an' one of 'em was shoutin' the odds an' upsettin' the customers. I didn't take no notice at first, but then one bloke knocked against ole Fred Dougall an' Fred told 'im ter mind what 'e was doin'. This bloke goes an' shoves the ole feller in the chest. That's when I jumped in.'

Danny had a smile on his face as he listened to Billy's account of the fracas. 'Yeah, go on,' he prompted.

'Well, I told the bloke ter pick on somebody 'is own age an' 'e 'as the cheek ter tell me ter piss orf,' Billy continued, 'so I told 'im in no uncertain terms ter be'ave 'imself. Terry Gordon came round the counter an' told 'em ter leave, an' wiv that, one o' the blokes picks up a bottle an' crowns 'im wiv it. There was blood everywhere an' Terry's missus was screamin' 'er 'ead orf. I grabs the bloke wiv the bottle an' floors 'im, then the ovver one jumps me. Ole Fred clouts 'im wiv a bar stool an' then the bloke grabs it from 'im an' aims it at the mirror be'ind the bar. After that the bloke staggers out the pub an' I couldn't get to im, 'cos I was detainin' the bloke I'd floored. The police came in an' told me ter come down the station ter make a statement, but it's all right, Danny, I ain't in any trouble.'

'Not unless those two come back lookin' for yer,' Danny replied.

Billy grinned. 'We'll be all right, Danny boy, we can 'andle 'em,' he said lightheartedly.

'We?' Danny queried.

Billy looked at his old friend with a bemused smile. 'Well, I rarely go in the pub on me Jack Jones. You're always wiv me,' he pointed out. 'I s'pose yer could always 'ide in the karsey if they do come back.'

Danny feigned to throw a punch and then slipped his arm round Billy's shoulders. 'C'mon, champ, they'll all be wonderin' where we've got to,' he said.

On Saturday night the rain started again and quickly turned into a storm that once more had the streets running with water as thunder crashed and lightning lit the sky. Children turned restlessly in their beds and adults winced at the loud thunder rolls. In Salmon Lane lightning struck a chimney and sent it crashing down onto the cobblestones, and in Page Street Maudie Mycroft sat in her parlour and held a hand to her cheek. 'It's the Lord's anger against the people who want war,' she told Ernest. 'The Lord's very angry.'

Her husband sighed. 'It's a storm, nuffink more,' he told her.

'Ernest Mycroft, you're a wicked man for disbelievin',' Maudie rebuked him.

'Look, luv, I'm not sayin' that the Lord ain't angry. We're all angry,' Ernest said quietly. 'What I'm sayin' is, the Lord ain't causin' the storm. It's yer actual elements. I don't fink we need ter go out an' build an ark.'

'Gawd fergive 'im,' Maudie said, raising her face to the ceiling. 'My 'usband is a wicked man, but Yer must fergive 'im.'

Ernest tried to hide a grin. 'I don't fink the Lord's too worried about me, Maud. 'E's got 'is work cut out at the 'Ouses o' Parliament ternight. The Cabinet's still sittin', accordin' ter the nine o' clock news.'

Dolly Dawson climbed the stairs to see if the thunder was disturbing her children and found that the two boys were sleeping peacefully.

60

Young Joyce must have been frightened, she thought, for she had curled up next to Leslie and was now sleeping soundly. Dolly went back down to the parlour and got on with her sewing, occasionally glancing over to where Wallace was sitting in an old armchair in his usual place in the corner facing the window. The drawn curtains were of a thick material but still the flashes of lightning could be seen through them.

The storm did not worry Wallace. He was engrossed in his weekly comic, his long legs drawn up under his chin as he stared wide-eyed at the coloured drawings of make-believe characters in a world of flowers and eternal sun. The looming war was not on Wallace's mind, nor were the problems of everyday living. The young man could not read and his damaged brain could not grasp the fast talk or the implications of the news bulletins which his mother listened to, and for which he had to be very quiet on pain of a cuff round the ear. He was happy in his own little world. When he was hungry he was given food and when he was tired he slept in a warm bed or beside the fire. Natural and basic needs did not trouble him too much, for when he felt an urge he simply followed his instincts. Other, more confusing feelings sometimes touched him but they soon faded, and only when a girl looked closely at him and smiled in a friendly way did Wallace feel a strangeness that made his neck hair tingle and his stomach churn. He would smile back, his lips struggling to form the necessary shape, and the smile would change to a leering, drooling laugh that reached up from his stomach and made his shoulders rise and fall rapidly.

Wallace was twenty-one, tall and gangling, with rounded shoulders, a pathetically friendly face, out of which stared the palest of blue eyes, and a ruddy complexion. His full lips were never still, constantly exposing his large white teeth. He was backward, brain-damaged from birth, and in the opinion of some folk who knew his father well, the product of a bad seed. Josiah Dawson had sired three normal children between his periods of incarceration in His Majesty's prisons, long after Wallace was conceived, and those same folk thought that it was quite likely they were not of his loins. Dolly would have been sorely hurt had she known what they were saying. She had only ever been with one man, and she had suffered his bouts of violence so as to receive the infrequent loving that he had to offer her.

Now, as she sat sewing Leslie's school trousers, she was feeling optimistic that her man would soon be released from prison. Word had it that many prisoners who were nearing the end of their sentences would be released now that war was inevitable. She awaited news of Josiah and dreamed of a repentant soul who would provide for her and the children, and give her the love she had missed for so long.

A clap of thunder louder than the rest made Dolly jump and she looked over at Wallace. 'C'mon, lad, it's time yer was abed,' she said, nodding her head towards the door.

Wallace put down his comic and unravelled his long legs from the chair. 'Milk,' he slurred.

Dolly was used to his simple way of speaking, and she had decided long ago that telling him off for not using courtesies would just confuse him. 'I'll bring yer some up,' she told him.

The storm was abating and Wallace lay awake beneath the bedclothes, his mind concentrating on noises. He heard the front door bolts slide, the sound of clinking glass as the empty milk bottles were placed on the doorstep, then the sound of bolts again. He heard the clatter in the scullery, the yard lavatory chain, and the back door bolts slide. The noise he was waiting for was the creaking of the stairs and the sound of the front bedroom door shutting. It was nearly time, he thought as he eased out of the bed and dressed. From the back of his bedroom door he took down a thick, grease-stained overcoat and scarf. One more noise would tell him that it was definitely time. He strained his ears and then he heard it, the sound of the bedsprings creaking in the front bedroom. With animal stealth Wallace let himself out of his room and crossed the landing. He knew that there was one stair which creaked loudly and he stepped over it. The bolts were simple to undo, and in no time he was walking briskly along the wet street listening to his footsteps echoing and the water gurgling down the drains.

It did not take him long to reach the river wall and it was there that he stopped, leaning his arms on the parapet, his eyes searching the darkness for the small tugs and the sea-scarred ships that came and went on the night tide. Here it was peaceful and secluded, and Wallace's mouth hung open as he saw the large dark outline of the Baltic freighter swinging slowly out into midstream from a point downriver of Tower Bridge. It was quiet tonight, but Wallace was not disappointed. He loved to watch the twinkling lights upriver and the red glow from the smelting works by Galleon's Reach; the river sounds held him in thrall, the soothing swish of muddy water lapping against the stanchions and the gurgling sound of bubbling mud. Nights like this touched a memory buried deeply in his mind of a time long ago, a Christmas when his mother carried him in her arms and his father was there with them. They had gone to the West End of London, and they stood watching the brilliantly illuminated fountains in Trafalgar Square splaying violet-coloured water into the icy pools. The splashing water shattered the light into spangles of changing colour like tiny glittering gems, rising and cascading endlessly. At that moment everything had been perfect.

As though guilty at tarrying too long, the young man turned away from the lights bobbing up and down on the river and set off for home, looking back once more before slipping his cold hands into his tattered overcoat and hurrying back along the deserted lane.

Chapter Eight

Rachel awoke early on Sunday morning and came down to the stone-floored scullery to light the gas over the large iron kettle. A few minutes later Carrie walked into the room and smiled sleepily at her daughter. 'I've 'ad a restless night,' she yawned.

Rachel sat down at the table and clasped her hands in her lap. 'Well, I reckon we'll know terday, Mum,' she said quietly.

Carrie sighed deeply. 'I would fink so,' she replied.

Footsteps sounded on the stairs and then Nellie walked into the scullery to join them.

'Don't tell me, Mum, yer didn't sleep very well,' Carrie said, a smile on her face.

Nellie tightened the wrap round her and sat down in a chair. 'I don't fink I got a wink o' sleep all night, what wiv the storm an' the news,' she said croakily. 'They said we'll know terday, Gawd 'elp us.'

Rachel turned out the gas jet and poured the boiling water into the teapot. 'Derek's gettin' a ship soon,' she said, stirring the tea. 'I'm expectin' a letter any day now.'

' 'E'll get leave before 'e goes, though, won't 'e?' Nellie asked.

' 'E's due fer seven days' leave, Gran.'

At that moment Joe came into the scullery scratching his tousled hair and yawning widely. 'I couldn't sleep a wink last night,' he groaned, leaning against the open door.

The two younger women laughed and Carrie stood up. 'I'd sit down if I were you,' she said with a warm smile. 'I'm gonna put the wireless on. There may be some news.'

Maudie, Sadie and Maisie sipped tea at the Sullivan house and Maudie had a worried look on her face. 'I didn't want ter say nuffink while Ernest was 'ere, but they've opened the crypt at the church fer a casualty clearin' station,' she informed them.

'I saw the police an' a warden comin' out o' that shelter late last night,' Maisie added. 'I 'ad 'alf a mind ter say somefink but I changed me mind. They wouldn't tell yer nuffink anyway.'

'The monastery, yer mean?' Sadie said with a crooked smile on her lined face.

Maisie looked peeved. 'I 'ope we don't ever 'ave ter use the place,' she said fearfully.

Maudie had decided to be brave, come what may. 'Well, if we do 'ave to, it'll be a lot better than sittin' in these places. A good shakin' an' the 'ole lot'll fall down round our ears.'

Sadie and Maisie exchanged glances at their friend's unusual forthrightness. 'I'll put the wireless on,' Sadie said as she got up, 'there may be some news.'

In the back yard, Fred Dougall, Ernest Mycroft and Daniel Sullivan were discussing the war crisis. 'They're makin' a big fing about these gas masks,' Ernest said. 'I don't reckon they'll ever use poison gas.'

'They used it in the last war,' Daniel told him.

'Yeah, but it wasn't used ter that extent,' Ernest persisted. 'I fink the Germans ended up gassin' 'alf their own blokes, what wiv the wind changin'. Besides, they'll get it back in double doses if they ever did use it, yer can bet yer life.'

The other two elderly men nodded in agreement and Fred pointed to the chicken coop. ' 'Ere, Daniel, is that a Rhode Island Red?'

Daniel shook his head. 'It's a bloody crossbred, if yer ask me,' he growled. 'I got it down Club Row. The bloke said it was a prize bird, but it ain't bin doin' much treadin' wiv my lot of 'ens. Four bloody eggs we got last week an' two of 'em was only the size of a pea. I tell yer what though, the bleeder must wake the 'ole street up wiv 'is cock-a-doodlin'. My Sadie reckons she's gonna wring its neck if it keeps on the way it is. The ovver day she said ter me, " 'Ere, Dan, that bird's jus' like you, all talk an' no do".'

Ernest chuckled and leaned against the lavatory door. 'I bin 'avin' a bit of a ding-dong wiv me ole woman,' he said. 'Well, not exactly a ding-dong but more like a difference of opinion. Yer see, she reckons we should go an' live wiv 'er sister in Kent. She's got the 'ouse to 'erself since 'er ole man died, an' Maud reckons we'd be better orf out o' Bermon'sey if the bloody balloon does go up. I told 'er I ain't budgin' but she can go if she wants to. Blimey, I couldn't live wiv 'er sister. She's a right scatty mare an' more nervous than our Maudie. I'd be a bundle o' nerves meself if I 'ad ter live wiv the both of 'em.'

Fred and Daniel grinned as they exchanged glances, and then they heard Sadie calling out. 'The Prime Minister's speakin' at quarter past eleven.'

'Well, we'll soon be put out of our misery, mates,' Daniel remarked.

In the house in Tyburn Square, George Galloway sat in the large front room overlooking the square. The sun's rays shone down onto the faded carpet and the black-leaded grate. Mrs Duffin the housekeeper had been in that morning and left the old man a cold lunch of cheese salad and pickles. Mrs Duffin had little to say. She would whisk round the place, leaving it spotlessly clean, and then prepare a midday or evening meal as required. She lived nearby and had been a good friend of Nora Flynn, George Galloway's previous housekeeper, and having been well versed in the likes and dislikes of the old man, she had so far managed not to antagonise him.

Now, as he sat alone in the house, George ruminated gloomily. It only seemed a short time since the last war, he thought. It had been a Sunday morning then, when the military called to tell him his elder son Geoffrey had been killed in action on the Somme.

He stood up and stamped his foot on the floor in an attempt to get the blood flowing again and then he walked over to the wireless cabinet and opened the doors. For a short while he twiddled with the knobs and then the high-pitched oscillation faded and the clear tones of a theatre organ rang out. He sat down again to await the Prime Minister, glancing at the decanter standing on the small table at his elbow. Normally he would not have a whisky until midday but this morning George decided that the situation called for an early, stiff drink.

Across the River Thames, in a quiet and leafy avenue on the edge of Ilford, Frank Galloway was reading the Sunday papers with a miserable expression on his fleshy face. He had had a bad week's racing and owed the bookmakers a tidy sum, and to add to that his wife Bella had been ill tempered and moaning at him at the least excuse. His daughter Caroline had been very testy lately too, and he was of the opinion that she should find herself a young man and flee the nest, preferably as soon as possible.

Bella was in the bedroom, still clad in a flowered wrap and with her hair swept up into a knotted white towel. She was in her mid-forties and beginning to look every bit her age. Her once beautiful face was lined around the eyes and mouth and her complexion was marked with patches of red on her cheekbones. Her blue eyes were puffy and she wore an irritated expression. War would certainly mean the closing of all the theatres in London, she reasoned, and her agent Hymie Golding had been less than helpful in finding work for her. What was worse, Barry Herrington had not been in touch and the rumour was that he had been seeing a young starlet lately. In addition to these tribulations, Caroline had come home very late the previous evening and boldly announced that she had finished with Desmond Controy. 'After all the hard work I've put in to get the two of them together,' Bella sighed to herself. After all, Desmond was progressing well in the theatre and there was talk of his getting a film part very shortly. True, a war would slow down his career but he had a good future, and he was shortsighted, a condition which would keep him out of uniform. Caroline was stupid to end the relationship, Bella fumed.

Frank put down the newspaper and leaned back on the settee. The last few weeks had been very trying for him. There had been masses of paperwork to get through and two of his drivers had decided to volunteer for the services. The war crisis had thrown everything into chaos. Nothing was clear at the moment regarding the transport; there was talk of a motor pool being set up to handle essential supplies, and the existing contracts hung in the balance. His liaison with Peggy Harrison was very shaky at the moment too. Some of the excitement had waned, and Peggy appeared to be blaming herself for her husband's illness. The shock of finding out about their affair on top of other problems concerning his business had caused his mind to snap, and Theo was now in a mental hospital with little likelihood of ever recovering.

Frank's thoughts were interrupted as Bella walked into the room and motioned to the wireless. 'Hadn't you better put it on?' she said irritably. 'The Prime Minister's speaking in five minutes.'

A strange stillness had settled over London as the sun climbed up into a cloudless sky. In the riverside borough of Bermondsey the quietness was broken by a tug whistle as it took up the strain on a brace of barges. Page Street and the neighbouring streets were deserted as everyone gathered round their wireless sets to hear the Prime Minister's broadcast.

The tired, flat voice of Neville Chamberlain carried out through open windows: 'I am speaking to you from the Cabinet Room at Ten Downing Street. This morning the British Ambassador handed the German Government a final note, stating that unless we heard from them by eleven o' clock that they were prepared at once to withdraw their troops from Poland, a state of war would exist between us. I have to tell you that no such undertaking has been received and that consequently this country is at war with Germany . . .'

Even before the Prime Minister had finished speaking folk were coming out into the street to talk with their neighbours. They huddled in little groups, occasionally turning their worried faces skyward, as though expecting an enemy air armada to appear at once. Others hurried along backstreets to their friends and scattered families, all anxious, fearful of the unknown and eager to seek comfort with those they loved.

At the Dawson household Dennis and Leslie were searching through their boxes of lead soldiers, Joyce was sitting in one corner talking to her one-eyed doll, while Dolly sat with her ear glued to the fading wireless, listening to the Prime Minister and occasionally waving frantically for the two boys to be quiet. Wallace was sitting in the back yard, his large feet resting on an empty beer crate, his face turned towards the warm sun. Suddenly a loud wailing started up, its rising and falling tone growing to a crescendo, and then it died away.

'Quick! It's an air raid!' Dolly screamed, grabbing up her daughter and shepherding her boys out of the house.

Wallace had hurried in, troubled by the unfamiliar noise, and he shuffled behind the rest of the family as they dashed along to the shelter on the elbow of Page Street, with people joining them on the way. Maudie appeared from her house on the arm of her husband, and Sadie Sullivan came trotting along beside Maisie. Fred and Daniel followed behind their wives and an ARP warden waved them down the gently sloping path into the entrance. Granny Massey slipped and was held up by her two daughters. Charlie Alcroft came down the slope in his carpet slippers, and the Mortimers from Bacon Buildings came hurrying along with their tribe of children swarming around them, the smallest hanging on to Ada Mortimer's shabby coat. Bringing up the rear was the Casey family. Ada Casey was a mousy-haired woman in her late thirties and with a cast in her left eye. She was a head taller than her husband Tom, a wiry individual in his forties with close-cropped hair and ears that stood out boldly. Two of the three children had casts in their left eyes, which had earned the family the unfortunate distinction of being known as the 'cross-eyed Caseys'.

Last to come into the shelter were the three Salter girls, looking around anxiously as they sat down together on a bench near the door.

'Where's that bloody farver of ours got to?' Brenda Salter growled to her younger sister.

'Gawd knows,' Lily replied, smiling sweetly at the staring Ada Casey.

' 'E's still up the Kings Arms, that's fer sure,' Barbara Salter cut in sharply.

'Just wait till 'e shows 'is face in 'ere, I'll give 'im what for,' Brenda said with venom. ' 'E knows 'ow we worry over 'im.'

'Give 'im a chance, Brenda,' Lily cut in. 'We've only just got 'ere ourselves.'

Brenda gave her younger sister a disdainful look. 'Anybody else would be out o' the pub like a rocket, but not our farver. If the bleedin' place was burnin' round 'is ears 'e'd still finish 'is pint.'

Suddenly the much maligned Maurice Salter slipped into the shelter, and as he caught sight of his three daughters he shook his head slowly before slumping down beside them. 'I knew it, I just knew it,' he said with emphasis.

'Knew what?' Brenda asked irritably.

'I knew yer'd all run out an' leave the gas on,' Maurice replied. 'I could 'ave bin killed runnin' back ter the 'ouse ter check. Didn't I warn you silly mares? Didn't I tell yer only the ovver night what could 'appen if yer leave the gas on?'

The three Salter girls looked shamefacedly at him and Lily patted his hand. 'It's a good job we've got you ter look after us, Dad,' she purred.

Brenda and Barbara exchanged meaningful glances and Maurice

settled down on the bench with a self-satisfied look on his broad face.

'Jus' remember in future. Yer can't be too careful wiv gas,' he said smugly, as he leaned his back against the damp concrete wall.

The shelter construction took the general shape of a wide tunnel, separated into two galleries by a thick concrete wall running down the whole length. The local ARP wardens had arranged with the police that the Bacon Street inhabitants should use the left-hand shelter and Page Street folk the right-hand one, so that should there be a direct hit on the shelter, identification would be that much easier.

Sadie had other ideas, however. ' 'Ere, Mais, did yer 'ear that copper tellin' the Bacon Buildin's mob ter go in the ovver shelter?' she asked as she made herself comfortable on the hard wooden bench against the wall.

'Yeah, I thought it was strange,' Maisie replied, scratching her left ear.

'It's ter keep us from arguin',' Sadie told her. 'There's one or two nasty so-an'-so's live in those buildin's an' they might start trouble.'

'What, like that Casey family?' Maisie ventured.

Sadie shook her head. 'Nah. They're a nice family,' she replied. 'Ada Casey's as good as gold. Mind you I ain't got much time fer that lazy git of an 'usband of 'ers. 'E's always orf sick, accordin' to Ada.'

'What's 'e do fer a livin'?' Maisie asked.

'As little as possible. 'E's a tram driver,' Sadie told her.

Maudie was sitting quietly, her ears pricked for the sound of falling bombs; whenever her friends looked in her direction she gave them a brave smile.

The last arrival walked into the gloomy, kerosene-lit interior and squeezed into the only available space, beside Brenda Massey, further along the cavern where she sat with her mother and sister.

'Yer Annie's 'usband Billy, ain't yer?' Brenda asked the sleepy-eyed newcomer.

Billy nodded, brushing a hand over his dishevelled hair. 'I slept late. The bloody siren frightened the life out o' me,' he grinned.

Brenda laughed nervously. She was an attractive brunette of forty with smiling eyes and prominent white teeth. 'My name's Brenda, an' that's me sister Rose,' she said. 'I 'ad a right job wiv Mum. She didn't want ter come down the shelter. It's a good job Rose was visitin'. She 'elped me get 'er out the 'ouse. Rose's two boys are evacuated an' 'er bloke's in the navy.'

Billy smiled at the friendly woman. 'Are you married?' he asked.

Brenda nodded. 'My ole man's in the merchant navy. We 'aven't got any children,' she replied.

Billy glanced around at the rows of anxious people chatting nervously. There were four rows of seating, long benches arranged along each wall and down the centre of the concrete cavern, the people on the middle benches sitting back to back. There was a strong smell of carbolic in the air and the temperature was rising steadily. Billy looked up at the ceiling. There were two small vents spaced some distance apart and he could see the smoky fumes from the kerosene lamps wafting up through them.

'It's gettin' stuffy in 'ere,' Brenda remarked. 'I 'ope we don't 'ave ter stay 'ere too long.'

At that moment the faint wail of the all-clear sounded and a cheer went up. The heavy stable-type doors were opened and a welcome draught of fresh air rushed in. People were already milling around at the entrance and Billy leaned down and took one of Granny Massey's arms. 'C'mon, gel, time ter go,' he joked.

Brenda took her mother's other arm while Rose gathered up the handbags. The old lady winced as the circulation came back into her legs and she sagged. 'I ain't 'avin' too much o' this, I can tell yer,' she moaned. 'Next time the bleedin' maroon goes I'm turnin' over an' puttin' the bedclothes over me 'ead. If yer ter go, yer'll go, no matter where you are.'

Brenda pulled a face at Billy, her eyes flashing. 'Annie's away wiv the kids, ain't she, Billy?' she asked.

He nodded, suddenly feeling a little uneasy. He was very lonely in the house at night. He missed the laughter of the children, Annie's warm body next to his and her arm over him as she slept. 'I'm goin' down ter Gloucester soon ter see 'em all,' he said quickly.

The exodus continued and Billy blinked in the strong sunlight as he helped the old lady up the slope and out into Page Street. There was time for a pint, he decided and then he had to present himself at the Tanners' house for Sunday dinner.

In Wilson Street the air-raid siren had precipitated similar scenes as everyone rushed for the shelter on the ground floor of the warehouse at the river end of the turning. The building had been reinforced with thick wooden supports reaching up to the high ceiling. Sandbags partially covered the entrance against blast and there was a large gas blanket that was pulled down over the heavy iron door. Like the shelter in Page Street, it was stuffy on that fine morning but the families here sat around more comfortably on sacks of nut kernels. The place smelled of spice and was lit by two unshaded electric light bulbs.

Danny Tanner sat with Iris while the children played unconcernedly. Seated next to Danny was an elderly man with a walrus moustache and wiry hair poking from the sides of his cap. Once or twice he looked hard at the younger man, and then after a while he said, 'Yer drink wiv young Sullivan, don't yer?'

Danny nodded. 'Me an' Billy are pals. We go back a long way,' he replied.

The old man wiped a finger along his thick moustache. 'I was in the Kings Arms the ovver Saturday when the trouble started,' he said. 'That pal o' yours can still chuck a right-'ander. 'E certainly put that monkey's lights out.'

Danny grinned. ' 'E was up an' comin' once,' he said proudly.

The old man nodded his head vigorously. 'I seen 'im box a score o' times,' he said, wiping his moustache again. ' 'E was in fer the title fight at one time. The war finished 'im though, like it finished a lot o' people. Don't you an' 'im train the kids in the gym?'

'We did once,' Danny replied. 'It's all bin stopped now though. They're usin' the place fer the ARP.'

The old man leaned towards Danny. 'I should keep yer wits about yer when yer in that Kings Arms, son,' he said in a low voice.

'Oh, an' why's that?' Danny asked.

'Look, son, I've bin livin' round this area all me life,' the old man went on, 'an' I've seen a few nasty characters come out o' the woodwork, but those two blokes Sullivan tangled wiv take the biscuit. They're what yer might call paid troublemakers. I was in the docks fer years an' when we 'ad the troubles in the twenties they brought a load o' scabs in ter break the strikes. Those two was scabs o' the first order. Musclemen, they was. We 'ad some set-to's wiv the likes o' them. I've seen 'em around, but it was the first time I seen 'em in the Kings Arms. It's got somefink ter do wiv that guv'nor. If yer ask me there's a few ole scores ter settle an' one was settled that Saturday. The lan'lord got a bottle over 'is 'ead an' they smashed the place up. If it wasn't fer Billy Sullivan, there'd 'ave bin a lot more 'arm done.'

'I know,' Danny replied. 'I went in lookin' fer Billy an' I saw the damage.'

The old man folded his arms and rocked backwards. 'Jus' take my tip,' he said quietly. 'Watch points when yer drink in there. I don't fink that's the last yer've seen o' those two monkeys.'

The blast of the all-clear brought a huge sigh of relief from the shelterers. Iris stood up and adjusted her coat. 'C'mon, kids, I got a dinner ter get,' she said, and to Danny she added, 'if yer goin' fer a drink, don't let Billy get too sloshed or 'e won't eat 'is dinner.'

Danny slipped his arm round Iris and pecked her cheek. 'I'll see yer 'ome wiv the kids first. We won't be late fer dinner,' he told her.

The all-clear was also greeted with a huge sigh of relief at the Maitlands' house in Salmon Lane. Nellie had collapsed on hearing the news that war had been declared and Joe had carried her into the back bedroom. She soon recovered, however, and she put the fainting fit down to lack of sleep. Carrie had seen the colour drain from her face and lips and she was afraid that it might be the start of a heart attack.

'I'm goin' fer the doctor, Mum,' she said firmly.

Nellie sat up in bed and grabbed her daughter's coat sleeve. 'Yer'll do no such fing,' she said, becoming agitated. 'I'll pop round ter see 'im meself termorrer. I only need a tonic.'

Carrie reluctantly bowed to her mother's wishes, and as she began preparing the dinner the air-raid siren sounded. During the warning period Carrie and Joe, along with Rachel, sat round the bed chatting to Nellie.

'What do I call myself now, Bradley or Maitland?' Rachel joked.

'Yer still yer farvver's child, Rachel,' Nellie told her.

'Poor Mum,' Rachel said feelingly.

'Why poor Mum?' Joe asked.

'Oh, an' poor Joe,' she said smiling at him with affection. 'You two are never gonna get an 'oneymoon now.'

Chapter Nine

The war was just two weeks old and already the opinion of many of the Kings Arms regulars was that it would be over in six months.

'We called their bluff an' they know they can't win,' one elderly docker remarked to his friend.

'I make yer right, Arfur. There's no way the Germans are gonna get frew that Maginot Line,' the friend replied. 'It's bloody laughable. Yer got two armies starin' at each ovver over them there fortifications an' neivver of 'em are gonna make any move. Yeah, I give it six months at the outside.'

One old man in a black seaman's jersey and cap puffed on his clay pipe and fixed the two friends with a contemptuous stare. 'It's gonna go on fer a long time, this war, mark my words,' he growled. 'All right, it might be quiet on the Western Front but it ain't all quiet at sea. Look at the ships what's bin sunk already. What about that passenger ship, the *Athenia*? It went down on the first day o' the war, an' what about the fishermen gettin' fired on while they're trawlin'?'

The first docker gave the old salt a look which told him to mind his own business. 'Wars are always gonna be fought at sea, mate, we all know that,' he answered in an offhand manner. 'It's bin like that from the year dot. It's 'cos we're a seafarin' nation, that's why. Take yer Nelsons an' yer Drakes. They went out ter do battle fer king an' country an' that's what's gonna 'appen in this war.'

'Queen an' country,' his friend corrected him.

'All right, queen an' country, but the trufe is, we're an island, an' there's no better navy in the world than the British.'

'Granted, but if yer fink it's all gonna be over in six months, yer got less sense than that bloody table,' the old seaman growled, turning his back on the pair.

Terry Gordon was busy serving pints, still looking a little out of sorts after his head injury, and he constantly cast his eyes over the gathered assembly for a strange face. His two attackers were known to him but he had refrained from saying so when he was interviewed by the police. He had been expecting some sort of trouble since the first day he took over the Kings Arms and it had not been long in coming. As he felt the tightness of his scalp where his wound was healing, it depressed him to think that there was still a lot of hate directed towards him.

Terry Gordon had been born in Dockhead, and when he was very young his family moved to the Elephant and Castle area. As a young man he had become a member of the McKenzie gang, a notorious family of villains who used protection rackets to control the local prostitutes, small shopkeepers and street bookmakers. At that time Terry's future wife Patricia was the girl friend of Dougal, the most sadistic of the brothers, but his ill treatment of her finally led her into the arms of the handsome young gang member, who had by that time become disenchanted with his way of life. When Dougal found out, he had him beaten up badly, but Terry was a determined character. He left the area, married Patricia and took over the management of a pub in Stepney, and for some time all was quiet. After a few years, however, when Terry and his wife decided to move back south of the river and buy into a very busy pub in Walworth, trouble reared its head once more. One night, Dougal and his brother Callum called into the pub and made Terry an offer of protection.

He refused to bow to their threats, and other business people in the area who were themselves paying extortionate rates to the McKenzies for so-called protection were given the lead that they needed; a rebellion was born. The area around the Elephant and Castle had recently been taken over by a tough Irish policeman who had vowed to clean it up, and Divisional Inspector Tommy O'Shay set about his task with relish. Dougal, Callum and one or two other senior members of the McKenzie gang finally got long sentences. Callum died in prison; Dougal McKenzie served his full sentence and came out a twisted, vengeful man, bent on seeking out those who had caused the gang's downfall.

When the Scot came back to his old haunts around the Elephant and Castle, he could see the changes. Most of his cronies had moved away and those left were older and wiser. Gone was the fear of the very name McKenzie, and the new young villains laughed behind the back of the heavily built, shuffling figure who had once ruled the area. There were still one or two loyal associates left, however, and Dougal started recruiting. He was in his forties now and slowing up, and whereas once he had been in the forefront of any violence, when word reached him that 'an old friend' had taken a pub in Dockhead, he sent in two hired musclemen to do the damage for him.

The landlord of the Kings Arms busied himself and worried. He had been very fortunate that Billy Sullivan was in the pub when the trouble started but it was obvious to him that Dougal McKenzie would not leave things as they stood. Maybe he should get a younger barman, he thought; someone who could look after himself and deter anyone from starting trouble. Maybe he should have a word with Billy Sullivan.

The Saturday evening was wearing on as Joe roused himself in front of the low fire. Carrie was sitting facing him, a newspaper resting on her lap.

'Did I fall asleep?' he asked, yawning widely.

Carrie smiled. 'Yer bin snorin' fer the past hour,' she chided him.

Joe sat up in his chair and looked at her closely. 'Is Rachel out?'

Carrie nodded. 'Carol called for 'er.'

Joe stared into the fire for a few moments then he looked up. 'D'yer know, it'd be nice if I could take yer ter the Kings Arms fer a quiet drink on Saturday evenin's but I daren't,' he said, lowering his eyes to gaze at his clasped hands.

Carrie folded the newspaper and dropped it on the floor by her feet. 'It doesn't bovver me in the least,' she replied. 'Do yer feel the need fer a drink?'

Joe shook his head. 'I like what I've got an' there's no way I'm gonna risk losin' it,' he told her firmly.

Carrie felt a sudden urge to hug him. He looked so childlike sitting there with his hair tousled and a very serious expression on his face. 'I'm very 'appy, Joe,' she said quietly.

He leant forward to rake the ash from the fire and then his face took on a thoughtful look. 'D'yer know what I'm finkin' about?' he said after a moment or two.

Carrie shook her head. 'No, I don't,' she replied with a warm smile. 'What yer finkin' about?'

'I was finkin' about the time when yer was gettin' that cafe on its feet an' yer came ter see me about some provisions,' he said, his grin broadening.

'In that little pub in Tower Bridge Road?'

'That's right, the Jolly Compasses,' Joe said. 'I remember lookin' at yer then an' finkin' ter meself 'ow beautiful yer was. There yer were, a young innocent in a nasty, grabbin' world, an' actin' like an 'ard-'eaded businesswoman. It certainly got me goin'.'

'Did yer see frew my bravado?' Carrie asked, smiling at him.

'Yeah, course I did,' he replied. 'There was no way I was gonna let yer not get a good deal that day though, Carrie. It was part o' the big plan.'

'Ter get me inter yer bed, yer mean?'

Joe looked down at his feet for a few moments and then his eyes came up to meet hers. 'I always knew yer were a little firecracker, ever since the time I saw yer pull that rearin' 'orse away from yer dad,' he said softly. 'I jus' wanted ter get ter know yer better at first, but sittin' there in that pub talkin' business wiv yer got ter me some'ow. I can't explain it but suddenly I wanted yer. Wanted yer like mad. I knew it was gonna 'appen eventually, I jus' knew.'

Carrie leaned forward in the chair with her chin cupped in her hand, her eyes sparkling. 'An' do I still excite yer?'

'More than ever,' he replied, his hand going out to hers.

The sound of the front door opening made them sit back with a grin, and Rachel walked into the parlour with a serious look on her face. 'Did yer listen ter the nine o' clock news?' she asked as she slipped off her coat.

Carrie and Joe both looked at her with anticipation.

'There's anuvver two ships bin sunk,' she told them. 'Carol got all upset. 'Er bruvver's at sea.'

Carrie knew what was on her daughter's mind. Derek would soon be at sea himself. 'Maybe the war won't last much longer,' she said softly, feeling at a loss for something to say that would ease Rachel's fears.

Joe stood up and put his arm round the young woman's shoulders. 'A couple more days an' Derek'll be 'ome, an' in the meantime I'm gonna put the kettle on fer a cuppa,' he said cheerfully.

Rachel's face brightened and she sat down in the chair Joe had just vacated. 'I was finkin', Mum. Would yer mind if me an' Derek went down ter Brighton fer a few days?' she asked suddenly. ' 'E wants ter see 'is Aunt Clara before 'e gets a ship.'

Carrie studied her fingernails for a few moments then looked up at her pretty young daughter. 'Rachel, I know you an' Derek are in love, it's obvious ter me, an' Joe,' she said in a soft voice. 'The problem is, yer both still very young. Gawd knows 'ow long this war's gonna go on for, an' yer young man's gonna be facin' a lot o' danger. Yer shouldn't take fings too fast. Don't do anyfing stupid, it could ruin yer life, both yer lives.'

Rachel leaned back in her chair. 'I know what yer mean, Mum,' she replied, her face colouring slightly. 'Yer fink I'll get pregnant on purpose, jus' so I've always got somefing ter remind me o' Derek if anyfing should 'appen to 'im.'

Carrie did not answer. The lump in her throat was rising and she averted her eyes to the fire.

'I want us ter get engaged, Mum,' Rachel went on. 'It's Derek who's draggin' 'is feet. 'E feels the same as you. 'E said we shouldn't do anyfing stupid an' we should wait till we see 'ow fings are gonna turn out.'

Carrie swallowed hard. 'Go ter Brighton wiv 'im, luv,' she said. 'Just be careful.'

Suddenly Rachel slipped onto her knees and buried her head in her mother's lap. 'I love yer, Mum, you an' Joe,' she said, 'an' I wouldn't bring any shame on yer. I jus' feel I'm very lucky ter 'ave yer both.'

Danny and Iris Tanner had just finished wrapping the last of the crockery in newspaper and packing it into a tea chest. Danny sat down on the edge of the scullery table and looked around.

'There's the breakfast fings ter wrap termorrer an' then we're ready,' he said with a satisfied smile.

Iris nodded. 'I'll be glad ter see the back o' this place,' she replied.

'It was our first 'ome,' Danny reminded her.

Iris came to him and slipped her arm round his waist. 'I'm not bein' 'orrible, Danny, but it's different fer a woman,' she said, looking up at him. 'I'm stuck 'ere all day wiv the kids an' it's a fankless task tryin' ter make somefink of it. Jus' look at that plaster, an' that gap in the door. The bedrooms are the same an' there's dampness everywhere. I'm worried fer the kids.'

Danny squeezed her to him. 'I know, luv,' he replied. 'The new place is a lot better than this, an' Billy's gonna 'elp me decorate it right frew. You'll be pleased when we've finished.'

' 'Ow many trips d'yer fink it'll take?' she asked.

Danny shrugged his broad shoulders. 'About two or three,' he told her. 'The wringer's the only problem. We'll 'ave ter make a special trip fer that. Not ter worry though. Billy's gonna give me an 'and.'

Iris leaned her head on her husband's shoulder. 'Well, luv, as this is our last night in this gaff, shall we 'ave an early night?' she said with a grin.

Danny looked briefly at the clock standing on the dresser and gazed through the window at the star-filled sky. 'If yer like,' he said, and chuckled. 'It's only twenty past one.'

Dolly Dawson took the letter down from the mantelshelf and read it again, then she hugged the paper to her ample bosom and sighed deeply. Her prayers had been answered. Josiah was being released from Dartmoor on Monday and he should arrive home late in the evening. She thought how nice it would be for the children and for Wallace especially. He missed his father badly and as long as Josiah stayed off the drink, things were going to be very nice in future. He was really a good man, Dolly told herself. It was just hard luck that he got himself into trouble at times. Maybe he had seen the error of his ways after his long sentence. The boys would remember him but Joyce had been just two years old when he went away and would not know him, she realised.

Wallace was lying awake in his room, dwelling on what his mother had told him earlier. He remembered his father being very angry and shouting at him when he broke a cup and getting a cuff round the ear, but there were good memories coming slowly into his mind too. He had been given a bright coin once when he was quiet, and then there was the time he went for a ride on the tram. No, that was a bad time, Wallace thought, not remembering exactly why. There was the man who shouted and it frightened him. The rattle of the tram had made his head

76

hurt and he was sick in the kerb afterwards. Wallace felt the pain starting up in his head again and he pulled the blanket right up over him and closed his eyes.

At closing time Billy walked back unsteadily from the Kings Arms to his empty house. In a week or two he would be going down to Gloucester to see Annie and the children but now time bore down heavily on him. He let himself into the house and went into the parlour. The fire had burned low and the room felt strangely cold. Billy looked around him, not bothering to sit down, and he sighed deeply. There was the piece of embroidery still lying on the shelf beside the armchair, and the photos of the children staring down at him from the mantelshelf. The drawn curtains looked crisp and fresh, one of the jobs his wife had done before leaving, and the grate was freshly black-leaded, another of Annie's weekly chores which she had done early on the morning she left, before the rest of the house was stirring. In the corner by the window was Mary Jane's old high chair, a piece of furniture that Annie would not part with, although Mary Jane had long since grown out of it.

Billy sat down heavily on the sofa and pondered what Terry Gordon had said to him that evening. 'Yer've got time on yer 'ands and in the evenin's now that yer missus an' kids are evacuated, Billy. Why don't yer put a few nights in be'ind the bar?' he had suggested.

Billy stared into the embers of the fire. Terry Gordon seemed a nice enough bloke, he thought, and his wife Pat was a friendly girl. The extra money would help too. He could take a few bits and pieces down to Annie and the kids on his visits, and maybe give her a few bob to help her out. Terry had been honest about the main reason behind his offer, too. There could be one or two undesirables coming into the pub and it would be Billy's job to see that they were shown the door. Terry wanted the Kings Arms to remain what it had always been, a family pub that was trouble-free. It had all been spelt out clearly, and what he had been told about the landlord's earlier life with the McKenzies and Dougal's hatred for him convinced Billy that Terry's life might well still be in jeopardy. The attack on him earlier could have been fatal, but fortune had smiled on him on that occasion.

As he sat in the quiet room, Billy thought about what Danny Tanner had told him a few days ago about the old man he met in the shelter. What the old man had said fitted with Terry's account. Well, if there was to be any comeback from the recent fight, maybe it would be better to meet it head-on from behind the bar instead of standing at the counter with his back to the door, Billy reasoned to himself. On that thought he turned off the gas jet over the mantelshelf and took himself up to his solitary bed.

In the large gloomy house in Tyburn Square the fire burned brightly in the spacious front room. The old man sat alone into the late hours, his face flushed with the heat and the whisky he had consumed. Since early evening, after his visitor had left, he had sat there mulling over the tragic events in his life and trying to make sense of it all. Just a few hours ago the past had been suddenly resurrected and it had shocked him to the core.

George Galloway poured himself another drink with an unsteady hand and took a large draught. The whole thing had started with a telephone message which his housekeeper had taken. 'A Mary O'Reilly would like to call round this afternoon at four. Very important,' the scribbled note said. George had picked the message up from beside the telephone when he got home at two o' clock. There was no phone number to ring.

At four o'clock exactly Mary O'Reilly arrived and George opened the door to her. He recalled seeing the frail, ashen-faced woman standing on his doorstep and immediately feeling uneasy. There was something in the woman's lifeless eyes which troubled him. What could she want with him?

'Yer'd better come in,' he said, leading the way into his front room.

The thin woman seated herself in the chair he directed her to and removed from her handbag a bundle of letters, securely tied with a thin red ribbon.

'I think yer should read these before I say anyfing,' she began. 'They're from yer son, Geoffrey, an' they were written ter me while 'e was in France.'

The old man looked at his visitor for a moment or two in disbelief, then without saying a word he undid the ribbon and stared down at the address on the top letter, written in what he recognised to be Geoffrey's spidery handwriting.

'They're in date order,' the visitor said quickly.

The old man read the letters, occasionally raising his eyes to glance at the frail woman facing him. He said nothing, but a shocked expression was frozen on his florid face. When he finally finished reading the dozen or so letters, he remained silent for a few moments, staring down at the last sheet of paper, while the woman sat quietly watching him and saying nothing.

Suddenly he looked up. 'The child. Is it livin'?' he asked quickly.

The woman nodded, a smile appearing on her ashen face.

'A boy?'

The woman coughed into her handkerchief and then reached into her handbag, taking out a dog-eared photograph. ' 'Is name's Tony an' 'e's twenty-one now,' she replied. 'That was taken when 'e was seventeen.'

George grabbed at the photograph and studied it intently for a while, trying to take in all he had just discovered. All his life the one thing he had wanted most since his two sons had grown up was a male grandchild to carry on the family name and the family business. His dearest wish had not been fulfilled, however, and he had resigned himself to the fact that the family name would die out. It had made him very sad. Now he had the letters that told him he did indeed have a grandson.

He looked up at the frail woman who had once been his dead son's mistress. 'Why didn't I ever get ter meet yer?' he asked in a gruff voice.

'I can't say fer sure,' she answered, quickly taking a handkerchief from her handbag. 'Geoffrey felt that yer never 'ad much time fer the few women 'e brought 'ome. I was married at the time as well, so that could 'ave bin why.'

'Why did yer wait all these years before lettin' me know I 'ad a gran'son?' George asked sharply.

Mary O'Reilly looked him firmly in the eye. 'Pride. Pride and anger in the beginnin',' she said. 'At first I was angry at Geoff dyin' while 'e was so young, so good an' kind. I loved 'im an' missed 'im. Then, when I got over the shock, I realised that I still 'ad a part o' Geoffrey wiv me an' I decided I'd bring the lad up ter be independent. My 'usband left me as soon as 'e found out I was carryin' anuvver man's child, but pride stopped me comin' ter you fer 'elp. Besides, I didn't know what yer reaction would be. I wasn't ter know yer'd take kindly ter bein' the gran'farvver of a bastard child. Fings are different now though. Tony's bin called up fer the army. 'E might get killed wivout knowin' the identity of 'is real farvver.'

'Yer mean yer never told the lad about my son bein' 'is farvver?' Galloway asked angrily.

Mary's eyes were watering as she tried to suppress her racking cough, and when she had composed herself she looked the old man squarely in the eye. 'I did tell Tony what 'is real farvver was like, an' 'ow much I loved 'im, when the boy was very young,' she replied. ' 'E'd seen yer son's name on the birth certificate as bein' the farvver, but I never told 'im that 'is farvver was the son of George Galloway the local cartage contractor. After all, yer not the only Galloway. Besides, I'd met a good man when Tony was a few months old. 'E treated the lad as 'e would 'ave done 'is own. 'E was killed in the docks when Tony was eighteen months old.'

George Galloway nodded. 'I see,' he said slowly. 'Well, I want ter meet 'im, yer understand? I'm the boy's gran'farvver an nobody can take that away from me. I loved Geoffrey dearly, despite what yer might fink, an' I want Goeff's son ter get 'is dues.'

The woman dabbed at the corner of her mouth with her handkerchief. 'There's anuvver reason fer me comin' ter see yer after all this time,' she said quietly.

'Oh, an' what's that?' George asked.

'I'm sufferin' from consumption,' she replied without emotion. 'I dunno 'ow long I've got. I wanna see my boy comfortable an' provided for. 'E's all I've got, an' I love 'im like yer loved your son.'

The old man stood up, his hard-heartedness softened by what he had heard. 'I'd like ter give yer somefink,' he said, turning away and going to the huge sideboard at one end of the room.

'There's no need, I can manage very well, fankin' yer,' she replied.

George opened a drawer and took out a folded wallet from which he withdrew two five-pound notes. 'Take this,' he said brusquely, waving away her protests. 'Yer should get somefink to ease that cough. Brandy's good.'

'Well, if yer insist,' she said, placing the money in her handbag.

'When can I see the boy, my gran'son?' he asked, trying to control the urgency in his voice.

'I'll get Tony ter come an' see yer as soon as 'e gets leave,' she told him. 'I've got yer phone number. I'll get 'im ter ring first.'

George showed Mary O'Reilly to the front door and stood watching while she walked slowly from the square, his mind still reeling.

The fire was dying now and George sat listening to the wind rustling the tall plane trees outside. For the hundredth time he cast his eyes on the bundle of letters lying on the small table at his elbow and he thought about the woman who had visited him and sat facing him in that room. His face was expressionless as he undid the thin red ribbon and once again read the contents. He picked up the one crucial letter that he had separated from the rest and held it in his gnarled hands, feeling its texture and trying to imagine how Geoffrey must have felt when he sealed that same letter shortly before he had been killed. It was sad that he never got the chance to see the boy. The lad had developed into a strapping young man, going by the photograph he had been shown. He did not seem to resemble Geoffrey to any large degree, but there was a similar bearing and colouring. Why had Geoffrey not brought his lady friend home before he went to war? George wondered. Would he have been so frightened of his own father? After all, he had stood up for himself at other times. He had intended to tell him, according to the letter, but he had not been given the chance.

Suddenly the hard old man collapsed into his leatherbound armchair and buried his head in his hands, sobbing like a child.

The room grew cold and dark. After a long time George stood up and composed himself, brushing a hand across his eyes as he poured another stiff drink. Soon he would meet Geoffrey's son, his own grandson, for the first time. There was much to be done.

Chapter Ten

On a Monday afternoon in early October Carrie stood with Joe at the yard gate in Salmon Lane and watched her daughter walking away down the street on the arm of Ordinary Seaman Derek Bamford. The young serviceman carried a suitcase and Rachel held a small zip-up bag as they hurried along to the tram stop.

'Young Rachel looks smart, doesn't she?' Carrie remarked. 'I thought the lad's lost a bit o' weight though.'

'So would you wiv the trainin' they get,' Joe said grinning, putting his arm round her shoulders.

'I 'ope I've done the right fing allowin' 'em ter go off like that,' Carrie said with a sigh.

'People are gonna talk anyway,' Joe reminded her. 'One day yer might be glad yer did agree.'

Carrie gave him a quizzical look. 'What d'yer mean, Joe?' she asked.

He merely shook his head. 'Jus' finkin',' he replied quietly.

At the end of the turning Rachel and Derek stopped to wave to them and then disappeared round the corner. Carrie sighed deeply and stepped back into the yard, and as Joe followed her she turned to give him a quick peck on the cheek.

'What's that for?' he asked grinning.

'Oh, jus' fer luck,' she replied.

At London Bridge the young lovers waited for their train to Brighton, both feeling happy and excited at the prospect of a whole week together. Servicemen and women stood around in large numbers and pairs of military policemen stalked the platforms, their eyes staring out mean and moody beneath stiff-peaked caps. Mothers with children, office workers and labourers waited alongside each other on the draughty platforms, looking tired and resigned. Bored porters pushed large laden barrows and station guards looking very important strutted along the platforms with green flags tucked under their arms.

An old lady walked onto the platform and put her small suitcase down near the two lovers. 'Is this the Brighton train?' she asked Derek.

He nodded. 'It'll be comin' in in a few minutes,' he told her.

The old lady smiled her thanks and arched her aching back. 'It's some time since I've bin ter Brighton,' she told Derek.

'That's nice,' he remarked, wondering what else he could have said.

'Not really,' she replied. 'Me daughter's livin' down there. She wants me ter stay wiv 'er. I live in Rovver'ithe, yer see. Margie finks it's a bit too near the docks fer comfort, what wiv the war startin'. Margie's me daughter. Nice gel. Nice 'usband too. Bert's 'is name. Got a gammy foot though. Nice-lookin' feller. Works in a bank. Shame about 'is foot though.'

Derek was getting embarrassed and he half turned to face Rachel, who was grinning widely.

' 'Ere, young man, I was wonderin' if yer knew my Albert,' the old lady asked, pulling on Derek's arm. ' 'E's in the navy like yerself. Looks really smart in 'is uniform, does Albert. 'E's turned a few gels' 'eads, let me tell yer. 'E looks a bit like you, but 'e's got a bit more meat on 'im. 'E's me eldest son, is Albert. I've got anuvver two boys. One's in the army an' the ovver, well, I don't talk about 'im much. Sammy's easily led. There's no 'arm in 'im really. Mind you though, that there Borstal soon sorts 'em out. When 'e gets out, my Sammy's gonna volunteer fer the army. It'll do 'im good, I should fink.'

Derek smiled patiently at the old lady and decided he would pay a visit to the toilet to escape her endless chatter.

' 'Urry up, Derek, the train's gonna be in any minute,' Rachel said with a grin, feeling sorry for him.

When Derek emerged from the toilet he saw that the old lady had moved on. Rachel was standing alone, being eyed by two soldiers. He quickly went over to her and slipped his arm round her slim waist, much to her delight and the chagrin of the two servicemen. The train was just pulling in to the station and Derek picked up the suitcase. 'I don't fink there's much chance o' gettin' a compartment to ourselves,' he said, taking hold of Rachel's arm.

The train had been shunted in from a siding and it was empty. Derek slid open a compartment door and took his time getting the cases stowed in the luggage rack, hoping it would stop other passengers choosing that particular compartment.

The whistle sounded and the train jerked out of the station. Rachel sat back in her seat and eyed Derek saucily. 'Well, we're alone,' she said. 'Gi' me a kiss.'

Derek looked towards the door before slipping his arm round her, and then their lips met.

The train gathered speed, and as the evening sun dipped away in the west, dark clouds were arriving to the east. The two young lovers stared out of the window, noticing the signs of war. Sandbags, steel police boxes, shelters and warning notices were apparent everywhere, and when the train began to leave the city behind, other preparations were just as evident in the countryside. Tank traps, barbed wire, concrete pillboxes and trenches sprawled across the fields and hedgerows, and as darkness descended the lights would be smothered.

The compartment door was suddenly flung opn. ' 'Ello, me dearies, I wondered if I'd find yer,' the old lady said smiling.

Derek groaned inwardly and Rachel gave the woman a polite smile. 'There's a nice young man mindin' me case,' she said. 'I'm jus' stretchin' me legs. They get a bit stiff what wiv the sittin'. They'll be all right though. Need ter get the blood flowin'. D'yer mind if I sit 'ere fer a while? I feel a bit tired all of a sudden.'

Derek leaned forward and took the old lady's arm, easing her down into the seat opposite him, and she gave him an appreciative smile. 'Yer do look like my Albert,' she said.

Rachel looked through the carriage window at the trees and fields which were gradually assuming the colours of autumn. She felt strangely at peace with everything and unconcerned at the woman's intrusion, unlike Derek, who appeared to be agitated and ill at ease.

' 'Ow long are yer stayin' in Brighton?' the old lady asked, clasping her hands in her lap.

'Just a week,' Rachel answered. 'Derek's due back on Sunday night.'

The woman smiled at the two young people, her eyes moving from one to the other. 'Are you two finkin' o' gettin' married then?' she asked suddenly.

Rachel nodded and gave Derek a quick glance to gauge his reaction but he merely shrugged his shoulders. 'There's a lot ter fink about,' he said, 'what wiv the war.'

The old lady sighed and leaned her head against the seat cushion. 'It's a tryin' time fer all of us, but it's 'arder fer young people,' she said quietly. 'None o' my children are married yet. Albert's engaged though.'

'We're finkin' o' gettin' engaged,' Rachel said, giving Derek a challenging look.

The young man smiled sheepishly. 'Yeah, we are, pretty soon,' he said, folding his arms and trying to look determined.

For a while the old woman stared out of the carriage window, then she looked at Rachel. 'Brighton's a nice place. I remember the last time I was in Brighton,' she said. 'It was a lovely summer's day an' I was walkin' along the seafront wiv me daughter. Anyway, there was this gypsy fortune-teller's place by the steps what led down ter the sands, an' my Margie ses ter me, "What about gettin' our fortunes told, Mum?" Well, ter be honest, I don't go a lot on them there people who look inter those crystal balls. I fink it's a load o' rubbish. Anyway we went in an' 'ad our fortunes told an' the gypsy said I'd be in fer a good spell o' luck durin' the next few months, an' she told me there'd be some money comin' ter me.'

'Was she right?' Rachel asked.

The old lady snorted. 'Luck? Gawd 'elp us, dearie, this past year I've 'ad nuffink but bad luck,' she replied. 'First me 'usband died of a stroke, then I fell down the stairs an' ended up in 'orspital fer nigh on four months wiv me back, an' ter crown it all me 'usband's insurance policy 'adn't bin paid up. I didn't get a penny. That wasn't all neivver. My Sammy got nicked and sent ter Borstal, an' if that wasn't enough, I lost the little cleanin' job I 'ad. Talk about luck.'

Rachel gave the old lady a sympathetic smile. 'We won't get our fortunes told, will we, Derek?' she said. 'I'd sooner not know if anyfink bad was gonna 'appen.'

The old woman nodded and eased her position on the seat. 'Mind you, though, some people carry luck around wiv 'em,' she said, looking at the two young lovers in turn. 'I don't mean them there little good luck charms yer can buy. I mean luck that seems ter be wiv yer all the time. Some people say them that's got it lead a charmed life, ovvers say it's the luck o' the devil. You look like yer carry good luck wiv yer, if yer don't mind me sayin' so, dearie.'

Rachel smiled. 'I 'ope yer right,' she replied.

'Like I say, I don't believe in them crystal balls fortune-tellers,' the old lady went on. 'Ter be honest, I fink the only way ter tell yer fortune properly is ter look in yer 'and. I really do. Yer see, when yer in the womb an' the good Lord gives yer life, 'E also gives yer yer fortune. 'E puts it in yer tiny little 'ands an' the print of it is there when yer actually born. We've all got it. Now there's some that can read the signs what's there. It's a gift, yer see. People 'ave told me I've got the gift, but I don't do much palm-readin' now. I'd read your palm though, if yer like.'

Rachel shook her head. 'I'd be scared yer'd see somefink,' she replied.

Derek put his hand on Rachel's arm. 'Go on, let 'er do it,' he said grinning.

The old lady leaned forward and took Rachel's hand in hers, pressing downwards on the young woman's fingers, stretching the palm. For a few moments she stared down, her face expressionless, then she smiled briefly. 'Yes, it's 'ere. I can see it clearly,' she said. 'I can see yer carry good luck, an' the life line's very strong. There's somefink else too. Yer goin' ter be very 'appy in life, provided yer strong, but there's goin' ter be a decision ter take. There's money. Yes, I can see money, but it's not very clear accordin' ter the lines. I fink the best fing I can advise is ter follow yer intuition. Be bold and firm, dearie.'

Rachel withdrew her hand from the old lady's limp grip and leaned back in her seat, smiling at Derek. 'Right, I've 'ad my fortune told, now what about you?' she said.

Derek looked at the old lady. 'Would yer do mine?' he asked.

She reached out to him and took his right hand in hers and suddenly her face took on a puzzled expression. 'That's strange,' she said. 'I can't seem ter get a readin'. Tell me, are yer left-'anded?'

Derek nodded, looking a little surprised. 'I am as a matter o' fact,' he replied.

When the woman took his left hand she stared down for a few moments, as with Rachel's reading, but this time her face took on a look of concentration. 'There's good signs, but yer must be careful,' she said. 'I can't see money, but yer'll be 'appy in life.'

'What's me life line show?' Derek asked with bravado.

'It's strong,' the old lady said, releasing her grip on his hand and leaning back against the seat cushion. 'Yer know, readin' palms takes a lot out o' me,' she said, rubbing a hand over her brow. 'I get very tired. I fink I should be gettin' back, or that young man who's mindin' me suitcase is gonna be worried I've fell orf the train or somefink.'

As soon as the old lady had left, Derek turned to Rachel. 'Yer don't believe in that load o' twaddle, do yer?' he asked with a smile.

'Course I don't,' she replied. 'It was just a bit o' fun.'

Derek leaned towards her and planted a quick kiss on her cheek. 'Well, it seems I'm never gonna be rich,' he laughed.

'Just stay safe, that's all I want fer yer,' Rachel replied, letting her head dip onto his shoulder and closing her eyes.

Dolly Dawson hummed happily to herself as she rubbed the wet whitening stone on her front doorstep. Life had suddenly changed for the better, and she could hardly believe it. Josiah was home and had found himself a labouring job with a local builder. He had changed more than she had dared to hope, and he really seemed to be trying his best to be patient with the children. Wallace had hugged him when he arrived home and where once Josiah would have pushed him away, he held him tight and patted the young man's back reassuringly. The boys were soon chatting happily to their father and young Joyce seemed to be at ease with him after her initial coyness. When the children had been put to bed and Wallace had gone to his room, Josiah had kissed her passionately and sworn that his bad days were over for good.

Dolly smiled to herself as she remembered the way he had held her hand, something he had not done since their courting days, and led the way to their bedroom. He had been ill at ease at first, but with her prompting he had loved her fully, and then slept with his arms round her like a frightened child. Josiah was like a child really, Dolly thought. He was a simple man who found it difficult to read and write and converse with his neighbours, though he had chatted away quite comfortably with the young man next door. They seemed a nice couple, and their children were well behaved. It was just as well she had forewarned them about Wallace though. He was harmless of course, but he tended to be misunderstood. He certainly had been by the last people who lived next door. That miserable old man and his busybody of a wife had not been friendly at all, and they seemed to think that Wallace had deliberately tried to burn their house down. Anyway, that was in the past now. It was going to get better from now on. The people in the street seemed very friendly. Maisie's nice, Dolly thought, and that Sadie too, though I wouldn't like to fall out with her. Maudie seemed friendly, but she was a bundle of nerves. Still, she couldn't help that. I must remember to warn Wallace again about playing with those matches in case there's an accident, Dolly told herself. We can't afford to fall out with that nice family next door.

Carrie leaned back in the office chair and rubbed her eyes. She had finished the wages and had completed the task of sorting through the new batch of official forms that seemed to be for ever coming through the letterbox. She had been pleased at the initial response to her application for deferment for her clerk Jamie Robins, but had been a little taken aback by his seeming lack of enthusiasm when she told him that there was a good chance he could stay on at the firm. Jamie had appeared to be preoccupied lately, and she had often noticed a worried look on his thin face as he worked away at his desk. She had been tempted more than once to ask him if there was anything troubling him but she felt he might think she was prying into his personal business.

Carrie kicked off her high-heeled shoes and rubbed her aching feet. It had been a very tiring day but at least the transport was running well, she thought with a sigh of thanks. Paddy Byrne had taken to driving the Leyland as though he had been driving lorries all his life and he was now on the regular contract with the rum merchants. Tom Armfield and Tubby Walsh were driving the new five-ton Fodens, and Ben Davidson, the new driver, seemed to fit in very well. He was experienced on the roads and seemed to know quite a lot about the mechanics. He would come in handy, she thought.

The wintry evening was chilly and darkness was falling as Carrie sat thinking in the quietness of the office. How things had changed, she sighed. Marrying Fred had been right, despite her reservations, and the guilt that had once tormented her was dying away now. He had been a very good husband and she really had grown to love him. Not in the very physical way that she now loved Joe, but in a more ordinary, everyday sort of way. He had provided for her, and it was through her partnership with Fred and hard work that she had finally been able to get her parents out of that terrible slum Bacon Buildings. It had allowed her to purchase this business and to prosper, she could never forget that. There had been a lot of sadness since then too; Joe leaving her, and her father dying. Seeing those horses being walked up into the horseboxes and driven away had brought tears to her eyes. It would have upset her father too, had he lived to see it, there was no doubting that. At least they had not gone to the knackers yard like some of the other local firms' horses. It was sad about Sharkey Morris too. He had been ailing of late, and losing his wife had affected him very badly. The job had got too much for him and reluctantly he had stopped working at the yard. At least he had said he would call in occasionally for a cup of tea and a chat.

Carrie left the office and crossed the yard, glancing back to the open space where the stables once stood. Two days it had taken the demolition men to knock the stables to the ground, and all that was left to remind her of the horses was the watering trough at the rear of the yard and a couple of iron hitching rings on the back wall. Everything else was gone for ever, she thought sadly; the nightly sounds of the animals moving in their stalls and the sharp metallic clip of iron hooves on cobblestones, the bellowing of the horses into their nosebags and mangers, and the sound of chaff-cutting and clatter of the wagons as they rolled in and out of the yard. Now there was the throaty noise of the lorries warming up and the roar as they pulled out through the gates. Times were changing, Carrie thought with some regret, and now a new menace faced everyone. The war was only a few weeks old and apart from battles at sea, it was peaceful and quiet. How long could it last? Would the expected bombing come one night and destroy everything? Would she and her loved ones survive to see peace once more?

'Carrie?' Joe called from the front door. 'What yer standin' there for? Yer look miles away.'

She gave him an embarrassed smile. 'I was jus' lookin' at those old 'itchin' rails, Joe,' she replied. 'I was finkin' 'ow quiet it is now the 'orses 'ave gone.'

She walked over to him and he put his arm round her. 'Are yer 'appy, Carrie?' he asked. 'Are yer really 'appy?'

She reached up and kissed him. 'I'm very 'appy, darlin',' she answered. 'Just worried about the war, an' Rachel. Will she lose that young man ter the war?'

'We can only pray, sweet'eart, we can only pray,' Joe said softly.

The little tea room was empty apart from two couples who sat chatting at their separate tables. The elderly couple were dressed in country tweeds, the large man with a bright red face occasionally shaking his head as he listened to the constant chatter of his thin-faced, grey-haired female companion.

'It really is disgusting,' she was saying. 'I was only talking to that nice Mrs Greenidge who lives at Rose Cottage in Sandy Lane. She has two billeted with her. Do you know they wet the bed? Goodness gracious me, it's too much. Those children had head lice too. Mrs Greenidge was telling me she had to teach them how to hold a knife and fork. They sat down to their tea and started eating with their fingers. Their clothes were filthy and their manners absolutely appalling. It really is too much. They're little monsters, they really are.'

'Guttersnipes,' was all the large man had a chance to say before the thin-faced woman resumed her attack on Goudham's most recent arrivals from London.

The other couple were seated by the window, both incensed at what they were overhearing. Billy Sullivan gritted his teeth and Annie sat with an angry look on her pale face, aware of her husband's jaw muscles clenching.

'The children are really settling in nicely,' she said, in an effort to divert Billy's attention. 'They've made a lot of friends and I'm managing to get some more training in at the home. What about you, Billy? You look tired and drawn. Are you eating properly?'

Billy glanced across at the two villagers and scowled darkly. Annie quickly took his hand in hers, squeezing it tightly. 'Look, Billy, there's no need to get yourself worked up over the likes of them,' she said quietly. 'They're not typical of the people around here. I've got to know lots of folk who've got evacuees billeted with them and they're really wonderful. Just ignore them. They're not worth spoiling our few hours together over.'

Billy let his shoulders sag and he gave Annie a bright smile. 'Yer right, luv. Sorry, what was yer sayin'?'

'I said you were looking pale and drawn, and I asked if you were eating properly,' she said with a slight note of irritation in her voice.

'Of course I'm eatin' well,' he replied. 'Iris an' Danny make me go ter their place every Sunday fer me dinner an' I often call in to 'ave a chat wiv 'em in the evenin's.'

'Well, see you keep it up,' Annie said firmly.

The village couple were leaving and the large man was still nodding in dutiful agreement with his wife's complaints as the two walked out through the door. As soon as they had left, the young waitress came over to the window table. 'I do hope they didn't upset you,' she said, addressing Annie. 'I know you come from London by your husband's accent.' She looked briefly at Billy and smiled. 'They really are a detestable pair. We've got two little boys staying with us and they're really sweet.'

Annie touched the waitress's arm in a warm gesture. 'Thank you,' she said quietly. 'I'm sure most people here are very friendly and understanding towards the evacuees. I've found it so.'

Billy had relaxed more now that they were alone and he was looking around the little tea room with interest. Old pictures hung on the walls and delicious-looking homemade cakes were displayed on circular glass stands on the counter. Blue chintz tablecloths and matching curtains reminded him of a doll's house, and the raffia mats on the well-scrubbed wooden floor added to the charm of the little establishment. He could smell baking and it reminded him of the rock cakes and apple pies his mother used to make when he was living at home.

Billy sighed. There was so much to tell, so much to say, and so little time. One thing was sure though, he resolved. He would definitely not tell Annie about his new evening job at the Kings Arms.

'Come on, Billy. We must get back to the children,' Annie said suddenly. 'I want them all to give you a big kiss before you leave. I'd like to say goodbye too, and I expect more than a kiss.'

Chapter Eleven

Carrie crossed the yard with the mid-morning tea for Jamie Robbins and Rachel, wondering what it was the young clerk wanted to see her about. He had approached her as soon as he arrived that morning, looking a little uncomfortable as he made his request. Carrie had been busy with the daily delivery sheets and had promised to see him as soon as she could.

She entered the office and Jamie looked up, glancing briefly at Rachel, who gave him an encouraging smile.

'Drink yer tea an' then we can talk,' Carrie told him, noticing the look which had passed between him and her daughter.

Rachel leaned back in her chair and sipped the hot tea, her eyes straying to the nervous-looking young clerk. She felt a wave of pity for him and wondered what had made him come to the decision. He was such a quiet, studious young man and pathetically shy. He must be feeling frightened. What pressures had been exerted on him to make him come to such a decision? she wondered.

Rachel swung her chair round to face the pile of papers on her desk and pretended to study them. Poor Jamie. How different he was to Derek, she thought. Her young man had excelled himself during their brief few days at Brighton. He had been a wonderful lover, attentive and considerate, as well as being very careful. She smiled to herself as she remembered how she had finally managed to get a promise from him to approach her mother on his next leave to ask about getting engaged.

Carrie had slipped out to talk to Joe who was busy in the yard, and when she returned Rachel got up and left the office to go over to the house, leaving Jamie alone with her mother.

'Yer wanted ter see me, Jamie?' Carrie asked, sitting down in Rachel's office chair.

The young clerk coloured slightly as he turned his swivel chair round to face her. 'I was wonderin' 'ow much progress yer'd made wiv the exemption papers, Mrs Bradley,' he said.

'It's Mrs Maitland now,' she reminded him with a disarming smile.

Jamie got more flustered. 'I'm sorry, I . . .'

'It's all right, I've got ter get used to it meself,' she laughed. 'Yer want ter know about the papers. Well, I've filled in the application form an' they've sent back anuvver form fer me ter fill in. It's gonna take some time, Jamie, but I shouldn't worry too much. I fink we'll manage it.'

The young man fiddled with his pen and his face became more flushed. 'I'm sorry, Mrs Bradley, I mean Mrs Maitland, but I've decided ter volunteer fer the army,' he said, looking down at his ink-stained fingers.

Carrie was taken aback and she stared at him for a moment or two before replying. 'But why, Jamie?' she asked, puzzled.

'I couldn't live wiv meself if I dodged the call-up,' he replied. 'Most o' the young men my age are goin' in the services an' it jus' wouldn't be right.'

'What about yer parents, Jamie? Who's gonna support 'em?' Carrie asked. 'You're the breadwinner. It takes a lot o' courage fer a young man like you ter support a family. Yer not a coward, an' in any case yer shouldn't take notice o' what people might say.'

Jamie looked up at her. 'My dad's got work now, an' I can send a few shillin's 'ome. Then there's the army allowance fer me muvver,' he replied. 'They'll be no worse off than a lot of ovver people.'

' 'Ave yer told yer parents what yer intend ter do?' Carrie asked.

Jamie nodded. 'They understand. I 'ad a long talk wiv 'em over the weekend. The only fing I'm worried about is lettin' yer down.'

Carrie gave him a reassuring smile. 'Well, I'm not gonna say I won't miss yer, Jamie,' she told him, 'but I wouldn't try ter dissuade yer, if yer sure yer know what yer doin'.'

'I'm sure,' he said firmly. 'I wanted ter tell yer before I actually go ter the recruitin' office. I'm sorry, Mrs Maitland, but it's somefing I've gotta do.'

'That's all right, Jamie,' she replied. 'Jus' remember ter keep in touch. Come an' see us when yer get leave. Oh, an' remember there'll be a job 'ere fer yer when the war's over.'

'Fank yer, Mrs Maitland, I really appreciate it,' he said, sagging a little with relief for having unburdened himself.

Rachel walked back into the office at that moment and stood between Jamie and her mother. 'So 'e's told yer,' she said smiling broadly. 'Our Jamie's gonna be a soldier.'

Carrie could see the young man's obvious discomfort and she gave her daughter a disapproving look. Rachel was always pulling Jamie's leg, which tended to embarrass him, though Carrie knew that there was no malice intended and in fact Rachel really felt very fond of him. 'Well, now we've got everyfing sorted out, what about you gettin' those wages done, Rachel, and lettin' Jamie get on with the accounts,' she growled. 'Remember I've got a business ter run.'

Dolly Dawson had collected the children from school and when she walked back into the house there was a surprise awaiting her. On the parlour table she saw a steel helmet, a service gas mask and whistle complete with a white lanyard. The helmet was emblazoned with the letters ARP. Dolly sat down heavily and stared at the equipment with concern. Dennis and Leslie were already fighting over who should wear the helmet while Joyce was puffing on the whistle trying to produce a noise. 'Now leave 'em alone, can't yer?' Dolly screamed at them. 'If yer farvver sees yer playin' wiv those there'll be trouble.'

' 'As Dad joined the army?' Joyce asked her mother.

'Don't be silly,' Leslie shouted at her. 'It ses ARP on there,' he pointed to the helmet.

'What's ARP mean?' Joyce asked, scratching at her head.

'I dunno,' Leslie said, snatching the whistle from his young sister. 'It's nuffink ter do wiv the army though. Besides, Dad can't be in the army, 'e's an ole lag.'

'What's an ole lag?' Joyce asked, still scratching her head.

'It means yer too old fer the army,' Dennis butted in.

Dolly pulled her daughter towards her and quickly searched through the child's hair. Suddenly she clicked her tongue. 'That's the second time this week she's come 'ome wiv nits,' she growled to the boys. 'Right, Dennis, run down the oil shop an' get us a pint o' paraffin. Leslie, put the kettle on. I must find that toof comb. Now where'd I put it?'

Joyce watched her mother searching through the dresser drawers and she started crying, knowing the tortures in store for her. First there would be a hard head wash, then the paraffin would be put on and combed through her tangled hair. Last of all, and the worst torture, was the fine-toothed comb, which pulled down on her hair and hurt her already tingling scalp. 'I don't want it washed, Mum,' she moaned.

'Now don't give me any trouble, Joyce, I gotta delouse yer, or we'll all be cooty before the week's out,' Dolly shouted at her.

Joyce settled down in one corner with her favourite doll, quietly awaiting her ordeal while Dolly turned out another drawer. Soon Dennis came running in with the paraffin.

'Mum, Mum, there's a big bloke got 'old o' Wallace an' 'e won't let 'im go,' he shouted.

Dolly let the drawer contents clatter onto the floor in her vexation. 'Where is 'e?'

' 'E's up by the paper stall,' Dennis replied, still gasping for breath.

Dolly sighed deeply as she slipped on her coat and hurried from the house. Things had been too quiet of late, she told herself. Something had been bound to happen.

As she rushed up to the end of the turning, Dolly could see a group of people standing outside the corner shop and in the centre was Wallace, standing quietly with his head bowed. Beside him was an elderly man who had hold of the young man's forearm and looked the more frightened of the two. On the other side of the turning, Dolly saw Maudie Mycroft and Maisie Dougall standing together watching the spectacle.

'What's 'e done?' she asked them breathlessly.

'I dunno, luv,' Maisie answered. 'I 'eard the bloke say 'e's pinched a bunch o' bananas from Gosnell's the greengrocers.'

'Poor little sod,' Maudie said with feeling.

Dolly pushed her way into the circle. 'I'm 'is muvver. What's 'e done?' she asked.

A large woman wearing a coarse apron with a money belt sewn into it put her hands on her lips belligerently. ' 'E come in my shop while I was busy an' picked up an 'andful o' bananas,' she shouted at Dolly. 'The cowson didn't fink I see 'im take 'em, but I did. We've sent fer the police. Mr Roberts caught 'im, didn't yer, luv?'

The elderly man nodded, wishing now that he had not taken any notice when the large woman shouted at him to stop the young man as she came waddling after him.

'Where's the bananas, Wallace?' Dolly asked him in a quiet voice.

The young man's face contorted as he wriggled to get away from the clutches of the elderly man and saliva dripped down onto his coat lapel. 'I ain't got bananas,' he slurred, his eyes looking appealing towards his mother.

'All right, let 'im go,' Dolly said firmly. 'Yer can see 'e ain't got any bananas on 'im. Yer must 'ave made a mistake.'

'Well, 'e took 'em, 'cos I see 'im take 'em,' the large greengrocer said with venom.

'Well, 'e ain't got 'em now, so where's yer proof?' Dolly asked her.

'P'raps 'e's ate 'em,' a bystander remarked.

'Chucked 'em more like,' another cut in.

'Bloody idiot wouldn't know what ter do wiv 'em anyway,' a scruffy-looking woman with a headful of curlers butted in.

'Who you callin' an idiot?' Dolly screamed at her.

People began milling about as the arguing intensified and the elderly gent decided it was an opportune time to lose his grip on Wallace's arm. Dolly meanwhile was being pulled away from the scruffy-looking woman by other bystanders and by the time the police car pulled up she had managed to grab a handful of curlers from her opponent's head. The elderly man had made a discreet exit and Mrs Gosnell was picking herself up from the pavement after one of Dolly's flailing arms had sent her sprawling.

'Now what's all this?' a policeman said sternly, hands on his belt.

Mrs Gosnell brushed herself down as she confronted him. 'This bloody idiot come in my shop an' pinched an 'andful o' me best bananas,' she shouted. 'I gave chase but Mr Roberts caught 'im.'

93

'Who pinched yer bananas?' the policeman enquired, beginning to feel that he had been sent on a fool's errand.

Mrs Gosnell looked around. 'The bleeder's scarpered,' she shouted, glaring at the crowd. 'Didn't any o' yer see 'im go?'

'I did. 'E went that way,' Maisie called out, pointing in the general direction of Jamaica Road.

'Ooh, Maisie, be careful,' Maudie whispered to her friend, knowing that she was giving the police false information.

'Did yer recover the bananas?' the policeman asked the greengrocer.

'Mr Roberts caught 'im,' she replied.

'Yeah, but did yer get yer fruit back?' the exasperated constable asked.

'No.'

'But yer caught 'im.'

'Mr Roberts did.'

'Did 'e recover the bananas?'

'Mr Roberts 'as scarpered too,' one of the onlookers chimed in.

'Now look, I can't stand 'ere all day over a bunch o' bloody bananas,' the policeman sighed. 'Yer got no culprit, no witness, an' no evidence. What am I s'posed ter do?'

'Go an' find the fievin' git,' Mrs Gosnell shouted at him.

'All right, give us a description,' he asked, pulling out a tatty notebook from his breast pocket.

' 'E was a dopey-lookin' git, about this 'igh,' the greengrocer said, holding her hand up, 'an' 'e pulls faces.'

' 'Ere, that's my boy yer talking' about,' Dolly shouted at the woman, trying to push her way in front of the policeman. 'My Wallace ain't dopey at all, 'e's just a bit backward. There ain't a bad bone in 'is body.'

'Right, that's enough,' the policeman said loudly, turning to Dolly. 'Now let's 'ave yer name an' address.'

'Look, I'll pay fer the bananas ter save any trouble,' she offered.

Mrs Gosnell looked slightly abashed, beginning to feel that perhaps people would consider her petty if she took things any further. 'There's no need fer that,' she said puffing. 'I jus' want 'im ter keep out o' my shop in future.'

The policeman put his notebook away. 'Right then, let's all move on,' he said firmly. 'Yer blockin' the pavement.'

Dolly walked over to Maisie and Maudie. 'Fanks fer that, luv,' she said to Maisie. 'That son o' mine's gonna drive me into an early grave, I'm sure of it.'

'The lad didn't mean any 'arm,' Maisie said kindly. ' 'E could 'ave forgotten ter pay.'

'It's only 'er word 'e took the bananas,' Dolly replied.

' 'E took 'em right enough,' Maisie told her with a large grin. 'The lad come scootin' round the corner an' 'e took the bananas out from under 'is coat an' chucked 'em in Mrs Perry's front door. Jus' then ole

Mr Roberts came out o' the shop there. That Gosnell woman shouted fer 'im ter grab yer lad an' 'e did. Mind you, the boy was jus' standin' there grinnin'. Ter be honest, luv, I 'ad ter laugh. Ole Roberts looked scared out of 'is life.'

'Gawd 'elp us,' Dolly groaned as she rubbed her forehead, picturing Wallace cowering under the stairs that very minute.

Maudie had been listening to Maisie's tale of the event and suddenly she nudged her friend. 'Talk about the Lord providin',' she said. 'Look over there.'

Mrs Perry's two youngest had emerged from their house and were sitting on the kerbside, both munching on a huge banana.

'I don't fink the poor little sods 'ave 'ad many o' them, if yer ask me,' Maisie remarked with a chuckle.

Josiah Dawson had decided long before he regained his freedom that he was going to put his past life behind him and become a good husband and father. He had also decided that upon release he would work hard to become a good citizen and upstanding member of the little community in which he now lived. The first step was to get a job, which he had managed to do very soon after his return from Dartmoor. It was hard work labouring for a builder, but he had built up his muscles working in the slate quarries in Devon and he found that he could cope with the demands of digging and mixing cement. Being a devoted husband took a little more thought and expertise, he realised, and to that end he had promised himself that first and foremost he would not get drunk any more. After all, it had been the cause of all his troubles in the past.

Josiah kept his promise, remembering how Dolly had been the recipient of a few backhanders in the past, always when he was the worse for drink. Things were looking very good at the moment, he thought to himself. Dolly was showing him a lot of loving, and she had been very loyal. She might well have taken a lover while he was incarcerated, and it would have been understandable. Dolly was a hot-natured woman, he knew, and she had been alone for quite a lengthy period of time. She had assured him, however, that he was the only one for her, despite everything, and Josiah believed her implicitly.

Being a devoted father was even harder than being a devoted husband. The children were growing up and needed his time, which was already trying his patience. Then there was Wallace. The young man was slowly deteriorating, according to Dolly, and Josiah knew she was right. He was constantly falling against the furniture as he ambled about the house and his speech was getting more and more slurred. He was finding it difficult to hold a knife and fork properly and Dolly now had to cut up his food into manageable pieces. Wallace was trying his patience to the limit, but Josiah had sworn to himself that never again would he chastise the lad with the back of his hand as in the past.

Instead, he would try very hard to be more like Dolly, who he felt had the patience of a saint and never seemed to let things get her down.

As for becoming an upstanding member of the community, Josiah was working hard in that direction. He had never been a regular church-goer, although he came from a Catholic family. He did, however, visit the church hall in Wilson Street during his midday break and offer his services as street warden for Page Street. Much to his surprise he was duly accepted and enrolled for instruction on the very many tasks which he might have to perform in the near future. One immediate task was to ensure that the blackout regulations were enforced and Josiah had to give this some considerable thought. He could no longer adopt a belligerent attitude with people, because of his police record. He would have to be firm but polite.

One thing worried Josiah. Would Dolly take kindly to his new-found duties as street warden, and the demands they would make on his time after being out at work all day? Well, he would soon know. He had finished work early that afternoon and when he got home and deposited his new equipment on the parlour table he was prepared for some hard talking. Dolly was out collecting the kids from school, however, and Wallace was nowhere to be seen, which gave him time to slip along to the Co-op shop and buy her a quarter of her favourite jelly sweets, hoping it would soften the blow.

Josiah had already decided that if he was going to be a credit to the community, one of the things he would have to do was make himself more aware of what was going on around him. That would mean talking to his neighbours, instead of shunning them as he had always done in the past. Small talk did not come easily to Josiah, but when Mr Jolly stopped him in Jamaica Road he was prepared to try his best.

'Didn't I see yer wiv a warden's 'elmet in Page Street a few minutes ago?' Bert Jolly asked.

' 'S'right,' Josiah replied.

'I was talkin' wiv yer good lady a couple o' weeks ago an' she said yer was workin' away,' Mr Jolly informed him.

'Oh yeah,' Josiah replied.

'So yer back now then.'

' 'S'right.'

'Are yer gonna be our street warden then?'

' 'S'right.'

'Yer gonna be makin' sure we don't let any light out at night?'

' 'S'right.'

Mr Jolly was beginning to think that the new street warden was a very anti-social sort of a bloke and he made to walk away.

Josiah gritted his teeth and tried a little harder to be friendly. 'What's yer name, mate?' he asked.

'Bert Jolly,' the dapper pensioner replied. 'I live at number twenty-three. I'm a widower. Me ole dutch died ten years ago, come next spring.'

Josiah was encouraged. 'Lived in Page Street long then?' he enquired.

'More 'an forty years, come next May first. I've seen a few comin's an' goin's, I 'ave,' Bert told him.

Josiah found that it wasn't so difficult after all. 'We live next door ter the Tanners,' he continued.

Bert Jolly's face broke into a smile. 'That's Danny Tanner, that is,' he said. ' 'E's married ter Knocker Brody's daughter Iris. Nice kid, she is. They both are, come ter that. I used to be mates wiv Will Tanner, Danny's farvver. Lovely bloke, 'e was. Terrible shame when 'e died. The Tanners are well known an' respected in this area. Young Carrie Tanner married ole Fred Bradley, 'im who 'ad the cafe in Cotton Lane. 'E died of a stroke, yer know. She's married again. Married a bloke who used ter lodge in the turnin'. Joe Maitland 'is name is. Nice bloke.'

Josiah could see that his patience and forbearance were beginning to pay off. He now felt that he knew almost everyone in the turning. Mr Jolly was not finished, however.

'She was a nice ole gel, too, that Mrs Axford. That was who Joe Maitland lodged wiv,' Bert went on. 'Snuff-taker she was. Took pounds o' the stuff. I reckon that's what killed 'er in the end.'

Josiah listened patiently for some time while Bert went on with his stories of the comings and goings in Page Street over the years. When he was finally able to drag himself away from the man's chattering, he continued on his way to the Co-op shop.

He whistled quietly to himself as he walked back along Jamaica Road. It was easier than he had imagined to get talking to people, and if the present trend continued he would soon know virtually everything about his neighbours, he thought.

'Wotcher, mate. I jus' got me evenin' paper,' a voice called out.

Josiah groaned as he spotted Bert Jolly. There was only so much a bloke could take in one day, he felt.

' 'Ere, I fergot ter tell yer. There was a right ole set-to along 'ere earlier,' Bert said. 'There was this young feller runnin' along tuckin' a bunch o' bananas under 'is coat an' there was ole Mrs Gosnell the greengrocer chasin' after 'im. Waddlin', I should say, that'd be more like it. Anyway, there was a bit of a crowd gavvered on the corner o' Page Street. I fink they caught 'im. I stood there lookin' an' I saw a police car draw up. I s'pose they nicked 'im. Funny-lookin' bloke 'e was. Sort o' stupid. As a matter o' fact I've seen 'im in the turnin' once or twice. I don't know if 'e lives there or not.'

Josiah's heart sank. His first reaction went against his promise to himself and he took a couple of deep breaths to strengthen his resolve. Knocking Wallace about the head was only going to make him more silly than he already was. No, he would have to use a little more guile in dealing with his wayward son. Josiah walked home gritting his teeth, his hands clenched into two almighty fists.

During October, women left their Bermondsey backstreets clutching ration books to register with a grocer and those who had not already collected their gas masks now did so, following repeated warnings that air raids could start at any time. Every night folk gathered round wireless sets to listen to the nine o' clock news, and those who did not have a wireless usually listened to the broadcasts at a neighbour's house.

In the early hours of 14 October the battleship *Royal Oak* was sunk in Scapa Flow by a German U-boat, with heavy loss of life. At nine o' clock that night the Tanner family gathered round the wireless, anxiously waiting for more news. Rachel's stomach was knotted with dread as the newscaster read out an Admiralty bulletin. Derek had gone up to Scotland only a few days previously to join a ship, and now as she sat listening, Rachel recalled the old lady on the train. She had looked strangely at Derek when she read his palm. Had she seen something there, some terrible tragedy in the lines of his hand? No, it was stupid even to think of it, she told herself. Derek was going to be all right. He would write to her soon.

Joe got up to make the tea and Carrie wrapped her arms round her very frightened daughter. ' 'E's gonna be all right, you'll see,' she said softly.

Rachel could not bring herself even to talk about the train episode, and as much as she tried to dismiss it as nonsense, the old lady's face kept reappearing in her mind, and it terrified her.

'I'm scared, Mum,' she said. 'S'posin' it was the ship Derek joined? The news said there was only a few survivors?'

Carried hugged her daughter tightly, finding little to say, no words that would comfort her and take away the fear. In the other fireside chair, Nellie sat quietly sewing, her glasses resting on the end of her nose, and when she looked up, the concern was evident on her face. 'The good Lord listens ter prayers, Rachel,' she said. 'All we can do is pray fer the lad's safety.'

Chapter Twelve

Billy Sullivan had settled in to his new evening job at the Kings Arms and things had been very quiet. There had been no repercussions from the recent brawl and Terry Gordon was beginning to feel that maybe his long-time enemy had decided to let bygones be bygones. Terry was very happy with his new barman's progress. He had taken to the job admirably and it was a comforting thought to have a local man behind the counter, one who could handle himself in an emergency.

Terry's pretty wife Patricia was also pleased to have Billy installed behind the bar. She had been intrigued by the stories that abounded of the handsome man's exploits over the years and decided she should get to know him a little better. Opportunity seemed to be presenting itself. She would have to be careful though, because Terry was very jealous. On Tuesdays when he took his night off, that would be the time to chat at length to Billy. In the meantime she would play it cool.

During Saturday evening the public bar had been buzzing with the news of the *Royal Oak*'s sinking, and at ten o' clock two strangers walked in. Billy was immediately on his guard and he reached under the counter for the comforting feel of the pickaxe handle he kept concealed there. The two men were heavily built and in their forties, he guessed. They both wore expensive overcoats and silk scarves, and the taller of the two had a trilby hat on. It was unusual for well-dressed strangers to frequent the public bar, Billy thought, unless they were looking for someone in particular, someone they knew would be in that particular bar.

'Give us two gin an' tonics,' the taller man said, glancing around at the customers.

Billy slipped the glasses under the optic, glancing through the opening to the saloon bar as he did so. He could see Terry talking to his wife; he would have to put him on his guard.

'Is Terry in?' the tall man asked casually.

Billy knew that the men would not have spotted Terry through the bar from where they were standing and he smiled disarmingly. ' 'E 'ad ter slip out a while ago. I don't fink 'e's back jus' yet, but I'll find out for yer,' he replied.

Terry's face hardened when Billy told him about the two men asking after him. As he followed his barman into the public bar his face brightened. ' 'Ello, boys. Long time no see,' he grinned, adding to Billy, 'it's all right, they're ole friends.'

Patricia had popped her head round the bar and she breathed a sigh of relief when she saw Terry laughing with the two. 'Fanks, Billy,' she said, giving him a smile and a quick wink. 'Yer never know who they're likely ter be. It's a relief ter know you're 'ere.'

Billy smiled back and shrugged his shoulders. 'You all right in there?' he asked, nodding towards the saloon bar.

'I'd feel better wiv you in there wiv me,' she said with another suggestive wink.

Billy got on with serving and chatting to the customers, and when the two strangers left just before closing time Terry went back into the saloon bar. One or two of the regulars had had too much to drink and were cursing loudly about the war, and one old man had fallen asleep at the corner table. Billy sighed as he began the task of getting the bar cleared. He gently shook the old man's shoulder to rouse him. 'C'mon, dad. Time fer beddy byes.'

The old man woke with a start and shook himself. 'Gawd, I must 'a' fell orf ter sleep. I was 'avin' this dream,' he said pulling a face. 'I was in this bloody great field an' it was full o' taters. There was this farmer an' 'e was an ugly-lookin' git. Anyway 'e told me I 'ad ter pick all the spuds before I could leave. I tell yer, Billy, there was fousands o' these tater plants an' me back was fair breakin' after a few minutes. I said ter meself, Jack, I ses, yer never gonna pick all these spuds terday, not wiv yer back bein' the way it is. Fair cripplin' me it was. Must 'ave bin the way I was sleepin'.'

Billy chuckled as he helped the old man to his feet. 'G'night, Jack,' he said. 'Mind 'ow yer go in the dark.'

When the last of the customers had left, Billy set about wiping the counter down and emptying the ashtrays. The potman had already cleared the glasses and was bolting up as Billy slipped into the small back room to collect his coat. He could hear raised voices coming from upstairs and then Terry hurried down. His face was set hard and he merely nodded goodnight as Billy took his leave through the side door.

On Sunday morning Nellie went to church. She was going to say a special prayer for Derek and as she walked along the quiet Jamaica Road she thought about her two lost sons. How different the two lads were, she recalled. James had always been the lively one, for ever talking and passing comment on something or the other, while young Charlie sat quietly reading in a corner. James had fallen in the Great War, and she doubted that she would ever see Charlie again now. He was so far away, and with his own family now. His last letter had said that he was retiring from the army, but perhaps he would stay on now that war had broken out. He would be forty-six and too old to fight, but he might stay on to train the young soldiers, she thought.

Nellie took her usual detour through Page Street and noticed how clean and tidy the little turning appeared. The front doorsteps were whitened and lace curtains hung in almost all the windows. There were a few empty houses and Nellie sighed sadly. People had gone, fearing what might happen to the riverside borough. The more hardy folk remained, however, and she saw Maisie standing at her front door chatting to the plump Dolly Dawson. Nearby was Maudie Mycroft, in earnest conversation with Sadie Sullivan, who seemed to have aged quite rapidly. Nellie rubbed her hand along the lapel of her coat as if to reassure herself that she was dressed smartly and held her head high.

'Mornin', Sadie, Maud,' she said as she passed.

'Orf ter church?' Sadie asked.

Nellie nodded. 'Young Rachel's worried about 'er bloke,' she told them. ' 'E's in the navy an' 'e's up in Scotland. I'm gonna say a prayer fer 'im.'

Sadie smiled. 'I've jus' got back. Daniel didn't go this mornin' though. 'E's in bed wiv bronchitis.'

'Sorry to 'ear it, Sadie. I 'ope 'e's better soon,' Nellie replied as she carried on.

Sadie watched Nellie walking away for a few moments then she turned to Maudie. 'She's beginnin' ter look 'er age,' she remarked. 'The poor cow's never got over losin' 'er William.'

Maudie pulled her coat tighter round her lean figure. 'Oh well, I'd better get goin',' she announced. 'I'm goin' round wiv the collection plate this mornin'.'

Nellie approached Maisie and Dolly. 'Mornin', ladies,' she said briskly. 'Can't stop, I'm orf ter the service.'

Maisie gave her a friendly smile. 'Dolly was just tellin' me about 'er Wallace,' she said. 'Tell 'er, Doll.'

Nellie was always keen to hear the latest gossip and she decided that maybe she could spare a few minutes after all. 'What's 'e done?' she asked.

Dolly briefed Nellie on the banana episode and told her what happened afterwards. 'Yer can imagine 'ow I felt,' she went on. 'I could 'ave died wiv shame. Anyway, when I got indoors I found the bleeder 'idin' under the stairs. Shakin' like a leaf 'e was. Ter be honest, Nell, I was gonna give 'im such a tannin', old as 'e is, but when 'e ups an' tells me that 'e stole the bananas ter give ter those Perry children I could 'ave cried. Wallace might be simple-minded but 'e's so feelin'. I dunno what I'm gonna do wiv 'im.'

Nellie shook her head. 'It's a shame, Doll,' she replied. 'Pity 'e can't get some sort o' job ter keep 'im out o' mischief.'

Dolly sighed. 'I've tried. Before we moved 'ere I got 'im a job at the market. Yer know the sort o' fing, 'elpin' the costers an' runnin' fer tea an' suchlike. Well, 'e only lasted a day. One stall'older sent 'im fer the tea an' 'e was gone over two hours. They found 'im sittin' in the park feedin' the birds, wiv the tea beside 'im. Stone cold it was.'

Nellie was aware that she was going to be late for the service and she brushed her hands down her coat once more. ' 'E'll be all right,' she said sympathetically. 'Yer jus' got ter persevere wiv 'im, that's all.'

As she walked away Maisie shook her head. 'She's beginnin' ter look 'er age,' she remarked.

Maurice Salter was a widower, and he had brought up his three daughters and his only son unaided ever since his wife died of peritonitis when she was in her early thirties. Maurice had never remarried and he earned his living as a stoker at the gasworks in Rotherhithe. His daughters had all grown into attractive young women, self-assured and outgoing, which Maurice felt had a lot to do with the relaxed, broadminded way he had brought them up. Brenda, the eldest, was twenty-six, and like her two sisters she was still unmarried. She was dark-haired, brown-eyed and had a bubbling personality. Barbara was twenty-four, with brown hair and a warm smile, and she was inclined to be the quiet one of the family. Lily, the youngest of the girls, was twenty-two, fair like her mother, and the prettiest of the trio. The girls worked together as machinists at the clothes factory near Tower Bridge and were terrible flirts, driving the young men wild with their antics and earning a rather dubious reputation as a result.

Robert Salter was the baby of the family at twenty-one, short and stocky like his father with a mop of dark wavy hair and brown eyes. He had been cosseted and teased mercilessly by his sisters until he began to assert himself and now he was missed terribly by the family, having been called up into the Royal Air Force. He was currently undergoing gunnery training for air crew and had suddenly found himself very popular with the rest of the trainees after he pinned snapshots of his three sisters onto his locker.

Maurice Salter was dark of complexion, short and stocky, with thick, greying hair that tended to curl up under his cap. He had found the upbringing of his four children a tremendous struggle and he had often been required to 'duck and dive', as he described it, to provide adequately for them. He had no sense of guilt about his sometimes devious activities. Ducking and diving was a means to an end as far as he was concerned, and the only way he had been able to keep his family together. He was an imaginative man, with an eye for the main chance and never afraid to take a gamble, and nowadays his children were concerned about the sort of things he might get himself involved in. They felt that as they were all working now the days of hardship were over and he should not feel obliged to be for ever on the lookout for a few extra shillings. But old habits died hard, and anyway Maurice enjoyed the excitement of the deal or dodge.

As he busied himself with polishing his shoes in the scullery on that Sunday morning, Maurice was deep in thought. Outside in the yard was a bale of blackout material which he had come by and he was calculating in his head the profit margin if he added the usual three farthings per yard to the agreed price of two shillings and elevenpence per yard. 'Brenda,' he called out. 'What's seventy-five three farthin's come to?'

His eldest daughter was sitting in the parlour busy with curling tongs and she sighed with exasperation as she realised the tongs had gone cold. 'I dunno, ask Barbie,' she told him.

'Barb. What's —'

'Why don't yer ask three shillin's an' be done wiv it?' Barbara called from the back bedroom.

Maurice sighed. 'Material is always sold wiv three farthin's stuck on the end o' the price,' he informed them. 'I don't want people ter fink it's come the ovver way.'

'They wouldn't dream of it, Dad, now would they?' Lily chipped in, checking the heat of the iron by holding it near her cheek.

'I shouldn't 'ave asked,' he said. 'I get no 'elp from you lot.'

'What yer mumblin' about, Dad?' Barbara called.

'I was jus' sayin' ter meself that I should 'ave took more care wiv yer schoolin'. There's none o' yer can add up,' he shouted.

Later, as Maurice left his house for his Sunday constitutional at the Kings Arms, Lily planted a kiss on his cheek. 'It's four an' eightpence farthin', Dad,' she said with a sweet smile.

Eastwards across the fast-flowing River Thames, in suburban Ilford, Frank Galloway sat listening to Bella's outpourings, a surly look on his heavy-jowled face.

'You've got to be practical, Frank,' she was going on. 'Your father's an old man now. Supposing the bombing did start. Who would look after him? You should get him to sell that house of his and move away. He could stay with you, now that I won't be here. The house should raise quite a decent sum. After all it's in a good spot, even if it is Bermondsey.'

Frank grimaced. Bella had always thought of Bermondsey as an area to be avoided at all costs. She had never been happy about visiting his father, not that she did very often. The factory smells and the sight of grimy warehouses and wharves always seemed to give her one of her migraines.

'Another thing you should consider is the will,' Bella continued, staring into a small mirror she had extracted from her handbag. 'You ought to make sure he's made a proper will. Why don't you ask him?'

'Be reasonable, Bella. I can't just come straight out with something like that,' Frank replied with a sigh.

'Why not? He is your father,' Bella said, dabbing at the corner of her mouth with her little finger. 'And you're all the family he's got. The problem would be if anything should happen to him and no will has been made. It could hold things up.'

'I'm not exactly stupid,' he replied. 'I know the problems. In any case, Father's told me more than once that I'm the only beneficiary. He must have drawn up a will.'

'Can't you ask his solicitor?' Bella persisted.

'I'll do no such thing,' Frank growled. 'Look, when the time's ripe, I'll out with it and ask him, but until then I don't want to hear any more about it.'

Bella gave him a blinding look and continued putting the finishing touches to her make-up. Frank ignored her and took up the Sunday paper once more. Bella was in her element, he thought with disgust. A tour of factories and military camps with a second-rate revue was not something she would have contemplated a few years ago, but things were different now. It was the first part in a show she had managed to get for quite a considerable length of time and she was ecstatic. There would be the usual johnnies hanging on like a lot of leeches as well as the other camp followers. Bella was going to have a whale of a time, and he would be left alone to fend for himself, now that Caroline had been packed off to that stupid finishing school.

Frank grimaced. If Bella thought he was going to sit in the house twiddling his thumbs every night pining for her she was wrong. She was right about his father's will though, he had to admit. The silly old fool was just as likely to have put off making a will, thinking he was immortal. He would have to find a way of bringing the subject up without upsetting the old boy. Perhaps he should try to encourage his father to move out of London, maybe to one of those country hotels which had been advertising in the newspapers lately. That was it, he decided. He would speak to him the following day.

Bella jumped up from her seat as the front doorbell sounded. 'There's my taxi,' she said excitedly. 'Now you will take care, darling, and write to Caroline soon, she'll be expecting a letter. Oh, and do get an early night, you look awful. 'Bye, darling, wish me luck. It'll be a terrible bore without you, but at least I'll have the satisfaction of knowing I'm doing my bit for the war effort.'

Frank watched the taxi pull away from the front door with a scowl on his face. The only thing Bella would get satisfaction from would be doing her bit for that infantile producer and his cronies. As for the tour being a terrible bore, it would be more like one round of pleasure, if Bella had any say in it. Never mind, he smiled bitterly. At least her absence would give him the opportunity to pursue his own interests without constantly having to make excuses. Perhaps he should call

Peggy this evening. He could play the poor neglected husband and father. She had always been a soft touch for that sort of thing. Or maybe he would write a quick letter to Caroline and then go off down to the pub and get well and truly plastered.

Frank went back into the house and flopped down on the divan. Maybe he should phone Peggy right away, he thought. The letter could wait for another day or two. The little bitch had not even bothered to answer his last letter.

George Galloway walked slowly out of Tyburn Square, leaning heavily on his silver-topped walking cane. He was wearing his black overcoat, with a Homburg covering his white hair and a silk scarf lying loosely round his bull neck. The old man's pinstripe trousers had razor-sharp creases and his black button-up boots were highly polished, presenting a general appearance of affluence and self-esteem. George was a very proud person, who insisted on always being immaculately turned out whenever he took his Sunday constitutional.

The public house that George used was the Saracen's Head in Jamaica Road, a small establishment which had an exclusive saloon bar frequented by the business fraternity of the area. The bar was well furnished and there was an open fireplace covered with brass and copper ornamentation. The landlord and his staff maintained a discreet attitude towards their saloon bar clientele, allowing them complete privacy to discuss their business without interruption. The arrangement suited the old man and it was the place where he often conducted his private matters.

When he entered the saloon bar, George was greeted by his solicitor and personal friend, John Hargreaves. The elderly solicitor was the senior partner of Hargreaves and Symons, an old-established company which handled the legal affairs of many of the local businessmen. Hargreaves was a tall, thin man with a large head and domed forehead. He was a hard-drinking man with a preference for good Scotch malt whisky, and his consumption of the spirit was a subject of awe by many who knew him well. The two men had a good deal of respect for each other, reinforced by mutual admiration of their capacity for the hard stuff.

Suitably supplied with double tots, the two found a quiet corner and sat talking.

'I've managed to draft the document, George,' the solicitor said, sipping his drink. 'It covers the properties you specified, and it sets out the disposal clause. You'll need to sign it, of course, and I've arranged a witness.'

George eyed the solicitor warily. 'This witness, is 'e reliable?' he asked.

'Reliable? I don't understand,' Hargreaves queried.

Galloway put his drink down on the polished table-top and leaned forward, his hands cupped over the silver knob of his cane. 'Listen, John,' he began. 'Yer know of the changes in the will, an' 'ow it affects my son Frank. There'll come the day when 'e's gonna be sittin' in on the readin' of it an' that day will be soon enough fer 'im ter learn that 'e's not the sole beneficiary. There's no need whatsoever fer 'im ter know about the gran'son now. So yer see, it's important that the witness is reliable. I don't want no bloody chancer witnessin' the changes, somebody who might pass the information on ter Frank, fer gain I mean.'

Hargreaves sighed as he shook his head slowly. 'George, you really are a crotchety old cuss at times,' he said with the ghost of a smile appearing on his thin face. 'You need have no fear. The witness will be unimpeachable, so you can rest easy.'

George allowed himself a grin as he swallowed the contents of his glass. 'Anuvver?' he asked.

The solicitor watched his old friend make his way to the counter with a sigh. It must have been a terrible shock for him to be suddenly told that he had a grandson, he thought, and at his time of life too. Frank would be in for a shock as well, when he eventually found out. George's caution was entirely understandable in the circumstances. If Frank ever found out prior to his father's death, it would do more than sour the already precarious relationship the two had.

George returned with more drinks and grunted loudly as he sat down in his seat once more. 'Goin' back ter what we was talkin' about, John,' he began, 'yer know the position wiv Frank. 'E's got 'imself in trouble with the bookies in the past, an' that's 'cos of 'er, as well yer know. I don't want 'im sellin' orf those properties ter pay 'is debts. 'E'll 'ave the business, an' if 'e works 'ard at it 'e'll 'ave a tidy bit o' collateral. The properties in Page Street an' Rovver'ithe are gonna set up Geoffrey's son. I reckon there's a good chance in that direction o' keepin' the Galloway name goin', providin' the lad gets a break, an' that's exactly what I'm givin' 'im.'

'That's commendable, George,' his old friend replied. 'I think you've made the right decision. Those properties are going to fetch a tidy sum one day, when this war's over of course. The land itself is going to rise considerably in value, and that's a generally accepted view by people who know about these things. The option to sell without constraints imposed was a courageous move, if I may say so.'

George nodded. 'I see it as a calculated risk,' he said. 'I'll know 'ow much of a risk when I meet the lad next week. I'll be puttin' it to 'im about startin' up in business. What sort o' business 'e chooses is fer 'im ter decide. As long as 'e uses the family name I don't care. At least 'e'll 'ave the money ter start.'

Hargreaves sat back in his seat and toyed with his glass thoughtfully for a few moments before looking up at his old friend. 'Don't mind me asking, George, but is there a possibility that Frank and his wife will split up?' he asked.

'Get divorced, yer mean?'

'Yes, that's what I mean.'

'I dunno,' George answered, shaking his head. 'If 'e does, it's more than likely it'll be fer adultery. Frank don't say too much about 'im an' 'er, but I can tell by the way 'e talks that they're not 'appy tergevver. She's got 'er own circle o' friends an' she's never 'ome. I can't stand the bitch,' he growled.

'The reason I asked was, would it make any difference to your thinking should Frank divorce Bella?'

'No, it wouldn't. That will is definitely my last will an' testament,' George said firmly. 'Yer know, John, there was one occasion when I said ter Frank that in my opinion I lost the wrong son in the war. I was very angry at the time an' maybe it was a terrible fing ter say, but I stan' by it. That boy o' mine is gonna ruin 'imself if 'e's not careful. Geoffrey would 'ave bin a different proposition. All right, maybe it was my doin'. I should 'ave made Frank come inter the business the way I did wiv Geoff, instead o' lettin' 'im go 'is own way. It's that bloody pansy crowd 'e got in what's changed 'im. Gawd almighty, John, that boy o' mine lets Bella walk all over 'im. 'E should 'ave laid the law down soon as they were married. A few spanks an' she'd 'ave soon changed 'er tune, an' as fer that daughter of 'ers, she's turnin' out a right spoilt little cow.'

John Hargreaves leaned forward over the table. 'I'll tell you something, George,' he said quietly. 'Men of our age should be mellowing, like this fine Scotch. It doesn't do us any good to rankle inside, through harbouring grudges or thinking on what might have been or should have been. Let go, George. Think about the good things, like getting to know that grandson of yours. Take the advice of an old friend. Let go, before it kills you.'

George stroked the gold medallion that hung from his watch chain. 'Don't worry, John,' he said, chuckling. 'It won't kill me. I'll live till I die an' I'll go when it's time. Is it your turn or mine?'

The short ring of the gate bell was followed by a longer note, and when Joe returned he was accompanied by a hollow-eyed woman holding a handkerchief to her mouth. 'Get Rachel,' he said quietly to Carrie. 'This is Derek's mum. She got a telegram this mornin'.'

1940 − 1

Chapter Thirteen

The first Christmas of the war was a very quiet occasion for the people of Bermondsey, and for the Tanner family it was also a very sad time, with Rachel spending many hours alone in her room. She had become hollow-eyed and pale, and unwilling to make conversation. During the day she worked as usual in the yard office but after the evening meal, which she barely touched, she would either go to her room very early or occasionally slip out to see her childhood friend Amy Brody. It seemed to Carrie that her daughter was heading for a complete breakdown and she said as much to Joe one evening after Rachel had gone to bed.

'I don't know what ter do, Joe,' she sighed. 'I feel so 'elpless. What can we say? How can we 'elp 'er?'

Joe hugged her tight. 'There's nuffink we can say,' he told her. 'It'll take time. It's early days yet, an' we've got ter realise she's still not over the shock.'

'But she's gonna go down wiv a bang if she's not careful,' Carrie said urgently. 'I've tried ter get 'er ter see the doctor but she just nods. I wish she would. P'haps 'e could give 'er a tonic or somefink.'

Joe ran his fingers through Carrie's hair and stroked her back gently, feeling at a loss for any words of wisdom. 'Maybe it might be a good idea if you an' Rachel got away fer a few days. I could look after the business,' he suggested.

'Where would we go at this time of year?' Carrie asked.

Joe thought for a while, and then his face brightened. 'Yer could go ter Canterbury. It's not that far an' yer should be able ter book in somewhere now Christmas is over.'

Carried sighed deeply and nodded her head. 'I dunno. I'll talk ter Rachel about it anyway, an' fanks, Joe. It might be a good idea.'

Sadie Sullivan was walking back from the market chatting to her friend Maisie.

'D'yer know what, Mais, that was the worst Christmas I've 'ad since the year my two boys fell in the first war,' she told her. 'What wiv the blackout, the rationin' an' the shortages. Then there was Daniel in bed wiv 'is bad chest. I tell yer, I was glad when it was all over.'

Maisie nodded her agreement. 'I make yer right, Sadie. What wiv one fing an' anuvver. There was Nellie's gran'daughter losin' 'er feller, an' that Mrs Allbury in Bacon Buildin's losin' 'er boy the same way. Then there was poor ole Mrs Bromsgrove goin' like she did.'

Sadie puffed loudly. 'Fings are gettin' steadily worse,' she moaned. 'They're rationin' bacon, sugar and butter now.'

'They're callin' up the twenty-sevens now, too,' Maisie said.

'Did yer 'ear on the wireless about those subs of ours what got sunk?' Sadie asked her.

Maisie nodded again. 'I'm gettin' frightened ter listen ter the news, it's so bleedin' depressin'. Maudie was tellin' me she's finkin' o' packin' up an' goin' down ter stay wiv that sister of 'ers in the country.'

Sadie chuckled. 'What, an' leave Ernie?'

' 'E'd go wiv 'er, I s'pose,' Maisie said.

'No fear. 'E can't stand the woman,' Sadie replied. ' 'E was tellin' my Daniel that 'er nerves are a sight worse than Maudie's. 'E wouldn't go wiv 'er, not Ernie.'

It was Maisie's turn to chuckle. ' 'Ere, Sadie, get a look at 'im.'

Sadie glanced in the direction her friend was nodding and saw Wallace hurrying along the turning carrying a plank of wood on his shoulder. 'What the bleedin' 'ell is 'e doin' wiv that?' she said out loud.

'Gawd knows,' Maisie answered. ' 'E's up ter no good, I bet.'

Sadie stopped at her front door and pulled on the doorstring. 'Fancy a cuppa?' she asked.

The fire was burning bright in the cosy parlour and the two friends sat chatting together for a while. Soon they were joined by Maudie and a little later by Dolly Dawson, who had managed to wheedle her way into the exclusive meetings during the past few months.

'I've just come from the corner shop,' she announced as she made herself comfortable near the fire. 'Ole Albert Lockwood's ravin'.'

'Oh, an' why's that then?' Sadie asked.

'Well, 'e was plannin' on paintin' 'is name over the shop when 'e shut fer dinner, an' was sayin' 'ow 'e'd managed ter borrer a couple o' ladders an' a plank. 'E said 'e'd mixed the paint up, sorted out 'is brushes an' a pair of overalls, an' when 'e turns round, what d'yer fink?'

'Don't tell me,' Sadie chuckled. 'Somebody nicked the plank.'

Billy Sullivan leaned against the counter and idly watched the domino players. Charlie Alcroft was eyeing the rest slyly while Tom Casey was studying his pieces carefully. Maurice Salter sat back with a triumphant look on his face while the fourth player Bert Jolly seemed bored with the whole procedure. Dominoes were placed down and then when Tom Casey laid a piece, an argument ensued and Maurice decided to act as mediator. Tempers rose and Billy grinned to himself as Tom Casey threw down his hand and came to the bar. 'Give us a pint, Billy, will yer,' he said, looking very aggrieved.

After Tom Casey had been persuaded by Maurice to rejoin the group, the game got under way again and Billy polished a few glasses. Tuesday evenings were invariably quiet sessions. His mind turned to Annie and the kids. The last letter Annie had sent home worried him. Brendan had gone down with mumps and the eldest lad Patrick had been getting into a few scraps with the local boys at his school.

'Yer look a bit serious, Billy.'

He turned to see Patricia smiling at him. 'I was jus' finkin',' he said casually.

'Annie an' the kids?'

'Yeah. Brendan's gone down wiv mumps.'

'I am sorry,' Patricia said, eyeing him in a way that made him feel uneasy. 'It must be a worry.'

Billy shrugged his shoulders. 'It's goin' back ter that empty place gets me,' he said, taking up another glass to polish.

The attractive landlady came up close to him and leaned on the counter, her full breasts prominent beneath the tight blouse she was wearing. 'Yer don't necessarily 'ave ter be alone ter feel lonely, Billy,' she said quietly. 'I get that feelin' sometimes.'

Billy held the polished glass up to the light to inspect it. 'It's the quietness that gets ter me,' he replied.

Patricia straightened up and spent a long time tucking her blouse into her tight skirt, still standing close to him. 'It wasn't always like it, wiv me,' she went on. 'Terry was a lovely feller at one time. I blame the pub life. Yer both workin' tergevver all the time an' it gets borin'.'

Billy was glad when Maurice came to the counter for a round of drinks, but after looking into the saloon bar, Patricia soon came back. 'There's only two sittin' in there by the fire an' they've only bought one drink each,' she told him.

'Is Terry likely ter be back late?' Billy asked innocently, knowing that Patricia had become nervous of being alone in the pub.

' 'E might be,' she told him. ' 'E's playin' darts wiv a few of 'is pals. Yer'll 'ang on till 'e gets back, won't yer, Billy?'

'Yeah, there's no rush,' he replied. 'I can 'ave a tidy-up while I'm waitin'.'

Patricia laid her hand on his forearm. 'I do appreciate it,' she said smiling sweetly at him. 'Since that trouble I'm scared o' bein' left wiv no one 'ere.'

He moved away, taking up another glass to hide his discomfort and vigorously polishing it. 'I don't fink yer need worry,' he said reassuringly. 'If there was gonna be any comeback it would 'ave 'appened before now.'

'Yer don't know the 'alf of it, Billy,' Patricia sighed.

'Do I need ter know?' he queried.

'Yeah, I fink yer should,' she replied. 'Look, we can talk over a cuppa when we've closed up, if yer like.'

The domino players had become rowdy again and Maurice seemed to be at the centre of the altercation. 'I didn't see yer 'and,' he was insisting. 'Honest, Tom, I wouldn't do such a fing. Gawd 'elp us, mate, I've got the beatin' o' you lot wivout resortin' ter cheatin'.'

Charlie started shouting and Bert joined in with arms waving.

'Right, you lot. If yer don't shut up I'm gonna chuck the lot o' yer out, d'yer 'ear me?' Billy growled menacingly.

Tom gave him a doe-eyed stare and Maurice looked pained. Charlie stood up and buttoned up his tatty overcoat. 'I'm orf 'ome,' he said offhandedly. 'Bloody cheatin' spoils a game.'

Time was called and the few remaining customers drifted home. There was very little clearing up to do and while Billy swept the bar, Patricia went into the back room to make the tea.

'Look, Billy,' she began as the two of them sat in front of the dying fire in the saloon bar. 'I don't want yer ter say anyfing ter Terry about what I'm gonna tell yer. Is that a promise?'

'Yeah, it's a promise,' he replied, wondering what new intrigues he was going to discover.

'Well, yer know those two smartly dressed blokes that's bin in 'ere a few times lately? Well, they're 'tecs.'

Billy raised his eyebrows in surprise. 'A few times?' he queried. 'I've only seen 'em once.'

Patricia nodded. 'They've bin back. They come in the saloon bar now an' again.'

When he first saw the two strangers Billy had taken them to be old acquaintances of Terry's, from the criminal fraternity. Later, when Terry was chatting comfortably with them, he had wondered whether it was something to do with what had happened back in September. Billy was soon proved right on one count.

'It's all ter do wiv the McKenzies,' Patricia went on. 'It seems that there's bin a lot o' trouble flarin' up again at the Elephant an' Castle.'

'Terry told me all about those Jocks,' Billy cut in.

'Not all,' she corrected him. 'It seems that Dougal McKenzie's not runnin' the gang any more. Dougal's card's bin marked, as they say. 'E's got a police record an' they're watchin' 'im closely. Besides, 'e's gettin' a bit too old now. It's Bruce, the youngest bruvver. 'E's the danger now. Bruce McKenzie 'asn't got a record an' 'e's a lot younger than Dougal. What's more, Terry was told by those two 'tecs that 'e's got a powerful team o' villains tergevver. They're be'ind most o' the trouble in the Elephant an' Castle area.'

'But what do those two coppers want wiv Terry?' Billy asked, looking puzzled. 'Are they tryin' ter force 'im ter press charges against those two monkeys who set about 'im?'

114

Patricia smiled mirthlessly. 'Listen, Billy,' she said, looking at him wide-eyed. 'Those two coppers are not ordinary 'tecs, they're top coppers. They're inspectors, I fink. They're well pleased that Terry's not pressin' charges, 'cos it suits their plans.'

Billy shook his head. 'I don't foller yer.'

Patricia leaned forward in her chair. 'Bruce McKenzie must be about thirty or so now, but when Terry was involved wiv the gang 'e was just a kid. 'E idolised Terry an' 'e did 'is best ter stop 'im gettin' beaten up when 'e left the gang fer me. I reckon that if it wasn't fer Bruce my bloke would 'ave bin killed. Now d'yer see the link?'

Billy shook his head. 'Look, I'm not exactly stupid, but it's all beyond me, Pat,' he said sighing.

She smiled indulgently. 'Terry's not gonna press charges against those two villains that beat 'im up, so when they come up before the beak they're on their own. Dougal McKenzie won't be involved, even though it was 'im that paid the two of 'em ter sort Terry out.'

' 'Ow d'yer know fer sure 'e was be'ind it?' Billy asked.

'The coppers told Terry. They got the word from one o' their grasses,' Patricia explained. 'Now, Bruce is gonna be pleased that 'is bruvver's in the clear, an' 'e knows perfectly well that it's down ter Terry.'

' 'Ang on a minute,' Billy cut in. 'I fink the penny's jus' dropped. Those two coppers want Terry ter renew old acquaintances wiv Bruce an' then once 'e's got in wiv 'im again they'll use 'im as a grass.'

Patricia smiled. 'Yer got it,' she said.

'There's one fing not right though,' Billy went on. 'What about Dougal? 'E's obviously still bearin' a grudge, or 'e wouldn't 'ave sent those two bruisers after Terry. Won't 'e 'ave somefink ter say about 'im comin' back inter the fold?'

'From what those coppers told Terry, there's bad blood between the two bruvvers,' she explained. 'Dougal feels 'e's bin shoved aside, so it's not likely that Bruce is gonna take any notice o' what 'e ses.'

' 'Ow does Terry feel about all this? If it was me I'd tell 'em ter piss orf,' Billy said firmly. 'It's too risky. If the mob found out Terry was a plant they do 'im in fer sure.'

'Don't yer fink I know that?' Patricia said with passion. 'The tragedy is, Terry's got no choice.'

' 'Ave they got somefink on 'im, then?' Billy asked, already knowing the answer.

She nodded slowly, and for the first time since they sat down to talk she seemed not to be fully in control. Tears started to well up in her eyes. 'It was down ter me, really,' she said quietly. 'When we were in the pub in Walworth there was a lot o' crooked stuff goin' around. It was me that encouraged Terry ter get involved. We were buyin' an' sellin' a lot o' bent gear, then one day we got some ladies' fur coats.

They'd bin nicked from a ware'ouse over in the City. They were too 'ot fer us to 'andle really, but we took a chance. Yer can call it greed an' I s'pose it was. Anyway, we got tumbled wiv 'em an' it looked like Terry was in fer a stretch, but that's when those two coppers came on the scene. Fer certain information they let Terry off. They even let 'im sell the couple o' coats 'e 'ad left so as not ter cast suspicion on 'im when they collared the gang that was nickin' all the stuff.'

'So Terry was forced ter grass on the gang then?' Billy said.

Patricia nodded sadly. 'Trouble is, they won't leave 'im alone,' she sighed. 'If 'e tells 'em ter piss orf like yer said they'll put the word about ter the villains that it was Terry that grassed 'em. 'Ow long would 'e last then?'

'What a mess,' Billy said sympathetically.

Suddenly Patricia dropped her head into her hands and wept. Billy stood up and leaned over her, patting her back comfortingly, then she was on her feet and in his arms, her head buried in his chest.

'Look, there might be somefink we can do,' Billy told her softly. 'Yer mustn't give up.'

She looked up at him with tears staining her cheeks, then suddenly her arms went round his neck and her lips found his.

Billy was startled, but the feel of her warm body against his and the softness of her lips was overpowering and he pulled her tightly to him. She was breathing faster now, and anxious pangs of guilt pierced Billy's mind as he felt her rubbing against him. With a sudden movement he gripped the top of her arms tightly and pushed her back from him. 'Terry's gonna be comin' in at any minute,' he gasped.

Patricia let herself go limp in his grasp and her hand came up to her forehead. 'I'm sorry, Billy,' she said sighing. 'I got carried away.'

'Yeah, so did I,' he said, moving away from her. 'This can only bring us a lot o' trouble.'

She did not answer him, she just sat down heavily in a chair and looked up at him with wide eyes.

'Look, Pat, I want yer to understand that yer can count on me fer any 'elp I can give,' Billy said reassuringly, 'but yer gotta realise that unless Terry stands up ter those coppers they're gonna walk all over 'im. 'E'll 'ave ter call their bluff sooner or later. Maybe they won't carry out their threat.'

'Yeah, an' maybe they will,' Patricia replied.

'What about Terry seein' a good solicitor?' he suggested.

'I've already talked to 'im about gettin' a solicitor,' she told him, 'but 'e don't seem too keen on the idea.'

There was no more time to talk, for they heard a key going into the lock and in a few moments Terry walked in. 'Sorry I'm a bit late,' he said. 'I was on a winnin' streak. 'As it bin quiet?'

Patricia nodded and gave him a wan smile. 'Billy's swept the bar up, it'll save a job termorrer, an' I've bin busy sortin' out the optics,' she lied.

Terry watched as Billy put on his coat and made for the side door. 'Fanks fer 'angin' on. See yer termorrer,' he said.

As soon as his barman had left, Terry turned to Patricia. 'I've made arrangements ter see Bruce McKenzie,' he said flatly, sitting down heavily in a chair.

Patricia looked at him with fear showing in her eyes. 'Fer Gawd's sake be careful, Terry,' she implored him. 'Yer gonna get in so deep the only way yer gonna get out is in yer box.'

He laughed cynically. 'Don't worry, Pat, I'm gonna lay it on the line ter McKenzie. Maybe we can work somefing out between us.'

She sighed deeply. 'Yer can't tell Bruce what the coppers 'ave got on yer, can yer?' she said. 'It seems ter me it's playin' two ends against the middle, an' your the one who's gonna be squashed.'

Terry laughed. 'I can't fink about it ternight. Let's get ter bed, Pat. Don't ferget we've still got a pub ter run.'

Josiah Dawson put on his coat and hat, slipped on his ARP armband and took up his gas-mask case and helmet. 'Well, I'm orf, Doll. Shan't be too late,' he told her.

Dolly looked up from her sewing. 'Don't ferget yer gotta be up early fer work, luv,' she reminded him.

Josiah nodded dutifully and let himself out of the house. It was dark in the street, with the moon obscured by heavy clouds, and as he made his way towards the elbow of the turning he saw a chink of light showing from one of the houses to his left. Josiah thought about his scant training. The first step was to call out in a loud voice for the culprit to 'Put that light out'. If that did not do the trick then the second step was to knock at the door and remind the tenant that he or she was breaking the blackout regulations. And if that did not work, the police had to be called.

Josiah felt that he was rapidly earning the respect and friendship of the Page Street folk and was loath to do anything that would upset the delicate balance, but he knew very well that he had an important job to do and he was determined to carry it out to the best of his ability.

His gentle tap on the front door brought no response, and the street's warden wondered whether he was correct in forgoing the first step. His second and louder knock brought a rapid response, however; the door was flung open and he found himself being glared at by a somewhat ruffled tenant.

'What the bleedin' 'ell d'yer want at this time o' night?' Maurice Salter growled. 'Piss orf.'

Normally that sort of attitude would have landed someone in hot water, or rather on his back with a sore jaw, but Josiah was determined

117

to be a model warden. 'I'm sorry, Maurice, but there's a chink o' light showin' frew the winder,' he said meekly.

Maurice drew breath. He suddenly realised that it was Josiah Dawson, and he had been taking a chance addressing him in that fashion. He had heard much about the man's past life and his quick temper. Maurice was a proud man, however, and he eased himself out of the dangerous situation by blinking once or twice and stroking his chin. 'Well, I don't know 'ow that's come about,' he replied. 'My Brenda got the blackout down the market an' the bloke on the stall told 'er it was best quality. In fact 'e said it was the same stuff they've got up in Buckin'am Palace.'

'Well, yer'll 'ave ter get it sorted out, mate,' the warden told him. 'I've got a job ter do, yer know.'

Maurice was a very enterprising character and he suddenly realised that he might be able to turn this embarrassing situation into something profitable. 'Well, of course yer dead right, Josiah,' he said, beaming. 'If it wasn't fer the likes o' you I dunno where we'd be. I'll fix it straight away, an' ter show there's no ill feelin', 'ow about you poppin' in fer a cuppa. Yer mus' be cold walkin' the street on a night like this.'

The warden nodded. 'Yeah, all right,' he replied, taking off his cap as he walked in the house.

Maurice showed him into the parlour and after removing newspapers, a handbag and various bits and pieces from the armchair he bade Josiah make himself comfortable. 'It's me daughters, yer see,' he said by way of apology. 'They're the most untidy gels yer could wish ter meet. It's not a bit o' good me tellin' 'em, they jus' ignore me. Mind you, they're a bit too old ter spank now,' he laughed.

Josiah nodded. He had seen the Salter girls on numerous occasions in the street and he had been struck by their grace and attractiveness. 'I s'pose yer right,' he replied.

Maurice left the room and called up the stairs. 'Can one o' you gels drag yerself away from yer chattin' ter come down 'ere an' make a pot o' tea? We've got a visitor.'

One by one the three girls popped their heads round the door to see who could possibly have called at such a late hour, then they disappeared into the scullery to carry on talking while the kettle was heating up. Maurice rubbed his hands and hummed slyly to himself as he went out into the back yard. The girls exchanged knowing glances.

'Gawd, I 'ope 'e ain't tryin' ter flog that blackout stuff ter Josiah,' Brenda remarked.

' 'E'll end up in the nick if 'e's not careful,' Barbara groaned.

'I wouldn't mind, but it's so thin yer'd need ter double it fer it ter be any good,' Lily said, raising her eyes to the ceiling.

Maurice came back into the scullery carrying the large roll of cloth and as he slipped past the girls he was still humming to himself.

Josiah could hear giggling coming from the direction of the scullery and was beginning to wonder whether it was a good idea to accept the offer of a cuppa, and when Maurice walked back into the room beaming from ear to ear, he felt decidedly uncomfortable.

'I s'pose yer get a lot o' people wiv dodgy blackout, don't yer, Josiah?' Maurice asked him.

'Yeah, as a matter o' fact I do,' he replied, wondering how much longer the tea was going to be.

'Well, I fink I've got the answer,' Maurice told him. 'Out there in the passage I've got a roll o' the best blackout material that money can buy. It's far superior to that rubbish they sell at the market. In fact I was finkin' that maybe me an' you could go inter partnership wiv that roll o' cloth.'

' 'Ow d'yer mean?' Josiah asked suspiciously.

'Well, it's like this,' Maurice began. 'Whenever there's light showin' out o' the 'ouses an' you 'ave the uncomfortable job of knockin' at the doors, it might be better if yer can give 'em a bit of advice. Yer know what I mean, tell 'em that the rubbish they've got up at their winders don't conform ter blackout regulations, an' when they look at yer as though they've bin struck dumb, all yer gotta do is tell 'em yer can get 'em the best stuff available. You take the orders an' I'll deliver the material.'

Josiah looked a little sceptical and Maurice leaned forward in his chair. 'I tell yer what I'm prepared ter do,' he said, taking a deep breath. 'I'm prepared ter give yer a commission of one penny fer every yard o' cloth yer sell. Of course, I'm gonna be out o' pocket, but it's gonna be werf it if it makes yer job that bit easier. After all, mate, us blokes 'ave got ter stick tergevver, an' it's 'elpin' the war effort in the bargain.'

Josiah thought about the offer over his cup of tea, and when he finally left the Salter house he was trying to work out just how many yards of blackout material it took to shut out the light in one of the Page Street houses.

Calculations were taking place in the Salter house too.

' 'Ere, Brenda, if I knock a penny orf o' two an' elevenpence three farthin's, that leaves me wiv two an' tenpence three farthin's, right?'

'Blimey, you are a clever ole cock,' Brenda teased him.

'So what's seventy-five times two an' tenpence three farthin's come to?' he asked.

Brenda looked puzzled as she stared down at her spread fingers, then she leaned her head round the door. 'Lily, Dad wants yer.'

Chapter Fourteen

Carrie pushed back the pile of papers she was working on and stared out of the window, her chin resting on her cupped hand. She glanced over at Jamie Robins, saddened at the thought of losing him. Jamie had told her that morning about someone in his street of the same age who had received his call-up papers and he was expecting to hear very shortly.

The young man was engrossed in bringing the ledger up to date and he occasionally grunted nervously, his thin shoulders hunched. He seemed so young and frail and the thought of him going off to fight in the war filled Carrie with dread. How many other young men like Jamie would soon be putting on a uniform and going off to the war, she wondered, their heads held high and their shoulders thrown back as they prepared to face the unknown horrors awaiting them? It had been like a grand parade in the last war, she remembered; her brothers going off to France along with many other local young men, the bands playing and people standing at the kerbsides waving Union Jacks and cheering loudly. This time it was different though. The young men left their homes quietly, with little fuss, only a few tears and kisses as loved ones said their goodbyes.

The February morning was cold and bleak, with a threat of snow in the heavy clouds. Outside the warm office the yard was quiet now that the lorries had left. Carrie turned away from the window and her contemplation of the thin spiral of chimney smoke drifting up into the greyness. Her mind seemed to be filled with worries on that cold winter morning. Her mother was going through one of her bad periods and for the last few days she had hardly left her bedroom at the back of the house, preferring to sit at the window staring down at the back yards of the adjoining houses and the pickle factory yard beyond. Rachel, too, was causing Carrie a great deal of concern. She was still taking her loss very badly, and only that morning she had suddenly announced at breakfast that she wanted the morning off to take care of something. Not wanting to pry, Carrie had told her not to worry, and Rachel had left her and Joe exchanging puzzled glances as she hurriedly left the table.

Footsteps in the yard roused Carrie from her thoughts and she looked up as Joe entered the office.

'It's started ter snow,' he said, nodding briefly to Jamie as he sat down in the one vacant chair.

Carrie glanced out of the window at the sudden flurry of snowflakes and sighed. 'I wonder where Rachel's gone,' she said anxiously.

Joe shook his head and toyed with the paper knife at his elbow. 'I 'ope she's not gone too far, wiv the wevver turnin' nasty,' he replied.

Carrie looked down at the pile of papers in front of her. There was so much to be done but on this particular morning she felt unable to put her mind to it. There were forms to be filled in, an application for the monthly petrol ration, and a large document to be completed concerning a Government transport pool that was being set up to enable essential supplies to be moved around the country in an emergency. There was also a form requiring further information about her exemption application for Jamie Robins, and Carrie removed it from the pile and dropped it into the wastepaper basket at her feet.

'By the way, Carrie, did the rum contract letter arrive?' Joe asked.

She shook her head. It was the first letter she had looked for that morning, mindful that the most important contract she had was up for renewal and there were other local firms interested in winning it away from her. There were enough problems with that contract as it was. When she had spoken to the rum firm's transport manager he had told her that imports of the spirit might have to be switched to West Country ports, should London be bombed. It seemed that Bristol would most likely be the port of entry and it would mean competing against the railways, as well as applying for an extra petrol allowance for the long journeys involved. It was all very worrying and the fact that no letter had arrived made Carrie feel that it was quite possible she had already lost out to another transport firm who had made a short-term offer.

Joe grunted and leaned back in his chair, his eyes searching Carrie's and reading the misgiving reflected in them. 'Don't worry, luv, it's not the end o' the world. It might come termorrer,' he told her with a smile.

Carrie nodded. 'I'm not worried,' she lied. 'There's still a week ter go yet.'

'Well, at least the rest o' the contracts are safe fer the time bein',' Joe said encouragingly. 'Then there's the casual pool. There's always a chance of a day's work if we're stuck any time.'

Carrie gave Joe the smile he was waiting for. It was true, she thought. The leather contract was safe for at least another year and it provided the occasional extra load or two per week, now that the leather factors were supplying the armed services. Both the new Foden lorries were being used on regular contracts with local food factories, which guaranteed her a regular petrol ration. Things could be much worse, she had to admit.

Heavy footsteps sounded on the cobbles outside followed by familiar whistling which brought a happy smile to Carrie's face. Her younger brother Danny was always a very welcome visitor to the yard, though his visits were usually very brief.

'Wotcher, folks,' Danny said as he came in, grinning broadly. 'I'm jus' orf ter work. Any chance of a cuppa? I've got 'alf an hour ter spare.'

Joe got up from his seat and motioned towards the house. 'Come on over an' spread yerself in front o' the fire fer a few minutes. I'll put the kettle on,' he said cheerfully.

Ten minutes later Jamie Robins left to go home for his lunch and Carrie locked the office and joined the two men who were chatting in the cosy parlour.

'We're gettin' more barges comin' upriver than ever,' Danny was saying. 'Mind you, a lot o' the cargoes are bein' transhipped from the ocean-goers onto trampers round the coast. They're frightened the big ships are gonna get trapped in the London docks if the bombin' starts.'

' 'Ow's Iris an' the children?' Carrie asked as she reached for the teapot.

'They're fine, apart from young Charlie,' Danny replied. ' 'E's got tonsillitis.'

'Don't let on ter Mum,' Carrie warned him. 'She'll be tellin' yer about those bread poultices she used ter put on us when we 'ad sore froats.'

'Joe was tellin' me she's not bin feelin' 'erself lately,' Danny said. 'I'll pop up an' see 'er before I leave.'

Carrie stirred her tea thoughtfully for a few moments then she looked up at her brother. 'We're worried about young Rachel,' she said, frowning. 'She's gone off somewhere. She left at breakfast time, said there was somethin' she 'ad ter do. She's still takin' the news about Derek very badly.'

Danny shook his head sadly. 'Bloody shame that. I only met 'im once. 'E seemed a nice young lad.'

Joe poked at the fire and then leaned back in his chair. ' 'Ow's those next-door neighbours of yours, Danny?'

The rugged features of the lighterman broke into a grin as he looked up from the fire. 'They're a bloody weird mob, that lot,' he replied. 'Mind you though, they're no trouble to us. In fact the kids 'ave made friends wiv their tribe. Dolly Dawson an' my Iris get on very well, though the woman's a real nosy ole cow. 'Er ole man's the street warden. 'E tried ter sell us some blackout stuff the ovver day. Said it was the best yer could get. Bloody stuff was useless.' Carrie and Joe exchanged smiles as Danny went on. 'It's a shame about their eldest boy, Wallace. 'E's simple-minded. 'E's a friendly lad, though. My kids fink the world of 'im, though Jamie tends ter torment 'im sometimes.'

'Can't 'e work?' Carrie asked.

Danny shook his head. ' 'E 'as to be watched all the time or 'e's liable to wander orf an' forget what 'e's s'posed to be doin'. It's a bloody shame really. Dolly reckons 'e'd be much better if 'e could get a steady job an' bring in a few bob a week.'

'We could get 'im ter sweep up the yard fer a few bob a week,' Joe joked.

Carrie had heard about Wallace from her mother and she nodded. 'P'raps we could give 'im a try. We need somebody ter keep the place clean,' she said.

Joe's face became serious. 'I was only jossin',' he said quickly.

'I know yer was,' Carrie replied, 'but we was only sayin' the ovver day we could do wiv a chap ter keep the yard clean now that ole Sharkey's gone.'

'Yeah, but yer can't expect somebody like that ter keep the place clean,' Joe told her. 'The poor bleeder could get knocked up in the air wiv those lorries in an' out the yard all the time.'

Carrie turned to her brother for support but Danny shrugged his shoulders. 'Don't involve me,' he said, glancing over to Joe. 'I wish I 'adn't mentioned 'im now.'

'Remember ole Jack Oxford?' Carrie said, turning to Joe. ' 'E was tuppence short of a shillin' but 'e kept that stable yard spotless. There were 'orse an' carts in an' out there all day as well.'

Joe raised his eyes towards the ceiling and then shrugged. 'Well, it's up ter you, Carrie,' he said with a sigh of resignation, 'but give it some thought. We don't want the poor sod gettin' run over.'

Carrie gave the two men a smile which told them she had won the argument. 'Danny, tell Mrs Dawson ter pop round termorrer sometime. I'll 'ave a chat wiv 'er.'

Danny got up from his chair and stretched. 'Well, I'd better be orf,' he announced.

As soon as he had left, Carrie turned to Joe, expecting him to be angry, but he merely smiled at her as he came close. 'D'yer know, Carrie, yer've got a big 'eart,' he said, reaching out and taking her in his arms. 'I only 'ope yer know what yer doin','

Carrie let herself relax, as if her worries might melt away as she felt him holding her tightly. 'You'll watch out fer the lad, won't yer, Joe?' she sighed.

'Don't worry, luv, I'll keep both eyes on 'im,' he replied, stroking her back gently.

'Yer a good man. Joe,' she sighed, resting her head against his chest. 'Yer'll never leave me, will yer?'

Joe squeezed her tightly, breathing in the sweet smell of her long blonde hair. 'C'mon now, Carrie,' he whispered into her ear. 'I could never leave yer. Yer got me fer good.'

She sighed deeply as she clung to him. 'Sometimes I get scared, Joe, 'specially wiv the war an' all. I wonder 'ow it's all gonna turn out. I couldn't live wivout yer.'

Joe eased his grip on her, moving his hands up to clasp her shoulders. 'Is this you I'm listenin' to?' he said, holding her at arm's length and gazing into her frightened blue eyes. 'The girl who's built up a successful cartage business an' who's got the rest o' the transport concerns around 'ere worried silly?'

Carrie gave a dismissive smile. 'I was motivated, Joe, yer know I was,' she said softly. 'It was the need fer revenge that spurred me. The need fer revenge an' ter take care o' me mum an' dad. Now, though, I know I mustn't let the 'atred burn inside me. Like me mum said, George Galloway is an old man now an' it don't do ter bear grudges ferever. I feel less bitter now, an' it's changed me inside. Can yer understand what I'm tryin' ter say?'

'I fink so,' Joe replied. 'Remember I 'ad ter change too. There was a time when I wanted revenge against those who got me sent ter prison. I wanted revenge so badly it almost destroyed me. I can live wiv meself now, an' I don't need the prop that drink gave me. I need you though. You're the only prop I need.'

Carrie moved close to him and her lips found his in a long, delicious kiss. All the cares and worries seemed to evaporate in that fleeting moment and she knew that come what may, she would have the strength to cope, providing they were together in love.

Billy Sullivan bent his head over the stone sink in his tiny scullery and thought of Annie and the children. He was missing them terribly and the regular letters that he received only made him feel more alone. They were all doing well in Gloucester; Annie was now an accepted and valued member of the church establishment for unmarried mothers, and the children were all getting on nicely at the local school there. Billy was looking forward to his monthly visit and as he dried his rugged face on a rough towel he thought about the embarrassing situation he was in here, and the lack of judgment which had got him into it.

The chance of earning a little extra money working at the Kings Arms had seemed sensible at the time; he was not to know just how things were going to turn out. Terry Gordon was now spending two nights a week with his cronies and Patricia was taking advantage of his loneliness. She had been very open about the fact that she wanted him and it seemed to Billy that unless he gave up working at the pub, things could get out of hand in a weak moment. Patricia was a very attractive woman and he was very lonely. He would have to be careful not to encourage her in any way, but could he trust himself? It would be best if he left the job, he realised. He could tell her that he found it was too much for him after a hard day's work, but that wouldn't cut any ice with her. No, he would have to be honest with her and tell her the real reason why he should leave. But then they would have to make up a good excuse to give to Terry.

Billy slipped on a clean shirt which Danny's wife Iris had washed and ironed for him and as he brushed his thick hair in front of the mirror his face was set in a serious expression. It was Terry's night out and no doubt Patricia would make the most of it as usual. He would have to be careful that none of the regulars noticed anything. There might be one who bore a grudge and would take the opportunity to write to Annie. It wouldn't be the first time that some troublemaker had broken up a marriage by penning poisonous gossip.

Billy let himself out of his house and walked along Page Street deep in thought. The evening was bitterly cold and a coating of fresh snow blanketed the hard cobbles. Ahead he could see the lights from the corner pub shining out into the empty turning and he hunched his shoulders against the cold. There were other considerations to take into account too, he thought. Terry was playing a very dangerous game in consorting with Bruce McKenzie and his mob, and Billy knew that he would be in the firing line should things go wrong. Danny had warned him to get out while he still could and he was right. His old pal would be there beside him if he could be, but it was not right to involve him. There was Iris and the children to consider.

When Billy walked through the door of the Kings Arms he immediately sensed that something was wrong. Patricia was behind the bar as usual but she looked very worried. As he lifted the counter flap and walked through, she nodded towards the saloon bar.

'There's a couple o' strange faces in there an' they've bin askin' a lot o' questions,' she said in a low voice.

'What sort o' questions?' Billy asked.

A customer walked over to the counter and Patricia shook her head. 'I'll talk ter yer later,' she said quickly, giving the elderly man a forced smile.

Billy took off his coat in the back room and rolled up his sleeves before going back into the bar. The few hardy customers who had braved the cold weather sat around the small room, their faces inscrutable, apart from one old lady who bit on her bottom lip and occasionally shook her head as though reminding herself of the dangerous times they were all going through.

Suddenly the door opened and an angry-looking Josiah Dawson stormed into the bar. He looked around for a few moments and then approached Billy.

' 'Ere, mate, 'as Maurice Salter bin in yet?' he asked quickly.

Billy shook his head. It was the first time he had seen Josiah Dawson inside the pub and if the look on the warden's face was anything to go by, Maurice Salter was in for trouble.

'I've just started work. 'E might 'ave bin in earlier,' Billy told him with a disarming smile.

'Well, if yer see 'im tell 'im ter get 'imself round ter my place quick as 'e can, if 'e knows what's good fer 'im,' Josiah growled.

Billy watched the irate man leave the bar then he turned towards Tom Casey who was sitting by himself in the corner. 'What's all that about?' he asked.

Casey scratched his bald head and stared back at Billy. 'Search me,' he said.

'Blackout,' a voice piped in.

'I beg yer pardon,' Billy said, turning to look at the dapper Bert Jolly.

'Blackout, that's what I said,' Bert repeated. 'I bought four yards meself an' the bloody stuff ain't werf a carrot. Yer can see right frew it. I reckon them there fifth-columnists are be'ind it. Wait till I see Maurice Salter, 'e'll 'ave a bit of explainin' ter do, mark my words.'

Billy grinned and got on with polishing glasses, until Patricia suddenly popped her head round the corner. 'They've gone,' she said with obvious relief.

Billy walked over to her. 'What's goin' on?' he asked.

She laid her hand on his bare arm and squeezed it. 'I thought they were 'tecs at first,' she said in a shaky voice. 'They was askin' a lot o' questions, then I realised they was villains. They asked me about where Terry was and then they said do I get any 'tecs in 'ere. They fair scared me. One of 'em 'ad this funny look.'

'Funny look?'

'Yeah. The short bloke 'ad this funny eye,' Patricia told him. 'It was all faded, sort o' milky lookin', an' 'e kept grinnin' at me. That evil leer of 'is sent shivers down me spine.'

Billy looked around the bar to make sure he would not be overheard, then he turned to Patricia. 'Yer'd better tell Terry soon as 'e gets in,' he said. 'If I'm not mistaken they'll be part o' the McKenzie mob an' they've come ter let yer know they're weighin' the place up.'

Patricia's face turned pale and she bit on her lip in anguish. 'I wish I knew what was goin' on,' she groaned. 'Terry won't tell me much an' every time I bring up the subject 'e tells me ter shut up. I'm fair worried fer the both of us, Billy. Fer you as well, come ter that. I couldn't blame yer if yer got out while yer still can.'

Billy blew deeply and then gave her a reassuring smile. 'I'm not leavin' yer while fings are the way they are,' he told her, immediately wishing he had not said it. 'It'd be different if Terry didn't leave yer alone in the pub.'

Patricia's face took on a firm look. 'Well, I'm 'avin' it out wiv 'im when 'e comes in ternight. I can't stand much more o' this,' she said, her voice faltering.

The rest of the evening seemed to drag on for Billy, with only a few

126

customers to take care of, then at ten o' clock Maurice Salter walked in the public bar.

'Gis a pint o' bitter, Billy,' he said, leaning his forearms on the polished counter.

Billy pulled down on the beer pump and out of the corner of his eye he spotted Bert Jolly approaching. He could also see Tom Casey and Charlie Alcroft exchanging expectant grins.

'Jus' the bloke I wanna see,' Bert said, leaning on the counter close to an apprehensive-looking Maurice. 'That blackout curtainin' yer bin peddlin'. It's bloody rubbish.'

Maurice had just finished his late shift at the gasworks and was feeling tired. He had also been stopped on his way to the pub by one of the neighbours who informed him that an angry Josiah Dawson was looking for him. He knew now that his little venture into the drapery business had not been such a good idea after all. He remembered that his three daughters had been quick to warn him that he was trading on very dangerous ground recruiting a man like Josiah to act as his agent. Maurice, being a man of considerable resourcefulness and guile, had already realised that things needed thinking out carefully, and by the time he had finally reached the Kings Arms he felt reasonably able to deal with the looming crisis.

'You're quite right,' he told an irate Bert.

'Oh?' was all the startled pensioner could say.

'Yeah, Bert. The bloody stuff is rubbish, in the normal manner o' fings,' Maurice went on, sipping his frothing pint.

'So yer admit it then?' Bert said.

Maurice wiped the froth from his lips with the back of his hand and grinned cheekily at the pensioner. 'Yer see, Bert, we're not talkin' about the normal manner o' fings in this case,' he said in a low voice.

'Ain't we?' queried Bert, puzzled. 'I thought we was talkin' about four yards o' blackout curtain that's so bleedin' skimpy it don't shut out any light whatsoever. What's more, Josiah Dawson told me yer was sellin' the best blackout stuff money could buy. Two an' elevenpence three farthin's a yard yer charged me. Bloody 'ell, I could 'ave bought better stuff orf a stall fer less than that.'

Maurice hid his irritation. He realised he might well have to return the pensioner's money, and there was no way he was going to be able to get the fourpence commission back which he had already paid to the street warden. He leaned his elbow on the counter and winked at his angry neighbour.

' 'Ave yer ever 'eard o' Shantung silk?' he asked.

'What?' Bert said, shaking his head.

'Well, Shantung silk comes from China, but yer can't buy it these days, not since the Japs overran Shantung,' Maurice started to explain. 'They used Shantung silk ter make dresses fer the upper-crust women.

Cost a fortune, it did. Anyway, the stuff I sold you was Chunking silk, which is even better than the ovver stuff. It's very fine fabric, that's why the light shows frew it.'

Bert frowned and looked disbelievingly at Maurice. 'Yer 'avin' me on, ain't yer?' he growled.

Maurice held both hands up. 'Would I do that ter you, Bert?' he asked. 'Now look. Let me explain. Before Chunking was overrun by the Japs, the Chinese merchants dyed all their rolls o' Chunking silk black, so as ter disguise it, in case it got nicked, yer see. Then they transported it 'alfway across China, realisin' that when it got there they could boil all the colour out of it an' Bob's yer uncle. Trouble was the stuff got mislaid durin' the long journey an' it was sold as blackout material ter this country by certain exporters who didn't know their arses from their elbows.'

'So what yer tellin' me is, I got four yards o' Chunking silk up at me winders,' Bert cut in.

' 'S'right,' Maurice said grinning broadly.

'But it ain't no bleedin' good if it don't keep the light in,' Bert said, his anger rising again.

Maurice laid his hand on Bert's arm reassuringly. 'Just fink fer a minute,' he urged him. 'That blackout material I sold yer is an investment. Buy anuvver four yards an' double it up. That'll do the trick. Then, when this bloody war's over, yer can boil it ter take the colour out, an' crash bang wallop, yer got yerself eight yards o' the finest silk money can buy. All the young ladies are gonna want new dresses when this lot's over, that's fer sure. Yer'll make a fortune.'

'Well, if that's the case, why d'yer sell it in the first place?' Bert asked him. 'Why don't you make the fortune?'

Maurice kept the pensioner waiting while he took another large gulp from his glass. ' 'Cos I'm a man o' principle, that's why,' he finally said with passion. 'Josiah Dawson got me all the orders an' I couldn't let the man down, nor the customers, now could I?'

'But yer must 'ave told Josiah it was blackout stuff fer 'im ter get yer the orders,' Bert argued.

'I didn't know at the time,' Maurice said, looking aggrieved. 'I only found out meself by accident. Young Brenda boiled the curtains an' while she was at it she done the blackout as well. Very thorough is my Brenda. Anyway, there it was starin' us in the face. She couldn't believe it when she took it out o' the copper. Reco'nised what it was straightaway, she did. I was sick, ter tell yer the trufe, but what could I do, bein' a man o' principle. Some yer win, some yer lose.'

'Well, in that case yer better sell us anuvver four yards then,' Bert said.

At that minute Josiah Dawson walked into the pub. 'Jus' the bloke I wanna see,' he growled at Maurice.

The hassled wheeler-dealer put his empty glass down on the counter and turned to face Josiah. 'Look, I can't stop now. Bert Jolly'll explain everyfing,' he said, making for the door.

Chapter Fifteen

As the bitterly cold winter days dragged on, Carrie became increasingly worried. There had been no letter from the rum factors to renew the contract, and to add to her problems Rachel had returned home late one afternoon to announce that she had volunteered for the WAAF. There had been tears and pleading from Carrie for her daughter to reconsider, but it was to no avail.

'It's no good, Mum, I've made my mind up,' Rachel had said quietly. 'I need ter get away. Not from you an' Joe, but from this area. Everywhere I go I can see Derek. It's as though 'e's still 'ere wiv me. Yer've got to understand.'

Carrie recalled the heartbreak she had felt as she hugged Rachel, and the hard tone Joe had adopted with her when she tried to use the business as an excuse to keep her daughter at home.

'Look, Carrie, yer not bein' fair ter the gel,' he had told her. 'She's spent enough years cleanin' an' fetchin' an' carryin' when yer farvver was ill. We can manage the paperwork between us. Don't make the gel feel guilty about leavin' us. Besides, she's right about gettin' away from around 'ere. It'll be good fer 'er.'

Carried could still remember clearly the way it hurt him when she barked back at him, 'It's all right fer you, she's not your daughter.'

He had turned away with a sad look on his handsome face but she pulled on his arm quickly and then melted into his arms, her apologies for her hasty words dissolving into sobs. He had held her close and stroked her back, the way he always did to give her comfort.

'I'm sorry, Joe,' she told him. 'Yer've bin like a dad ter Rachel an' she loves yer every bit as much as I do. I'm so sorry.'

Carrie was grateful for the comfort Joe had been to her these last few months, and now, as the deadline for the rum contract arrived, he was as supportive and optimistic as ever.

'It could be in the mail,' he said. 'Everyfing's late these days. Even the postmen are gettin' called up.'

Carrie laughed at his pathetic excuse but she knew that he was as worried as she was. The contract must have gone to another transport firm, but she wondered why. Her rates were competitive, and Paddy

Byrne her regular driver for the contract was beyond reproach. There had never been any complaints about his work, and he had told her only a few weeks ago that there didn't seem to be any reason why the contract would not be renewed.

'There's got ter be a reason why we've lost that business,' Carrie said as she sat with Joe beside a roaring fire on Friday evening.

'I s'pose we've bin underbid,' Joe said, staring into the flames.

'I can't see that,' Carrie replied. 'Our rates are rock bottom. If any firm went lower they'd 'ave no margin o' profit, or very little. Yer can't go any lower than us an' survive fer long, I'm sure o' that.'

'P'haps money's changed 'ands,' Joe volunteered.

Carrie shook her head emphatically. 'It can't be that. It's always bin a board decision. They wouldn't all be open ter bribes, surely?'

Joe shrugged his shoulders. 'It beats me,' he said, still staring into the fire.

The sound of the gate bell startled them and Joe eased himself out of his chair and hurried from the room. Carrie frowned. Rachel was in her room and her mother had been in bed for the past few days with bronchitis. It was very rare that anyone would call at this time of night, she thought.

Joe returned with Dolly Dawson, who nodded cheerfully to Carrie.

'I'm sorry ter trouble yer at this time o' the evenin', luv, but I bin finkin' over what your Danny said about the job fer Wallace,' she said, standing in the doorway. 'At first I didn't fink 'e was up to it, that's why I never come round ter see yer, but it was your Danny who got me ter change me mind.'

Carrie motioned Dolly to a seat by the fire. ' 'Ow did 'e manage that?'

'Well, it was like this, yer see,' Dolly began. 'This mornin' your Danny asked me if I'd come ter see yer an' I 'ad ter tell 'im no. Then 'e asked me whyever not. Don't get me wrong, luv, Wallace is not a wilful sort o' lad. 'E's good as gold when 'e's left alone, but 'e is inclined ter get excitable, especially when people take the piss – I mean the rise out of 'im. I was finkin' the drivers might take it out of 'im, Wallace bein' the way 'e is, if yer understand me meanin'. Then I wasn't sure if the lad was up ter sweepin' the yard an' keepin' it clean. Your Danny said there'd be no trouble from yer drivers, 'cos they'd be out all day, an' 'e said that 'e was sure Wallace could keep the place clean. 'E's a lovely boy, your Danny. So is 'is wife Iris. And those kids o' theirs. A credit ter the two of 'em, they are.'

Carrie and Joe exchanged amused glances and Joe took the opportunity to make his getaway. 'I'll put the kettle on,' he said.

Dolly was feeling comfortable in front of the roaring fire and she folded her arms as she leant back in the armchair. 'What done it was Maudie Mycroft,' she explained. 'D'yer know Maudie?'

131

'I know 'er,' Carrie replied, wondering how Maudie could be involved in the saga.

'Well, Maudie slipped over in the snow terday,' Dolly went on. 'Right outside my place it 'appened. Bruised all 'er leg, she 'as. Fair shook 'er up, but she'll be all right. Josiah pulled 'er up on 'er feet an' 'e gave 'er some of 'is 'orse liniment ter rub in. 'E believes in 'orse liniment fer bumps an' bruises, does Josiah.'

'Yeah, but what's Maudie fallin' over got ter do wiv Wallace?'

'Well, I'm comin' ter that,' Dolly answered. 'Maudie wouldn't 'ave slipped over if Danny 'ad bin at 'ome.'

'An' why's that?' Carrie enquired, by now totally confused.

' 'Cos your Danny always sweeps the snow away from our front doors when 'e's at 'ome. 'E was at work when Maudie slipped over.'

'Oh, I see,' Carrie replied, still bewildered.

Dolly's face was starting to glow with the heat of the fire and she stretched out her legs, much to Carrie's dismay, who felt that at this rate Dolly Dawson was going to stay all night. 'Anyway, ter cut a long story short,' Dolly went on, 'I was talkin' about poor ole Maudie ter my Josiah an' 'e ses ter me, "Why don't yer see if yer can get Wallace ter sweep the snow away from our doors?" Well, I got ter finkin'. If our Wallace done a good job wiv the snow sweepin', then 'e'd surely be able ter keep a yard clean, now wouldn't 'e?'

Carrie nodded, finding it difficult to maintain a semblance of interest. 'I s'pose 'e would,' she agreed.

'Well, I give Wallace this big yard broom,' Dolly continued, 'an' I tells 'im what ter do. Then I went back indoors ter get on wiv me ironin'. A great big pile it was, mostly the kids' stuff but there was Josiah's shirts an' underwear as well, an' the sheets orf the kids' beds. Anyway, I finished the ironin' an' I come over all tired. Yer know 'ow yer get sometimes when yer doin' yer ironin'.'

Carrie nodded and wished Joe would hurry up with the tea. 'Yeah, I know,' she said, stifling a yawn.

'Anyway, I must 'ave dozed orf,' Dolly chatted on, 'an' suddenly I woke up wiv a start. It was about time fer the kids ter come in from school. All of a sudden in they come, all groanin'. "Where's all the snow gone?" they shouted. Well, I looked out me winder an' what d'yer fink? There was 'ardly any snow left in our end o' the street. Wallace 'ad swept the bleedin' lot away, cobbles an' all. 'E must 'ave bin at it fer more than three hours by my reckonin'. So yer see, luv, I'm sure you'll get a good job done if yer decide ter take 'im on.'

Joe arrived with the tea, and by the expression on his face Carrie knew that he had been listening to what Dolly had been saying.

'All right, Dolly, I'll give 'im a try,' Carrie told her. 'Tell 'im ter come in on Monday at ten o'clock. Joe'll keep 'is eye on 'im an' make sure 'e knows what ter do. Wallace can finish at four an' I'll start 'im at thirty shillin's a week. If 'e settles down all right, I'll up 'is wages ter thirty-two an' six. 'Ow's that sound?'

Dolly's face lit up. 'That's very fair, luv. Wallace will be pleased when I tell 'im,' she said smiling broadly.

On that Friday morning, in the Galloway yard in Wilson Street, an expectant Frank Galloway opened a letter and then grinned triumphantly to himself. The official contract from the Associated Rum Merchants was his. All that was needed was his signature. 'Well, well,' he said aloud. 'Isn't that Tanner woman going to be disappointed.'

The smile widened still further when George Galloway hobbled into the yard office later that day. 'We got the rum contract, Father,' Frank announced. 'There it is. Will you sign it, or shall I?'

The white-haired old man reached into his waistcoat pocket and took out a pair of silver-rimmed glasses. For a while he studied the document and then he nodded. 'I must say yer did a good job there, Frank,' he remarked, taking the pen his son had offered him. 'It's regular work, an' it might bring us in more cartin' jobs, once they switch the trade ter Bristol. There'll be a lot of imports switchin' ter Bristol.'

Frank felt happy with the way things had turned out. His father seemed pleased for a change, he thought, and so he should. It wasn't every day a contract like this came along. What was all the more pleasing was that the new business had been taken away from that Tanner girl. It was only justice, after all. She had filched that little rat Robins and used his knowledge to undercut them. Well, Jamie Robins was going to remember his little indiscretion for a long time, he chuckled to himself.

George puffed as he spread his bulky frame in the large office chair. He was finally going to meet his new-found grandson for the first time very soon and he was looking forward to it. The lad was coming home on leave after training and then apparently going off to join a regiment in France shortly. George frowned suddenly as he fingered the gold medallion hanging from his watch chain. What if the lad met the same fate as his father? he wondered anxiously. No, it couldn't happen, he told himself. It would be too cruel.

Frank had been watching his father closely and wondered whether now would be a good time to open up the subject of the will. He had been meaning to talk to him about it for some time but the old boy had not been very approachable of late. He was getting bad on his legs and looked to be breaking up fast. Anything could happen. He could take a heavy fall in the snow or maybe his kidneys would finally pack up with all that whisky he was throwing down. It was only right to get things sorted out, Frank felt. After all, he had taken over the firm when his elder brother Geoffrey was killed in France and he had done his best to cushion the old man from the day-to-day worries. It had not always been easy, he told himself. The old man should recognise the fact and give him his just rewards. Now was as good a time as any to bring it up, Frank decided.

'As soon as the collections shift I'll be putting an advert in the trade paper saying we're doing regular runs to Bristol,' he informed his father.

George nodded and took off his glasses, running his thumb and forefinger over his eyelids. 'That sounds good,' he said with a sigh.

'By the way, Father, I think there's something we should discuss while you're in the office,' Frank began. 'Look, I don't want to sound morbid, and I don't want you to take this the wrong way, but shouldn't you be bringing me into your confidence a little more?'

George's eyes narrowed. 'What exactly d'yer mean?'

'Well, Father, you involve me in certain of your business affairs when a problem arises, such as the Page Street properties, but you tend to keep me in the dark about your other assets. Remember, I'm your son, and I feel that I do have some rights. Besides, supposing you suddenly became ill and were unable to look after your business affairs properly. I would have to assume the responsibility, just as I look after the transport side of it. I should be kept informed, don't you feel?'

George leaned forward in his chair, his two hands clasped over his silver-topped walking cane. 'Let me ask yer somefink,' he said, his heavy features flushing slightly as his temper rose. 'What about the past deal yer did wiv that Macedo bloke be'ind me back? An' what about those gamblin' debts yer got yerself into? Would yer say that was bein' open, 'cos I wouldn't.'

Frank looked down at his fingernails for a moment and then met his father's hard gaze. 'I didn't want to worry you about the debts, Father,' he said quietly. 'And as for that business with Macedo, it was a long time ago, and I did explain all about it.'

'Yeah, after I dragged it out o' yer,' the old man growled.

'All right, Father, forget I mentioned it,' Frank said, raising his hands in front of him.

The elder Galloway's face relaxed slightly and a ghost of a smile crossed his heavy features. 'Look, Frank,' he began. 'When I go you'll get yer inheritance. It's all taken care of. I've drawn up a will an' it's lodged wiv my solicitor. So yer shouldn't fret on that score. You'll be well provided for.'

Frank's expression did not change as he struggled to hide his satisfaction. 'I'm not talking about a will, Father,' he lied. 'I'm just concerned about being in the dark over things.'

George nodded. 'Well, now we know where we are,' he said, taking out his watch from his waistcoat pocket. 'I've got ter go. I'm meetin' somebody shortly. Phone fer a taxi, will yer?'

* * *

Jamie Robins looked at the letter his mother handed him as soon as he got home from work and prayed that it was the one he was waiting for. His mother watched with trepidation while he opened it and she could see by his expression that it was his call-up papers.

'When are yer goin'?' she asked.

'Next Thursday,' he replied. 'The Royal Artillery, Catterick.'

Jamie's mother took out a handkerchief from her flowered apron and dabbed at her eyes. 'Yer didn't 'ave ter go,' she said, fighting back the tears. 'Yer could 'ave got an exemption.'

Jamie sighed and put the letter against the mantelshelf clock. 'Look, Ma, we've bin all over it time an' time again,' he said quietly. 'I can't stay out of it, I jus' can't.'

'Well, go an' wash yer 'ands, dinner's nearly ready,' she told him crossly.

Jamie walked out into the scullery feeling very relieved. The last few weeks had been terrible. It had been hard to look his employer in the eye without wanting to tell her everything, even though she would never have forgiven him for what he had done. But what else could he have done? He had been caught like a rat in a trap by his own stupidity, and there had been no way out, except to do as he had been told. It was hard to believe it had happened to him, but it had, and volunteering for the forces was the only thing he could think of in the circumstances. At least now he would not have to face Carrie, who had been so very good and kind to him.

Jamie splashed cold water over himself and sighed as he buried his wet face in a rough towel. One day Frank Galloway was going to have to pay for what he had done to him, and to the Bradley firm.

Billy Sullivan slipped the bolts as soon as the last customer had left and then proceeded to collect the empty glasses from the tables. Patricia was busy in the saloon bar and he hoped that her husband would return home before she was finished. Terry had come home on a couple of occasions and found them chatting together in the public bar. He hadn't seemed at all put out but Billy felt guilty, thinking how Patricia had been making up to him. He had tried to dissuade her but she only laughed at him and said that Terry had other things to occupy his mind. She seemed to have got over the visit of the two strangers very quickly and she had told him that when she approached her husband about it he had assured her there was nothing to worry about.

Billy felt otherwise. He had noticed one or two strange faces in the bar recently. Outwardly there appeared to be nothing wrong. Strangers did occasionally come in, and they would not attract much attention, but it had seemed to him that these particular strangers were very watchful. Their eyes darted about the bar and they seemed interested in everyone who came in. Maybe it was his imagination, he thought. Perhaps he was getting unduly nervous in his old age, but try as he would, Billy could not dismiss the nagging feeling that something very unpleasant was going to happen soon, and he was going to be inevitably drawn into it.

Patricia came into the bar and sighed as she looked around her. 'Leave the rest of it, Billy, I wanna talk,' she said.

Billy walked over to her and leaned on the counter, keeping his distance, but she moved up close to him.

'Don't yer find me attractive?' she asked, her blue eyes widening.

He puffed. 'Of course I do, but yer know the score, Pat. We're both married. It'd be wrong ter start anyfing.'

She reached out and stroked his bare forearm. 'I've a feelin' yer've bin avoidin' me lately,' she told him in a low, seductive voice. 'I've watched yer. Yer turn away when I look at yer an' yer always findin' fings ter do.'

Billy moved his arm away and straightened up. 'Be sensible, Pat,' he said sharply. 'I'm well known around 'ere. If I start makin' up ter yer while I'm workin' 'ere the customers are gonna notice. The next fing yer know my Annie's gonna get a letter. I know 'er, she'll be on the next train 'ome. I can't take the chance o' ruinin' our marriage.'

'Listen, Billy, it doesn't 'ave ter be like that,' she said. 'I could talk ter Terry, tell 'im I need a night off. We could meet somewhere. Annie would never know.'

He shook his head. 'No, Pat. I'm not takin' a chance. I can't.'

She moved closer, her hands reaching up to his shoulders and her eyes boring into his. 'Tell me yer don't fancy me. Tell me I don't get yer excited. Yer can't, can yer?'

He tried to push her away but her lips pressed against his and for a fleeting moment he let her mould herself against him, his lips responding to her kiss and his arms holding her tightly. Then suddenly there was the sound of a key in the lock and footsteps in the side passageway. They moved apart only just in time as Terry came into the bar. He looked away and said nothing, but it was obvious to Billy that he had noticed something.

'What's goin' on?' he asked after a moment or two, his eyes flitting from one to the other of them.

Patricia smiled disarmingly. 'What d'yer fink's goin' on? We were jus' talkin' about Billy's wife an' kids,' she said coolly.

Billy had to admire her. Her calmness had taken the edge off what could have been a nasty confrontation. She went over to Terry and led him further into the bar. 'Billy wanted ter get away early ternight but I asked 'im ter stay till yer got in,' she explained. 'I'm frightened o' bein' alone 'ere, Terry. I'm glad yer not late.'

Billy slipped on his coat and mumbled a goodnight, feeling the cold night air on his hot face as he stepped out into the empty street. That does it, he told himself. He would have to leave now, before he got in

136

over his head. After all, it was Terry's responsibility to look after his wife, not his.

Inside the Kings Arms, Patricia faced her angry husband, her hands on her hips as she glared at him. 'Nuffing was goin' on,' she shouted. 'I've already told yer once. Billy's never said a word out o' place. We was jus' talkin', that's all. Anyway, if you didn't keep goin' out, yer wouldn't 'ave nuffing to worry about, would yer?'

Terry turned away from her and sat down heavily on a chair. 'Look, Pat, yer know what I'm up against,' he sighed. 'I've got them two monkeys leanin' on me an' they're gettin' impatient. I've told Bruce McKenzie everyfing. 'E knows the score now.'

'Did yer tell 'im about 'ow the coppers got ter yer?' she asked incredulously.

He nodded. 'I told Bruce straight that if I didn't play along wiv their little scheme they was gonna put the word around that I was the grass who put that ovver crowd away, but I swore to 'im it wasn't true.'

'And did 'e believe yer?' Pat asked.

Terry nodded. 'Yeah, at least 'e seemed to,' he said, staring down at his feet. ' 'E told me not ter worry an' that 'e'd fix those two 'tecs.'

Patricia felt a sudden pity for him. He had been a good husband, and very loving towards her, until he had fallen foul of those two policemen. It had been that which had soured their marriage and made her feel unwanted. She had sought comfort with Billy, knowing that he was lonely and vulnerable. She had done wrong in leaving Terry to face his problems alone.

She reached out and squeezed his shoulder. 'Why don't we get out, luv?' she said. 'Let's move away. Let's get right away from all this trouble an' aggravation. Let's do it fer us, before we ruin what we've got.'

Terry's eyes came up to meet hers. 'Is that what yer really want?' he asked in a low voice.

'I can't see any other way out of it, if we're gonna 'ave any sort o' future tergevver, Terry,' she sighed.

He closed his hand over hers. 'I'm dog tired, luv. Let's sleep on it. We'll talk about it in the mornin'.'

Chapter Sixteen

Carrie was hard pressed to find work for Paddy Byrne now that she had lost the rum contract, but with a lot of phoning around she managed to get casual work most days. Sometimes there was the odd extra load available at the food factories and leather factors, who seemed to be kept very busy supplying the armed forces. Paddy remained as cheerful as ever and Carrie reassured him that he would be kept on the payroll as long as she could still get the work. Paddy responded with his usual grin. 'There'll be somefing comin' up shortly, gel,' he said. 'I shouldn't worry too much.'

Carrie was very concerned about losing the contract. The short letter from the company merely thanked her for her good service over the years and said that they had been forced to make other arrangements for the future. It was obvious to her that she had been undercut, and that the successful transport firm must have put in a dangerously low bid. But then she had done the same thing herself in the past, just to keep things ticking over until something better came along.

Carrie learned from one of her drivers who had won the contract. Tom Armfield brought the news in one evening and it both shocked and angered her.

'I saw a Galloway driver unloadin' at the rum vaults in Tooley Street, Carrie,' he said. 'I thought yer'd better know.'

All the old bad feelings towards the Galloways were rekindled by the news and Carrie was still seething when she talked it over with Joe later that evening. 'It wouldn't 'ave mattered if it 'ad bin any ovver firm, but Galloway, it jus' sticks in me chest like I've bin punched,' she said angrily.

' 'E can't be earnin', if the bid was lower than yours, surely?' Joe replied.

'It must be a short-term contract, until they sort out where the imports are bein' switched to,' Carrie remarked. 'If Galloway's got the contract, 'e'll be more likely ter get the Bristol trade. 'E'll get the petrol ration 'e needs an' it'll open up ovver contracts to an' from the West Country.'

'If that's the case, 'e won't mind runnin' this contract at a loss,' Joe said darkly.

Carrie leaned back in her chair and moved her bare feet nearer the fire. 'I bet Frank Galloway took a lot o' comfort when 'e got that work, knowin' 'ow 'e feels about the way I've outbid 'em in the past,' she said frowning.

Joe's eyes were full of concern as he studied her. 'Yer not gonna brood on this, are yer?' he asked. 'There's enough ter do now that Jamie's left an' Rachel's goin' soon.'

Carrie smiled. 'Don't worry, luv, I'm not gonna let it get ter me. I wouldn't give Galloway the satisfaction,' she said firmly. 'The first fing ter do is get somebody ter replace Jamie as soon as we can.'

Joe stood up and stretched. 'C'mon, luv, let's get ter bed, it's nearly twelve.'

Carrie took his hand as she got up and he slipped his arm round her waist, then they heard the floor above them creak and Nellie's voice from the top of the stairs. 'When yer get a minute, I'd like anuvver cuppa, Carrie. That last one got cold.'

George Galloway sat facing the young man in uniform whom Mrs Duffin had shown into his large front room. He had shaken the soldier's hand with a strong grip and then motioned him into a chair while he poured himself a drink. 'I mus' say yer favour yer muvver,' he said, eyeing him closely.

The young man smiled and returned the gaze. 'I never saw a photo of me real farvver,' he said awkwardly. 'I never knew what 'e looked like.'

George Galloway knew that he was going to say that. 'I've got a picture o' Geoffrey in uniform,' he replied, taking the photo from his wallet and passing it over. 'That was jus' before Geoff left fer France. 'E was killed soon after.'

Tony O'Reilly studied the print. ' 'E looks very smart,' he said quietly.

'Yer on embarkation leave, I understand,' George said, as the young man gave him the photo back. 'D'yer know where yer goin'?'

'We don't know fer sure, but it looks like France,' Tony replied.

The old man nodded, his rheumy eyes appraising the young soldier. He was a chip off the old block, he thought. He would be about Geoffrey's height, though not quite so stocky. He had an open face like Geoffrey, too, and there was something in his manner that reminded George of his long-dead son. It was his hands, that was it. Geoffrey used to sit the same way with his hands spread on his knees and his back upright.

'Yer'll be careful, won't yer?' the old man warned him sternly. 'You're the only male heir. There's nobody else apart from you, which brings me ter the business I wanted ter talk ter yer about.'

Tony sat quietly watching the old man. In her last letter his mother had told him all about her visit to George Galloway. It had been a shock to learn finally who his grandfather was, and to find out that Galloway's dead son Geoffrey was his real father. Tony felt very uneasy in the old man's presence. He had never given much thought to who his real father might have been but he knew his mother was anxious that he should finally learn everything about the past and he could understand why. She was slowly dying of consumption and he knew she wanted to make peace with herself. It must have been very hard for her, he thought. She had told him that she had been determined to bring him up without seeking help from the Galloway family, but now that he was of age and going off to war he had a right at least to meet his grandfather.

'If my son 'ad survived the war I would 'ave passed over my business an' properties to 'im before now,' George began, 'but it wasn't ter be. I've got anuvver son, Frank. 'E runs my cartage business but there's no son from 'is marriage. Between you an' me there's very little marriage anyway, as far as I can make out. Frank's missus is a no-good money-grabber an' their daughter's a spoilt little cow. But anyway, that's of no concern ter you. What I'm sayin' is, Frank's bin taken care of. The business is gonna be 'is when I'm no longer around. There's ovver properties that I own, 'owever, an' I'm not lettin' that schemin' whore of a wife of 'is get 'er greedy 'ands on 'em. I'm puttin' 'em in your name. They'll be yours when I'm gone.'

Tony looked shocked. 'I dunno what ter say,' he muttered.

'There's nuffink to say,' the old man replied, a ghost of a grin touching his lips. 'When this war's finally over, I want yer ter fink 'ard about startin' up on yer own. Yer look a sensible lad who could get on in business, an' yer'll 'ave a sight more than I started wiv. Yer'll get 'elp as well from my solicitor, who also 'appens ter be a good friend. If 'e's still around 'e'll advise yer, or at least 'is firm will. There's a clause in the will which allows yer ter sell the properties ter raise the necessary money ter start up. Ter be 'onest wiv yer, there was no legal reason ter put in the clause. Once the properties are yours yer'll be entitled ter do what yer like wiv 'em. I only put the clause in so that Frank'd know o' my wishes, that yer got my blessin' ter sell the properties orf.'

The young soldier shook his head slowly. 'I can't believe it,' he said almost inaudibly.

'There's two conditions I will be insistin' on,' Galloway said, staring at him. 'I want the business to bear the family name, Galloway, an' I want yer ter promise me yer'll not start up in a transport business in this area. Is that agreed?'

Tony could only nod for a moment and then he blew hard as he slumped down in his chair. 'I still can't believe it,' he said in a quiet voice.

Galloway got up to refill his glass. 'I'll want yer promise, lad,' he said, 'an' we'll drink on it. That'll be good enough fer me. Geoffrey was a

140

man of 'is word an' I expect 'is son ter be the same.'

Billy Sullivan went to Gloucester to see his family once more and on the train going there he wrestled with his problem. Should he tell Annie about the barman's job he had, or should he wait until he had left? She would have to know sooner or later. Someone would eventually tell her anyway. One thing was certain though. He was going to leave after that weekend. His marriage was at stake, and his health would be too should Terry's cronies decide to turn on him. The prospect seemed likely, considering the devious game he was playing. Sooner or later the two police inspectors were going to want some results from their efforts. Terry would not be able to palm them off indefinitely.

The weekend was a very happy time for Billy. The children were delighted to see him and he spent time taking them on walks in the country lanes, his eyes opened to the beautiful scenery everywhere, so unlike the grimy backstreets of Bermondsey. Annie, too, was very happy and during their very brief time together after the children were put to bed she clung to him, her eyes hardly leaving him. Billy realised how much he loved her and how stupid he had been ever to allow Patricia to pierce his armour. She had almost made him forget the treasures he had in Annie and the children, and his jaw muscles tightened as he thought about it.

It was as he was leaving that he finally told Annie about his job.

'It seemed a good way ter get a few extra shillin's fer you an' the kids, luv,' he said, seeing the worried look on her pretty face.

'That's not important,' she replied. 'What is important is your health. You work hard all day, without working at nights.'

'Well, yer've no need ter worry any more,' Billy said smiling. 'I'm leavin'. I decided ter pack it in before I came down ter see yer. Danny an' Iris 'ave bin naggin' at me ter pop in an' see 'em a little more often.'

Annie squeezed his arm and laid her head against him. 'Make sure you do pack it in, Billy,' she said quietly. 'Besides, I don't want you getting familiar with all those barmaids.'

Their long, lingering kiss and the feel of Annie's slim body against his told Billy all he needed to know. Like it or not, the Gordons were going to have to get themselves another barman as from tomorrow, he vowed.

Maurice Salter had been under considerable pressure from his three daughters to get rid of the remaining blackout material.

'Yer know, Dad, yer just too stupid fer words at times,' Brenda, his eldest, told him one evening as he sat at the parlour table after work. 'Fancy comin' out wiv such a silly story. Who'd be stupid enough ter believe yer in the first place?'

'Bert Jolly did,' Maurice replied, looking dejected.

'Apart from Bert Jolly,' Brenda went on. 'Yer must 'ave realised yer couldn't get away wiv such a fantastic story. People are gonna find out sooner or later. Christ, yer gonna make it difficult fer us three to 'old our 'eads up around 'ere. "Oh look, there's the three Salter gels. Their farvver's a con man," they'll say.'

Barbara, the next eldest, was sitting darning one of her father's socks and she raised her dark eyes to join in the condemnation. 'Dad, you really are the limit,' she scolded him. 'That Josiah Dawson was a real nasty bit o' work at one time, accordin' ter what I've 'eard. 'E could get really nasty wiv you if yer not careful.'

Lily, the youngest, added her piece as she wound her fair hair in a towel. 'Why don't yer give 'em their money back?' she said, looking a little sorry for her beleaguered father. 'That way they can't say anyfing. Tell 'em yer sorry.'

'It's already bin taken care of,' Maurice told them. 'I've given 'em all a double amount o' material an' I've told 'em that if they're not satisfied I'll give 'em a refund. I can't be no fairer than that, now can I?'

'But what about Josiah?' Brenda asked. ' 'E's gonna be upset when yer ask 'im fer yer commission back.'

Maurice knew that there was no way the Page Street warden was going to part with his hard-earned commission, whatever else happened, and he started to look even more dejected as he slouched at the table.

Lily was always the one who showed her affection most and she came over and put her arm round his neck. 'Poor Dad,' she purred. 'Yer was only tryin' to earn a few coppers extra.'

'Don't encourage 'im, Lil, 'e'll be sellin' orf the 'ome next,' Brenda said scathingly.

Maurice drew breath. He had been negotiating the sale of his piano for the past few weeks but without much success, apart from one possible buyer. It seemed that no one wanted uprights these days. It was a good piano too, he thought. Not a mark on it, a useless bit of good-condition furniture that took up most of the parlour. It wouldn't have been so bad if the girls bothered to play it now and again. That would have been a reason to hang on to it. Brenda played fairly well, and Barbara could knock out a tune or two. Young Robert played it really well, but he was in the RAF now and had other things on his mind. Just as well to get rid of it, Maurice thought.

As if to mock him, Brenda sat down at the piano for the first time in ages and started tinkling.

' 'Ere, Bren, play " 'Ome sweet 'Ome",' Lily requested.

' 'Ow's it go?' Brenda asked.

'No knocker on the door, no carpet on the floor, ours is an 'appy 'ouse, ours is,' Lily sang.

Maurice was beginning to feel like the world was against him. He had arranged for the prospective buyer to come and look at the piano later that evening, and he felt that maybe it was time for him to slip up to the Kings Arms for a pint or two.

' 'Ere, can yer play "Broker's Man"?' Lily asked.

Brenda gave her younger sister a blinding look. 'Where did yer learn all these stupid songs?'

Lily leaned her elbow on the table and studied her fingernails. 'They're not stupid, they're funny,' she said, looking aggrieved.

'Go on then, sing it an' I'll play it,' Brenda told her.

Lily stood up straight and gave a short bow to Maurice as he left the room:

> Down came the poker on 'is nut,
> An' the leg of an old armchair,
> They shouted murder an' police,
> But there wasn't no policemen there.
> Up came one wiv the fryin'-pan,
> An' anuvver wiv the leg of a chair,
> An' they played chimmy-chase all round the place,
> Wiv the poor ole broker's man.

Maurice could hear the loud giggling as he hurried from the house, hoping that the prospective buyer might suddenly have changed his mind.

'Yer know, we do go on at Dad, an' 'e's a real love,' Lily remarked later that evening.

'Look, Lil, we all love 'im, but 'e's gotta be told,' Brenda replied. ' 'E's got about as much chance o' makin' money wiv 'is buyin' an' sellin' as Barbara 'ere 'as o' datin' Ronald Colman.'

Barbara stood up and flaunted herself in front of her two sisters, her hand on her hip and her lips pouting. 'Ronald Colman wouldn't be able ter resist my charms,' she purred, as the other two fell about laughing. The first timid knock on the door went unheard by the giggling girls, but they heard the louder knock.

'Be careful, Brenda, it could be anybody,' Lily warned her.

Brenda opened the front door to a diminutive-looking man wearing a mackintosh and a bowler hat. 'Yes?'

The man coughed nervously. 'Er, I've come to see the item,' he replied in a cultured voice.

'Yer'll be wantin' ter see me dad, but 'e's gone out,' Brenda told him.

'Mr Salter did say this evening,' the man replied. 'He said he wanted to get rid of it as soon as possible. Never mind, perhaps I'd better come back another time.' He touched his hat.

Brenda felt a little sorry for him. 'Look, Mr, er . . .'

'Mr Forbes,' the man said quickly.

'Well, Mr Forbes, I don't know what me dad's told yer, but it ain't exactly first quality,' she informed him.

'He did say I wouldn't be disappointed,' Mr Forbes said, stroking his chin.

'Did 'e tell yer it came from China?' Brenda asked him.

'No, as a matter of fact he didn't,' the man replied, looking surprised.

'Well, that's a relief,' she sighed.

'Mr Salter did say that he'd be well rid of it,' the visitor told her. 'He said it's taking up a lot of room and he wouldn't be asking too much. I can't afford to pay a lot, but I would like to surprise my wife. She doesn't ask for much and it would be the ideal gift. It's her birthday soon, you see. Yes, she's very talented, is Vera, and she'd enjoy just looking at it, I'm sure.'

Brenda could not understand how anyone could get any joy from looking at blackout material, but each to their own, she decided. 'Yer can 'ave a look at it if yer like,' she said, feeling sorry for the timid-looking individual. 'It's in the scullery. There's not much of it left I'm afraid. Me dad's bin cuttin' bits off of it.'

'Oh dear,' Mr Forbes sighed. 'I do hope he's not ruined it. Mr Salter told me it was immaculate. He said that if we could agree a price he would get it delivered by a friend of his who's got a horse and cart.'

'Where d'yer live?' Brenda asked. 'If it's not too far 'e could pop it round 'imself, it'd be no trouble,' she said smiling. 'Or 'e could get on a bus wiv it.'

Mr Forbes was very puzzled and not a little frightened as Brenda let him in the house. He was even more apprehensive when he saw Lily and Barbara eyeing him as he walked through into the scullery. 'Where is it?' he asked.

Brenda pulled out the remainder of the blackout material and laid it down on the table. 'It's very skimpy,' she said.

'But there's no piano here,' he remarked, removing his bowler and scratching his bald head.

'Well, it's not surprising, is it?' Brenda said, feeling as though she'd made the bad mistake of letting a lunatic into the house.

'Could I see the piano?' Mr Forbes asked meekly.

' 'Ow did yer know we 'ad a piano?' Brenda asked him.

'Mr Salter invited me to come and look at it,' he replied, flushing slightly.

Brenda suddenly turned to her two sisters who had sauntered into the scullery. 'We've bin at two purposes, me an' Mr Forbes,' she told them, 'but that's nuffink ter what us an' dear Farvver's gonna be when 'e gets 'ome. Jus' wait till 'e does show 'is face in 'ere. Our mum would turn in 'er grave if she knew. Fancy tryin' ter get rid of our pianer.' She turned to Mr Forbes. 'I'm sorry, but it's not fer sale. 'Ere, there's a consolation prize though.'

A very disappointed Mr Forbes walked away along Page Street with the roll of blackout material tucked under his arm, only to be accosted by the dapper Bert Jolly.

'That's not Chunking silk,' he said. 'It's jus' second-quality blackout material.'

Mr Forbes hurried on, thinking that he had stumbled into a street of idiots and the quicker he got out of the turning the better.

Back at the Salter household the three young women were having a serious talk. Brenda and Barbara were fuming while Lily felt a little sad for her father. 'Don't go on to 'im when 'e comes in,' she pleaded. 'Yer know 'ow 'e gets melancholy when 'e's 'ad a drink.'

Barbara scowled at her sister. ' 'E'll be the ruin of us one day,' she said bitterly.

Brenda was equally irate. 'I jus' can't understand what possessed 'im,' she moaned. 'Fancy tryin' ter sell our pianer. 'E'll be sellin' the mats from under our feet next.'

Lily usually managed to cool the atmosphere at such times but tonight she realised she was going to be hard put to it to save her father from the others' wrath. 'Look, we all know that Dad's a bloody idiot an' 'e don't fink before 'e does these fings, but be fair, 'e's not all bad,' she said quietly.

'Well, 'e's overstepped the mark ternight,' Barbara retorted, her dark eyes flashing.

Lily got on with rolling her hair into pipe cleaners. 'I don't fink 'e's well,' she remarked.

' 'Course 'e's well,' Brenda said quickly. ' 'E's well enough ter go around sellin' the 'ome up, an' knockin' out that bloody blackout stuff. The trouble is, 'e finks 'e's gotta be the provider all the time. We all know 'e works 'ard at the gasworks. We don't want 'im ter drive 'imself inter the ground wiv all this duckin' an' divin'.'

'That's my point,' Lily rejoined. 'Let's jus' give 'im the time to explain before we jump on 'im.'

'I reckon the best fing that could 'appen ter Farvver is fer 'im ter get 'imself a lady friend,' Barbara cut in. ' 'E must be lonely.'

' 'E's got us lot,' Brenda said quickly.

'Yeah, an' 'alf the time we're takin' the piss out of 'im or bawlin' at 'im fer the fings 'e does,' Lily reminded her.

'We could sort of let 'im know that 'e's got our blessin' ter go out wiv some nice lady, providin' she is nice,' Barbara said.

'So we 'ave ter vet 'er first,' Lily said sarcastically.

'I don't mean that,' Barbara replied. 'We all want fer 'im ter be 'appy. That's all we want.'

The sound of Maurice coming in the house halted the conversation and when he appeared in the doorway he looked a little shamefaced as well as being slightly the worse for drink. 'Any visitors?' he asked casually.

'Only one, dad,' Brenda replied archly. 'Some feller who wanted ter look at the pianer.'

'Oh, that silly sod,' Maurice slurred, making a meal of taking his coat off. ' 'E got the wrong end o' the stick. I was only jokin' wiv 'im about the fact that I've got three talented kids an' none of 'em 'ave the time ter play their ole dad a tune or two. I told 'im I might as well sell the bloody fing, not that I would, of course.'

'No, of course not,' Barbara replied, glancing at her two sisters.

'Anyway, sit down, Dad, an' we'll make yer a nice cheese an' onion sandwich,' Lily said with a sweet smile.

Maurice was feeling much happier now. It looked to him as though he had weathered the latest storm, and now it was time for the good news. 'By the way, I've sold the rest o' that blackout stuff,' he announced.

'Who to?' the girls chorused.

'Josiah Dawson's bought the lot fer chickens,' he said triumpantly.

'Chickens?' his daughters repeated.

' 'S'right,' Maurice told them. 'It seems that a bit o' curtainin' over the cages makes the chickens fink it's time ter sleep. This double British summertime is knockin' 'ell out o' their layin'. A bit o' blackout over the cage also stops 'em cluckin' inter the early hours, accordin' ter Josiah.'

The three young women went suddenly quiet, and after supper they slipped off to bed earlier than usual, with the exception of Lily, who had been given the task of explaining about the blackout material.

' 'Ere, Dad, yer won't be angry, will yer? But . . .'

Chapter Seventeen

After his visit to see Annie and the children, Billy Sullivan took the first opportunity to call in at the Kings Arms. Monday evening was his night off but he sometimes went down to the pub for a pint. When he walked into the public bar Terry greeted him. ' 'Ow was Annie an' the kids, Billy?' he asked.

'They're all fine,' Billy replied, leaning on the counter while the landlord filled his glass.

'I bet that country air is doin' 'em good,' Terry remarked, and he noticed that his barman looked preoccupied. 'Is everyfing all right?' he added as he put the frothing glass of ale down on the polished counter.

Billy took a swig of his drink and then put the glass back down. 'I gotta talk ter yer, Terry,' he said.

Terry gave him a questioning look then put his head round the corner and motioned to Patricia who was chatting to a customer in the saloon bar. 'Keep yer eye on the public bar fer a few minutes, will yer, luv,' he told her. 'I'm goin' in the back room to 'ave a chat wiv Billy.'

Once they were seated in the small back room, Billy came straight to the point. 'Terry, I'm gonna 'ave ter give me notice in,' he said.

Terry looked surprised. 'Is there any particular reason why?' he asked.

Billy shrugged his shoulders and stared down at his clasped hands. 'There's a lot o' work goin' on at the buildin' site an' I'm feelin' a bit tired in the evenin's, Terry,' he replied.

The landlord looked hard at him. 'No ovver reason?'

'No, like I say. I'm feelin' like I need the rest in the evenin's,' Billy answered.

Terry leaned back in his chair and folded his arms. 'Yer not worried about us gettin' a visit, are yer?' he asked.

'If yer mean from that Elephant an' Castle mob, the answer's no,' Billy replied, returning the stare. 'I would 'ave bin away before now if that 'ad worried me, Terry.'

The landlord leaned forward in his chair and glanced quickly at the door to make sure Patricia was not within earshot. 'Listen, Billy,' he said in a low voice. 'I appreciate yer lookin' after fings while I'm away from the pub in the evenin's an' it's a comfortin' feelin' ter know you're be'ind the counter. Trouble is, I've got meself in deep wiv certain people. It was over somefing that 'appened a long time ago, which I won't concern you wiv. Suffice it ter say, I'm bein' 'eld over a barrel, but I'm sortin' it out. I need more time though, an' ter be honest I need yer ter back me fer a little while longer.'

' 'Ow much longer, Terry?' Billy asked sharply.

'A few more weeks, just a few more weeks.'

Billy shook his head. 'I dunno,' he replied. 'A few weeks might stretch inter months.'

Terry had an appealing look in his eyes as he went on, 'Look, Billy. This fing is big, very big. I'm up ter me ears in it an' I'm gonna spell it out ter yer. I'm bein' used as a go-between for a black market set-up an' two bent coppers. I gotta tread very carefully or I'm done for. A few more weeks is all I ask.'

Billy recalled what Patricia had told him in confidence not so long ago, and he realised that Terry was not overstating his position. He was obviously in real danger. 'All right, Terry,' he replied. 'I'll stay on fer a few more weeks, but only a few weeks, understood?'

The landlord sagged down in his chair. 'That's wonderful, Billy,' he said, sighing deeply with relief. 'That's all I ask, an' I'll feel better if I know yer be'ind the bar while I'm out durin' the evenin's. Yer won't need ter wait fer me ter come in, jus' do the usual clearin' up an' then 'ave it away. I'll tell Patricia ter put the bolts on as soon yer gone an' I can knock on the door. Yer won't lose by it, I promise yer.'

The Page Street women got on with their daily lives complaining about the rationing, the cold weather and the shortage of money, and whenever they gathered together they complained about each other. Maudie Mycroft moaned about the foul-mouthed Mrs Gorman whom she occasionally met at the market and who had been expelled from the mothers' meetings because of her verbal abuse of other women, and Sadie Sullivan complained about Maudie's constant griping. Maisie complained about her husband Fred getting under her feet since he retired, and Dolly Dawson complained about the people who complained about her Wallace.

'The boy don't mean any 'arm,' she grumbled to Sadie. ' 'E jus' don't seem to realise what's what.'

Sadie was going through a rough patch caring for her husband Daniel who was laid up in bed with a bad bout of shingles and her temper was short. 'Wallace 'as ter learn, same as anybody else,' she replied. 'Look at the ovver day. Maisie told 'im orf fer chuckin' milk bottles at the trams as they went past the street, an' then 'e chucked one at 'er as she walked away.'

'I know,' Dolly sighed. 'I really told 'im orf about that, but 'e told me 'e didn't actually chuck the milk bottle at 'er, only near 'er jus' ter scare 'er.'

'Well, it scared the bleedin' life out of 'er,' Sadie retorted. 'An' what about that day Wallace walked be'ind ole Mrs Passmore pullin' faces? Frightened 'er too, 'e did. I tell yer straight, Dolly, your Wallace wouldn't 'ave got away wiv it if it'd bin me.'

'I know, Sadie, but the boy don't mean no 'arm,' Dolly pleaded.

'Anyway, p'raps 'e'll be'ave 'imself now 'e's got that job wiv young Carrie Tanner,' Sadie remarked, suddenly beginning to feel a little sorry for Dolly.

The harried woman pulled the collar of her coat up round her ears against the wind. 'I don't know so much. Nellie Tanner called in yesterday to ask if I'd pop round ter see 'er Carrie. I don't know what Wallace 'as bin up to but I 'ope it's nuffink bad.'

Maisie Dougal was doing her share of complaining too. 'I went up ter Lockwood's this mornin' fer Fred's Woodbines an' 'e told me 'e was right out of 'em,' she told Violet Passmore. 'Strike me if I don't see ole Bert Jolly comin' out o' there ten minutes later wiv a packet in 'is 'and. 'E took one out o' the packet an' lit it up right in front o' me eyes.'

Violet stared at Maisie through her thick-lensed spectacles and touched her newly permed hair as though to reassure herself it was still in place. 'Yeah, but that don't mean 'e bought 'em in there,' she remarked.

'I bet 'e did,' Maisie insisted. 'There's too much o' this under-the-counter business goin' on, an' the prices they're askin' is bleedin' scandalous. Talkin' about under-the-counter stuff, did yer 'ear about ole Bradshaw's?'

Violet had heard the story but she knew she was going to hear it again, despite nodding vigorously.

'This ole lady walked in Bradshaw's the ovver day an' asked 'im fer a tin o' corned beef,' Maisie began. ' 'E told 'er 'e was out of it but 'e 'ad some special offers under the counter. Twice the price it was. Anyway, this ole gel told 'im what 'e could do wiv it an' Bradshaw give 'er a load of abuse.'

'Yeah, I 'eard about it,' Violet sighed impatiently.

Maisie was too keen on finishing her tale to get the hint. 'Anyway,' she went on, 'this ole gel walked out really upset an' when she got 'ome she told 'er ole man. Up 'e goes an' calls ole Bradshaw everyfing from a pig to a dog. Bradshaw picks up a carvin' knife an' wiv that the bloke crowns 'im wiv a great big brass weight 'e picked up orf the counter. There was blood everywhere, accordin' ter Mrs Groombridge.'

Violet had heard three different versions of the story but not the outcome. 'What 'appened ter the bloke who done it?' she asked.

' 'E comes up at Tower Bridge Court next week, by all accounts. 'E'll get six months at least, what wiv the beaks they've got there,' Maisie informed her.

Violet got home a little later than planned and complained about Maisie's inane chattering to Mr Passmore, who being a very perceptive person told her that for most people chattering and complaining were outlets for their anxiety. 'The war is gonna get very nasty soon an' everybody knows it,' he said. 'Everybody's scared an' comin' tergevver fer support. Once yer realise that, yer get more tolerant o' people.'

Violet felt comforted after her husband's explanation. He was so calm and self-assured, she thought. His few words made her feel a little more well disposed towards Maisie Dougal. Meanwhile, Fergus went off to the pub and complained to his cronies about Mrs Passmore.

Carrie showed Dolly Dawson into her tidy parlour and offered her a cup of tea, hoping that what she had to say would not upset the woman too much.

'I've tried, Dolly, we both 'ave, but it don't seem ter be workin' out,' she said kindly. 'Wallace was fine the first mornin'. Joe told 'im what ter do an' there was no complaints. 'E swept the yard up really well. Then Joe got 'im to 'elp wiv puttin' up the new shed fer the lorries. It was only fetchin' an' carryin' an' Wallace seemed ter be gettin' on fine. We let 'im go early, too, the first day, an' the next day 'e came in on time an' wivout bein' told 'e swept the yard a treat. Trouble was, when Joe went ter get 'im ter give 'im an 'and, the lad 'ad disappeared. 'E's not bin in since.'

Dolly looked puzzled. 'But I bin makin' sure 'e goes out on time. 'E's always back fer 'is tea in the evenin'. Mind you, I can never get much out of 'im at the best o' times.'

'Well, I thought yer should know,' Carrie said with concern.

Dolly finished her tea and stood up. 'I'm grateful that yer gave 'im a chance, Carrie, many wouldn't 'ave,' she said with a brief smile. 'I wouldn't worry about 'im, I fink I know where 'e'll be.'

Dolly left the transport yard in Salmon Lane with a heavy heart and walked towards the river wall. The day was bright and cold, with little cloud to bar the winter sun. She could see the tall cranes swinging to and fro and dipping down into the barges and grimy freighters' holds, tugs puffing up and down the river and the sound of traffic trundling over the white-stone Tower Bridge. The tide was high and beginning to ebb, with patches of oil caught in the middle of spinning eddies. The heart of London was beating strongly, but it held no attraction for Dolly. She was frightened of the river, terrified that one day it would take Wallace to its bosom, close over him and bear him away.

She could see him now, his feet dangling over the river wall and his back arched. He was staring ahead, as though mesmerised by the swishing sound of the muddy water against the old stanchions. He wore a cap which was pulled down on his ears, the peak unbuttoned and covering the whole of his forehead. Dolly drew breath and moved back. It was not the time to go to him, to remonstrate or scold him. He was there, alone with his thoughts, happy and unaffected by the hustle and bustle beneath him and all around him. Wallace was at home.

Dolly turned and walked away, back to Page Street, to Josiah and the children. Wallace would come home later, tired and hungry, and he would eat his fill and then sleep when sleep took him, borne away by the sound of the swishing, swirling waters of the River Thames flowing through his child's mind.

Dougal McKenzie stepped down from the tram in Jamaica Road and pulled his trilby further down on his head. The night was dark with the moon obscured by cloud and the still air felt cold. Dougal was in no hurry. His informants had done their work well and he knew all he needed to about the layout of the Kings Arms and the habits of its tenants and customers. Last to leave usually were a couple of pensioners who always stood talking for a few minutes before making their way home. Tuesday was always a quiet night, one of the two nights when Terry Gordon was absent. Usually Terry came home around eleven thirty, mostly by tram, but if he was late he invariably arrived in a taxi.

Dougal hummed quietly to himself as he strolled through the dark night and thought about the job in hand. It wouldn't have been possible to arrange it this way a few weeks ago, he knew. The stumbling block would have been Billy Sullivan the barman. Dougal knew from his informant that the publican had picked a tough, hard man to keep an eye on the pub, a local man who had once been a very good fighter and was well respected by all who knew him. Dougal also knew that it was Billy Sullivan who had stopped the fight and very nearly killed one of the men he had sent to cause trouble at the pub. Things were different now, however. Billy Sullivan did not wait until Terry Gordon returned home, instead he was out of the pub by eleven fifteen, twenty minutes past at the outside, then Patricia put the bolt on the side door and awaited her husband's double knock.

Dougal prided himself on his efficiency. The man he had used to keep the outside of the pub under surveillance had been told to make a note of when the local policeman walked past on his beat, as well as any other regular occurrences between closing time and midnight. Things had not worked out too well the last time he plotted against the publican, and there was no margin for error on this occasion. Everything had to be planned down to the last detail.

Dougal glanced at his wristwatch as he strolled past the Kings Arms. It showed ten minutes to closing time. So far so good, he told himself. No one would be likely to walk out of a pub at that time of the evening and the night was dark. No one would recognise him in this area anyway. He would be able to accomplish what he had set out to do and be off, like a thief in the night.

He reached the first junction in Jamaica Road; it had taken him just five minutes. Another five minutes in the same direction, then he would turn round and walk back at the same pace towards the Kings Arms. By that reckoning he would reach the opposite side of the road to the pub at ten minutes past the hour, little time to wait, and little time to be noticed, before Sullivan left the place. It was a stroke of good fortune that the barman now left earlier, he thought. His man had told him of the rumours he had heard. It appeared that Sullivan and Patricia had been getting over-friendly towards each other and Terry had become suspicious and warned his barman off. There was a further benefit to be had from such rumours, Dougal thought. If all went well, then Billy Sullivan would be the prime suspect.

The Scot turned back and walked steadily towards the Kings Arms. When he arrived at nine minutes past eleven he could see the two pensioners still chatting away. 'They're late, why don't they shove off?' he cursed aloud. As if hearing him, the two old men turned and began to walk away from the pub, and then five minutes later Billy Sullivan emerged from the side door which led out into Page Street and walked briskly away down the turning.

Now, thought Dougal. There must be no slip-ups. This time it was for real.

His two knocks were answered by Patricia, and when she saw him and tried to scream he stifled her with his large hand over her mouth. He leaned back against the door to close it then took the heavy service revolver from his overcoat pocket and pressed the barrel against her temple. 'I'm ganna take my hand away from ye mouth, woman, an' if ye utter a sound I'll kill ye where ye stand. Understood?'

Icy fingers of fear grasped her insides and Patricia nodded in panic. Dougal put his face closer to hers as he held the gun against her head. 'I'm serious, lassie, so be warned,' he snarled.

She nodded again with terror in her eyes, staring at the revolver held in his large fist.

'Right then, put the bolts on,' he commanded.

Patricia knew Dougal only too well. He had a sadistic streak to his nature, and she had been on the receiving end of it more than once in the past. Her mind was racing. He was out to kill Terry, and her too, she had no doubt. What could she do? She must warn her husband somehow.

Dougal's cold eyes dared her to resist him as she slid the bottom bolt first then reached up to slide the top bolt, her body between him and the door. Her free hand made a short movement before Dougal spun her round roughly and backed her along the short passageway into the small room which divided the two bars.

'Sit down and be quiet,' he ordered.

'What d'yer want wiv us, Dougal? We've not 'armed yer,' she said, her voice shaking with fear.

'That scum of a husband took ye from me,' Dougal hissed. 'Not content with that, he's after fixing young Bruce. I'm on to him though, lassie, be sure o' that. I've got a present for that no-good scum-bag o' yours. He'll get it right between the eyes,' he snarled, waving the revolver inches away from her terrified face.

'Terry's workin' wiv Bruce, not against 'im,' she cried. 'Go an' talk ter yer bruvver, 'e'll tell yer.'

'Bruce always had a soft spot for that Sassenach,' Dougal growled. 'He's been took in, but I'm not. I can see through it all. Bruce'll come to thank me one day.'

Patricia sat rigid in the armchair. Maybe there was a chance to catch Dougal off guard and run for it, she thought, but there would be no time to slide the bolts before he reached her. Her eye caught the large glass ashtray on the table. Maybe she could stun him, just long enough for her to reach the street. It was a slim chance but better than waiting for Terry to walk into a bullet.

Dougal had noticed her glance. 'Sit back in that chair,' he grated, pulling the other armchair round until it was between her and the open door of the small room. 'We won't have long to wait, so let's spend a few minutes talking about us,' he said quietly.

Josiah Dawson was beginning to feel at home being the street's warden. Most of the folk in the turning knew him and nearly everyone passed the time of day, or in his case the time of evening, as he went about his business. He had been careful not to antagonise the more volatile tenants with his requests for them to keep within the blackout regulations, and he had come to terms with his problem of talking to people. He had tried hard, and now his range extended a little further than the basic grunts he once made to get away quickly. He had even engaged Sadie and Maisie in polite conversation on more than one occasion recently, and as he prepared to do his rounds he felt in control.

'Try not ter be too late, there's a dear,' Dolly told him. 'I've got a nice pot o' soup simmerin' over the gas.'

Josiah whistled to himself as he walked along Page Street, but as he passed the Salter residence he scowled. How could a clown like Maurice Salter sire such beautiful daughters? he pondered. But then he and Dolly had sired Wallace, and there was nothing wrong with him and Dolly. 'It must be the luck of the draw,' he concluded aloud.

As Josiah neared the Kings Arms he spotted a glimmer of light showing through the thick glass portlight in the top of the side door. It was unlike the Gordons to be so careless, he thought. Well, they'd have to be told just like everyone else. The warden hoisted his gas mask and helmet higher onto his shoulder as he stopped at the door of the pub, preparing his few civil words of warning.

Inside, Patricia was fighting back her tears. 'I've bin on ter Terry ter get away from it all,' she faltered. 'Why can't yer leave us alone? We'll move away an' be no trouble to you or yer family.'

'It's too late for that,' Dougal growled, his cold eyes glaring at her.

The gentle double tap on the door galvanised the Scot into action and he motioned to Patricia with his revolver. 'Remember, lassie, I'm right behind ye. One wrong move and ye'll get it first, understood?'

Patricia's heart was pounding. The tap on the door was not Terry's. He always knocked firmly. She could feel the gun in her back as she walked fearfully to the front door and reached for the bolts, hoping against hope that the purposely displaced blackout curtain had caused Josiah or the local bobbie to investigate. She opened the door and saw the street warden standing there, and the look of disbelief on his wide face as he caught sight of Dougal standing behind her.

'Good Gawd! I don't believe it! I jus' don't believe it,' Josiah cried. 'Dougal McKenzie. What the bloody 'ell are you doin' round these parts?'

Dougal had been caught off balance by the sight of Josiah standing in the doorway. 'Just a friendly call, we're old acquaintances,' he said awkwardly.

Patricia suddenly moved sideways, her back slamming against the passage wall. 'Mind! 'E's got a gun!' she cried out.

Dougal stood facing the heavier man, not knowing what to do next, and the street warden shuffled his feet, his face suddenly wreathed in a stupid grin.

'What the bloody 'ell's goin' on 'ere?' Josiah asked.

Dougal made to push his way past him and into the street but the warden's large hand pressed against his chest. 'Is 'e troublin' yer, gel? Dougal was always troublin' somebody,' he growled. ' 'E was the same on the Moor. Tried it on me once, 'e did, till I put 'im in 'is place.'

Dougal's hand came up and the revolver was pointing in Josiah's face. 'Move out of me way, Dawson, or I'll use this,' he snarled.

Patricia slipped forward on a dead faint and as Dougal flinched, Josiah grabbed the gun with one hand, forcing it upwards and away from him and at the same time threw a punch from his shoulder with the other hand. The blow caught Dougal under the chin, snapping his head backwards. The gun went off, sending ceiling plaster crashing down as the Scot sagged. Josiah had a firm grip on the gun now and his strength was too much for the ageing villain. Soon Josiah had wrenched the gun free and another carefully placed blow with his clenched fist sent Dougal onto his back, his head slamming against the lino-covered floorboards.

Suddenly people were at their front doors having heard the blast of the gun. Albert Lockwood came hurrying over with an overcoat thrown over his pyjamas. 'What's goin' on?' he shouted.

'Phone the police,' Josiah ordered, feeling very important at that minute as he stood over the supine Dougal, one foot resting on the mobster's chest.

As Albert hurried back to his shop, a taxi pulled up in the turning and Terry Gordon stepped down, his face going white as he saw the commotion and then spotted his wife lying in the doorway. 'Oh my Gawd!' he cried out.

'She's jus' fainted, she'll be all right,' Josiah said reassuringly. 'We've 'ad a spot o' trouble 'ere wiv the blackout ternight, but it's all under control.'

Chapter Eighteen

The cold winter slowly gave way to a warm spring, and with it came the early flowers blossoming in window boxes and in back-yard tubs. By May the sky was usually blue, with high drifting clouds and light refreshing breezes which carried away the smells of the factories, the river mud and the spice wharves. Council water carts soaked the dry backstreets and children played hopscotch and knock-down-ginger missing their young friends who had been taken away to less dangerous surroundings. Women stood on doorsteps discussing the mild weather, Germany's invasion of Denmark and Norway, and Maurice Salter.

'I say good luck ter the bloke,' Maisie remarked. 'After all, the man's bin on 'is own fer a lot o' years an' 'e's brought them gels up a treat. Credit to 'im, they are.'

'That's all very well,' Sadie replied, 'but the woman's already got an ole man.'

'Be honest, Sadie, when was the last time yer saw 'im?' Maisie snorted. 'All right, I know the feller's in the merchant navy, but I fink they've split up anyway.'

Sadie tucked her hands into the armholes of her flowered apron. 'P'raps yer right,' she replied. 'I can 'ardly remember what the bloke looks like. I know 'e 'ad a mop o' ginger 'air.'

'Well, I say good luck ter the both of 'em,' Maisie persisted. 'After all, yer gotta take yer pleasures while you can. None of us knows what's in front of us.'

Sadie sighed deeply. 'It's a long time since I've 'ad any pleasures, Mais. It takes my Daniel all 'is time ter get up in the mornin' these days. Mind you, 'e's bin a good 'un. Never shied away from work, when it was goin'. Trouble was, there never was enough of it. Still, we managed ter bring our tribe up. All nicely settled they are, but I still worry about my Billy. 'E's missin' Annie an' the kids.'

'Is Billy still workin' at that barman's job?' Maisie asked.

'Yeah, 'e's still there,' Sadie replied. 'I've lost count o' the times I 'eard 'im say 'e's gonna pack it in. I 'ope 'e ain't got 'is eye on that landlady. Yer know what men are like. Can't be on their own fer more than a few weeks.'

'They're not all the same,' Maisie countered. 'Maurice Salter ain't bin walkin' out wiv anybody before this one, not ter my knowledge.'

' 'Ow would you know?' Sadie said sharply. 'The Salters ain't bin livin' in the street more than five minutes.'

'Dolly Dawson told me that Maurice wouldn't look at anuvver woman after 'is wife died,' Maisie replied. 'Dolly used ter live near the Salters.'

Sadie sniffed contemptuously. 'I should't take all she says fer gospel, Mais. The woman does go on a bit, an' since 'er ole man got 'is name in the paper fer that turn-out at the Kings Arms, she's bin struttin' around like a bloody peacock in season.'

Maisie merely nodded. She had always found Dolly to be a very friendly soul who would do anyone a good turn. Dolly had a lot to put up with, she thought. Wallace was constantly causing her problems and the poor woman had been very upset when he walked out of his job. Sadie Sullivan was getting bitter in her old age.

'Well, I'd better get meself indoors,' Sadie said. 'There's a pile o' washin' waitin' ter go in the copper an' 'e'll be wantin' 'is tea.'

Maisie smiled her goodbye and Sadie went into her parlour. She flopped down in the comfortable armchair to rest her feet on the fender. 'Maisie Dougall's gettin' more and more gullible in 'er old age,' she said to herself.

On Friday evening there was a family gathering at the transport yard in Salmon Lane. Carrie was in the scullery with Danny's wife, brewing tea, while the men sat together in the parlour with Nellie who was busy working on a piece of embroidery. Billy Sullivan was there too. He had been invited along by Danny who was well aware of his friend's painful loneliness.

'So what d'yer reckon's gonna 'appen now, Billy?' Joe asked.

Billy shrugged his shoulders. 'That turn-out wiv Dougal was a blessin' in disguise,' he replied. 'Apparently there's a lot o' reporters sniffin' around at the Elephant an' Castle an' everybody's stayin' quiet till it cools off a bit. Terry don't say much these days but I reckon 'im an' 'is wife are gonna get out o' the pub soon as they can. I've 'eard a few words dropped 'ere an' there.'

'I thought you was gonna get out yerself before now,' Danny cut in, winking quickly at Joe.

'Terry asked me ter stay on fer a while longer,' Billy replied, looking a little embarrassed. ' 'E was worried about anuvver visit.'

'From what yer've told me, I'd say that bloke's asked fer trouble,' Danny said plainly. ' 'E can't expect you ter keep the peace. If they come round mob-'anded, yer'd be in the shite.'

'Well, I don't expect it ter be fer much longer,' Billy replied.

The ladies came into the parlour, Carrie carrying the tea tray and Iris the sandwiches, and for a while the affairs of the Kings Arms were forgotten. The conversation turned to Rachel, and Carrie's face brightened. 'We got a letter yesterday from 'er,' she said. 'She's nearly finished 'er trainin' an' then she's bein' posted. We expect 'er 'ome in a week or two.'

' 'Ow does she seem?' Danny asked.

'Well, it's 'ard ter tell,' Carried replied, 'but she's bin to a few dances at the camp. I fink she's slowly comin' ter terms wiv losin' Derek.'

Danny smiled fondly as he looked up at the mantelshelf and saw Rachel's photo. 'I'll always remember that night we 'ad that do fer Ellie Roffey at the gymnasium,' he said. 'Rachel looked really beautiful in that green dress wiv 'er 'air piled up on top of 'er 'ead. I remember all the lads was fallin' over themselves ter get a dance wiv 'er. Christ, it seems years ago.'

Carried nodded. 'She's all grown up now, Danny. I'm dyin' ter see 'er again. I do 'ope she's gonna be all right.'

Joe slipped his arm round Carrie's shoulders. 'She's gonna be fine,' he said quietly. 'She'll meet someone else pretty soon, mark my words.'

Billy was staring at Nellie's nimble fingers as they worked at the embroidery, his thoughts far away. Annie's last letter had intimated that she was thinking of returning to London if things remained quiet. He had a momentary feeling of elation at the thought of her sharing his bed once more, but in his heart he knew that it would be a mistake for her to come back now. The war was going badly and he felt that it would only be a short time before London and the other big cities were bombed. He had talked about it to Danny and he had said that he was thinking of persuading Iris to get out of London with the children.

' 'Ow's the business goin'?' Danny asked Carrie.

She gave her younger brother a look that said he shouldn't have asked. 'I've got regular work fer two lorries an' day-ter-day contracts wiv the ovver two,' she told him. 'Paddy Byrne's gettin' fed up wiv 'angin' around the yard. 'E's spent two days last week cleanin' the lorry. I need regular contracts if I'm gonna make it pay. It was a bad day when I lost that rum contract, an' a worse one when I found out that Galloway 'ad filched it.'

'Did yer get ter the bottom of it?' Danny asked.

'I got word that I'd bin undercut,' Carrie replied, her face darkening. 'Galloway 'as never bin able ter match me before.'

'We know the reason,' Joe cut in. 'It's the long-distance work 'e's after. 'E'll suffer a loss until the trade moves ter Bristol. Then 'e'll put up the rates, knowin' that the rum merchants are tied to 'im because o' the petrol rationin'. They won't be able ter pick an' choose their carriers then.'

Nellie had been quietly working away as though oblivious of the conversation but she suddenly put down her embroidery and sighed.

'Let the man 'ave the work, Carrie,' she said. 'There's no need ter feel angry about it.'

Joe and Carrie exchanged glances and Danny looked surprised as he stared at his elderly mother. Billy remained distracted, his thoughts still on Annie and the children.

'I wish I didn't feel angry, Mum,' Carrie replied, 'but I can't 'elp it. It gives me sleepless nights.'

'That firm is doomed,' Nellie said in little more than a whisper. 'I can feel it sure as I've ever felt anyfing. Let 'em destroy themselves, don't you be party to their downfall.'

Carried looked closely at her mother and saw the half-hidden glint in her eye. It made her grow cold and she shivered involuntarily.

Danny turned to Billy, hoping to lighten things. 'What about me an' you goin' ter see the church people again, Billy?' he suggested. 'Maybe we could get 'em ter let us open the gym once or twice a week. There's still a few kids round 'ere an' there's more comin' back.'

Billy's face brightened somewhat. 'We could try, I s'pose,' he replied.

The loud ring of the yard bell made Nellie jump and she looked up anxiously. 'Who would that be at this time?' she asked.

Joe got up and went to answer it, and when he returned his face was serious. 'Billy, yer wanted,' he said.

Carrie gave Joe a quizzical look and his eyes bade her to remain silent.

'Who is it?' Billy asked, getting up quickly.

Joe did not answer but followed him out of the room. When he returned alone he sat down heavily in a chair and stroked his chin thoughtfully. 'It was Annie,' he said.

'Annie? Billy's Annie?' Carrie gasped. 'Why didn't yer bring 'er in?'

Joe frowned. 'She looked very upset an' she asked me ter send Billy out,' he told her. 'It might be one o' the kids an' she couldn't face us all.'

Carrie looked at Danny pleadingly and her brother stood up. 'I'll go back 'ome an' then I'll pop in later,' he said. 'Somefink must 'ave 'appened ter bring Annie back ter London.'

The Sullivans' parlour was clean and tidy and the hearth had been black-leaded. The fire was laid and in one corner a pile of fresh washing was folded ready for ironing. Billy sat facing Annie, his body arched forward in the easy chair as he stared down at the note she had handed him. Annie gazed down at her clasped hands as she waited for his reaction, fearing that he would be unable to deny what had been written on the lined sheet of notepaper. Her heart was heavy to breaking and the sickness in the pit of her stomach felt like it would be there for ever.

Billy looked up at her, his eyes cold and menacing. 'If I ever find out who wrote this letter I'll choke the life out of 'em,' he grated.

Annie held his gaze, tears filling her eyes. 'You've not denied it, Billy,' she replied, her voice faltering. 'Tell me it's not true.'

He stood up, fighting to control the anger that threatened to overwhelm him. 'Do I need to?' he said in a loud voice.

'Yes, you do,' Annie cried. 'I need you to tell me the truth, Billy. You've already lied to me once. You told me you'd packed up the job, and now you've admitted that you're still working at the pub. Then I get this letter. What am I to believe?'

Billy reached out for her but she backed away. 'Tell me! I need to know!' she shouted at him.

He sat back down in his chair and drew breath, upset by Annie's reaction. 'Look, luv, I know I told yer I'd packed the job up, but it was ter stop yer worryin',' he said quietly. 'I'm gonna pack it in soon anyway. Terry asked me ter stop on fer a few weeks more jus' fer Patricia's sake. They're plannin' ter leave the pub as soon as they can.'

'But what about that letter?' Annie asked, her eyes widening. 'It says you're having an affair with Patricia.'

'It's not true,' Billy said with feeling. 'It's just a poison-pen letter written by somebody who don't even 'ave the guts ter put their name to it. All right, I've waited be'ind in the pub until Terry came in, but it was never more than 'alf an hour or so. I don't even do that now, since I said I was gonna pack up. Surely yer don't believe that evil rubbish, do yer?' he asked, glaring at her.

Annie looked down at her hands and then her eyes came up to meet his again. 'When I got that letter yesterday I was sick, physically sick,' she began. 'I lay awake all night thinking about it, wondering about you, wondering about us and the life we've made together. I didn't believe it could be true about Patricia and you, but being so far away from you, not being able to talk to you, got to me. I could see all sorts of things happening in my mind. Why should I feel that way? Why didn't I just burn that evil letter and cast the whole thing from my mind?'

Billy sighed and leaned back in the chair, putting his hand up to his forehead. 'Look, I've never lied ter yer, Annie,' he said slowly. 'What I'm tellin' yer now is the trufe, or may I be struck down fer lyin'. When you an' the kids left fer Gloucester I felt more lonely than I've ever done in me 'ole life. I used ter pace the floor when I got 'ome in the evenin's. I missed the kids' laughter and chatter. I missed us all sittin' around the table at mealtimes, an' I missed the warmth of yer beside me in bed at nights. Danny an' Iris made me feel comfortable in their 'ome when I visited 'em, an' they've bin really good ter me, but it's not the same. I still 'ad ter come 'ome ter the silence, the loneliness o' this place wivout yer. That barman's job Terry offered me 'elped a bit. I could talk ter people, be amongst old friends. Patricia felt more safe wiv me bein' there while Terry was out and she chatted wiv me when it was quiet.

We got on well an' she went as far as sayin' that 'er an' Terry weren't all that 'appy tergevver. I could 'ave picked up on that an' asked 'er out, if I'd wanted to, but I told 'er I was 'appily married an' would never do anyfing be'ind yer back.'

'You mean she tried to get you into her bed?' Annie asked.

'Yes, she tried,' Billy replied, looking her squarely in the eye. 'But there was nuffink out of order, nuffink fer you ter worry about, an' that's the trufe, so 'elp me Gawd.'

For a few moments Annie stared at him and then she looked down at the letter still held in his clenched fist. 'Give me that,' she said firmly.

Billy held out his hand and Annie snatched the note from him and tore it up into little pieces. 'That's the last time we will ever talk about this,' she said, dropping the bits of paper into the hearth and touching them with a lighted match. 'I'm tired an' I've got to catch the early train back tomorrow. I want you to come to bed now. I want you to hold me in your arms and make me feel good. I want you to love me, Billy.'

He stood up and reached for her, his arms encircling her, his cheek against her soft dark hair. 'There could never be anyone but you, darlin',' he whispered. 'I love you and the kids more than life itself. Nuffink could ever come between us.'

Annie gave a long, deep sigh and nestled to him. She could feel his hands gently stroking her back and his lips nuzzling at her ear. 'I love you, Billy Sullivan,' she whispered.

The light tap on the front door made them both start and Billy chuckled as he released her. 'I'll bet that's Danny,' he said.

In the Salter household a delicate matter of the heart was uppermost in the three young women's minds as they sat together one evening in early May.

'Well, as far as I'm concerned, Brenda Massey ain't right fer Dad,' Barbara announced.

'I agree,' Brenda said. 'There's the difference in ages fer a start. Bloody 'ell, 'e's twenty years 'er senior.'

'I don't see as that matters too much,' Lily cut in. 'Dad don't look 'is age an' that Brenda looks all of 'ers. Besides they seem 'appy tergevver. At least Dad is.'

'She's also a married women, Lily,' Barbara added.

'Brenda Massey told me that she's separated from 'im, an' 'as bin fer years,' Lily replied, working away at her fingernail with the edge of a matchbox.

'Well, I don't feel too 'appy about it,' Barbara went on. 'People are bound ter talk.'

'Sod the lot of 'em,' Lily said sharply. 'It's no business o' theirs anyway.'

161

Brenda sighed. 'I know we all wanted Dad ter find somebody nice but I fink 'e's in fer a disappointment wiv that one,' she said, snatching the matchbox away from Lily.

'What d'yer do that for?' Lily grumbled.

' 'Cos yer could poison yerself doin' that. Besides, it's irritatin',' Brenda told her.

The sound of the street door opening and closing was followed by a cheerful humming and then Maurice walked breezily into the room. He was carrying a large bunch of flowers wrapped in soggy newspaper and he laid them down on the table. 'I got away early ternight,' he announced. 'What's fer tea?'

'There's some brawn in the cupboard, Dad, or there's a bit o' cheese left. Mind it ain't gone mouldy though,' Barbara told him.

'Fanks fer the flowers, Dad,' Lily called out as he went into the scullery to wash his hands.

Maurice darted back into the room. 'Those are Brenda's,' he said quickly.

'Fanks, Dad,' Brenda said, smiling sweetly at him.

'Not you, my Brenda,' Maurice said, rolling his sleeves up higher on his thick arms.

'I always thought I was your Brenda,' his daughter said, feigning disappointment.

'Look, I ain't got time ter muck about,' he chided her. 'I've got ter get ready. Me an' Brenda are goin' out ternight. It's 'er birfday an' we're 'avin' a meal out, an' then we're goin' ter the pictures.'

'Shall I put 'em in water?' Lily asked him.

'Nah, they're wet enough,' Maurice said as he walked out of the room.

'They're not all that's wet,' Barbara mumbled to her elder sister.

'Don't be 'orrible,' Lily growled at her. 'As long as 'e's 'appy.'

'I really don't know why dad bovvered ter buy 'er them flowers,' Brenda said. 'Granny Massey'll chuck 'em out soon as 'is back's turned. She's a bloody ole witch.'

' 'E bought Brenda those flowers because 'e's a romantic. I wish I 'ad a feller that would buy me flowers,' Lily replied with a deep sigh.

Barbara sniffed the air once or twice. ' 'Ere, what's that funny smell?' she asked.

Brenda pulled a face. 'It smells like drains.'

'No, it's more like sulphur,' Lily said.

Brenda leaned down and sniffed at the paper covering the flowers. 'It's that,' she announced.

' 'Ere, dad, where 'ave these flowers bin?' Lily called out to him.

'Why's that?' Maurice called back from the scullery.

' 'Cos they stink, that's why,' Lily told him.

Maurice came back into the room, his face covered with shaving foam. 'It's all right. I got 'em durin' me dinner break an' one o' the lads put 'em in water fer me,' he said smiling.

'Well, yer better 'urry up an' get 'em round ter Brenda,' Barbara told him. 'They're wiltin'.'

Maurice pulled the newspaper to one side and puffed angrily. 'I'll murder that Jackson. 'E's put 'em in the sulphur tank, the bloody idiot.'

The girls laughed aloud and Lily picked up the flowers. 'I'll rinse 'em off an' rewrap 'em,' she said helpfully.

Maurice finally left the house looking very spruce. He had on his best suit, a blue, double-breasted pinstripe, and he wore a white shirt with a navy-blue tie. His shoes were polished and his thick greying hair had been well groomed and layered with brilliantine. He carried the bunch of flowers wrapped in white paper which Lily had found in the scullery. She had folded the paper over the top of the flowers and sealed it with a small safety-pin.

Maurice had not dared to tell his daughters that the flowers were not for Brenda. He had decided to buy them for Granny Massey as a peace offering, but he doubted whether it would make any difference to how the old girl felt about him. She had become a bane to his courting of Brenda and had openly told him that he was not the right sort of person for her daughter. The old lady had taken to calling out from her bedroom whenever he and Brenda settled down in the lounge for a little kiss and cuddle and Maurice felt that he would have to win her over somehow if he was ever going to make real progress with Brenda.

The evening was warm and sultry as Maurice knocked on the Massey front door, observed by Maisie and Sadie who were talking together.

'Nice evening,' he called out, and was rewarded by a smile and a nod from Maisie, and a scowl from Sadie.

Brenda opened the front door and gave Maurice a sweet smile as she took the flowers from him, then she caught sight of the two onlookers and flashed them a forced grin.

'They're fer yer mum,' Maurice told her.

Rachel Bradley leaned back against the cushion and idly watched the passing countryside as the train puffed towards Euston Station. The other occupants of the carriage, two elderly gentlemen and a young soldier in the Royal Armoured Corps, were nodding off to sleep and she stretched out her legs. It was good to be finished with the training camp, she thought. If she was lucky she would be posted to a fighter or a bomber station. It would be much better than being sent to one of those supply camps she had heard about, where nothing ever happened to break the monotony. Maybe her training as a telephonist would be useful at a fighter station. She would just have to hope for the best.

The young soldier's head slipped sideways and he woke with a start. He smiled sheepishly at her and closed his eyes again. Rachel returned her gaze to the greenery beyond the window, trying to get a clear picture in her mind of Derek. It was strange, she reflected. Since his death in action, and until she enlisted, she had been able to see him clearly in her mind, but now the memory of his handsome features was beginning to fade and the image in her head was misty. Maybe it was a turning point, she thought. Perhaps her decision to enlist had been the right one, despite her fears to the contrary during the first few weeks of training. She had missed her mother and Joe, and Uncle Danny and Aunt Iris, and even the carmen, who always had a smile and a few words for her. She had often buried her head beneath the itchy blankets and cried silently into her pillow with loneliness and sadness over her loss. The mornings had forced her to forget herself though. From just after dawn when reveille sounded the recruits were kept on the go, from the dining hall to the parade ground, the lecture room to the gymnasium. All through the day loud voices barked, cajoled, screeched and bullied as the recruits were turned from diverse individuals into an efficient working unit.

The train was passing the outskirts of London now and houses with back gardens took the place of rolling fields and wooded hills. The soldier was stirring, along with the elderly gents, and Rachel glanced at him. He was about her age, she thought. He had dark hair cut very short, with a shadow of stubble running round his square chin. He looked tall sitting slumped in his seat, and his thick neck and wrists gave her an impression of strength.

It was not long before the train was puffing into the centre of London. Buildings rose up on either side, and the familiar grime and bustle of the metropolis made Rachel feel that she was really coming home.

She stepped down from the stationary train and walked briskly from the platform, carrying her service gas mask and steel helmet slung over her shoulder. The soldier who had shared her carriage was a little way in front and Rachel noticed the confident swagger of his broad shoulders. She had been wrong about his height though, she realised. He was just an inch or so taller than she was.

Outside the bustling railway station Rachel turned left and walked on towards King's Cross. The soldier was still in front, walking quickly and lengthening the distance between them. At King's Cross, Rachel hurried across the wide thoroughfare and turned into King's Cross Road. Ahead was the bus stop and standing there was the young soldier. He grinned at her as she reached the stop and spoke to her for the first time.

'Are yer goin' over the water?' he asked casually.

Rachel nodded. 'Bermondsey.'

'So am I,' he replied.

There was no more time for conversation as the 63 bus drew up.

'On top only,' the conductor called out.

Rachel hurried up the stairs and slipped into a seat towards the back of the upper deck, while the soldier was forced to go along to the front of the bus.

The journey home through familiar surroundings seemed to be over very quickly and at the stop before the Bricklayer's Arms the young soldier alighted, giving her a cheery grin as he hurried past her. 'Good luck,' he said simply.

At the Bricklayer's Arms, Rachel got off and decided against waiting for the tram which would take her to Dockhead. It was a warm Friday evening and there was little traffic about. She knew the backstreets well and she was soon nearing the lengthy St James's Road which led out to the wide Jamaica Road. She could see the Kings Arms now and the still cranes on the river beyond. The sky above was slowly turning a glorious golden hue, and she was suddenly aware of the tang of spice and the sour smell of the river mud. She was home now, back among the folk she had grown up with. She could see the tall spire of St James's Church, set back from the road, and she remembered the time she had walked through the church gardens with Derek's arm round her waist. She could see him now in her mind, but mistily.

Chapter Nineteen

Frank Galloway poured himself another drink and glanced irritably at the wall clock. It had been a hard, trying day and now it looked like Gloria was going to let him down. He needed to talk to her urgently and as he sat down again in his comfortable leather armchair and sipped his Scotch, he felt worried.

Gloria would have been able to get him the information he needed. After all she was a street-walker and she had the right contacts. He had met her by chance one evening in a public house near the river and had gone with her to the Rotherhithe flat she rented. That evening he had persuaded her to do a job of work for him and had been pleased at the way in which things had worked out. Gloria had been well paid and Frank had expected her to jump at the chance of another tidy sum. He knew that she could be relied upon to be discreet, and with the new job of work he had in mind for her, discretion was paramount.

Frank sipped his drink with a moody expression on his broad face. His day had started with two of the drivers off sick, and then he had received a message from Mrs Duffin which said that his father was very poorly and he should call round as soon as possible. He had gone along to Tyburn Square expecting to find his father breathing his last but the old man was sitting up in bed with a glass of whisky in his hand smoking a large cigar.

'It's me leg,' George had said gruffly. 'Can't put any bloody weight on it an' Mrs Duffin called the doctor in. It seems I've got trouble wiv me sciatic nerve, whatever that may be.'

'Should you be drinking at this time in the morning?' Frank asked.

'It's me leg not me bloody stomach,' George replied sharply. 'Anyway, at my age what's the use o' takin' notice o' those quacks? They're all the bloody same wiv their advice. If they 'ad their way we wouldn't be able ter do anyfing 'cept give up the ghost.'

Frank could see that his father was as hale and hearty as ever and he attempted to make his excuses and get away. George had other ideas, however. 'Pull up a chair, Frank,' he said benignly. 'I want ter talk ter yer.'

Frank did as he was bid. 'I've got problems at the yard, Father,' he said before George could start. 'There's two of the drivers out sick and the rum merchants got a bit shirty because we were late getting a vehicle there. I'm running near to the bone with that contract and if we lose it due to the penalty clause we've lost our investment.'

George seemed uninterested in his son's predicament and he reached over to the bedside table and picked up his watch and chain. ' 'Ow's Bella and young Caroline?' he asked.

Frank was surprised at the question. It was not often that the old man showed any interest in either of them. 'They're doing well,' he replied. 'Bella's on a countrywide tour of the service camps and Caroline's settled in the West Country.'

'It was a shame she couldn't sire a boy,' George said, winding the watch slowly. ' 'E would 'ave bin finkin' about comin' in the business by now.'

Frank nodded, feeling that the business was the last thing he would inflict on a male offspring. 'That's how it goes,' he muttered.

George put the watch to his ear and then fiddled with the gold medallion hanging from the chain. ' 'As there bin any more news about that extra petrol supply?' he asked.

Frank shook his head, watching with irritation as his father's fingers worked over the medallion. It was a habit the old man had had for years and it seemed more pronounced when he was fishing for answers.

'Anything troubling you, Father?' Frank asked suddenly.

The old man chuckled. 'I can see this irritates yer, boy, it always 'as done. But I wouldn't be parted wiv this medal. It's brought me a good deal o' luck through the years.'

Frank bit back an angry retort. He remembered well when it was stolen from the office years ago with the watch and chain and then recovered from the thief after he had been killed by a train. It had hung in a pawnbroker's window before eventually finding its way back to the yard, surviving the fire which killed its third keeper. Frank remembered, too, the police inspector saying that the pawnbroker had told him it was a runic reproduction and had something to do with a Nordic fire god. It had brought nothing but bad luck to the men who had carried it around with them, except for his father.

'Did I ever tell yer about 'ow I came by this?' the old man asked.

'You took it from a toff in the Old Kent Road,' Frank replied.

'That's right, I did. It was a question o' survival in those days,' George said with passion. 'Me an' Will Tanner slept under the arches and stole from the markets to eat. Many a night we slept wiv our stomachs rumblin' wiv 'unger. It's different now though. Yer don't see the starvin' kids 'angin' around the markets these days.'

Frank was keen to get back to the yard office and he stood up. 'I'd better be off,' he said.

'Pity there wasn't a son from yer marriage,' George said, toying with the medallion.

Mrs Duffin was lingering near the bedroom and as Frank came out and shut the door she approached him. 'I'm sorry ter bovver yer, Mr Galloway, but yer farvver asked me ter post these letters so they'd catch the midday post an' I can't leave the 'ouse, the doctor's due back this mornin' wiv some medicine an' 'e's late. I don't want ter miss 'im, yer see.'

Frank nodded. 'All right, Mrs Duffin, I'll post them,' he replied, taking the half-dozen or so letters from her.

'Yer farvver was most concerned about that one,' she said, pointing to the top letter. ' 'E told me ter make sure it got posted safely.'

'All right, Mrs Duffin, leave it to me,' Frank told her. 'Don't mention that I posted them. You know how fussy he is about such things. If he asks, just tell him you slipped out and posted them yourself.'

Mrs Duffin smiled her thanks. It was a load off her mind to know that the letters were in safe hands.

Frank had returned to his office directly, with the letters still in his coat pocket. As soon as he was seated at his desk he opened the one Mrs Duffin had pointed out to him. It was addressed to a Mrs Mary O'Reilly and the contents intrigued him. Folded in the paper was a five-pound note and the letter urged the woman to get a good tonic with it. It also asked for George's best regards to be sent on to 'young Tony' and said that the lad would be well looked after in the future.

Frank sat brooding over the message which he had resealed and sent on. What was the old man playing at? he wondered. Was the boy a love child? Was Mary O'Reilly one of his many women? It seemed a very likely possibility, he thought, bearing in mind how the old man had harped on about him and Bella not being able to produce a male child. It would be just like the silly old fool to give the boy a part of the business.

The doorbell interrupted his anxious speculation, and when Gloria was made comfortable with a large gin and lemon, Frank had some serious questions to put to her.

Loud music was blaring out as Rachel and her friend Amy Brody walked into the Samson dance hall in Rotherhithe. Rachel was wearing her uniform, reluctantly, after realising that she had gained a few pounds in weight since joining the WAAF and her two dance dresses no longer fitted her. Amy had dragged her out on her first night home, saying that servicemen and women got in half price and that women in uniform were always being asked to dance. Amy herself was working as a machinist at a factory engaged in making uniforms and she had not been able to enlist in the ATS, much to her chagrin. 'Some gels get all the luck,' she moaned to her best friend.

'It's not all it's cracked up ter be,' Rachel said. 'In our camp there was a couple o' those manly women. One tried ter cuddle me in the washroom and there was anuvver who tried it on wiv one o' the ovver gels. She got reported.'

''Ow 'orrible. It makes me go cold finkin' about those sort o' women,' Amy said with a shudder.

'They're in every camp, so I've bin told,' Rachel went on, enjoying Amy's discomfort. 'They're really nice gels most of 'em, it's just that they don't like men. One o' my friends in camp is a bit like that.'

'Yer don't let 'er cuddle yer, do yer?' Amy asked in a shocked voice.

'Course not. We're jus' good friends,' Rachel told her, trying to keep a straight face.

Amy was feeling a little better now about not being able to join up and she looked around the large hall for a suitable partner. ' 'Ere, Rachel, I like the look of 'im,' she said giggling.

The lad in question was dancing confidently with a large partner who towered over him. He glanced over at Amy and appeared to smile at her.

'Did yer see that,' Amy said excitedly, nudging her friend. 'I fink 'e's interested.'

The music was lively and the two friends soon had partners. Rachel danced first with a bespectacled youth and then with a tall gangling lad who trod on her feet. Amy was enraptured by the attention her admirer was paying her. He seemed to have deserted the large young woman for good and as they danced round the floor, Amy could see the hard looks she was getting.

The crowded hall quickly became stuffy, and after the third dance Rachel motioned her friend to go with her to the bar which was on the upper floor overlooking the dance area. Amy was feeling thrilled at the prospect of being taken home by her attentive companion and Rachel was pleased that her clumsy dance partner had found another young lady to stamp on.

As they reached the bar, Amy's partner came up to her. 'Would yer care ter join me fer the next dance? It's fer a spot prize,' he said excitedly. 'We stand a good chance ter win it. It's a foxtrot.'

Amy hurried away to take part, leaving Rachel standing alone at the bar. People were milling about waiting to get drinks and the bar staff were kept busy. By the time Rachel managed to order a shandy, the spot dance was finished and a disappointed Amy walked from the dance floor seething. She and her partner had been beaten by the large young woman and her new partner. Rachel meanwhile had taken her drink and passed over the money, only to be told that the drink had been paid for. She looked around in surprise and suddenly caught sight of the young soldier standing at the far end of the bar, the young man who had shared her compartment on the train. He was with a group of friends, some in uniform. He smiled and raised his glass then suddenly turned away. Rachel felt her face grow hot and she sipped the shandy self-consciously, glad when Amy rejoined her.

'It wasn't fair,' Amy was going on. 'We were definitely the best couple. I'm sure that fat pig knows the manager. She kept makin' eyes at 'im.'

The soldier was looking her way again and Rachel realised that he was trying not to arouse the suspicion of the young woman by his side. Rachel made a pretence of listening to Amy's incessant chatter. The music started up again, an excuse-me waltz, and Amy was whisked off by her new-found beau. The young woman with the soldier went off to dance with another member of the group and then the soldier came over to Rachel, smiling broadly.

'I was surprised ter see yer 'ere,' he said, leaning on the bar counter. 'D'yer come 'ere often?'

'I used to,' Rachel told him. 'What about you?'

'This is the first time fer me,' he said. 'As a matter o' fact I'm on compassionate leave fer forty-eight hours. Me mum's ill in 'ospital an' me friends dragged me out ter cheer me up.'

'I'm sorry,' Rachel replied. 'Is she very ill?'

He nodded. 'Yeah. I was 'opin' ter get a longer leave but it looks like our lot are gonna be movin' off very soon.'

'That's a shame,' Rachel said, feeling sorry for him.

Suddenly the young soldier touched her arm. 'I gotta go,' he said quickly. 'The girl friend's jus' bin excused. Talk ter yer later if I get a chance.'

Rachel watched him walk away with his pronounced swagger and while he was chatting with his friends she stole a few furtive glances his way. He was certainly good-looking. His dark hair tended to curl and his square features were open and friendly. He had a charming smile, too, and his relaxed way of talking had made her feel at ease with him and almost forget that he was a stranger.

Amy had returned, and during her constant chattering Rachel still took the odd moment to look over at the group. The soldier occasionally glanced over towards her too and once or twice their eyes met very briefly. The girl he was with giggled a lot and seemed flighty, appearing to be out to impress the whole group with her loud talk. Rachel took an immediate dislike to the young woman and began to wish that the soldier would come over and ask her to dance. He had not gone onto the dance floor at all, she noted, and it seemed as though he was not really interested in the dancing.

Rachel was asked to dance by one or two young men, however, and when at last she had managed to encourage Amy to go for another drink at the bar she was disappointed to find that the group were no longer there. Amy was bubbling, though, as she had made a date with her new-found dancing partner.

The two friends finally left the dance hall and caught the tram back to

Dockhead, and all the while Rachel thought about the soldier at the dance. He was the first man she had found herself remotely interested in since Derek, although she had attended a few camp dances where there were many opportunities for her to date young men. She told herself that it was just as well things had turned out the way they had. The soldier was going off to fight and she would be posted somewhere, maybe miles away from London. To get involved now with anyone would be unwise, and she leaned back against the tram seat and tried to put the brief encounter out of her mind. There were other things to think about.

Maurice Salter had enjoyed the evening and was feeling very hopeful. It had not been easy for him to form an attachment with a woman after his wife died and he had concerned himself with bringing up his three daughters to the best of his ability. Now he had new interests.

Lily had been the one who suggested to him that it was about time he found himself a nice lady friend who would make him happy. Brenda and Barbara, too, had agreed that it was a good idea for him to have some pleasure instead of moping around the house. Maurice knew full well that the girls loved him and wanted him to be happy, but he knew also that his choice of lady friend would be a subject of discussion among his daughters. He knew that Brenda Massey was not their idea of a good companion for him and they had told him so in no uncertain words. Brenda thought that her namesake was a man-eater and Barbara thought that she was flighty, and likely to cause him pain before long. Only Lily gave him her unqualified approval. 'She seems a nice woman, Dad. Good luck ter yer,' she had remarked.

Maurice had been very careful not to rush Brenda into getting between the sheets, although she seemed keen to progress with their courting. The fly in the ointment, as far as Maurice was concerned, was Granny Massey. She was a nasty, interfering old battleaxe, for his money, and she had made it plain to him that he wasn't her choice of a suitor for her daughter. Brenda told him he should not take any notice of her ageing mother's attitude and at forty she was old enough to make up her own mind about the men she went out with. Granny Massey did not share her daughter's opinion, however, and she did all she could to thwart the courtship. Tonight was no exception. As Maurice and Brenda travelled back to Dockhead on the late tram, Granny Massey was ready and waiting.

'I enjoyed the film, Brenda, didn't you?' Maurice asked.

'Yeah, an' the fish an' chips went down well,' Brenda told him. 'The pub was a bit packed though,' she remarked.

'Still, we got a seat, eventually,' he said.

Brenda slipped her arm through his as they sat on the upper deck of the tram and leaned against him provocatively. 'I wish we 'ad

171

somewhere ter go where we could be really private,' she said in a husky voice.

Maurice pulled a face. 'We can't go ter my place, the gels are always poppin' in an' out,' he groaned.

'I can't relax at my place,' Brenda frowned. 'I'm always frightened Mum's gonna come down an' walk in on us.'

Maurice had thought about tying a rope across the banisters or maybe connecting Granny Massey's bedroom doorknob to the electricity supply, but he felt that Brenda wouldn't take too kindly to it. After all, the old witch was her mother, bad as she was. The alternative was to cosset the old girl and win her over; hence the flowers.

Brenda let herself into the house and immediately sensed that all was not well. Her usual greeting was not answered and she gave Maurice a worried frown as he followed her into the passage. 'Mum never goes ter sleep before I get in,' Brenda remarked.

'Don't I know it,' Maurice mumbled.

As she entered the parlour to hang up her coat, Brenda gasped. Granny Massey was sitting back in the easy chair beside the empty grate, a blanket thrown over her frail shoulders and a handkerchief held up to her mouth. On the table there was a glass of water, a bottle of smelling salts, and the flowers Maurice had given her. All the blooms had dropped from the stems, which were laid out as though for inspection.

'Whatever's wrong?' Brenda asked, kneeling down at her mother's side.

'I came over queer as I was turnin' in,' Granny whispered. 'I came down fer a glass o' water an' must 'ave fainted. When I come round I dragged meself inter the chair an' all I could see was those bloody fings there on the table. That's what made me ill, them,' she croaked, pointing to the withered flowers.

Maurice would have gladly strangled the old lady there and then, but he knelt down beside Brenda and gave the old woman a cheery smile. 'I'm sorry, luv,' he said. 'They was lovely when I bought 'em.'

'When was that, last month?' Granny chided him.

'I'm sure Maurice couldn't 'ave known they'd die off so soon,' Brenda remarked.

'Oh yes 'e did,' the old lady replied. ' 'E did it on purpose. 'E's never liked me. I'm only in 'is way. I know.'

Brenda had wanted this evening to be special; she had been prepared to allow Maurice into her bedroom, as soon as her mother went to sleep. Now, though, she felt that it had all been spoilt because of her mother's unreasonable behaviour. 'Maurice wouldn't do that, Mum, 'e really likes yer,' she said with feeling. ' 'E wanted ter please yer wiv those flowers.'

'Please me?' the old lady croaked. ' 'E done it on purpose, I tell yer.

Just smell 'em. 'E's put some poison on 'em. Go on, smell 'em.'

Brenda reached for the stems and sniffed them. Her face suddenly darkened and she turned to glare at Maurice. ' 'Ow could you?' she said with passion. 'Of all the dirty, wicked tricks. Maurice Salter, I never want ter see yer ugly face again as long as I live. Get out!'

Maurice sadly made his way home, feeling that he should have stuck to his ducking and diving instead of dabbling with the unfamiliar pastime of chasing the ladies.

Gloria Simpson took a pocket mirror from her handbag and studied her face once more, her thoughts centred on the meeting she had had with Frank Galloway a couple of nights ago. The Horse and Groom public house was filling up and she felt a little less conspicuous. Being conspicuous normally never troubled Gloria, in fact it aided her in her profession, but tonight she had good reason to want to blend in with the surroundings. Since Frank had come into her life, things had changed for the better. It was in this very pub that she had solicited him when he called in looking very sorry for himself. He had allowed her to approach him and he had bought her a drink before he realised that she was a professional woman of the streets. Taking him back to her seedy flat in Rotherhithe for the night was the best thing she could have done. Instead of wanting to climb into bed as quickly as possible like all her other clients, Frank Galloway seemed more inclined to talk. He was very drunk and obviously feeling very miserable. He had wanted a sympathetic ear and Gloria did not mind in the least. Her house rule was that men paid her on entry to her flat and Frank obliged without question. The fact that he spent two hours talking to her was no problem for Gloria, and when he had exhausted himself with his ramblings and fallen into a drunken sleep on her sofa, she covered him with a blanket and went off to bed. Next morning he could hardly remember any of the evening and she played her part very well. The bruises on her arm and leg had been caused by a previous client who took pleasure in brutalising her and Gloria used the marks of violence to good effect. Frank Galloway was full of apologies for being so rough with her and asked to see her again.

The chance encounter had worked out very well for her, and Frank had now become a regular visitor to her flat. Recently he had taken her home to his smart house in Ilford and arranged a job of work for her. The payment was more than Gloria could have hoped to earn in a full week on the streets and Frank Galloway was very pleased with her performance. Now he had given her another job to do and she was eager to make a success of it, after he had promised her a handsome reward.

The public house in a little backstreet near the Surrey Docks was frequented by merchant seamen from Scandinavia and Russia who crewed the timber ships, as well as the local dockland folk. Frank

Galloway had gone there that first evening to talk business with a prospective customer who had not shown up, and he had met Gloria instead.

She gazed casually round the bar and sipped her gin and tonic. Her friend was late and she did not want to attract the attention of a prospective client before she arrived. Gloria operated from the Horse and Groom and would have preferred to have the meeting elsewhere but her old friend knew the whereabouts of the pub and had insisted that they meet there.

A couple of the customers who knew her were sniggering at one end of the bar and a middle-aged man in a dark pinstripe suit occasionally lifted his head from the evening paper and gave her an inquisitive glance. Gloria looked up at the large clock at the back of the counter and decided to give her friend another ten minutes.

It was exactly eight minutes later when Lola Fields walked into the Horse and Groom. She looked flushed and out of breath and as she spotted Gloria she sighed with relief. 'I thought I'd missed yer, Gloria,' she said, sitting down heavily in the chair.

'I was just about ter leave,' Gloria replied a little irritably.

'There was a tram breakdown an' the bleedin' fings were lined up all along as far as the tunnel,' Lola told her. 'I 'ad ter walk most o' the way.'

'Anyway, yer made it,' Gloria smiled, taking an envelope from her handbag and putting it down on the table. 'Now listen,' she began. 'I want yer ter get me some information. I know yer work the Ole Kent Road pubs, so yer shouldn't 'ave much trouble gettin' me what I want. There's money in there fer yer trouble, an' if yer do a good job there's a bonus ter come.'

Lola's eyes lit up and she reached for the envelope, but Gloria stopped her by placing her hand over it.

'Before yer take this job on, there's one or two fings yer should know,' she said in a low voice. 'First of all, nobody, an' I mean nobody, must know what yer doin'. Is that understood?'

Lola nodded her head vigorously, beginning to feel excited.

'Next, I want yer ter memorise the address an' instructions then get rid o' the paper,' Gloria told her. 'I don't want the police askin' questions if they pull yer in fer solicitin'. Is that clear?'

Lola nodded again, and then Gloria handed her the envelope. 'Put that in yer bag, an' I'll get yer a drink,' she said.

'What's it all about?' Lola asked as they sipped their gins.

Gloria gave her old friend a steely look. 'Survival, Lola.'

Chapter Twenty

On Friday evening, 10 May, Fred Dougall hobbled down Page Street holding the *Evening Standard* in his hand. 'They're on the move!' he told Maudie Mycroft as he passed by her front door and saw her cleaning the windows.

Maudie went in and woke up her husband Ernest who was snoozing in his favourite armchair. 'They're on the move!' she told him.

'Who are?'

'I dunno, somebody must be.'

'Who said?'

'Fred Dougall.'

'Well, 'e should know,' Ernest mumbled.

Fred's wife Maisie was standing at her front door talking to Sadie and when she saw Fred approaching with a serious look on his face, she nudged her friend. 'Somefink's up,' she said.

Sadie, like Maisie, was now in her mid-seventies and not easily excited by trivalities, but she too could see by Fred's serious expression that something important was happening. 'Wonder what's goin' on,' she said.

'They've invaded 'Olland an' Belgium,' Fred announced as he reached them.

'Who 'as?' Maisie asked.

'Well, it's not us, yer silly mare,' Fred said sharply.

The two women stared at the headlines. 'Gawd! It looks bad,' Sadie remarked.

'It's all gonna blow up now, mark my words,' Fred told them. 'They're gonna put the ARP an' civil defence services on the alert.'

'Does that mean we're gonna be invaded too?' Maisie asked him.

'Course it don't,' Fred said quickly, trying to reassure the frightened-looking pair.

Maudie hurried up to the group. 'It's jus' come over the wireless,' she said excitedly. 'The Dutch 'ave opened the floodgates. They're floodin' the 'ole country.'

'What they doin' that for?' Maisie asked.

'Ter stop the Germans,' Fred replied.

Maisie and Sadie exchanged puzzled glances while Fred walked into the house to hear the rest of the news. Maudie looked worried, her eyes going from one to the other of her old friends, hoping for some comment from them that would make her feel easier, but the two merely stared down the turning as though waiting for the hordes to appear.

'I jus' bin talkin' ter that man at the fruit stall,' Maudie said. ' 'E made me go cold all over wiv what 'e said.'

'What did 'e say?' Sadie asked, hardly interested.

Maudie pulled a face. ' 'E said that if the Germans got 'ere, 'e'd cut all 'is children's froats sooner than let them get 'em.'

' 'E should be locked up fer sayin' such fings,' Maisie growled.

'Yer don't fink we'll be invaded, do yer?' Maudie asked them, her eyes flitting nervously from one to the other.

'Course not, yer silly cow,' Sadie replied quickly. 'Not jus' yet anyway.'

Maudie picked up her shopping bag. 'I'm gonna 'ave anuvver word wiv my sister an' see if me an' Ernest can go an' stay wiv 'er,' she mumbled. 'I fink we'll be better orf away from London.'

'Where's she live?' Maisie asked.

'Pratt's Bottom.'

'Never 'eard ot it.'

'It's in Kent.'

'Yer might be all right there,' Sadie cut in. 'I don't s'pose the Germans 'ave 'eard of it eivver. They might give it a miss if they do invade.'

Maudie walked away mumbling to herself and her two friends exchanged grins. 'I do feel sorry fer 'er sometimes,' Maisie remarked.

'I do too, the silly ole cow,' Sadie replied.

Joe Maitland locked up the yard gate and went into the house just in time to hear the news. 'It looks bad,' he said.

Carrie sat back in her armchair and stared into the empty grate with a serious look on her face. 'There's bin no letter from Rachel,' she said. 'I'm gettin' worried.'

Joe turned down the wireless and sat down facing Carrie. 'I shouldn't worry too much, luv,' he said quietly. 'She did say she was gonna be posted. It'll take 'er a time ter get settled. Yer can't expect 'er ter write too often.'

Carrie shrugged her shoulders. 'I dunno what ter fink,' she sighed.

Nellie walked into the parlour and Joe got up to give her his chair. 'I'll make us a nice cuppa,' he said.

'That's Joe's answer to everyfing,' Carrie smiled at her mother.

Nellie took her seat and reached down for her needlework. 'I'm gonna go round an' see our Danny an' Iris later,' she announced. 'The way fings are goin', those kids o' theirs should be evacuated.'

176

'They'll 'ave ter make their own minds up, Mum. Yer can't interfere,' Carrie replied, sounding a little sharp.

Nellie looked sternly at her daughter over her steel-rimmed spectacles. 'Well, I fink they should 'urry up an' make their minds up,' she said. 'If yer farvver was 'ere 'e'd 'ave somefink ter say about it.'

Carrie felt disinclined to continue the conversation, considering her mother's mood, and she settled down to read the evening paper.

'I dreamed about yer bruvver Charlie last night,' Nellie said suddenly. ' 'E was standin' in this field an' there was all people around 'im. I waved to 'im but 'e just ignored me. It was the first time fer ages I've dreamed about 'im. Last time I did there was a letter from 'im a week later.'

'P'haps yer'll get a letter soon, Mum,' Carrie said encouragingly.

Nellie put down her embroidery and reached for her handbag which was lying at her feet, rummaging inside it until she found the dog-eared photograph of her middle son. ' 'E looks thin in that picture,' she remarked. 'Mind you, it must take the weight off yer in that sort o' climate. In 'is last letter 'e promised ter send some new photos of Lorna an' the children. They must be gettin' big now.'

Carrie looked up from the paper and saw that familiar wistful look on her mother's lined face. She had often said that she never expected to live long enough to see her son again and she could well be right, Carrie thought. The war looked as though it would drag on for years and her mother was getting exceedingly frail.

Joe came into the room carrying cups of tea, and as Nellie sipped hers noisily, her eyes stared ahead, her mind going back through the years. Charlie was leaving for India and there was so much she wanted to tell him, so much to say, but the lump in her throat had choked the words and the tears had misted her last look at him. She remembered his heavy tread down the old wooden stairs of the tenement block, and she remembered in her misery cursing the very name of the man who had been the cause of his leaving.

Billy Sullivan had been true to his word and no longer worked at the Kings Arms. Terry had asked him to remain for a little longer but Billy was adamant. The parting was amicable and Billy still used the pub, along with his old friend Danny Tanner. On a warm Friday evening at the end of May, they were sitting together in the public bar discussing the latest bad news.

'They've got fousands out already an' accordin' ter the paper they reckon they'll get most of 'em 'ome,' Billy said, sipping his pint.

Danny nodded. 'I was lookin' at the map o' Dunkirk in terday's paper,' he remarked. 'It's not far from some of our ole battlefields.'

Billy nodded. 'Once France falls, they'll be facin' us over a very narrer strip o' water, Danny,' he said raising his eyebrows.

'Me an' Iris 'ave decided about the kids,' Danny said, picking up his pint.

'Are yer sendin' 'em off?' Billy asked.

'No, we've decided against it,' Danny told him. 'We give it a lot o' thought an' we came ter the conclusion that we'll keep 'em wiv us. Iris can't bear ter be parted from 'em an' she said that if anyfing 'appens to us then we'll all go tergevver.'

Billy nodded slowly. 'Yer know, that was the way I saw it,' he replied. 'It was different wiv me an' Annie though. She got the chance ter work at that 'ome and she's still wiv the kids. I don't fink she could bear ter be parted from 'em eivver. I know I miss 'em all somefing terrible.'

Danny drained his glass and stood up. 'Same again?'

Glasses refilled, the two sat in silence. Now in their middle years, the two old friends could sit together, comfortable and pensive, without the need to make undue conversation.

The beer dwindling, Danny looked across at his friend. 'Let's 'ave a stroll down ter the gym,' he suggested.

Billy nodded, and after they had drained their glasses the two left the pub and set off along the quiet Jamaica Road.

The evening was balmy, with birds chattering noisily in the tall plane trees that stood back from the road. Above them the evening sky was turning red and gold, and smells of spice and fruit drifted from the nearby wharves. Billy walked with his usual pronounced stoop, his shoulders rolling, while Danny walked upright, his head held high.

'Yer know, I sometimes wonder why I bovver ter go in that pub again, after the poison-pen letter Annie got,' Billy told his mate.

'If yer'd stopped out o' there, whoever sent it would 'ave beat yer,' Danny replied.

Billy nodded. 'Sometimes I look around at those familiar faces an' find it 'ard ter fink that any of 'em could 'ave done such a fing,' he said.

'Well, somebody did,' Danny replied. 'I wouldn't worry about it though. Yer'll probably never get ter the bottom of it.'

They had reached Wilson Street and as they turned the corner they could see the red-brick building standing out against the evening light. They strolled up slowly, hands in pockets, and saw the civil defence sign by the front door. Next to it was a poster reminding people to carry their gas masks about with them and yet another poster warning against careless talk. The front entrance was shielded with sandbags, and a criss-cross of paper strips covered all the windoes.

Billy sighed as he stared at the building. 'I wonder what ole Farvver Murphy's finkin' about all this?' he said.

Danny hunched his shoulders. ' 'E's prob'ly lookin' down an' groanin' at the blood stupidity of it all,' he replied.

'We 'ad some good times 'ere,' Billy reminded him with a grin. 'D'yer remember when we brought those two jack-the-lads back 'ere an' duffed 'em up?'

Danny smiled at the memory. 'We come near ter doin' it all wrong that night, ole pal.'

Billy walked up to the front door and stood on the wide stone step, remembering the dream he had had, a dream nurtured and brought to fruition by the unsparing efforts of the much-loved old priest, Father Murphy. He turned to face Danny. 'Remember the brick-stackin' contest, an' the look on Wally Walburton's face when we offered ter buy 'im a pint afterwards?' he asked.

' 'Ow could I ever ferget,' Danny grinned.

Billy tried the locked front door and then walked back to the entrance that had once had an iron gate. 'I'm finkin' that by the time this war's over, me an' you'll be too bloody old ter go back trainin' the kids,' he remarked.

Danny shrugged his broad shoulders. 'It can't go on fer ever, Billy. C'mon, let's get goin'. I'm on early shift termorrer.'

Dusk was settling over the Bermondsey backstreets as the two strolled back to Page Street.

'Come in fer a bit o' supper,' Danny suggested.

Billy shook his head. 'No, it's all right,' he replied.

Danny slipped his arm round his friend's shoulders. 'C'mon, mate. Iris told me not ter take no fer an answer.'

As they stepped inside the front door of the Tanner house, a lone figure shuffled out of the turning, heading for the solitude of the evening river, unable to understand why there were now no lights over the quays or shining from the high stone towers of the bridge that moved up and down.

During the first week in June a visitor called at the Bradley transport yard, introducing herself as Mrs Robins and saying that she would like to speak to the owner in private. Joe showed her into the office where Carrie was busy with the worksheets and left the two women together. A short time later Carrie came over to Joe as he was fixing tarpaulin to the roof of the newly erected vehicle shed and beckoned him down. Her face was set grimly and when Joe reached the foot of the ladder, he could see she was holding back tears.

'That was Jamie's muvver, Joe,' she said quietly. 'Jamie got back from Dunkirk yesterday. 'E's bin wounded an' 'e's asked ter see me.'

'Is 'e badly wounded?'

'Bad enough. 'E's lost a leg.'

'Good Gawd,' Joe groaned. 'The poor little bleeder.'

'I can visit this Sunday. Come wiv me, Joe. I need yer wiv me,' Carrie said, gripping his arm.

'Of course,' he replied. 'What 'ospital is 'e in?'

'Woolwich Military. It's afternoon visitin'.'

On a bright Sunday morning George Galloway decided he coul[...] manage the short walk to his favourite pub. He leaned heavily on hi[...] silver-tipped walking cane and when he reached the Saracen's Head an[...] stepped into the cosy saloon bar, he was greeted by his old friend John Hargreaves. The two found their favourite corner and sat togethe[...] drinking large Scotches.

'That Dunkirk turnout was a masterful piece of organisation,' Hargreaves said. 'At least we got most of our army back in one piece.'

George nodded. 'My gran'son got back safely, fank Gawd,' h[...] replied. 'I got word from 'is muvver yesterday.'

'Will you be seeing him, George?' the elderly solicitor asked.

'Soon as it can be arranged.'

'How's the lad's mother? She's not very well I remember you saying.'

'It's consumption,' George told him. 'The woman's neglected 'ersel[...] over the years. She should 'ave come ter me before now.'

'Pride, George, it's all a question of pride,' his friend remarked. 'W[...] all have our pride.'

'Well, she's payin' the price now fer 'er stupid pride,' George growled. 'Still, the boy's a strappin' lad. A chip off the old block righ[...] enough. Yer can see it in the way 'e carries 'imself. Proud lad, 'e is. Lik[...] 'is farvver. Geoff cut a fair dash in 'is time. I'll tell yer what, John, i[...] I'm around I'll make sure that lad gets the right advice about settin[...] 'imself up in business when this lot's over.'

'That's if the lad has the inclination.'

'Inclination? 'Course 'e will,' George stormed. ' 'E's a Galloway.'

'Well, there's a war to be fought first,' Hargreaves pointed out, 'an[...] by the way things are going it'll be a long, hard struggle.'

George sipped his drink without saying anything. John Hargreaves i[...] a bloody old fool, he thought. Always looking on the dark side.

'How is the application for extra petrol going?' the solicitor asked[...] breaking the silence.

George allowed himself a smile. 'Pretty good,' he replied. 'The firs[...] rum consignment inter Bristol docks is due in next month. It looks lik[...] we've got a transportation licence, providin' the railways don't put thei[...] oar in.'

'I wish you luck,' Hargreaves said, holding up his glass. 'By the by[...] the landlord tells me the Scotch is in short supply. Whose round is it?'

On that bright Sunday afternoon Carrie and Joe caught the train t[...] Woolwich Dockyard and then hailed a cab to the large military hospita[...] some distance away. She carried the bunch of flowers Joe had bough[...] outside the railway station and they joined the many anxious civilian[...]

180

hurrying through the high gates and making their way to the brightly painted wards bedecked with flowers.

Carrie held onto Joe's arm as they walked into a high-ceilinged ward on the first floor and scanned the beds. She spotted the white-faced lad lying back against the pillows. His bedclothes were raised over a steel frame and there was a handgrip suspended just above his head. Carrie handed the flowers to a nurse hovering nearby and leaned over the bed. ' 'Ow's our soldier boy?' she asked, kissing his forehead.

Jamie looked embarrassed as he grasped the handgrip to pull himself up against the pillows. 'I'm well, Mrs Maitland,' he replied.

Joe leaned forward and took the lad's hand in a firm grip. 'We're pleased ter see yer, Jamie,' he said.

'Did me mum tell yer?' Jamie asked, nodding towards the mound of bedclothes.

His visitors both nodded and as Carrie sat down in the chair beside the bed, she touched the lad's arm. 'Is there much pain?' she asked him.

Jamie shook his head. 'I wanted ter see yer soon as possible, Mrs Maitland, because there's somefink I want yer ter know,' he said in a low voice.

Carrie gave him a smile of encouragement but Jamie dropped his eyes to the bedclothes and then glanced up at Joe. 'I thought it'd be easy,' he said falteringly, 'but I don't know 'ow ter start.'

Carrie could see his plain unease as his eyes flitted back and forth between her and Joe. She gave her husband a quick wink and turned to the ashen-faced young man. 'Would it be easier if Joe waited outside?' she asked.

Jamie nodded. 'Would yer mind, Mr Maitland?' he said.

Joe gave him a reassuring smile and walked away towards the corridor, Jamie's eyes fixed on him until he reached the door of the ward. Finally the young man turned to Carrie, tears filling his eyes. 'I done yer wrong, Mrs Maitland. I let yer down,' he said in a low voice.

Carrie patted his arm reassuringly. 'No yer didn't, Jamie,' she said. 'Yer felt it was right ter go an' do yer bit. I understood, so did Joe.'

Jamie shook his head slowly. 'Yer don't understand. It wasn't that at all. I betrayed yer, betrayed the trust yer put in me, an' after all the kindness yer showed me.'

Carrie's face took on a puzzled look. 'What is it, Jamie?'

'It was me that cost yer the rum contract. Me,' he groaned.

'Go on,' she urged him.

'I gave Frank Galloway all the information he needed to undercut yer,' Jamie told her, his eyes averted from Carrie's gaze. 'That's why yer lost the contract.'

'But why, Jamie? Why would yer do such a fing?' Carrie asked, shocked at what he was saying.

'It's a long story,' he sighed. 'I don't know where ter begin.'

'At the beginnin', Jamie. That's where it usually starts,' she said, looking at him kindly.

He took a deep breath, his eyes coming up to meet hers. 'When yer was tryin' ter get me a call-up exemption I was really pleased,' he began. 'I was worried about me mum an' dad, me bein' the breadwinner an' all. Anyway, it wasn't long before the snide remarks began. Who d'yer know ter get out o' the fightin'? Are yer a pansy boy? Then there was the same sort o' remarks made ter me parents. At first it didn't worry me, but then it slowly got ter me. I started goin' out ter the pub in the evenin's. Jus' fer a couple o' drinks ter make me feel better. One night I met this young lady. She seemed very nice.'

'Yer met 'er in the pub?' Carrie cut in.

Jamie nodded his head slowly. 'She came up an' asked me fer change so she could make a phone call,' he went on. 'She told me 'er name was Gloria an' we got talkin' about work an' fings. Then she asked a lot o' questions about me, like where did I work an' was I joinin' up soon. I was flattered by 'er interest an' I bought 'er a drink.'

Carrie's forehead was creased in a frown but she said nothing and let him go on, aware that he was now trembling noticeably.

'Gloria told me that she worked in an office an' that it was a small world because 'er dad was Jack Simpson who used ter work fer yer,' Jamie continued. 'We 'ad a few more drinks an' I was beginnin' ter feel light-'eaded. I wasn't used ter more than a couple. Anyway, I walked 'er 'ome an' I suddenly felt really sick. Gloria let me stay at 'er place fer a while, an' then we made arrangements ter see each ovver again. I got serious an' wanted ter see 'er all the time, but she told me she 'ad ter take turns of lookin' after 'er sister who was ill. One night we went back to Gloria's flat an' I stayed the night. I loved 'er, Mrs Maitland. I really loved 'er,' Jamie said, his voice suddenly faltering.

Carrie gently gripped the young man's arm. 'Take yer time, Jamie,' she said softly.

After a few seconds he continued, 'I only made love wiv 'er twice but then Gloria told me she was pregnant. I was naturally upset but I told 'er I'd do the right fing by 'er 'an marry 'er. It was then that she told me she was already married an' that 'er 'usband was away in the army. She said 'e was a violent man an' that 'e'd kill the pair of us if 'e found out. She said she needed money ter get rid o' the baby an' that it was my responsibility.

'I 'ad no money, Mrs Maitland. I didn't know what ter do an' I was worried sick. That was when I went an' volunteered fer the army. Gloria told me I'd 'ave ter find the money or she'd write an' tell 'er 'usband that I'd raped 'er an' got 'er pregnant. Then she came up wiv this idea about gettin' the money from Frank Galloway. She said that 'er farvver told 'er all about the bitterness between you an' the Galloways, an' 'ow yer got a lot o' their contracts by undercuttin' 'em. She asked me ter go an' see Frank Galloway an' tell 'im I'd sell 'im the information 'e needed ter do the same. She said it was only right, considerin' 'e'd lost out by bein' undercut. I wouldn't do it. I couldn't face the man, but Gloria said she'd go an' see 'im for me. I jus' needed time, Mrs Maitland, 'opin' me call-up papers would arrive, so I put 'er off fer a week or two, but then she said 'er 'usband was comin' 'ome on leave soon an' she'd 'ave ter tell 'im that I'd raped 'er. I 'ad no choice, I 'ad ter give 'er the information.

'So now yer know the 'ole story. I sold yer out, betrayed yer fer money. I wish now that that shell 'ad taken me 'ead off, instead o' me leg. I really do.'

Carried reached out to him and held his hands in hers. Her shock at his disclosures was tempered by the sight of him crying like a baby. Tears fell down his cheeks and onto his chin, and his eyes focused on hers appealingly. There was no anger in Carrie, only a sadness for the weak and immature young man, now so brutally maimed.

'It's all right, Jamie, it's all right. Yer couldn't 'ave done much else ter raise the money,' she told him kindly. 'There's no ill feelin'.'

Jamie tried hard to compose himself and then he squeezed up the bedclothes in an angry fist. 'I jus' said that yer know the full story now, but yer don't, Mrs Maitland,' he went on. 'Gloria finished wiv me as soon as I gave 'er what she needed. I saw 'er wiv Frank Galloway in a pub the night before I went inter the army. She an' 'im looked very friendly. They set me up, Mrs Maitland. They planned the 'ole fing between 'em. She told me openly when I begged 'er ter come back ter me.'

Carrie felt a familiar cold anger rising in her chest. Once again a Galloway had cheated and manipulated to get what he wanted. It went much further than a normal business rivalry when the lives and the emotions of people were disregarded, used and then thrown away to gain a cheap advantage. It was because of such cynical callousness that Jamie was lying there now with one leg missing. There would be a price to pay, though. She would make sure of that, she told herself, remembering the vow she had made to herself in her early years, the vow that only recently she had tried to forget, that one day she would witness the end of the Galloways.

Joe held Carrie's arm tightly as they left the hospital, having been told all that Jamie had said. He was quiet, angry at Frank Galloway's dirty scheming and the damage it had caused to a lad he had grown fond of, and mindful of his wife's simmering rage. He knew that whatever happened now, whatever pressures were brought to bear on Carrie, she would strive single-mindedly and relentlessly to outgrow and outlive the Galloway concern. He knew that in the past she had always had a good business sense and acted responsibly; his only fear was the one he had once heard voiced by Nellie, that hatred could sometimes eat into a person's soul and destroy everything that was good.

Chapter Twenty-One

The Bermondsey backstreet folk saw out the long June days with a good deal of trepidation, fearing an invasion at any time, their conversations always returning to the expected invasion.

'They've took all the signposts down,' Ernest told Maudie.

'What difference does that make?' she asked him.

'It's ter fool the Germans if they arrive,' he replied.

'But the signposts are in English, not German,' Maudie said.

'Well, I s'pose there's a few Germans that can read English,' he sighed, wishing he had never mentioned the signposts.

Daniel was feeling better by now and he ventured up to the Kings Arms for a pint one evening, only to be cornered by Bert Jolly.

'What they could do is come up the Thames in a submarine,' Bert remarked, 'land at Westminster pier an' they'd be in Parliament before yer knew it. After all, there's only one copper standin' on the gate, an' all 'e's got is a bloody gas-mask case. What would 'e be able ter do ter stop 'em, smash 'em wiv 'is gas mask?'

'Who yer talkin' about?' Daniel asked.

'Why the Germans o' course,' Bert replied.

'That wouldn't work, the tide changes too quick,' Daniel told him.

'I know that, an' you know that, an' the bloody Germans will too, what wiv all those fifth columnists we've got,' Bert went on. 'They could come up on the tide, take over the Parliament an' Bob's yer uncle.'

'An' Fanny's yer bleedin' aunt,' Daniel growled. 'I've never 'eard so much tosh in all me life. Submarines up the Thames indeed.'

'Well, they got one in Scapa Flow, didn't they?' Bert persisted.

'Scapa Flow is a bit wider than the Thames, an' a lot deeper,' Daniel said. 'They'd be better orf rowin' across the Channel, comin' up on the *Brighton Belle* an' doin' the London bit by Underground. Mind you, that wouldn't go down well wiv the passengers. Fancy 'avin' ter give yer seat up ter some scruffy German soldier.'

Bert realised that his perspicacious idea was being ridiculed and he turned his attention to the domino team. Daniel settled himself by the counter sipping his pint of ale and soon he was joined by Maurice Salter, who was feeling depressed by the day's events.

'I knew I should 'ave stayed in bed terday,' he groaned.

'Why's that then?' Daniel asked.

'Well, I was on early shift this mornin' an' I thought I'd try out me new bike,' Maurice said.

'Yer got a new bike, then?'

'Well, it ain't a new bike really, only a second-'and one, but it's a good runner,' Maurice told the ex-docker. 'Got four speeds, it 'as. The cogs need a good oilin', but it's in fair condition. Trouble was, the bleedin' dynamo packed up this mornin' before I got ter work, an' the bleedin' coppers stopped me fer 'avin' no lights. Anyway, I thought ter meself, Maurice, I said, yer better fink of a good excuse or yer in fer a fine. One o' me stoker mates got fined twenty shillin's last week fer no lights.'

'What did yer tell 'em?' Daniel asked, beginning to wish he had stayed indoors and sent Sadie up to the jug bar for a pint of each.

'Well, I said that I wasn't on early shift this week but there was a shortage o' stokers due ter sickness and the guv'nor sent fer me ter do an extra shift,' Maurice told him. 'Anyway, the coppers seemed satisfied wiv me explanation, 'specially when I said that me guv'nor told me I was ter get ter work as quick as possible.'

'So yer got orf, then?' Daniel asked.

'Nah, I got nicked,' Maurice replied.

' 'Ow comes?'

'Well, as I started pedallin' away, me saddlebag fell orf the back o' the bike,' Maurice told him.

'So?'

'All the tins o' corned beef fell out in the road.'

'So yer got done fer black-market stuff, then?' Daniel asked.

'I'm bailed to appear on Monday,' Maurice replied.

'There's a bit in the paper terday about a bloke gettin' nicked for black-market corned beef,' Daniel told him. 'Six months' 'ard labour, 'e got.'

Maurice groaned aloud and leaned his elbows on the bar counter dejectedly. 'Six months' 'ard labour!' he repeated.

'Don't fret,' Daniel told him. 'Breakin' stones on Dartmoor can't be much 'arder than shovellin' coal at the gasworks.'

Maurice finished his pint and left the pub, wondering what his daughters would have to say about the latest in his catalogue of disasters.

Rachel Bradley had been posted to an emergency airfield that had only just been set up in Kent and she joined the plotting team. West Marden was home to a Spitfire squadron and Rachel found the job different and exciting, taking calls from various sources and passing the information to colleagues who plotted the positions and strength of aircraft activity over the Channel and south coast. The plotters used large rods to push and pull counters over a huge horizontal map of southern England, and all the time the activity was monitored by senior officers sitting on the balcony above the central area.

Rachel soon made friends with the other aircraftwomen, or ACWs as they were called, and got to know one in particular, a young woman named Mary Hannen from north London. Mary had a well-to-do boy friend called Timothy Jarman who came down by car to collect her on the two occasions she managed to get a weekend pass. They seemed a happy couple. From the snippets Rachel had picked up in conversation, he seemed to be working on something top secret. It figured, she thought, considering that the petrol rationing did not seem to affect the handsome young man, who looked fit enough to be in the armed forces.

Rachel's early days at West Marden were happy ones. She felt that she had finally come to terms with losing Derek, and she did not mind being away from home any more. She knew that her decision to join up had been the right one. She thought sometimes about the young soldier she had met while on leave and wondered what had happened to him. Maybe she would go along to the Samson dance hall in Rotherhithe on her next weekend leave, although she did not hold out much hope of seeing him there. Still, there were things happening here, she thought. The camp dance this weekend was likely to be a good one, with servicemen and women coming from other camps in the area.

On Friday there was a briefing during which the solemn-looking group captain warned all personnel to be on their toes, adding that there were likely to be mass raids on airfields and installations prior to an invasion attempt. All leave was cancelled, which upset Mary Hannen more than anybody, but the dance would take place.

Early on Saturday evening Rachel's friend confided in her. 'I really wanted to see Timothy this weekend,' she said sadly. 'He's going away for a few weeks on this special course. He was going to book us into a hotel up west.'

'I'm sorry,' Rachel replied, glancing into her hand mirror and pursing her lips. 'Still, I'm sure there'll be anuvver chance soon.'

Mary looked worried. 'Tim works with the War Office,' she said quietly. 'I shouldn't be telling you, but I know you'll not let on. It's something to do with bombs and mines. It's very dangerous work.'

Rachel smiled at her as she stood up and adjusted the collar of her uniform. 'Don't worry, Mary, yer secret's safe wiv me. Now 'ow about us gettin' over ter the NAAFI, or all the best fellers are gonna be spoken for.'

Gloria Simpson was feeling pleased with herself as she waited for Frank Galloway in the Lyons tea rooms at the Bricklayer's Arms. He had promised to meet her there at three o' clock that afternoon and she was sure that he would be pleased with the information she had gathered from her friend Lola. Frank had promised her a sum of money for her assistance, but Gloria felt that there were more substantial rewards in the offing, if she played her cards right. Frank's marriage was on the rocks and he seemed keen to progress with their affair. He was obviously a wealthy businessman, and there was a mysterious side to him which she found exciting. He was so different from the men she was used to associating with. With luck she would soon be able to give up the game and let Frank take care of her.

At ten minutes past three Frank hurried into the tea rooms and flopped down heavily on the chair facing Gloria. 'The old man held me up,' he moaned. 'He called in just as I was getting ready to leave the yard.'

Gloria put on her best smile and touched his hand gently. 'Never mind, luv, yer not late,' she said.

Frank hid his revulsion and rewarded her with a brief smile in return. 'Well, what have you got for me?' he asked, trying not to look too enthusiastic.

Gloria reached into her handbag, took out a small notebook and opened it. 'Right, 'ere we are,' she replied. 'Mary O'Reilly is in 'er late fifties. She's a widow whose ole man died some years ago. 'Er boy Tony is in the army an' jus' got back from Dunkirk. She lives alone at that address.'

'What about the boy?' Frank asked impatiently. 'Where's he live?'

' 'E lives wiv 'is muvver, when 'e's on leave,' Gloria told him.

Frank nodded. 'What about the woman's habits?' he asked.

'What d'yer mean?' Gloria queried.

'Well, does she drink, and if so what pub does she use? Is she in the habit of going to the music hall and suchlike?'

'Don't yer want ter know a lot,' Gloria remarked, smiling at him again.

Frank was not amused and he gave her a cold look. 'Now listen, Gloria,' he said. 'I've a very good reason for wanting to know all I can about the O'Reillys, mother and son. I can't tell you why just yet, but I will, when it's right. Suffice it to say that it's very important to me that I learn all I can as soon as possible. Now you go back and get what information you can. I'll contact you before the week's out.'

Gloria looked crestfallen. 'Ain't we goin' out ternight?' she asked him.

Frank was looking forward to an evening with one of Bella's younger and equally flighty friends, a very attractive lady who was the soul of discretion. 'No, I can't make it,' he said quickly. 'Something very important has come up. I'll see you soon. I promise.'

Gloria sighed in resignation. She would have to be patient, she realised. There was time enough.

* * *

The tenants of the Kings Arms found themselves kept very busy during the summer evenings. Patricia was breathing easier now that her husband was not leaving her to cope alone twice a week. Terry was making the most of his respite from harassment by the crooked police inspectors, but he realised that it would not last for much longer. He had played his part acting as a link man between them and Bruce McKenzie and things had started to move down at the Elephant and Castle. Already there had been a clampdown on the small fry with quite a few arrests, but Terry knew that time was at a premium as far as he was concerned. The inspectors would not feel safe while he was in circulation. He knew too much for his own good and one day someone was going to come for him, he felt sure. They would not stop at him either. Patricia was equally at risk. At the moment, though, things were quiet. The Dougal McKenzie case had not come to court yet and Terry did not think that any of Dougal's cohorts would pay him a visit until the trial was over. In the meantime, he was making his own plans. Hopefully he and Patricia would be well away from London before very long.

In a backstreet not very far away from the Elephant and Castle, Tony O'Reilly sat talking to his sick mother in their little parlour.

'What was 'e like?' he asked her.

Mary stared into the black-leaded grate as she answered him. 'Yer farvver was a gentle man, Tony,' she said. ' 'E was very different from 'is bruvver Frank. Geoffrey was the apple of 'is farvver's eye an' ole man Galloway brought 'im in to 'elp 'im run the business when 'e was little more than a lad. Geoff's bruvver Frank was allowed ter go 'is own way though, but ter be honest I don't fink George Galloway trusted Frank wiv the responsibility o' the business.'

Tony sat thoughtful for a few minutes, thinking of the second meeting he had had recently with George Galloway. Suddenly he looked across to his mother. 'Why didn't me farvver ever take yer ter see the ole boy?' he asked.

Mary smiled cynically. 'Geoffrey Galloway was a very 'andsome young man,' she replied. ' 'E 'ad 'is pick o' the young women, but 'e was quiet an' studious. The sort o' woman 'e was attracted to never seemed ter go down well wiv 'is farvver. Geoff told me once that 'e did take one or two young ladies 'ome ter meet the ole boy, but 'e give 'em the cold shoulder. George Galloway preferred the loud, brassy women, the sort Frank went wiv. I wasn't brassy in the least, an' I was married ter me first 'usband at the time, though our marriage was goin' wrong. Anyway, me an' yer farvver fell in love. I couldn't stop it 'appenin'. When I realised I was 'avin' you, Geoff was in the army an' about ter go overseas. I didn't tell 'im, but then when you was born, Geoff promised me 'e'd take me ter see 'is farvver. As yer know, Geoff was killed in action soon after an' I vowed there an' then that I'd manage wivout any 'elp from the Galloway family. It was pride, Tony. I wanted yer ter grow up independent. Fings 'ave changed now though. I'm ill an' I'm not likely ter get better. I want ter die knowin' yer've got a good start in life. That's all I want.'

Tony could see the tears welling up in his mother's eyes and he went to her, putting his arm round her thin shoulders. 'Yer gave me a good start in life, Mum,' he whispered. 'Yer did it your way, an' I'm proud of yer. We don't need the Galloway money. I can make it on me own.'

Mary sat up straight in her chair and shrugged his arm away. 'Don't talk such rubbish,' she said loudly. 'That money is yer right, yer 'eritage. Yer real farvver worked ter build up that business, an' if 'e'd 'ave lived yer would've got it one day by right. Look, son, whatever decisions I made as a young woman left alone wiv a child 'as no bearin's on what's transpired. I gave yer me reasons fer goin' an' seein' George Galloway. Take what's yours by right. Let me die 'appy, will yer?'

'Yer gonna be around fer a long time yet, Ma,' Tony said softly. 'But if it's what yer want, I'll go along wiv yer wishes.'

'Yer a good boy, Tony,' she said, wiping away a tear. 'Just do what's right. Use what money yer get wisely. That way it'll bring yer 'appiness, not misery like it's done ter the Galloway family.'

Tony looked up at his mother. 'Misery?'

'Yeah, misery,' she replied. 'Money didn't do the Galloways any good. George Galloway's wife died while she was still a young woman. 'Is young daughter committed suicide by jumpin' in the Thames. There was talk of 'er bein' in love wiv one o' the Tanner boys an' the ole man ferbid 'er ter see 'im. Then Geoffrey was killed. Talk to anybody who worked fer Galloway. 'E was a pig to 'is men. Ask ole Nellie Tanner what she finks o' George Galloway. 'E sacked 'er feller while the poor sod was orf sick, an' that was after more than firty-odd years o' loyal service. It cost the Tanners their 'ome too. People say that was the reason Carrie Tanner went inter the transport game, so she could try an' put the Galloways out o' business. Mention the name Galloway round Dock'ead an' see the look on people's faces. The reason I know so much about it is because o' Nora Flynne. She used ter tell me fings.'

'Who's Nora Flynne?' Tony asked.

'Nora was George Galloway's 'ousekeeper,' Mary told him. 'She went ter work fer Galloway just after 'is wife died. It was 'er that come ter me wiv the news about Geoffrey. She was a lovely lady an' we got quite friendly. She spotted straightaway that I was pregnant an' she advised me ter go an' see the ole man, but I wouldn't. She used ter bring me bits an' pieces an' parcels o' food now an' then. In fact it was Nora who arranged a midwife for me. It was one of 'er close friends who'd delivered 'undreds o' babies round the Rovver'ithe area. Yeah, she was a lovely lady was Nora Flynne. She brought George Galloway's kids up an' she was very close ter young Josephine, Galloway's only daughter. She was 'eart-broken when the girl drowned 'erself an' she blamed 'im fer what 'appened. Anyway, she left after the tragedy an' took rooms in Rovver'ithe near ter where I'd bin livin' when you was born. I 'ad ter move out after I 'ad you. It was a big 'ouse we were livin' in an' times were really 'ard. I couldn't afford ter pay the rent any more. Anyway, I managed ter find this place which was a lot less rent an' that's 'ow we come ter live 'ere.'

'Did yer see much o' Nora Flynne after that?' Tony asked.

'I bumped into 'er about a year later. You was still in the pram at the time. We got ter talkin' an' she told me she was 'avin' ter get out 'cos they was pullin' 'er place down, so I told 'er about some places fer rent near me. She moved ter New Kent Road an' we used ter see a lot of each ovver after that. She used ter come round ter see me an' we'd sit fer hours chattin' over the past.'

'What 'appened to 'er?' Tony asked.

'She got very frail as she got older an' then she finally went into an institution. Must 'a' bin about two years ago. There was nuffing else for it. She couldn't look after 'erself an' she was nearly eighty years old.'

'Did yer ever go an' see 'er, Ma?' Tony asked her.

'No, I didn't, more's the pity,' Mary replied. 'I know I should 'ave done.'

Tony stretched. 'Well, I'd better be gettin' ready,' he said. 'I'm due back before mornin'.'

Mary watched as her son gathered his kit together and she was filled with sadness. She had seen his father go off to war, never to return. Tony had gone off once and been lucky to get back from Dunkirk without a scratch. Would he be so lucky this time?

In the Salter household a conference was taking place. Three pretty young women sat round the parlour table with cups of tea and occasionally they dipped their hands into the biscuit barrel for the rapidly diminishing supply of plain digestives.

'Well, this time we gotta put our foot down,' Brenda said.

'What can we do? After all, 'e ain't a kid,' Lily cut in. ' 'E's old enough ter know better.'

'It'll be in all the papers,' Barbara remarked. 'I won't be able to 'old my 'ead up at work.'

'Sod 'em all,' Lily said quickly. 'Yer don't mean ter sit there an' tell me that none o' them at work 'as never done a bit o' black-market stuff. Look at Lucy What's-'er-name. The ovver week she come in four days runnin' wiv salmon sandwiches. Then there was that dirty ole git, Alf Dockett. 'E was braggin' about bein' able ter get just about everyfing at 'is corner shop.'

'Yeah, but that's different from bein' brought up in front o' the

191

magistrate,' Brenda said. 'It makes yer feel like yer farvver's a criminal.'

'Well, I reckon we ought ter lay the law down,' Barbara told her two sisters.

'What we gonna do, send 'im ter bed soon as 'e gets in?' Lily said sarcastically.

'No, we'll tell 'im that if there's any more duckin' an' divin' on 'is part then we'll stop our 'ousekeepin' money. That should make 'im sit up an' take notice.'

Lily took the last of the digestives and dipped it in her tea. 'It's a shame really,' she sighed. 'Dad seemed ter change fer the better while 'e was wiv that Brenda Massey. I wonder what went wrong between 'em?'

'Yeah, I 'ave to admit yer right,' Brenda said.

'Next time I see Brenda Massey, I'll ask 'er,' Barbara declared.

'Yer can't do that,' Lily said. 'It's none of our business.'

'We could say that Dad's bin ill an' not responsible fer 'is actions,' Brenda suggested.

Lily shook her head. 'That's no good until we know why they split up. We might make fings worse.'

The conference was brought to a hasty end when the girls heard the front door. Maurice came into the room looking very worried indeed and slumped down in the chair. 'Well, we'll know the result termorrer,' he said fearfully.

'Don't worry, Dad, we'll club tergevver an' 'elp yer wiv yer fine,' Lily said helpfully.

'Where we gonna get fifty guineas from?' Brenda asked.

'If yer do go away, can we come an' see yer?' Barbara asked.

'Don't be so 'orrible,' Lily chided her. 'Yer won't get sent away, will yer, Dad?'

Maurice shrugged his shoulders. 'Six months I should fink,' he groaned.

'Wiv good be'aviour it'll only be four months,' Barbara remarked.

Lily got up to pour her father a cup of tea and when she put it down in front of him, he delved into the biscuit barrel and his face dropped. ' 'Ave all the biscuits gone?' he asked.

'It's them fat pigs,' Lily said, glaring at her sisters.

'You took the last one,' Brenda said loudly.

'I only 'ad two,' Lily told her.

Maurice put his hands up for order, knowing that when they started bickering, it went on for hours. 'Now listen ter me,' he began. 'I might go away termorrer. After all, it's no use finkin' ovverwise. Now I'm gonna tell yer a few fings an' I want yer ter listen. First of all, I want no young men in 'ere while I'm away. Next I want yer ter keep the place tidy, an' no bickerin' between yerselves. All do yer share an' fings'll run along nicely. Last of all, I don't want any of yer ter come visitin', understood? Them places are not fer the likes o' my daughters, even if their ole man's there. All I can say is, I'm very sorry fer what's 'appened an' fer the worry it's caused yer all, but I'll try an' change when I come out. That's a promise.'

There was total silence for a few seconds while Maurice's words sank in, then Brenda spoke. 'We know yer did it fer us, Dad,' she said kindly. 'We don't fink any less o' yer, do we, girls?'

'Course not,' Lily and Barbara said together.

'Anyway, we'll just wait till termorrer, an' if yer get off wiv a fine, we'll all go up the Kings Arms ter celebrate,' Lily said.

'I'll bake yer a nice seedy cake an' put a file in it, just in case yer do go down,' Barbara teased him.

Lily glared at her sister, feeling that Barbara's sense of humour was getting more and more warped.

'Right then, I'm orf ter bed,' Maurice announced, 'an' if that bloke Casey comes round wiv them dresses, put 'em under the stairs out the way. We don't want 'em on show.'

Chapter Twenty-Two

On Saturday evening, Carrie hummed contentedly to herself as she laid the table in the parlour and then stepped back to admire her efforts. She had used her best calico tablecloth and brought out the blue willow-pattern dinner set. The knives and forks were placed neatly beside the china and in the centre of the table was a small vase of asters, arranged delicately in a spreading spray. Beside the dinner plates Carrie had placed the matching teacups and smaller plates, and looking at it all she felt pleased.

It had been a hard week, but now, with Rachel home on weekend leave and her mother perking up after one of her bad turns, Carrie wanted tonight's meal to be a special one. Joe had slipped out for the evening paper and she could hear her daughter moving around upstairs as she positioned the chairs round the table and went into the scullery to check on the food. The potatoes were browning nicely and the small joint of beef sizzled in the fat as she pulled it from the oven to baste it once more. The Yorkshire pudding was rising and as she stepped back away from the heat Carrie felt satisfied. All that was left to do was to finish off the minted peas and make sure that the carrots and swede were soft enough. So far so good, she thought, turning to see Joe coming along the passage holding the evening paper.

' 'Ow long? I'm starvin',' he said, slipping his arms round her waist and nuzzling her neck as she lifted the lid of the steaming pot.

Carrie felt the familiar shiver of pleasure as his chin rubbed against the side of her face and she let her head arch back, offering her throat to his lips. He kissed it and then tried to turn her round but she gently protested. 'Go an' check the table, Joe, there's a luv, I'm ready ter serve up.'

Nellie came down the stairs wearing her favourite blue dress with her hair set in tight waves, and when Rachel followed down soon after, Carrie felt a glow of pride flow through her. Her daughter looked beautiful with her flaxen hair set down in deep waves round her ears and shaped across her forehead. Her figure looked especially shapely in her tight-fitting olive-green dress, which was open at the neck and puffed round the shoulders. She was wearing the necklet with a small gold pendant with its tiny sapphire centred inside some intricate

194

etching, the piece her grandmother had given her for her sixteenth birthday, and it pleased Carrie. Nellie would notice it and make a point of reminding everyone that she had worn that same necklet on special occasions when she was a young woman. The family was reunited once more and Carrie savoured the special moment before going out into the scullery to serve up the meal.

The summer evening light filtered through the net curtains and the clock above them on the mantelshelf chimed the hour of seven as Joe leaned back in his chair. Carrie and her mother were discussing the new contract and what it would mean if it proved to be regular, while Rachel was beginning to look slightly concerned as she eyed the clock and then cast her eyes round the table at the dishes. Joe's face hid a grin as he caught her eye.

'Leave all the washin' up ter me, Rachel,' he said casually. 'Yer don't want ter splash that dress.'

Rachel gave him a wide smile of thanks for his understanding. 'I'm meetin' Amy at eight,' she told him. 'It should be a good dance ternight. There's a good band an' it'll be nice ter meet up wiv everybody again.'

Carrie glanced at her daughter inquisitively. 'Is there anybody special yer 'opin' ter see there?' she asked.

Rachel shrugged her shoulders. 'Only the usual crowd, Mum,' she said dismissively, her mind flitting back to the last time she and Amy Brody had gone to the Samson dance hall.

Joe began to gather up the plates and Rachel looked at the clock once more. 'I'd better be gettin' ready,' she said, feeling slightly guilty at leaving the table after the effort her mother had put into the meal. She stood up and went round to plant a kiss on her mother's head. 'That was a lovely meal, Mum,' she whispered. 'I must get ready now.'

Nellie gave the young woman a sharp look as she went to her with a fond kiss. 'You be careful, young lady,' she said.

Rachel smiled as she exchanged looks with her mother and then she hurried up the stairs to her room. What would her grandmother have thought, she wondered, had she known about the recent camp dances and the lonely young servicemen who attended them, away from home and loved ones, many of them inexperienced and seeking to learn about love before going off to fight? What would her grandmother have thought had she known of the carryings-on behind the NAAFI buildings and in the dark places where couples consorted, the men groping and clumsily striving to make love, their partners sometimes fighting desperately to ward off the advances and sometimes only too willing to be taken?

These were desperate times, Rachel thought with a frown. Tomorrows were so full of uncertainties. In the early morning light, young men took off from airfields on patrol and flew out over the narrow strip of water dividing the opposing armies. Ratings sailed off to face the U-boats, and soldiers boarded troopships or waited in camps, not knowing where they might eventually end up or what fate had in store for them. Even at the airfield ground control, there was always the danger of a sudden attack from enemy bombers seeking to destroy the country's defences.

Rachel sighed deeply as she sat in front of her mirror and studied her face. She was getting too serious, too morbid, she realised. The night was young and there was fun to be had. Let tomorrow come, she decided. Tonight was for living.

As the evening light started to fade, Maurice Salter rolled up his sleeves in the scullery and splashed cold water over his face. He had been given another chance, no two, he corrected himself. There must be no more tempting providence, nor any upsetting of Granny Massey, accident or otherwise. From now on he would be the model father and an impeccable wooer. He had exhausted himself in his efforts to stay away from the expected stone-breaking, and in talking himself back into Brenda Massey's arms. His good fortune had been aided to a large degree by his three daughters and Maurice knew that he was in their debt, and that they would no doubt remind him of it occasionally, or a little more often.

The court at Tower Bridge had been crowded that Monday morning. There had been two sentencings before he was brought in front of the magistrate, a surly-looking lady in metal-rimmed glasses who he decided was definitely a man-hater. She had corrected the solicitor, criticised a court usher, had words to say about the mumbling in court, and last but not least moaned about the stuffiness of the place. Windows had been opened, the usher and solicitor concerned had apologised and the public were hushed before Maurice took his turn in the dock, shoulders hunched in disgrace.

'It was an act of charity, really, that led me inter this place, your worship,' he began. 'I 'ave three grown-up daughters who are careful to eat the right sort o' food an' they decided some time ago that they would not eat any more meat. I'm on shift work an' I get the shoppin' before I turn in, yer see.'

'Turn in?' the magistrate said shrilly.

'Go ter bed in the mornin's,' Maurice explained.

'Go on,' she prompted him.

'Well, bein' tired an' exhausted when I do me shoppin' I kept fergettin' that me daughters 'ave gone orf meat an' I still kept buyin' me ration o' corned beef,' Maurice went on. 'Anyway, one mornin' I looked in the cupboard fer some coppers that I keep in a tin there. I wanted it fer the street singer, yer see, an' I saw all these tins o' corned beef, yer worship. "Good gracious," I ses ter meself. "Fancy me bein' such a dunder'ead. I must stop buyin' this corned beef." '

'Will you please get on with it, I've got other cases to hear,' the magistrate complained.

'I'm comin' ter the point, yer worship,' Maurice added quickly.

'Be brief.'

'Well, wivout no more ado I put the tins in me saddlebag wiv the intention o' takin' the food ter the church ter be distributed amongst the poor an' needy, an' then if I don't get a message from me guv'nor ter say that some o' the men are orf sick and my presence is required there an' then ter keep the 'ome fires burnin'. I immediately did no more than get on me bike, bein' a patriotic citizen, an' pedalled as fast as I could ter work, only ter be stopped by the policeman who saw that I didn't 'ave no lights on me bike.'

'No lights?' barked the magistrate.

'It was me dynamo, yer see,' Maurice explained. 'I didn't 'ave time ter see if it was still workin'.'

The woman JP was beginning to wonder whether the defendant's own inner dynamo was still working. Impatiently she motioned to him to continue.

'It was then that the bag fell orf me bike an' the tins spilled all over the floor,' Maurice said obligingly.

'Is that all you have to say?' the magistrate asked, daring to hope.

'Jus' one fing more,' Maurice answered. 'I know yer've got yer job ter do, yer worship, an' whatever yer decide ter do wiv me is less important ter me that the plight o' the needy of our fine borough. Can yer see that the corned beef gets ter St James's Church? I want the poor ole sods – I mean people, ter benefit.'

The weary magistrate sighed loudly. 'It seems that this man should be in front of me for failing to display lights during the hours of darkness instead of being charged for attempting to distribute food to the needy,' she stated. 'I hope the arresting officer will take note of my remarks and make sure that the corned beef reaches the nominated church expeditiously. And in future refrain from wasting the court's time. Case dismissed.'

Maurice walked from court a free man, and into the arms of his delighted daughters.

'We've got a surprise fer yer, Dad,' Lily told him on the way home.

'Oh, an' what's that then?' Maurice asked.

'Jus' wait till yer get 'ome,' Lily replied.

Lily went into the house first, while her father was restrained at the front door by Brenda and Barbara for a few minutes. Then Maurice was almost pushed into the parlour and his daughters scurried off up the stairs.

' 'Ello, Maurice,' Brenda Massey said rather shyly as she stood up. 'I'm so glad yer got off.'

Maurice was taken aback and he could only stutter his thanks.

'I do 'ope we can be friends again,' Brenda said in a low voice.

'Of course we can,' Maurice replied beaming.

Brenda motioned him into a chair. 'Just you rest awhile. I can see you'll need some takin' care of from now on,' she said. 'Are yer feelin' all right now?'

Maurice had never felt better in his life but intuition told him to be careful. 'Well, I'm much better, now,' he said with emphasis on the last word.

Brenda slipped her coat back on. 'I've got ter get back ter work,' she told him with a smile. 'Can we see each ovver ternight?'

Maurice nodded. 'I'll be privileged,' he said, bowing slightly.

Lily, Brenda and Barbara gathered together in the parlour after Brenda Massey had left.

'What's s'posed ter be wrong wiv me?' Maurice asked them, grinning ear to ear.

'Breakin' up wiv Brenda caused yer to 'ave a collapse at work,' Barbara told him. 'The doctor tole yer it was 'eartache.'

'So 'e did,' Maurice grinned.

'Yer won't be grinnin' when yer get the bill,' Lily added.

'What bill?' her father said in alarm.

'One large bunch o' flowers fer Granny Massey an' a pair o' woolly bed socks. Then there was the box o' chocolates fer Brenda.'

'Flowers? Bed socks?' Maurice enquired.

'Barbara managed ter get ter see Brenda Massey an' she found out a few fings,' Lily said.

'Like Granny 'avin' cold feet in bed, I s'pose,' Maurice groaned.

The three young women nodded and then Maurice stood up with a very serious look on his face.

'Now I want yer ter listen ter what I 'ave ter say,' he began. 'I expect the lot o' yer are waitin' fer some sort o' praise. Well, I can tell yer now that what yer done fer me wasn't very nice. It was bloody marvellous! So on Saturday night I'm takin' yer all up the Kings Arms ter celebrate.'

Laughter rang out in the Salter household, and when the frivolity finally died down, Maurice turned to Lily. ' 'Ere, luv, are those dresses from Tom Casey still under the stairs?'

Now, as Maurice got ready to take his three daughters to the Kings Arms for the Saturday night celebratory drink, he addressed himself in front of the cracked scullery mirror. 'Maurice, if yer store any more bent gear under the stairs may the devil jump out o' there an' do fer yer.'

Then, as he turned his back on the mirror and slipped on his coat Maurice pulled a face. 'The next lot o' stuff goes under me bed,' he mumbled aloud.

* * *

The band was playing a waltz and Amy Brody danced dreamily in the arms of her current boy friend. Rachel, too, was on the floor, wincing now and again as her partner trod on her toes. Heavy-footed dancing partners seemed to be her lot at the Samson dance hall, she thought ruefully. She was feeling slightly disappointed with the evening. Hardly any of her old friends had turned up and the one or two who had were preoccupied with their partners. There had been little opportunity to chat and whenever Rachel took a breather Amy gushed on about her new beau.

'I never did worry about men wearin' glasses,' she went on. 'Some men look really attractive in glasses. Take Albert fer instance. 'E looks quite nice in those glasses 'e's wearin'.'

Rachel nodded, looking around at the motley gathering and feeling rather bored.

'Albert was really upset when 'e failed 'is medical,' Amy was saying. ' 'E wanted ter join the marines.'

Rachel nodded again, glancing over at the young man in question and noticing that his suit hung from his slim shoulders and his Adam's apple showed prominently above his loose shirt collar. She suppressed a smile, feeling that she was perhaps being unkind towards the young man. He might have made a good marine with training.

'Albert works in the City. 'E's a messenger fer a bank,' Amy continued. ' 'E's very romantic. 'E bought me a big bar o' chocolate last week an' then this week 'e came round wiv a bunch o' flowers. We might get engaged next year.'

The romantic young man had left his friends and was making his way over to Amy for the dance which had just struck up. Rachel took the opportunity to head off towards the bar, preferring that to the attentions of Albert's clumsy friend. As she reached the foot of a wide flight of stairs, she saw the young soldier. He was wearing his uniform with his forage cap tucked through his jacket lapel. Rachel felt her face go hot as he smiled broadly at her and she almost slipped on the steps.

'Well, if it ain't my carriage companion,' he said as he came up to her. 'It sure is a small world.'

'I was jus' goin' fer a drink,' Rachel replied, suddenly at a loss for words.

'Let me buy yer one,' he offered, taking her arm as they climbed the stairs.

Down on the dance floor Amy nestled in her young man's arms as they weaved in and out of the less competent couples, and Rachel watched her as she waited for her escort to collect the drinks. Occasionally she looked his way, making sure he did not see her appraising him. Finally he came back and placed the gin and orange at her elbow.

'My name's Tony,' he said as he sat down. 'Tony O'Reilly.'

'I'm Rachel,' she replied.

'I know. Rachel Bradley,' he said.

Rachel looked surprised. ' 'Ow did yer know my name?' she asked.

Tony grinned. 'I 'ope yer don't mind, but I bin makin' enquiries. My ex knows yer family.'

'Ex?'

'Yeah. We sort o' parted. We 'ad a row the last time I saw yer. Janie seemed ter fink I was payin' too much attention to yer.'

'I'm sorry,' Rachel said quickly.

'Oh, don't bovver ter be sorry,' Tony grinned. 'I was goin' back off leave an' Janie wasn't too 'appy about that eivver. Apparently she's found a new boy friend.'

'I remember yer tellin' me it was compassionate leave,' Rachel said. 'Yer mum was ill, wasn't she? 'Ow is she now?'

'She's not too bad at the moment,' Tony replied.

'Where yer stationed?' Rachel asked.

'We're regrouping up in Catterick,' he replied quietly. 'We got decimated at Dunkirk.'

'You were at Dunkirk?' she said surprised.

'I was one o' the lucky ones,' Tony said, looking down at his clasped hands. 'A lot didn't make it back, an' there was a lot wounded while we were waitin' ter be taken off the beaches.'

Rachel thought of Jamie Robins. 'I know a young man who lost a leg at Dunkirk,' she said sadly.

Tony shuddered and quickly downed his drink. For a few moments he sat looking at the dancers, but Rachel could see his mind was elsewhere. Suddenly she felt very close to him, wanting to take the young man to her and hold him tightly. At that moment it seemed as though they were the only two at the dance hall and a feeling of elation possessed her. She could feel her face growing hot once more and she struggled to relax, breathing slowly and deeply.

'Are yer all right?' Tony asked, his eyes upon her.

Rachel nodded and smiled. 'Let me buy yer a drink,' she said.

Tony shook his head. 'I'll get 'em,' he replied, standing up and reaching for the glasses.

Suddenly, almost without thinking, Rachel caught his hand in hers. 'I got a better idea,' she said breezily. 'Let's dance.'

Tony shook his head in embarrassment. 'I don't dance,' he said quickly.

'Anybody can dance, at least wiv me they can,' Rachel told him.

Tony reluctantly allowed himself to be led to the edge of the dance floor and as Rachel held up her arms he slipped his arm round her waist.

'That's fine. Now put yer arm up higher, jus' below me shoulder,' she urged him. 'Now just 'old me 'and loosely but firmly. That's better.'

They moved across the polished floor, and as Tony began to relax Rachel found him to be light on his feet. She could smell lavender water and Lifebuoy soap and he breathed in the perfume she was wearing and the sweet aroma of her hair. They danced closely, yet not holding too tightly, their thighs touching as she prompted the movements. Tony sighed to himself at the very pleasure of the dance while Rachel closed her eyes, wanting to savour the moment. He was a natural, she felt.

The evening wore on and Rachel found herself drawn to the young man more and more. He did not try to assert himself, but through his modesty and friendliness he made a strong impression on her. They talked of the war and its effect on people's lives, and of Rachel's family, about whom Tony seemed very interested. When she asked him about his family he became less talkative. She did not try to press him, and when another waltz finally started up, the young soldier was the first to get to his feet.

The night had settled over the river and the backstreets that adjoined the docks and wharves as Tony walked along beside Rachel. They had left Amy and her boy friend at the tram stop, preferring to stroll through the quiet streets together. Tony chatted easily, his dark eyes flashing at her occasionally.

'Yer know, we was destined ter meet,' he told her. 'Jus' fink of all the people I could 'ave sat wiv in that train an' it 'ad ter be you.'

Rachel smiled. 'Tell me somefing,' she said. ' 'Ow come yer went ter that dance ternight? After all, yer don't live in Rovver'ithe.'

'My ex-girl friend does though, but that wasn't why I went there ternight,' he hastened to add. 'I went there in the 'ope of seein' you.'

'I was 'opin' ter see you too,' Rachel said, surprised at her own forwardness. 'I wondered over the weeks where yer were, if yer'd gone overseas.'

'Can I see yer termorrer?' Tony asked suddenly. 'I'm due back on Monday.'

'If yer'd like to,' she replied.

'I'd like to very much,' he said.

They walked on, past the plane trees through which they glimpsed the dark, eerie shapes of the high cranes, their footsteps sounding loudly on the empty pavement. Rachel had not taken his arm, though she was walking close to him, and it was only when they crossed the main road that Tony briefly held her by the elbow. Rachel shivered and slipped up the collar of her beige coat, less against the elements than her own emotions. Tony had excited her and reawakened secret feelings that seemed to have died after the tragic death in action of her first love.

Tony too, was feeling strangely excited. He found the beautiful young woman very warm and friendly, with a sense of fun hidden behind her serious demeanour. He had already learned something of Rachel's family during the long talk with his mother, who had repeated the warning issued by George Galloway that he should not tell anyone of the plans made on his behalf.

They reached Salmon Lane and as they turned into the street Tony moved over to be on the outside, a little courtesy that pleased Rachel and she smiled at him.

'What time termorrer?' she asked.

'Let's spend the day up town,' he suggested. 'I could call fer yer early, say ten o' clock.'

Rachel felt a surge of excitement running through her but she pretended to think about it for a moment or two. 'Yes, all right, I'll be ready at ten.'

There was no goodnight kiss, only a brief hand on her arm as he turned to leave. 'I really enjoyed this evenin',' he said.

Rachel stood at the yard gate and waited until he had reached the end of the turning and passed out of sight. What did the future hold for them both? she wondered, pressing her finger on the yard bell-push. Was it sensible to think about what was to come in times like these? She heard Joe's footsteps in the yard and, with a brief look up into the star-filled sky, Rachel made a secret wish.

Chapter Twenty-Three

At breakfast time on a bright morning the following week, Rachel sat chatting with her friend Mary Hannen in the dining hall. The sky above West Marden was clear, with only a wisp of cloud, and an early sun shone through the dirty windows onto freshly scrubbed tables. The two friends were both on early shift that morning and during the few minutes' free time left to them Mary listened with keen interest as Rachel talked excitedly about her budding romance.

'We took the early tram ter the Embankment an' walked all around the West End,' she told her. 'Then we went inter this posh cafe fer coffee, an' then we went inter St James's Park. It was really romantic.'

'Did you have a kiss and cuddle in the park?' Mary asked with a grin.

' 'E put 'is arm round me an' we chatted a lot. 'E's really nice.'

'What did you do then?' her friend pressed her.

'Well, we stayed in the park fer quite a time,' Rachel replied, 'then we walked along Piccadilly an' went ter see this exhibition that was on. It was all about sculpture.'

Mary pulled a face. 'I bet that was boring.'

'No, it was really good,' Rachel said. 'We went ter the pictures in Leciester Square after that ter see *North-West Passage* wiv Spencer Tracey. It was smashin'.'

'What about when Tony brought you back home? Did you let him kiss you, passionately?' Mary asked with a saucy smile.

Rachel nodded, feeling her face getting red. She remembered that Tony had seemed reluctant to make the first move but then, when he suddenly came closer and slipped his hands on her waist, he had certainly kissed her with passion. Rachel recalled the feeling she had experienced as his body pressed against hers. It was delicious, and her heart pounded as his lips met hers in a long, lingering kiss which left her breathless.

'Well? Was it nice?' Mary repeated, enjoying her friend's embarrassment.

'Course it was.'

'Did he try to get you going?'

' 'Ow d'yer mean?'

'You know, did his hands start wandering?'

Rachel flashed her friend a quick look. 'No, they didn't. Tony was very proper,' she said indignantly.

Mary grinned back at her. 'Tim wasn't. The first time we went out together he was all hands. Men are all the same. It just takes some of them a little longer to get round to it.'

Their conversation was interrupted as the orderly officer came over to the table. 'You're wanted in admin, Hannen,' he said in an unusually quiet tone.

Mary shrugged her shoulders at Rachel as she hurried away. A few minutes later, as Rachel was making her way from the mess hall to the plotting room some distance away, the air-raid siren suddenly wailed out.

'Take cover!' a voice screamed out.

Rachel saw the officer running and at that instant she heard the loud roar of planes. Suddenly she saw them swooping down over the airfield, flashes of light coming from their wings. Personnel were throwing themselves flat, caught out in the open and unable to reach the dugouts in time.

Rachel turned towards a nearby mound of sandbags piled round a gun emplacement and threw herself down just in time as the first Messerschmitt passed over her. Other planes screamed low out of the clear blue sky and she pressed her hands tightly over her ears and gritted her teeth, her heart pounding madly, expecting any second to be blasted from her meagre hiding place.

The planes roared off, climbing high now, leaving behind them the first casualties West Marden had experienced. Someone was screaming out for help and as Rachel raised her head above the sandbags she saw the carnage. Two aircraftmen were lying still, their bodies twisted in grotesque positions, and one young aircraftwoman was sitting upright on the edge of the runway, holding the top of her arm and crying for help. Everyone seemed to be running now and the gun crew opened up beside Rachel, the deafening noise making her ears hurt.

'Get in the dugout quick as you can!' a flight sergeant ordered her as he hurried past.

Rachel dashed for the shelter while there was still a lull and as she hurried down the steep steps, she heard the roar again. This time it was more of a scream and a voice from the dugout shouted, 'Stukas!'

The dive bombers were dropping almost vertically and as they pulled out of the dive their bombs were released. One blasted concrete and earth skywards, leaving a large crater in the middle of the runway. Other bombs hit the hangar and another explosive turned a parked Hurricane into a ball of flame.

The Messerschmitts were returning, strafing the airfield with their machine-guns. Spurts of earth and tarmac shot up as the bullets hit and the planes climbed quickly, turning to make another run over the almost defenceless airfield.

Some pilots were able to take off before the airstrip was put out of action and they joined combat high over the Kent fields. A Stuka crashed in flames and another seemed to disintegrate in mid-air. White, shocked faces peered from the dugouts at the inferno, and as the roar of the attacking Messerschmitts increased, Rachel saw Mary. She was walking towards the billet, totally unconcerned by all that was taking place around her. It was as if she was in a trance, sleepwalking through the carnage, her head held low as though deep in thought.

Rachel screamed out her name but it had no effect on her. She walked on as the roar reached a new crescendo. Bullets spurted around her and one of the mechanics suddenly left the safety of the dugout and ran as fast as he could towards her, his head thrust forward. As he reached her he threw her to the ground, covering her with his body. All around them debris flew up into the air from the planes' cannon and bullets, and flames licked at destroyed aircraft that had been caught in the surprise attack.

The enemy planes climbed high towards the Hurricanes and Spitfires in combat above them, and Rachel gave a cry of joy as the two prone figures on the tarmac started to move. Mary was gripping a piece of paper as she was quickly led into the dugout and made to sit.

'You could have got killed!' the mechanic shouted at her angrily.

Mary looked through him, her eyes dull and lifeless. 'It doesn't matter,' she whispered. 'It just doesn't matter.'

The mechanic was about to say something more but Rachel shook her head at him. 'What is it?' she asked Mary quietly.

Mary just stared into space and Rachel reached for the paper clutched tightly in her hand. 'Let me see,' she said gently.

Mary clasped the piece of paper even more tightly, and then the orderly officer hurried into the dugout. 'Get her to the sick bay,' he ordered.

Rachel reached down to take her arm but the officer pulled her back. 'Not you, Bradley,' he said. Other willing hands guided Mary from the dugout and then the officer turned to Rachel. 'You're her best friend, I'm told,' he said.

Rachel nodded. 'Yes, sir.'

'Hannen got a telegram this morning. It seems her young man was killed yesterday,' the officer said quietly.

'Oh my Gawd!' Rachel uttered, sitting down heavily on the bench.

'Hannen's going to need you now,' the officer told her.

' 'Ow did it 'appen, sir?' she asked.

'It was some experimental work that went tragically wrong. That's all we know, all we're allowed to know,' he said.

The Battle of Britain was at its height over southern England when Bert Jolly walked along Page Street with the evening paper under his arm.

'They've shot down 'undreds,' he told Sadie.

'I know,' she replied. 'I jus' bin listenin' ter the wireless.'

Maisie came hurrying along the turning. ' 'Ere, Sadie, there's 'undred an' forty-four bin shot down, accordin' ter the wireless,' she said breathlessly.

'Ours or theirs?' Sadie asked.

'The Jerries, o' course,' Bert chimed in.

'I ain't talkin' ter you,' Sadie replied abruptly, giving him a sharp look.

Bert decided to leave them to it while Maisie leaned against Sadie's doorpost, glad of an excuse to leave the ironing.

'That silly ole sod is always pokin' 'is nose in where it's not wanted,' Sadie moaned.

Maisie nodded. ' 'Ere, Maurice Salter's back wiv that Massey woman,' she said, slipping her arms through the front of her apron. 'I saw 'em the ovver night. Bold as brass they was. She was all over 'im as they walked down the turnin'.'

'Don't it make yer sick,' Sadie remarked. 'That affair's bin on an' orf like a cock sparrer on a crust o' bread.'

' 'E's 'eadin' for a fall, if yer ask me,' Maisie replied. 'She's got a right name round 'ere.'

Dolly was busy in her front room and through the window she espied the two women deep in conversation. Being naturally inquisitive, she decided to take the women a new titbit to chew over. She slipped off her apron and put on the shabby coat she wore to go shopping before darting across to them.

'I'm just orf ter the corner shop fer Josiah's fags,' she lied. 'Did yer 'ear about ole Mrs Wishart in Bacon Buildin's?'

The two shook their heads.

'She got bound over ter keep the peace,' Dolly informed them.

'What was that for then?' Maisie asked.

'It was over whose turn it was ter do the stairs,' Dolly went on. 'Apparently ole Mrs Dalton ain't bin doin' 'em 'cos of 'er back an' when Mrs Wishart was scrubbin' 'em, Muvver Dalton trod dog shit all over the clean stairs. There was a bit of a bull an' cow by all accounts, an' then Mrs Wishart chucked the bucket o' water all over 'er. The police got called an' they nicked poor ole Mrs Wishart fer usin' bad language. Mind you, she can let it rip sometimes.'

'Well, I'd 'ave chucked more than the water over 'er if she'd 'ave trod shit all over my scrubbin',' Sadie said quickly. 'I'd 'ave crowned 'er wiv the bucket.'

'No, that's what Mrs Wishart done. She let go o' the bucket. That's why they called the police,' Dolly told them.

The three stood chatting for some time and when they saw Maudie approaching, Sadie sighed. ' 'Ere she comes, gloom an' doom.'

206

Maudie was looking very worried. 'There's bin bombs dropped in Croydon,' she said fearfully. 'I just 'eard it on the wireless.'

'It was on this mornin's news,' Sadie said offhandedly.

'I didn't listen ter the news this mornin',' Maudie said, holding her back. 'I 'ad a lay-in. Me back was killin' me.'

'It's those 'ard seats at the muvvers' meetin's what's doin' it, if yer ask me,' Maisie said, smiling at Sadie.

'I've stopped goin',' Maudie announced.

'Oh, an' why's that?' the women chorused.

'It's the new vicar,' Maudie explained. ' 'E's all fire an' brimstone. Scares the life out o' me, 'e does.'

'I like a bit o' fire an' brimstone,' Sadie said. 'Farvver Murphy was like that. 'E used ter rant an' rave at Sunday Mass. 'E's bin sorely missed around 'ere.'

Maudie decided that her back was not up to it and she took her leave. The three women continued their chat for a few more minutes then Dolly decided to get back home before Josiah came in from work.

'I feel sorry fer Dolly,' Maisie remarked as she watched her walking back to her house. ' 'Er Wallace 'as bin in trouble again.'

'What's 'e bin up to this time?' Sadie asked.

'They caught 'im pissin' on Mrs Brody's front doorstep an' 'er ole man give 'im a clip roun' the ear,' Maisie said. 'Dolly's ole man went roun' ter see the Brodys an' it nearly come ter blows, by all accounts. Then last week Wallace nicked the pram ole Mrs Webster uses ter collect the bagwash when she left it outside 'er front door, an' she 'ad ter go round an' see Dolly. They found it in Wilson Street the next day. All the wheels were missin'.'

' 'E'll get put away if 'e keeps that up,' Sadie told her. 'They can take 'em away if they're out o' control.'

'That's what Dolly's worried about,' Maisie said.

'She's got somefing else ter worry about too,' Sadie remarked.

'Oh, an' why's that?' Maisie asked her.

'She come out ter get 'er ole man's fags an' she's gone straight back indoors,' Sadie replied grinning.

'I tell yer, Danny, this 'eavy rescue squad they're formin' is a very good idea,' Billy Sullivan was saying over his usual weekend drink with Danny at the Kings Arms. 'What they're askin' for is buildin' workers an' carpenters an' all sorts o' construction workers ter volunteer. The likes of us know quite a bit about 'ow the places are made, an' should there be a bomb drop on a row of 'ouses, Gawd ferbid, we'd 'ave a bit more chance o' savin' lives when we're workin' in the ruins, proppin' up timbers an' such.'

'So yer goin' inter the 'eavy rescue then,' Danny said. 'Well, good luck ter yer, Billy, but I 'ope ter Gawd yer never 'ave ter put the idea inter practice.'

'I'll drink ter that,' Billy said with a serious face.

The pub was filling up as the two continued their chat, Billy talking about his coming visit to Annie and the children, and Danny telling him about his strange next-door neighbours the Dawsons. The piano was playing and a few of the regulars were singing. The balmy night and the sky full of stars formed a peaceful setting, far removed from war and the death and destruction soon to rain down on the little dockland community.

'I ain't seen 'im in 'ere before,' Billy said suddenly to his friend.

Danny glanced in the direction Billy nodded and shook his head. 'Nor 'ave I.'

Billy's face became serious as he studied the stranger. ' 'E seems ter be takin' a great interest in what's goin' on,' he remarked.

Danny regarded him cautiously. ' 'E could be lookin' fer somebody,' he replied, remembering what Billy had told him about the possible danger to both Terry and his wife Patricia. 'Anyway, it's none of our business.'

Billy continued to watch the stranger closely, noting how he constantly cast his eye around at the other customers from his table in the corner, and when he went to the counter to get his round he approached Terry. 'D'yer know 'im?' he asked.

Terry took a furtive glance in the stranger's direction and shook his head. 'Never seen 'im before,' he replied.

The evening wore on and half an hour before closing time, Maurice Salter walked in, nodding agreeably to one or two of his acquaintances. The stranger immediately got up from his seat and approached him. The two became engrossed in conversation and then the stranger hurried from the pub, and Maurice took his drink and sat down at the table next to where Billy and Danny were sitting. After a friendly nod to the pair he took out a notebook and scribbled into it for a few seconds.

'By the way, what size shoes do yer wives take?' he asked suddenly.

'Sixes, I fink,' Danny replied. 'Why d'yer ask?'

'I jus' done a deal,' Maurice said grinning cheerfully. 'I'm gettin' some small sizes. I'll let yer know when they arrive.'

Carrie had heard the news of the raids on southern airfields and she waited with bated breath until the phone rang early that same evening. Tears of relief welled up in her eyes as she heard Rachel's cheerful voice at the other end of the line. Joe sat down in the armchair and gave a huge sigh of relief. The war was moving closer, he realised. Soon the bombing of London would begin, and images of a terrible destruction, vivid in detail, plagued his sharp mind. He shuddered, feeling the need for just one drink to calm his grating nerves. He gripped his hands together tightly and stared down at them, fighting to ward off the dangerous desire that had suddenly assailed him.

Carrie looked at him, seeing the tension in him and willing him to be strong. No words were needed as their eyes met. She came to him, massaging his neck with her hands, her thumbs kneading the strong muscles on his wide shoulders. 'Is it bad?' she whispered.

Joe nodded, his eyes closed, his head held forward as the tension lessened. 'It's the first time fer ages,' he said presently.

'It's all right,' Carrie said softly, her hands and thumbs moving up his neck.

Joe let his body grow limp, his shoulders sagging and his head resting very low beneath Carrie's pressing fingers. 'It's passin',' he said in a low voice.

'I'm glad,' Carrie said, slowly going round to face him, her hands resting on his shoulders.

He reached out and took her to him, pressing his head into her round belly. She moved her fingers through his hair, urging him on with her desire. His hands slipped from her hips, down the length of her shapely thighs. He could feel her warmth, her reaction as she moved against him. He caressed her upwards now, inside her skirt this time, riding it up as his hands moved to the inside of her thighs. He remembered the earlier times, when they were new lovers, Carrie a young vibrant woman embarking on a new romance, and he felt the same hot desire for her.

Suddenly Carrie stepped back, her body just out of reach of his searching fingers, tempting him to come to her with a ghost of a smile touching her flushed face. Joe rose from his chair and clasped her, his arms encircling her, his body pressed against hers. His lips found her delicious neck and throat, her ears, her eyes. She sighed deeply, knowing that tonight was going to be special. 'Take me ter bed, Joe,' she groaned.

He swept her up in his strong arms, kicking the parlour door back as he carried her out through the darkened passageway and into the small bedroom.

'I want ter ferget everyfing ternight, Joe,' she whispered. 'Make me ferget.'

Very gently he put her down on the cool bedcovers, and in the darkness she moved against him as together they undressed each other, Joe kissing her bared breasts and stiffening nipples, his lips travelling down her body, brushing her heaving belly. He could feel her trembling and hear her panting breaths, coming faster now, as the tide of love flowed over her aching body. She arched herself and then like an explosion of passion she knew a new, wonderful love, and sank back, still trembling as he relaxed against her, his passion spent in the fulfilment of her desire.

Chapter Twenty-Four

On the first Saturday in September 1940 the sun shone down from a clear blue sky. Children were out early playing in the backstreets and women hurried back and forth from the market with laden shopping bags. The knife grinder pushed his contraption into Page Street early that morning and set it down on the bend of the road by the shelter gates, so that it was in view from both ends of the turning. A few curious children stood watching as the old man worked the treadle which set the stone revolving and sparks flying as he sharpened carving knives, blunt chisels, firewood axes and other implements that were brought out to him. Soon the children got bored and moved away, keeping their eyes open for the appearance of the ice-cream man, or the toffee-apple seller who always pedalled his bike into the turning with a loud cry that set the youngsters running. It began as a normal summer Saturday.

Billy Sullivan finished work at twelve noon and he met Danny at the Kings Arms for a lunchtime drink. Maisie finished her first round of shopping and made a cup of tea for herself and Sadie, the two sitting with their feet up in Maisie's parlour. Maudie sat in her parlour reading the *Daily Mirror* and worrying over the latest war news, while Dolly hustled the kids out of the back yard so that she could scrub it clean with the yard broom. Bert cornered a much mellowed Josiah and complained about kids clambering over the shelter roof and digging up the earth spread over the concrete, which in his estimation weakened the shelter, while Maurice Salter turned over in bed, trying to get a few hours' sleep after his night duty at the gasworks. His three pretty daughters painted their toenails and put their hair in rollers, wishing to make themselves attractive to the lucky men in their lives.

Round the corner in Bacon Street the old tenement block looked as grotty as ever, with the sun shining on the decaying brickwork, the rotting window frames and the leaning chimney stacks. The heat of the sun ripened the communal rubbish tip at the rear of Bacon Buildings and the stench began to drift out into the street. Children raced up and down the creaking wooden stairs and were told off by irate denizens who threatened them with unspeakable consequences. Elderly tenants of the eyesore tenement puffed up and down the stairs with shopping baskets, and opposite along the row of two-up, two-down houses, people stood chatting at their front doors, glancing up occasionally at the dirty windows and rotting sashes of their neighbours' flats. The rag-and-bone man came into Bacon Street and called out without much response, while children from the tenement block and the houses opposite sat together in the gutter, whipped coloured tops along the street or played marbles.

Not many streets away in the transport yard in Wilson Street, Frank Galloway sat with his foreman organising the Monday worksheets, and outside the yard man hosed down the cobbled yard. Lorries were returning and being parked for the weekend, the drivers arranging a drink together before going off home. At the end of the turning, children sat on the river wall watching the activity along the quays, the cranes swinging and the dockers shifting the cargoes, working in gangs and cursing the clumsy crane driver or the dithering carman. Tugs tooted and lightermen hauled on hawsers with scarred hands and leaned their body weight against the mooring poles.

In Salmon Lane the yard gates were secured open for the returning lorries and Carrie was busy in the office. Outside, Joe was tidying a pile of worn-out tyres, ready for the totter's call. Across the yard in the family house, Nellie sat at her bedroom window idly watching the men unloading a lorry in the yard of the pickle factory, while in the front bedroom Rachel was lying on her stomach on the bed, trying to apply herself to the difficult task of writing a letter to Mary Hannen. It was hard to convey in words just how sorry she felt for the unfortunate young woman, and she put down the pen and rested her head on the cool pillow. Mary was in a military hospital in Kent, recovering from a nervous breakdown following the tragic news she had received about her fiancé, Timothy. Rachel realised it was very unlikely that Mary would return to West Marden and she knew that she would miss her terribly.

Wallace had tired of playing with his brothers and sister, and as he sat hunched on the kerbside he watched the women hurrying back and forth with their shopping and felt it was time he took a walk to the market. There were usually apples lying under the stalls and he might be able to find a few to bring home. If he got some of those big apples that tasted nasty, he could smash them into pieces and take them to the river later to feed the swans that floated by when it was quiet. His attention was drawn to some children playing marbles in the gutter and one of the little coloured balls bounced over the cobbles and landed at his feet. Wallace picked it up and felt its smooth surface, watched by the children who were too frightened to ask for it back. He grinned lopsidedly and threw the marble across the cobbles, hoping they would ask him to play. The children hurried away and Wallace tried to remember what it was he had intended to do.

It was a normal summer Saturday.

At twenty minutes to five that evening Josiah Dawson was dozing in the parlour when he was rudely woken by a civil defence messenger who had pedalled furiously into Page Street.

'There's a red alert!' he gasped.

When he had roused himself properly by splashing cold water over his face, Josiah hurried out to Dolly who was putting her washing through the wringer in the tiny back yard. 'Keep them kids 'andy, luv, there's a red alert,' he said as casually as possible.

He strolled nonchalantly along Page Street, hoping he would not be stopped by any of his neighbours needing to chat. He whistled loudly as he reached the shelter gates, removed the padlock and then swung the gates back, only to be hailed by Bert Jolly.

'What yer openin' them gates for?' he asked the street warden.

'I 'ave ter test the 'inges every so often, in case they get rusted,' Josiah replied, feeling pleased with himself for his quick response.

'They should be kept greased,' Bert said knowingly.

Josiah walked off towards the main road without replying, to the annoyance of Bert who had intended to have a chat and find out something.

The roar of the air-raid siren sent the warden rushing back to his home. People were spilling into the street, startled by the frightening wail. Women came hurrying towards the air-raid shelter, holding on to scared children. Old men, young women, babies in arms, frail grannies and men in shirtsleeves converged on the corner of the turning. Josiah grabbed his daughter while Dolly took the hands of her sons, and together they hurried along with the rest of the community. A policeman stood at the shelter gates, urging everyone to keep calm, and as Dolly hurried down the slope to the shelter entrance, she turned to Josiah with a worried look on her face. ' 'Ave yer seen Wallace?' she asked breathlessly.

Josiah shook his head and Dolly raised her eyes to the heavens. 'That lad'll send me to an early grave,' she groaned.

Suddenly Wallace turned the corner and hurried past the Kings Arms, holding a splintered apple box in his arms. He caught sight of the policeman at the shelter gates and bit on his lip in anguish. Today he had found nice red apples, as well as some big sour ones for the swans. He stopped in his tracks, uncertain of just what to do, but a loud shout from one of the street folk jerked him into action. 'Don't stand there like a bloody idiot! Get in the shelter quick!' the voice commanded.

Wallace hurried on towards the shelter, his face red with exertion and fear of what the policeman was going to say about his apples. He need not have worried, for at that moment a drone filled the air and increased until it was a roar. Up above in the clear blue sky, black objects flew in close formation, breaking away as anti-aircraft guns opened up. Small puffs of white expanded high among the air armada and one plane seemed to blow apart silently.

The policeman was shouting at Wallace to hurry and the lad broke into a trot, his tongue hanging out of the corner of his mouth. The sound of exploding bombs mixed with the crash of anti-aircraft fire and black smoke climbed into the sky. Flames licked up and then a huge eruption of sparks burst into a wide spray, dropping to earth slowly.

'It's the Surrey! They're bombin' the docks!' Bert shouted as he hurried past the policeman.

Inside the shelter, people sat fearfully, listening to the din of battle. Children nestled against their parents, while Maisie and Sadie sat on each side of Maudie who was shaking violently. Dolly cuddled her brood close to her and a few feet away Iris Tanner gathered her children round her, talking in a low voice to reassure them. 'There, there. Now don't cry. It's our guns that's makin' the noise,' she told them.

Maurice had merely turned over in bed at the sound of the siren and it was his daughters screaming out for him to come down that woke him up properly. Together they had hurried to the shelter as the first bombs fell and Maurice was still cursing loudly at having his sleep interrupted.

In the adjoining cavern the Bacon Street folk sat together talking in low voices. Mrs Brown and Mrs Jameson were still puffing from their exertions after hurrying down from their top-floor flats. The elderly Mr Cuthbert sat studying the racing page, trying to look at ease but trembling inside. Tom Casey sat with his wife and their brood, making faces to allay the children's fears.

Bert had found himself a seat near Sadie and Maisie, who were still trying to comfort Maudie. 'Fousands o' tons o' wood in that Surrey,' he said with conviction. 'It'll burn like billy-o.'

'Shut yer noise, can't yer?' Sadie grated. 'Yer frigtenin' Maudie.'

Bert gave Sadie a hard look and left his seat to join the rest of the men who were gathered under the concrete canopy at the entrance to the shelter. Heads were peering out at the darkening sky as the huge pall of smoke spewed out and upwards from the doomed timber docks a little way downriver. The sound of fire engines added to the din. A messenger lad came pedalling madly into the turning and handed the policeman a note.

'Yer wanted at the warden's post soon as the raid's over,' the constable informed Josiah.

Bert nudged Tom Casey, who had come out of the stuffy interior for a breath of air. 'I feel sorry fer those poor bleeders downtown,' he said. 'They'll be blasted inter kingdom come.' Tom stared at Bert vacantly as he went on, 'If them bridges are down they'll be isolated.'

Josiah caught the elderly Job's comforter roughly by the arm. 'Keep yer voice down, yer'll frighten the women an' kids,' he growled.

' 'E's frightenin' me,' Tom said.

Danny Tanner stood on the deck of the speeding tug along with two other lightermen as the craft made its way to the conflagration that was Surrey Docks. He had seen Iris and the children safely into the shelter before answering the call to try to save as many barges as possible. As he watched the smoke and flames rising high into the red sky, he feared for the future. If this was a sample of what modern warfare was like, then God help us all, he thought.

The tug neared the flames and the heat was intense. Smoke drifted out into the middle of the river and burning resin from the seasoning timber poured down over the river wall and set the Thames alight.

'Those two!' the tug skipper shouted. 'There's not much time.'

Hawsers were attached to the barges and slowly they were turned and manoeuvred into midstream. One of the lightermen slipped in his haste and fell onto the edge of the barge rave. His colleague rushed over, barely managing to pull him back from a fiery death in the burning resin below him.

Danny had secured the other barge and was still standing aft as the tug hauled the brace from danger. Bombs were falling as the aircraft made yet another bombing run and one loud explosion nearer than the rest sent Danny sprawling. He managed to grab a hawser ring as his legs shot over the side of the barge and he held on, gritting his teeth as he slowly pulled himself away from danger. As soon as he recovered enough to sit up, he looked across at the other barge. The two lightermen had disappeared. Danny's heart sank and he hung his head in grief. He had known Mickey French and Lofty Barnett for a number of years. They were both his age, good, skilful lightermen, and they both had families.

Smoke was drifting along from the Surrey and it was difficult to see the tug clearly, but Danny knew that the skipper would not have been able to do anything to help his comrades, even if he was aware that the two men had fallen into the burning water. Danny held his head low as the barges were slowly towed away from the thick smoke and flames, occasionally glancing back to what looked like hell itself. The barges were to be moored at Butler's Wharf, just downriver from Tower Bridge, and as Danny prepared to jump ashore and secure the hawser, his heart leapt. His two colleagues were getting up from their prone positions on the other barge, their faces coal-black from the smoke. He had been unable to see them behind the rim of the hold and he had assumed the worst.

'Danny, yer look like a bloody chimney sweep,' his friend Mickey called out.

'You could do wiv a bar o' Lifebuoy yerself,' Danny shouted back as he hauled on the heavy rope.

George Galloway left the Saracen's Head public house and made his way slowly home, leaning heavily on his walking cane. The day was fine and warm, and George decided he would sit in the nearby St James's Park for an hour or so. His thoughts were centred on his grandson Tony, and he hoped that the lad would take heed of the advice he had been given. If so, there was a very good chance of the Galloway name being carried on now, the old man told himself. The lad had Galloway blood and would prosper, providing he survived the war. It was a shame about his mother, but it was not his fault she had left it so long to get in touch. In fact the woman should have come to see him when the lad was a baby. He could have been placed in a good school, got an education and the best start in life. George reached the park gates and he walked into the quietness of the trees and lawns. Provided he lived a few more years, and the war permitting, he would at least be able to instil a little bit of business sense into young Tony.

The early afternoon was warm and George settled himself in a seat beside a flower bed. The Scotch and the walk had made the old man drowsy and soon his head drooped. Suddenly he was woken by the wail of the siren and when he looked at his watch he saw it was five o' clock. He had slept for nearly two hours and his back and legs felt stiff. He got up slowly and hobbled out of the park towards Tyburn Square. The bombing started. George could see black smoke and flames rising into the clear blue sky. Without thinking, he rubbed the gold medallion between his thumb and forefinger, a habit of years whenever he was troubled or deep in thought. He hurried on a little, his walking cane tapping on the pavement, and when he finally reached Tyburn Sqaure the sky was turning purple with the flames and smoke. Cyril Botley was standing at the bottom of the short flight of steps to his front door, gazing skyward.

'You'd better come down to the shelter, Mr Galloway,' he called out.

George growled to himself. The man was a bloody nuisance. He had constructed a shelter in his basement with large timbers and girders, equipped it with armchairs and all the comforts he could think of for him and that silly woman of his, and had insisted that George share it with them in time of danger, as he put it. The elder Galloway had no intention of sharing a shelter with anyone, let alone that pair of wet blankets. He had decided that if there should be air raids, he would get drunk as quickly as possible and sleep through them. If the house was hit by a bomb he would know nothing about it anyway, and as far as the noise was concerned, a large quantity of good Scotch whisky would solve that little problem.

'No, it's all right. I'm goin' in fer a drink,' George replied.

'Nonsense, there's an air raid taking place!' Cyril said sharply. 'You'll be a lot safer down with us. Besides, I promised your son Frank I'd keep an eye on you.'

George swore under his breath. Frank was going to get a good telling-off for making other people think that he needed to be watched out for, he vowed.

'Come on, Mr Galloway, in you come,' Cyril insisted, going towards him and taking his arm.

'I need a drink,' George moaned.

'There's a drink in the shelter,' his neighbour told him with a wink.

Reluctantly George allowed himself to be shepherded into the house, down a flight of stairs to the dimly lit basement and into a low armchair facing Beryl Botley. As his eyes grew accustomed to the light, he saw that his neighbour had been very busy with his shelter. Carpet covered the floor and there was a cabinet in one corner, on which stood a wireless. The walls had been decorated with a flower-patterned wallpaper and the ceiling was freshly whitewashed.

'Mr Galloway needs a drink, dear,' Cyril said, standing beside the cabinet and waiting for her reaction.

'Very well then, but you'd better be careful, Cyril. You know what the doctor said,' Beryl reminded him.

Cyril grinned at George and poured a tiny amount of whisky into two glasses, then handed one to his guest. 'Here's to us,' he said jovially.

George looked disdainfully at the tiny measure and gulped it down before his host got his glass to his lips. 'Cheers,' he said sarcastically.

'Shut that cabinet now, Cyril,' Beryl ordered, holding her temple as though in pain.

'Headache, Beryl?' her husband asked.

'I've got a touch of migraine,' she answered.

'Can I get you a cold flannel, dear?' he asked dutifully.

'What she needs is a stiff drink,' George growled.

'I can't stand the stuff,' Beryl groaned. 'It makes me ill. Yes, get me a cold flannel.'

Cyril hurried up the stairs and George stared with open distaste at the thin woman sitting facing him, feeling that he would like to take his stick to her.

'Why don't yer put yer 'ead between yer legs?' he suggested with the beginnings of a crooked smile on his whisky-flushed face.

'I've a headache, I don't feel faint,' she told him sharply.

'Yer don't look too good,' George said. 'In fact yer look as white as that ceilin'.'

Beryl gave the old man a hard look and averted her eyes quickly, believing that she had made her dislike clear. Cyril was soon back, fussing over her.

George looked longingly at the drinks cabinet. 'That whisky was ice,' he said. 'I like a good whisky.'

Cyril was too busy holding the flannel to Beryl's brow to take much notice, but George was not giving up yet.

'Is that Irish or Scotch?' he asked nodding to his empty glass.

Cyril still did not take heed and George struggled up from his uncomfortably low armchair.

'Where are you going, Mr Galloway?' Cyril asked quickly. 'The air raid's still on.'

'I'm goin' back ter my place an' I'm gonna get pissed,' he replied, giving Beryl a blinding look. 'I'm not gonna get pissed 'ere, am I?'

As soon as he had left, Beryl threw the flannel down on the floor by her feet. 'I don't want that horrible man in here again, is that understood?' she said bitterly.

'But I promised I'd keep an eye out for him,' Cyril said meekly.

'The devil takes care of his own,' she replied.

In the adjoining house George settled down to another Scotch, reminding himself to have a word with Cyril Botley at the first opportunity. The man will have to threaten her with a good hiding or he'll end up making his life a misery, he thought, bringing his cane down heavily on the seat of the empty chair facing him.

Carrie and Joe had decided very early on that should there be air raids, they would take refuge in the cellar of the house. It had been reinforced with large timbers and some chairs had been left down there ready. Joe had run an electric cable down for lighting and placed sandbags against the narrow windows set in the base of the house to protect against flying glass. He was satisfied that they would be safe enough, unless the house suffered a direct hit.

When the bombs started to fall, Joe ushered Carrie and her mother into the cellar down the narrow, creaking stairs. Nellie was white-faced and trembling. Carrie was worried about Rachel, who had gone to see her friend Amy.

'She'll be all right,' Joe said to reassure her. 'There's a shelter right close to Amy's.'

When Joe had settled Carrie and her mother in the cellar, he went up the narrow flight of stairs and out into the yard. High to his right, clouds of black smoke blotted out the strong sun, and he saw sparks and flames above the rooftops of the adjoining houses. The stench of charred wood carried into the yard, and above the firing guns and explosions he could hear the constant clanging of fire bells.

The raiders at last turned for home, but the all-clear siren did not sound. The roar of anti-aircraft guns ceased and only the faint sound of a fire bell shattered the eerie silence that had settled over the little riverside streets. Carrie and Nellie emerged from the cellar and joined Joe in the yard, staring up at the angry sky.

A few minutes later Rachel hurried into the yard. 'It's all right, Mum, I was in the street shelter with Amy,' she said quickly, seeing her mother's concern. 'It's terrible. I 'eard the Surrey's bin destroyed and there's a lot o' people killed downtown.'

Nellie put her handkerchief to her mouth. 'Gawd 'elp us all,' she said in almost a whisper.

It had started as a normal summer Saturday and became a day that would never be forgotten by the folk in the riverside backstreets of Bermondsey and Rotherhithe.

Chapter Twenty-Five

After the bombers had left, the people of Page Street stood on their front doorsteps gazing up at the blood-red sky. Vast fires were still raging out of control at the Surrey Docks and more and more fire tenders were being brought in to fight the conflagration. Now and then someone came into the little turning with more information about the air raid, and the news was quickly passed along from one small group to another.

'The downtown bridges are smashed and there's fousands waitin' ter get away,' the lamplighter said as he pedalled his bicycle into the street gripping a small ladder and steering with one hand.

Old Mrs Haggerty was hard of hearing and she knocked on her neighbour's front door. ' 'Ave yer 'eard the news?' she said. 'There's fousands trapped downtown. Somefink ter do wiv the bridges.'

Mrs Watson hurried to tell her friend who lived a few doors away. 'There's tens o' fousands trapped downtown,' she told her breathlessly. 'It's the bridges.'

Ida Green was prone to exaggeration. 'There's 'undreds o' fousands killed downtown,' she told her next-door neighbour. 'On the bridges, by all accounts.'

Thousands of Rotherhithe folk were in fact waiting calmly and patiently to be evacuated from a devastated area around the Surrey Docks which was cut off from the rest of Rotherhithe by a navigable waterway linking the Russia and Greenland Docks to the Surrey Basin. The road bridges over the water had been damaged, and for the time being only fire tenders were allowed to cross. The downtowners, as they were called, had suffered badly and many of their riverside homes had been destroyed, but their plight was being magnified to such a degree that many folk in the dockland backstreets of Bermondsey were convinced that most of their downtown cousins had perished, and that they too were going to be wiped out in the next air raid aimed at the dock area.

People waited anxiously all evening for the all-clear siren to sound, but instead, when the hour grew late and darkness drew in, the drone of aircraft filled the angry sky: the second air armada that day was being guided to its targets by the red glow over London.

Bombs started to fall once more and the shelter in Page Street was soon filled to capacity. Babies cried incessantly and young children sat huddled against their mothers as the din of battle reached a crescendo. Outside the twin caverns, men stood around together in the scant safety of the concrete canopy and worried for their families and for their little homes that were sited in the shadow of the docks and wharves.

Billy Sullivan sat with the rest of the heavy rescue squad in a reinforced garage in Abbey Street, where phone lines were linked to a central control. The men waited for their first call, having been hastily assembled with little or no time for training. When it came, it concerned a tannery that had been hit in Bermondsey; there were shelterers trapped in the basement. The heavy lorry roared from the garage through burning streets and two minutes later they arrived at the factory.

The rescue workers, wearing blue overalls and steel helmets with the letters HR on the front, set to work immediately shoring up the entrance of the basement shelter with heavy timbers pulled from the debris. The squad leader Jim Davis took control and barked his orders to the team, joining in as the men struggled with the timbers. Jim Davis was a stocky individual with grey hair, pale blue eyes and a massive pair of hands. He was a site foreman for a large building company, and his knowledge of the building trade and ability to handle men made him a natural squad leader.

'I can 'ear voices,' one of the men shouted to him as they laboured among the ruins.

'Oi, you lot, shut yer noise a minute, will yer,' Jim barked out as he lowered his head to the ground.

The faint sounds of singing carried up through the rubble and the rescue team redoubled their efforts to force a way through the huge pile of debris, only too aware that the whole building was threatening to collapse on them at any minute.

' 'Ere's the door,' a worker shouted as he strove to move a huge block of concrete to one side.

Billy Sullivan lent his muscle to the task and finally the door was prised open. Jim Davis shone his torch down the flight of stone stairs and saw white faces staring up at him.

'Fank Gawd!' one shouted as they climbed up and were quickly led to safety, their spirits having been kept high during their ordeal by a large woman with bright ginger hair who had conducted the community singing and now led the way out.

'There's two still down there an' they won't come out yet,' she shouted to Jim Davis above the din of explosions and gunfire.

'What d'yer mean, yet?' Davis shouted back.

'See fer yerself,' she told him.

The squad leader beckoned for Billy to follow him and the two descended the stone stairs, treading carefully over the scattered debris. In the dim light of an oil lamp hanging from a rafter they saw two elderly men seated on empty boxes with playing cards spread out in front of them on a larger box they were using as a table.

'Oi, you two!' Jim shouted. 'Get yourselves up them stairs.'

' 'Ang on a minute, mate,' the smaller of the two called out. 'There's a few bob runnin' on this 'and.'

'Listen, yer dopey pair,' Jim growled at them. 'This buildin' is in danger o' fallin' down on top of us. Sod the money. Get up them stairs while yer still can.'

The smaller man gathered up the pile of silver and coppers and the two hobbled up to the surface.

'Don't put that sprasy in yer pocket, Titch. That's stake money,' his opponent growled.

'I ain't gonna do no such fing,' Titch replied. ' 'Ere, you mind it,' he said to the big squad leader.

Jim Davis gave the little man a blinding look. 'Piss orf an' find yerself anuvver shelter, Titch,' he said angrily. 'We've got work ter do.'

All night the bombs rained down and through the long hours people sat in stuffy shelters, mothers with children asleep on their laps and babies cuddled in their protective arms, and others caring for their aged parents.

Granny Massey sat between her two daughters Brenda and Rose and feigned sleep, her sharp ears alert for anything that might be said about her. Brenda sat staring up at the concrete roof and winced every time a gun roared or an explosion rocked the shelter. The bombs were getting nearer and occasionally dust fell from the roof as loud blasts seemed to lift the solid concrete structure. Earlier one or two of the Page Street folk had attempted a sing-song with their neighbours but now they all sat quietly, wondering if they would survive the night.

Granny Massey opened her eyes and looked around her. 'Me feet are cold,' she groaned.

Brenda adjusted the blanket Granny had round her but to no avail.

'I'm goin' back ter me bed,' she announced.

'Don't be silly, Mum,' Rose said sharply. 'The bombs are still fallin'.'

'I ain't worried about bloody bombs,' the old lady replied. 'When yer gotta go, yer gotta go.'

'Well, you ain't goin' nowhere, so shut up an' sit still,' Brenda told her.

Granny Massey dabbed at her eyes with a handkerchief. 'Nobody loves yer when yer old,' she moaned.

Brenda sighed in resignation and turned her thoughts to Maurice Salter. He had been on night shift for the past two weeks and their

221

meetings had been very brief. He had managed to mollify her mother somewhat, and now the old lady merely ignored him, much to Brenda's dismay. Maurice was a very nice man, she felt, with a heart of gold, but sadly a head full of ridiculous ideas for making money.

'I'm not sittin' 'ere all night,' Granny said suddenly. 'Soon as it gets a bit quiet I'm orf 'ome.'

Brenda and Rose exchanged exasperated looks and pretended they had not heard, which irritated Granny madly. 'That's it,' she announced, standing up. 'I'm goin'.'

'Look, Mum, yer can't go outside,' Brenda implored her along with Rose, trying to coax the old lady back on the bench.

'Leave me alone. I know what I'm doin',' she croaked.

Brenda was getting embarrassed at her mother's behaviour and she looked appealingly at Sadie Sullivan and Maisie Dougall who were sitting opposite. 'Tell 'er,' she urged them. 'Tell 'er 'ow dangerous it is outside. She don't understand.'

'Oh yes I do,' Granny said.

'Sit down, yer scatty ole mare, yer showin' yerself up,' Sadie scowled at her.

'Who you callin' a scatty ole mare?' Granny Massey shouted at Sadie.

'You, that's who,' Sadie shouted back.

'My mum's not a scatty ole mare,' Brenda told Sadie sharply.

'Well, yer could 'ave fooled me.' Sadie growled under her breath.

'Why don't yer try ter get some sleep, luv,' Maisie urged the old lady. 'It'll do yer good.'

'Sleep? What wiv all that racket goin' on outside?' Granny replied. ' 'Ow can anybody sleep?'

'You'll sleep in a minute if yer don't shut yer bleedin' noise up,' Sadie muttered.

'What did you say?' Brenda asked quickly.

'Sadie said yer muvver'll be able ter sleep if that noise shuts up,' Maisie cut in, trying to avoid further nastiness.

Granny Massey closed her eyes again and this time she went off into a deep sleep. Meanwhile Rose sat discussing her evacuated children with Brenda, while Sadie and Maisie stared at their feet and occasionally shifted uncomfortably on the hard wooden bench. The air was very stuffy and it was made even more close by the heavy gas blanket draped over the shelter door. The smell of carbolic drifted out from the makeshift toilet at the end of the cavern and the two suspended kerosene lamps gave off smoke fumes that hung in the air and stung the back of the throat. Still the bombs fell, some a muffled rumble, others louder and more frightening as the shelter shook. People tried to remain calm, but there were screams and shouts of terror whenever an explosion made the refuge lift and shudder, and the shelterers wondered whether

222

the whole place might be torn apart with them buried beneath it. Occasionally some of the men came in to see how their families were faring and they were asked how bad it was. Their shocked faces said it all as they shook their heads.

All through the first night of the blitz Carrie sat with Joe, Rachel and Nellie in the cellar of their house, fearing that at any moment the whole place was going to collapse over them. Joe tried to make light of their danger with small talk but even he lapsed into silence as the bombs got nearer. Rachel was holding onto her mother's arm, while Nellie sat in the armchair Joe had brought down and tried to get on with her needlework.

' 'Ow will yer get back ter camp if the railways are damaged?' Carrie asked her daughter.

Rachel shrugged her shoulders. 'I'll just report ter the RT office on the station. They'll sort it out,' she replied.

'P'raps they'll send yer back 'ome fer a few more days,' Nellie said without looking up from her sewing.

'I wouldn't fink they'd do that, Gran,' she laughed. 'They'll lay on buses or lorries ter take us back.'

After a while there seemed to be a lull in the bombing and Joe ventured up into the scullery to make a pot of tea. Rachel sat quietly thinking that it was likely to be less dangerous at camp than in Bermondsey from now on, and she knew she would be very worried about her family's wellbeing once back in West Marden. At least at the camp there was a job to do, and it was a vital one. She had friends at camp, and there were the occasional dances or social evenings to liven things up. She thought about Tony and where he might be at that particular moment. Would he be on guard duty and getting the news of the bombing of London? Was he thinking of her and wishing that they could be together? Thoughts hurried across her mind and Rachel sighed to herself. Tony had captured her heart and the very thought of him sent little shivers of pleasure running through her body. The regular letters she received from him were tender and romantic and she replied in the same vein. It had become a courtship by mail and she knew for certain that she desired him, needed him to put his arms round her and keep her safe. How wonderful it would be if he had been able to sit with her on this terrifying night and wrap her in his arms, she sighed.

Carrie had been quietly observing her daughter and sensed that she had her soldier boy friend on her mind. She had spoken to Joe about the sudden change in Rachel and Joe said that he had noticed the difference too. The old sparkle had returned to her eyes and she seemed more vital, more alive. Carrie had been delighted to see it but she knew that it could all end so suddenly. Derek had been cruelly taken from her at the time when she was happiest. Tony had given her back her old zest for life, but he too was a serviceman, and he could be taken from her just as swiftly.

' 'Ave you 'eard from yer young man lately?' Carrie asked, already guessing the answer.

'I get a letter almost every day,' Rachel replied, smiling.

'I don't know what yer find ter write about,' Nellie butted in.

'There's lots ter write about, Gran,' she told her.

'I 'ope yer not gettin' too serious, the way fings are,' Nellie retorted.

'They're just good friends,' Carrie cut in, eyeing her daughter and smiling at her.

'That's as it should be,' Nellie went on. 'I can't see the sense in gettin' too serious wiv a young man, especially when 'e's in the army. 'E could be sent overseas at any time, an' where are yer then?'

'On yer own, I should fink,' Carrie said jovially.

Nellie went back to her sewing. Joe came down with the tea and the guns opened up once more. They could hear the drone of planes overhead as a new wave began their bombing runs, then the house shook violently. Nellie cowered in her chair and Joe instinctively went to Carrie.

'That was a close one,' Rachel gasped.

Another loud explosion shook the house, and another in quick succession. Nellie was rocking to and fro in her terror and Carrie went to her, her arms encircling her, while Joe put his arm round Rachel's shoulders and let her nestle her head against his chest. The light faltered and then went out, leaving the family in complete darkness. Joe took out a box of matches from his pocket and struck one, searching for the oil lamp he had brought into the cellar for just such an emergency. A loud explosion rocked the house once more.

'It's the wharves,' Joe said as he lit another match and kindled the oil lamp. Dust filled the air and a strong smell of burning drifted through the cellar. 'I've gotta go an' see. It might be the lorries,' he exclaimed, hurrying up the stairs.

'Be careful, Joe, fer Gawd's sake,' Carrie called out after him.

As he stepped out into the open, Joe saw the flames rising high into the night sky from a burning wharf behind the yard. He shuddered as he watched, the flames becoming a huge shower of sparks as the wharf caved in. He could hear the sound of fire bells and running feet outside the yard.

'Wilson Street's copped it,' someone called out to a colleague.

'So's Abbey Street,' another shouted back.

Joe turned back into the cellar, knowing there was nothing he could do, other than comfort and try to protect the women. All around him flames were shooting skywards, and then another, louder roar of aircraft filled his ears.

Josiah Dawson knew that at times such as these people were looking to him, as street warden, for comfort and security. He had a position to uphold and he was a proud man, if somewhat headstrong. Tonight he had not spared himself. After making sure that Dolly and the children and Wallace were safely installed in the shelter, he did his rounds. The blackout regulations were being observed to his satisfaction and he had reported in to the ARP post in Jamaica Road. So far so good, Josiah thought to himself as he stood in the doorway of the corner shop to light a cigarette, his steel helmet down over his forehead to shield the light of the match. Explosions shattered windows and rattled doors as guns roared and shrapnel fell around him. Josiah gritted his teeth and hunched his shoulders as he hurried back along the turning, staying close to the houses for protection against the flying metal. Suddenly, in the eerie light reflected down the little turning from the burning wharves, he saw Maurice Salter pedalling his bicycle towards him and holding onto what looked like a torso on a pole.

Maurice pulled up outside his house and dropped his bundle onto the pavement while he removed his cycle clips, seemingly unconcerned at the din around him.

'Get yerself inside!' Josiah shouted at him. 'There's shrapnel comin' down.'

Maurice looked surprised at seeing the warden and he gave him a lopsided grin. 'I found it in the Ole Kent Road as I come past,' he said as he put his key into the lock. 'C'mon in fer a few minutes, I'll make us a cuppa.'

Josiah tucked the padded torso under his arm and followed Maurice into the scullery. 'What the bloody 'ell d'yer want this for?' he asked.

'Well, as a matter o' fact I thought it might come in 'andy fer Brenda,' he replied grinning. 'She's doin' dressmakin'. It's a tailor's dummy.'

'I can see that,' Josiah said. 'Anyway, what yer doin' 'ome at this time? I thought yer was on the night shift.'

Maurice had leaned his bicycle against the scullery door and was searching his pocket for matches. 'They caught the gasometer so we 'ad ter shut the furnaces down,' he replied. 'We're back in the mornin', please Gawd.'

Josiah winced as a nearby explosion rocked the house but his host did not seem in any way perturbed. 'I'll make us a nice cuppa,' he grinned, putting the match over the gas ring. 'Sod it, I fergot the gas was cut orf,' he said, shaking his finger as he dropped the burnt-down match.

Josiah made to leave but Maurice suddenly caught his arm. ' 'Ere, I know. There's a drop o' brandy in the cupboard,' he said lightly. 'Let's 'ave a snort.'

Two hours later the street warden left the Salter house feeling very unsteady on his feet. It was the first time he had let a drop of alcohol pass his lips since being released from prison and he felt ashamed of himself. That was a slip, but it won't happen again, he promised himself as he staggered towards the shelter.

The raiders had left, and in the early morning air Josiah could smell the sweet aroma of cordite, brick dust, and the acrid smell of smouldering timbers. Thankfully the street had survived, although all around there had been heavy damage. Fires raged at the wharves and warehouses and he could see the glow in the sky from a large fire, probably the gasworks, he concluded.

Back at the shelter Josiah tried to pull himself together. Dolly would be very upset if she thought that he had gone back on the drink, and being in a state of intoxication would certainly lose him much of his respectability among the street folk.

'You all right?' Tom Casey called out to him as he made his way rather unsteadily down the slope to the shelter entrance.

'Yeah, I fink so,' Josiah answered. 'I got caught in a blast. It's knocked me bandy.'

Willing hands helped the warden onto a bench and men gathered round him, eager to know the extent of the damage caused by the air raid.

'I 'eard Abbey Street copped it.'

'Is Bacon Buildin's all right?'

'Wilson Street's bin wiped out, by all accounts.'

Josiah put his hands up for silence. 'I ain't bin far from the turnin' but there's no gas on. The gasworks copped it, that much I do know,' he said, holding his head in his hands.

Just then the all-clear siren sounded, and as folk emerged shaken and white-faced from the shelter, someone called out to Dolly, 'Yer better get yer man 'ome, gel. 'E's bin blasted.'

'Yeah, get 'im 'ome, luv. That man's done us proud,' someone else piped in.

Dolly took Josiah's arm, their daughter holding on to her coat and the boys holding hands, the three youngsters yawning and pale-faced as they trooped home together in the early dawn light.

Chapter Twenty-Six

On Sunday morning the knife grinder pushed his contraption into Page Street and stood waiting for his customers to bring out their knives and choppers. He looked apprehensive, as though intruding upon the privacy of the little turning, but Sadie walked up to him with her carving knife and gave him a big smile.

'The bloody fing won't cut frew butter,' she told him. 'Put a good edge on it, I've got a joint fer dinner.'

Maisie took her blunt axe to him for regrinding and as she stood waiting alongside Sadie for the man to finish the job she shook her head sadly.

'Last night was a nightmare. I could 'ave kissed 'im when I saw 'im pushin' that fing inter the street,' she remarked.

Sadie gave her old friend a warm smile. 'Yer know, Mais, I was jus' finkin' the same fing,' she replied. 'It was like bein' reassured seein' 'im come round this mornin'.'

'I wonder if the ice-cream man'll come round?' Maisie said, slipping her hands inside her apron.

'Gawd knows,' Sadie replied. 'Anyway, the gas is back. At least we'll be able ter cook our dinners.'

Children stayed close to their front doors on that Sunday morning and the church bells were silent. Bells rang on the fire engines as they travelled to replace the tenders that had been at the fires through the night and ambulances sounded their bells as they rushed along neighbouring roads. Although many people were still unaccounted for and many others were known to be buried under tons of rubble, the news broadcaster gave out estimated figures of deaths and injuries. East End and south-east London hospitals had been damaged but nurses and doctors worked tirelessly to accommodate the constant flow of casualties. Tired, weary wardens and rescue workers took the opportunity to get some sleep, and women cooked their dinners on a low gas flame.

Brenda Massey took delivery of a tailor's dummy, and to keep herself calm she started work on a dress she had cut out from material Maurice had given her. Bert Jolly went for his Sunday papers and moaned about the shortage of tobacco, although Albert Lockwood the proprietor of the corner shop had saved him a half-ounce packet of Nosegay. Maurice

Salter caught up on his sleep, while his three daughters cleaned the house and prepared the dinner, and a few houses away Josiah slept off the effects of the drinking binge he had had with Maurice. In the Dawson's back yard Wallace sat looking through one of his brother's picture books, not really able to understand just what had happened to change everything. That morning he had been bullied into not going down to the riverside; he felt nervous and his eyes kept glancing up to the smoke-laden sky.

Frank Galloway called along Wilson Street to make sure the business premises were still intact, and then after looking at the row of houses opposite which had received a direct hit, he went along to see his father. A rather strained next-door neighbour greeted him and told him that the old man had insisted on staying in his own house all through the raid and had only just left, presumably for church. Frank smiled as he walked out of Tyburn Square. He could count on the fingers of one hand the number of times his father had gone to church and he made his way to the Saracen's Head.

In another local public house, the subdued customers drank their beer and related their own stories of the Saturday night of terror. Terry and his wife Patricia looked tired as they served pints of frothing ale and made small talk, and when Billy walked into the public bar with Danny, the landlord made his way over to serve them.

'We spent the night in the cellar,' he said stifling a yawn. 'Pat slept fairly well but I didn't get a wink.'

Billy leaned wearily on the counter. 'I was out most o' the night. We 'ad a bad 'un down at the tanneries,' he replied.

Danny, too, was feeling the effects of his labours on the river the previous afternoon and he sipped his pint quietly, listening to the conversation between Billy and Terry.

'Any strange faces bin in 'ere lately?' Billy asked.

Terry shook his head. 'There were quite a few o' Dougal's cronies at the trial but apart from a few dark looks they never made any threats,' he replied. 'Mind you, five years wasn't a bad result, considerin' the man's previous form.'

'Are yer still plannin' on gettin' out?' Billy asked in a low voice.

Terry looked sideways before replying. 'We're still sortin' fings out but it'll take a few weeks yet,' he said. 'It can't come quick enough fer me. It's gettin' a bit dangerous livin' in Bermon'sey, an' I don't only mean the air raids. I want a fresh start, some place where me an' Pat ain't known. Anyway, we'll 'ave a drink tergevver before we do go.'

Danny cast his eyes around the bar. The piano was not being played today and there were a few regular faces missing.

The domino team were sitting together drinking quietly, and when a bleary-eyed Maurice Salter made his appearance, they started a game. The usual shouts and arguments broke out at the table, and then a few minutes later old Mrs Watson fainted. They carried her out and sat her in a chair while she recovered, Bert Jolly supervising and insisting that she was suffering from high blood pressure.

' 'Ere, let me get at 'er,' he said, blowing a cloud of pipe smoke in her bright red face. 'That's the way ter bring 'em round.'

Mrs Watson coughed violently, and an argument started between the little pensioner and another elderly man.

'That stuff'll kill 'er,' the old man growled.

'Yer can't get a better bit o' baccy,' Bert said indignantly.

'She wants fresh air, not that bloody stuff down 'er insides,' the old man shouted.

Patricia separated the antagonists and administered a glass of water to the unfortunate Mrs Watson and she sat up straight, her eyes popping.

'There you are,' the old man said triumphantly to Bert Jolly.

'That's bound ter revive 'er,' Bert said dismissively. 'The silly ole mare's not used to it.'

Billy and Danny took their leave near closing time and walked along the quiet Jamaica Road towards Salmon Lane. Glass littered the pavement and they saw men boarding up shopfronts and other workmen sweeping the road and tramlines. Smoke still hung in the summer sky, and the birds in the tall plane trees did not seem to be singing like they usually did.

'Carrie said the food's gonna be on the table at 'alf two, so we'd better get a move on,' Danny said.

They quickened their pace a little, feeling hungry after the beer. When they reached the yard and stepped through the wicket gate, their mouths fell open in surprise. Carrie had set up a long trestle table in the shade just outside the front door and covered it with a spotlessly white bedsheet. The table was set with the best china and Carrie had placed a vase of flowers in the centre. Danny's children rushed to meet him and Carrie gave Billy a fond hug. 'C'mon, yer just in time,' she said with a smile.

Nellie sat at the head of the table with Joe facing her at the other end; Iris and the children were together on one side, and Rachel, Danny and Billy sat facing them. The meal of roast beef, roast potatoes, minted peas and Yorkshire pudding was consumed with relish and Carrie breathed a sigh of relief. The gas pressure had been low all morning and the Yorkshire pudding had been reluctant to rise.

They talked about everyday things, and everyone was trying to act as though the air raids had never happened. Billy made them all laugh with his account of the fainting and Bert Jolly's first aid, while Nellie relived old memories of her time in Page Street, telling the gathering about the time their driver got drunk on a street outing to Epping Forest and she had to drive the horse and cart home. Carrie talked about her childhood trips to the farms to fetch hay with her father and Rachel

spoke about some of her more light-hearted experiences on joining up
They were all doing their best to make the meal a happy one, all trying
desperately to put to the back of their minds the knowledge that las
night's air raid was only the beginning.

Billy was missing Annie and the children as keenly as ever, but he wa
glad that they were at least away from the bombing. Danny worried fo
Iris and his children's safety, wondering if they had made the righ
decision in keeping the family together during these increasingl
dangerous times. Carrie worried for Rachel who was leaving early tha
evening for her camp, and for her mother, who was getting ver
unsteady on her feet lately and looking very frail. Iris laughed with he
children and talked of happier days with Carrie and Nellie, an
occasionally she gave Danny a secret look. Joe sat quietly listening, hi
eyes straying to his beloved Carrie. All were trying to savour th
fleeting moment and fix in their minds the happy event, albei
shadowed by the drifting smoke high above them, and the acrid smell o
smouldering timbers that was carried into the yard on the light summe
breeze.

In Page Street the gas pressure had caused a problem and many
dinner was spoiled. Granny Massey sat grumpily eyeing Brenda as he
daughter pinned pieces of her dress together. 'I blame that bloke o
yours fer the gas,' she growled. 'What did 'e want ter put the furnac
out for?'

Brenda sighed resignedly. 'They 'ad to, Mum. The gasometer go
bombed. It wasn't Maurice's fault the dinner was late.'

'The bloody spuds weren't browned, an' as fer the meat, it fair mad
me jaws ache tryin' ter chew it. It was tough as ole boots.'

'You should 'ave put yer teeth in, Mum,' Brenda told her.

'Yer know I can't wear 'em fer eatin',' the old lady replied irritably
'They make me gums 'urt.'

Brenda sighed again and stood up to slip her creation over the padde
model in the corner of the parlour. For a while she worked at pinnin
and adjusting the length of the dress, and Granny nodded off. Brend
left the room to search for some suitable thread which was missing from
the needlework basket.

Granny woke up suddenly when her arm slipped from the side of th
chair. The sun had disappeared behind the rooftops and the light in th
parlour had grown dim. The old lady grunted as she adjusted he
position in the chair and then she saw the figure standing in the corner
'I fancy a cuppa,' she told it.

When it made no effort to go and get it, Granny became irritabl
again. 'Yer never consider my feelin's,' she moaned. 'I don't ask fe
much. I wouldn't mind if I was always askin' fer fings. A nice cup o' te
ain't too much to ask for, surely ter Gawd.'

There was no answer and Granny got even more cross. 'That's right us' ignore me,' she went on. 'I'd be better orf goin' in the work'ouse. At least they'd give yer a cuppa now an' then.'

In the dim light the old lady squinted at the tall figure standing in the corner. It seemed to be mocking her and she took out her handkerchief from the sleeve of her cardigan and dabbed away a tear. 'Go on, stand here like a dummy,' she ranted. 'Yer'll be sorry when I've gorn.'

Brenda finally found the desired cotton and when she came back into the parlour she saw that her mother was stirring. The old lady was in fact trying to get off to sleep again and she jumped when Brenda touched her arm.

'Would yer like a nice cuppa, Mum?' she enquired cheerfully.

'Poke yer tea,' the old lady growled. 'I ain't gonna beg fer a cuppa.'

Brenda sighed in dismay and went into the scullery to put the kettle on, wondering if the air raid had scrambled her mother's brains.

Darkness fell and the dreaded air-raid siren sounded. On this occasion folk were ready and the exodus from their homes in Bermondsey's backstreets took place in an orderly fashion. People carried pillows and blankets, flasks of tea and packets of sandwiches as they hurried out, ready for a long, terrifying night. Children took board games under their arms and babies cried at being woken suddenly as they were grabbed unceremoniously from their cots. Men shepherded their families into the safety of the shelter and stood guard under the concrete canopy, preparing for another dangerous night.

Soon the roar of planes was drowned by the crash of gunfire, and then the scream and clatter of falling bombs began. Explosions rocked the shelter to its foundations and people prayed to their particular gods for deliverance. All night the bombs fell, and all night folk strived to comfort their loved ones and catch some sleep. The hours of darkness were filled with unremitting terror for the shelterers, and on that night the Luftwaffe achieved what campaigners had failed to do for years. They destroyed Bacon Buildings.

Fires were started everywhere and an oil bomb landed in Salmon Lane, setting the pickle factory on fire. Down in the cellar of Carrie's home the sound of the explosion was deafening and when Joe ventured up to ground level, he saw that all the windows in the back of the house had been blown out. Down on the Thames a freighter was burning fiercely, and fire boats lay offshore on the ebbing tide spraying their hoses on the burning wharves. Fire tenders hurried back and forth round craters and debris, and rescue squads battled to save people buried under tons of masonry.

In Bacon Street the scene was horrendous. People forgot their own safety as they struggled to dig their neighbours out from the downstairs flats where some of them had been taking shelter. Bombs and shrapnel were still falling from the sky, which was as bright as day.

The raging inferno that was London could be seen for miles, and when Rachel took a well-earned rest from the frantic activity of the plotting room at West Marden, she stood gazing up at the red sky with an aching heart. Fear for her family turned her stomach over and she felt distraught. She knew that more raiders were on their way and tears of frustration filled her eyes. Janie Hall stood beside her, her arm round Rachel's shoulders. There was nothing she could say, nothing that would help to comfort her friend, and she too felt the tears coming.

A merciful dawn brought relief for the besieged river folk. There was work to be done, children to care for and meals to be prepared. Many people's homes had been destroyed and friends and relatives took on the burden of caring for them, but for other homeless it was the rest centre or Salvation Army hostels. Gas and electricity were cut off in many homes and tea was brewed over coal fires. Some folk were wandering the streets in a state of shock, and piercing cries rang out for dead loved ones as they scrabbled through the rubble that once was home, or just stood gazing emptily at the debris.

On Monday morning people went to work as usual, weary and frightened at the thought of the coming night. At the end of the day a tired work force shook hands with each other and wished their workmates and colleagues God's blessing.

Night by night throughout the first week of the blitz of London the air-raid siren sounded with dreadful regularity and bombs rained down. Countless fires were started and the beleaguered firefighters struggled vainly to contain them. Many burned out of control and others that were smouldering from previous nights flared up again. Hospital corridors were used as emergency wards and exhausted medical teams worked round the clock to tend the injured and give what comfort they could to the dying.

Late on the following Sunday night a bomb scored a direct hit on the Kings Arms, and it so happened that Billy Sullivan's rescue team was the one sent to the scene. Jim Davis was first off the lorry and he soon had his men in action.

'They'll be in the cellar!' Billy shouted as they set to work.

For a solid hour the men strained to move masonry and timbers, and finally they reached the stairway that led down into the cellar. One of the men eased himself down into the narrow opening and a torch was passed to him. Jim Davis leant over the hole. 'Are they alive?' he called out.

'There's nobody 'ere,' came the answer.

The squad leader caught sight of a wardrobe that had been knocked aside, causing the door to fall open. It was empty.

A policeman wearing a steel helmet came up to Jim Davis. 'Any casualties?' he asked.

Jim shook his head. 'Look at that empty wardrobe. They must 'ave gone ter shelter somewhere,' he replied, scratching his sweat-matted hair.

Billy Sullivan could not help grinning to himself. The Gordons' luck had held. They had picked the perfect night to take their leave of Bermondsey; they were most probably tucked up comfortably in bed far away from the carnage of dockland.

Later a policeman's report was sent down to the Elephant and Castle police station on request and it was read with much disappointment by two senior officers.

Gloria Simpson stood looking out from the bedroom window at the angry red glow in the night sky over dockland. If it had not been for Frank Galloway, she would have been plying her trade back there and maybe even lying maimed or dead under a pile of rubble at this very moment, she told herself. Yes, she had a lot to be thankful for, but would her good fortune last? Would Frank lose his patience and throw her out of his house when she failed to provide him with the information he wanted?

Gloria sighed deeply and lit a cigarette, her thoughts troubled. She had helped Frank once, and she had grown to regret it, ashamed of what she had done to curry his favour. He was using her, and the information she had only just got from Lola would no doubt send him into a frenzy. He seemed the sort of man who was capable of anything, and the thought of what he might do when he discovered the truth about Tony O'Reilly scared her. If he harmed the boy she would be as much to blame as him. She could not let that happen, even if it meant her going back to the mean and dangerous life she had led before. It was a question of survival and her own freedom, something she would lose if Frank did anything bad because of what she told him. No, she would have to stay silent, pretend she had heard nothing more. It was the only way.

'Draw the curtains and come back to bed,' Frank called out to her.

Gloria put on her best smile as she sauntered across the deep pile carpet and let the bathrobe fall from her as she slipped in beside him. 'Do I really please yer, darlin?' she purred.

'Of course,' he said, stroking her slim back. 'You've been very good, and I'm grateful.'

'Well, show me,' she whispered her hands going down to his round belly.

Frank winced as he turned to face her. There was a limit to his vital powers.

'Love me,' she sighed. 'Love me the way yer did last night.'

Frank screwed up his face in the darkened room as he prepared to pleasure her. It was becoming hard work, he found; there seemed no end to her desire.

233

Gloria squirmed and writhed, her breath coming in pants and her nails biting into his back as she enjoyed his lovemaking, and when he was finally spent she spread herself out on her back, threw her arms up over her head and slept like a baby.

Frank could not sleep, however, and Gloria's light snoring began to irritate him. He climbed from the bed and lit a cigarette, then he slipped on his dressing gown and moved over to the window. In the distance he could see the glow that was becoming brighter in the night sky and he thought about his father with anger in his heart. He had been a loyal son and had taken on the responsibility of running the business after Geoffrey was killed in action, but he had never been really appreciated. When he had tried to prise information from the old man he had been almost disregarded, merely being told that he was taken care of in the will. As much as he had come to detest Bella, he had to admit to himself that she was correct in what she said. He had good reason to know about the family's assets, they would be his by right one day.

Frank stubbed out his cigarette and immediately lit another. Gloria had not been very forthcoming with information on the O'Reilly woman and he could not suffer her company indefinitely. Bella would not be away for ever and he had to play his hand very carefully. If the marriage was going to end, as seemed very likely, then it must be Bella who was seen to be the guilty party, or he would be taken for everything he had left.

Dawn light was creeping into the bedroom when a very tired Frank finally climbed in between the sheets, and he groaned loudly as Gloria roused and turned towards him.

Chapter Twenty-Seven

All through the autumn and into November, the bombing continued relentlessly. Every night the Bermondsey folk made their way to the shelters early, carrying bundles of bedding and some sustenance to see them through until morning. Hollow-eyed, exhausted men sat beneath the scant cover of the shelter canopy and took turns to snatch sleep as they watched over their loved ones. Inside the shelter, women tried to get some rest in primitive conditions, huddled together on wooden benches, their children dozing fitfully at their feet in beds made up on boards or doors salvaged from ruins. The stale air reeked and every night the shelter rocked and shook from the bombs falling on the docks and wharves, the railways and the little homes and old tenement blocks. Hospitals were bombed and churches destroyed. There was no discrimination as the murderous explosives fell from the night skies, and there was little anyone could do, save pray and huddle together for comfort.

Heavy rescue squads battled in hazardous conditions throughout the night to free those trapped beneath the ruins of their homes, and fire tenders struggled to get to the blazes through rubble-strewn streets. Firewatch teams were set up and men raced back and forth to save their burning homes, often helpless as fires raged out of control. The WVS manned mobile canteens, and teenage lads still too young for call-up acted as messengers, pedalling through the bomb-torn streets between street wardens and command posts.

On a Sunday night early in November, a blanket of fog settled over dockland and for the first time since the raids started, many people slept in their own beds. Some, however, still huddled together in the shelter throughout the quiet night, not daring to risk staying at home.

The Dawsons had decided to take a chance that night and the children were packed off to bed early. Josiah was exhausted and he went to bed at nine o' clock, leaving Dolly sitting sewing in her tidy parlour along with Wallace, who had been unusually subdued of late. The young man sat at the table with a pile of the children's comics, and as he flicked through them quickly, Dolly watched him and worried. Until the blitz started, Wallace had gone about things in his usual way, strolling the streets by day and going down to the river to see the ships coming and going. He would sit on the river wall watching the activity along the quayside and then arrive home in the evening, tired and happy. Sometimes he would slip out late to see the lights upriver and Dolly would go off to bed, lying awake until she heard him return and let himself in with his key, which he kept fastened with a shoelace round his neck. There had been no opportunity for Wallace to go down to the river by night while the raids were on, but tonight he seemed a little restless and she felt that despite the fog he might well venture out.

Dolly finished sewing a button on a pair of Leslie's trousers and snapped the cotton with her teeth. It was no use trying to warn Wallace not to go down to the river. He had no understanding of the dangers that might arise. For him it was enough that he was not sitting in the shelter with the din of war hurting his ears. There was no danger in the quietness of the night, and he could not be made to see otherwise. Only his father seemed able to make him take notice, and that had come about through fear and pain, fear of the gruff voice and pain from the occasional cuff round the head. Josiah had changed now though, Dolly thought to herself. He was gentle and patient with the lad, but Wallace still remembered.

'I'll get yer some cocoa an' then yer'd better be orf ter bed,' she told him.

Wallace looked up briefly and then he returned to the comics, his eyes going up towards the ceiling as a distant foghorn sounded on the river. Dolly watched him for a few moments, gazing at the flatness of his wide face, his deep blue eyes and the tuft of mousy hair that was for ever standing up on the crown of his head. What thoughts were going through that lonely mind? she wondered as he sat staring at the coloured drawings. Was he happy or sad? Did he hurt inside? How she ached to ask him the questions and needed him to tell her, only too aware that it was useless to try. He never spoke more than a few simple words at any one time, and then only when he felt the need. He was grinning now at some secret thought, his mouth lopsided, saliva hanging from his bottom lip.

Dolly got up and went out into the scullery to make the cocoa. Maybe it would make him tired and ready for bed, she thought as she struck a match and held it over the gas ring. Maybe she should take the key away from Wallace and bolt up, but what would that achieve? He might attempt to climb out of the window, or he might find some other way to go out and be forced to stay out until morning. Josiah would know what to do, but she did not have the heart to wake him. Her man was exhausted from his warden's duties and bound to be short-tempered. Better if she did what she had always done and let the lad have his way. He would come to no harm, and return when he was ready.

A train puffed slowly into Euston over makeshift tracks and as it shuddered to a jolting halt at the buffers, servicemen hurried from the compartments, making their way quickly along the sandbagged platform with their passes held at the ready. A pair of military policemen stood at the ticket barriers watching the soldiers as they passed by, alert for the deserter or the unauthorised traveller.

The foggy night felt cold to Tony O'Reilly and he pulled up the collar of his greatcoat and adjusted his smallpack over his shoulder as he showed his pass at the barrier. He was looking forward to seeing Rachel once more, even if it was only for a few hours down at West Marden. She had written to him to say that she could not get any leave at the moment but if he could make his way down to the village while he was on leave she could get a few hours off. A few short hours would be better than nothing, Tony thought as he hurried down the stairs into the dark main road. First, though, was the visit to Guy's Hospital to see his mother. Her condition had deteriorated and she had been rushed there the previous night in the middle of an air raid.

Tony walked quickly along to King's Cross Road to the 63 bus stop, recalling the first time he had laid eyes on Rachel. She had boarded the same bus and exchanged a few words with him. It was not so long ago, but how much had happened since. He was in love with her, and hoped she felt as he did. They had spent a short leave together and their kisses were still deliciously vivid in his memory. Time was short now, he knew. Soon his unit would be going overseas, possibly to the Middle East, and he wanted to know in his heart that Rachel would wait for him. She had told him about her first love and its tragic ending, saying that she still needed time to adjust and it was no use them getting serious while the war was on. He had told her he understood her feelings, and they should allow themselves time, but that was before he realised he was hopelessly in love with her. He could not get her out of his thoughts since that brief time together and now his heart beat faster as he looked forward to holding her in his arms once more.

The bus was nearly full. Tony found a seat next to an elderly gent who was nodding off to sleep. Every time the bus changed direction, the man's head rested against his shoulder and Tony felt embarrassed. He need not have worried, for no one took any notice. The rest of the passengers stared ahead, all seemingly tired out, their eyes heavy-lidded and hollow.

Tony looked out of the window through the protective webbing and in the gloom he could see the bomb damage. Houses and shops lay in ruins and people seemed to be hurrying by more quickly, their heads held low and their eyes fixed down on the pavement in front of them. It was a picture of misery, he thought; anxious people hurrying home past the desolation before the fog closed in completely.

'They won't be over ternight, that's fer sure,' the conductor told a large woman who sat near the platform.

237

'I 'ope yer right,' the woman replied. 'I ain't 'ad me feet up since Gawd knows when.'

'Well, yer can get ter bed wivout worryin' ternight,' the conductor said. 'This fog's gettin' worse. We won't go all the way ter Peckham. They'll most likely turn us back at the Bricklayer's Arms.'

At the Elephant and Castle the man sitting next to Tony suddenly woke up and hurried off the bus. One stop before the Bricklayer's Arms Tony alighted, walking home through familiar backstreets that looked welcoming even in the swirling fog. When he arrived at his house, he saw a young woman crossing over towards him from the other side of the turning.

' 'Ello there. I'm Lola Fields,' she said, smiling at him. 'I'm a friend o' yer mum's. You must be Tony.'

He nodded. 'I'm 'ome fer a few days' leave. I'm goin' in ternight ter see 'er.'

'Well, give 'er my love, an' I do 'ope she's feelin' better,' Lola replied, giving him a wide smile.

Tony slipped the key into the lock and nodded in acknowledgement as he let himself into the quiet house. The place smelt of dampness and as soon as he took off his overcoat he set about building a fire. He went into the scullery and saw dirty teacups lying in the enamel bowl and a packet of margarine lying opened on the table. Dirty washing stood in a bucket and the curtains looked grubby and long overdue for changing.

He sighed to himself. There was a lot to do before he could go down to Kent to see Rachel. The whole place needed cleaning and he felt at a loss to know where to start. Well, it had better be a cup of tea, he decided, lighting the gas jet and filling the furred-up kettle.

Just then there was a knock at the door and Tony was surprised to see Lola standing on the doorstep.

'I do 'ope yer don't fink I've got a cheek,' she said smiling, 'but I did tell yer mum I'd come in an' tidy the place up while she was away. I got ter wonderin' if there was anyfing yer wanted at the corner shop.'

Tony shrugged his shoulders. 'I'm just makin' a cuppa. Yer welcome ter come in fer one, if yer like,' he told her.

Lola gave him another wide smile, showing large white teeth. 'It's the best offer I've 'ad all day,' she said, looking him up and down cheekily.

Tony led the way into the scullery and took down the teapot from the dresser, spooning tea into it. 'I've not seen yer before. 'Ave yer known me mum long?' he asked.

Lola sat down in a chair and crossed her legs, deliberately giving him a glimpse of her stockinged thigh. 'We met at the Castle. Yer mum uses the pub, as yer probably know,' she replied, eyeing him up and down again as she spoke. 'She's a nice lady, is yer mum. We got ter be friends pretty quick. She told me all about you. Very proud of yer, she is.'

238

Tony smiled amicably as he stood near the gas stove. 'I didn't know me mum was back drinkin'. She packed it up when 'er illness got worse,' he told her.

Lola studied her long fingernails for a few moments. 'She shouldn't drink wiv 'er complaint, an' I told 'er so,' she said after a while, 'but I s'pose it 'elps 'er in a way. Yer know she's very ill.'

Tony nodded. 'I know.'

The kettle started to boil and as he made the tea, Lola watched him closely.

'Look, why don't yer pop round the Castle when yer get back from the 'ospital,' Lola suggested. 'You are goin' in ter see yer mum ternight, ain't yer?'

Tony nodded. 'I might do that,' he answered.

'Let's 'ave that tea an' while yer gone, I'll get stuck inter this mess,' Lola said breezily.

The ward was lit by dimmed lights and the young nurse looked tired and jaded as she led Tony along to the end bed. 'I need to check on your mother's temperature,' she announced in a flat voice.

Tony looked down on the sleeping figure and his heart sank. His mother seemed to have become even more frail since his last leave. Her face was ashen and her hands little more than skin and bone as they rested over the white sheet.

The nurse touched her shoulder tenderly and Mary O'Reilly opened her eyes. 'You have a visitor,' she said softly as she took the thermometer from a glass of water, shook it vigorously and placed it under the sick woman's tongue.

Mary's eyes lit up as she looked up at her son and when the nurse had left them she weakly motioned him to sit down. Tony planted a kiss on her forehead and seated herself beside her, his hand going over hers. ' 'Ow are yer, Ma?' he asked quietly.

Mary was seized by a sudden attack of coughing, shaking her whole body. She sighed deeply. 'I've bin a naughty gel, son,' she said, a ghost of a smile touching her colourless lips. 'I went back on the bottle.'

Tony shook his head and patted his mother's hands. 'Yer know it's not good fer yer, Ma, in your condition,' he told her. 'Yer promised me yer wouldn't.'

'I know I did, but what wiv the bombin' an' all that, I jus' went in fer one ter steady me nerves,' she said, looking at him with sad eyes.

'Well, they won't let yer near any booze in 'ere, Ma,' Tony said grinning. 'Yer just gotta get well as soon as yer can.'

Mary chuckled and pointed to the space under her locker. 'They let me 'ave a Guinness every day,' she answered.

Tony leaned back in his chair. 'Ma, who's Lola Fields?'

239

'She's a good friend,' Mary replied. 'Why d'yer ask?'

'She came round soon as I got 'ome. She offered ter tidy up,' Tony told her.

Mary nodded slowly. 'That's Lola. She's a good gel, Tony. Don't mind what people say about 'er. She's a good 'un.'

'What do they say about 'er, Mum?'

'They say she's a Tom.'

'On the game, yer mean?'

'Yeah, that's right.'

'Is she on the game?'

Mary eased herself up on the pillows and clasped her hands together. 'I wouldn't be the one ter cast a stone, Tony,' she said quietly. 'Lola's a good 'un right enough. She found me on the floor an' it was 'er that looked after me till the ambulance came. What she does is no concern o' mine, nor anybody else's fer that matter.'

Tony looked at his mother's frail face. 'It's no concern o' mine neivver, Ma. I jus' wanted ter know, that's all.'

'She might sell 'er body ter live, son, but there's more goodness in that woman than in many o' the so-called paragons o' virtue I could name,' Mary said with conviction. 'We shouldn't be too quick ter judge people. Take ole George Galloway. That man's name don't go down very well wiv most o' the people who knows 'im, but 'e's looked after me since I first went ter see 'im. 'E's gonna take care o' you when I'm gorn, an' the way I'm goin', I don't fink it'll be long.'

Tony patted his mother's hands. 'Yer gonna be fine, Ma,' he said softly. 'Just do what the doctors tell yer, an' when yer do get out of 'ere, lay off the drink. That's what'll kill yer.'

Mary smiled cynically. 'Jus' livin' kills yer, son. Anyway, enough o' that. 'Ow long are yer 'ome for?'

'I'm on a seventy-two-hour pass,' he told her. 'I'm due back fer first parade Wednesday.'

'What yer gonna do while yer on leave?' she asked.

The young man shrugged. 'I'm goin' down West Marden in Kent termorrer mornin' ter see a lady friend,' he replied. 'I may get a room somewhere nearby so I can spend a bit o' time wiv 'er. Don't worry though, I'll come back ter see yer before I go back ter camp.'

'Don't yer worry about yer ole mum,' Mary told him with a smile. 'I'll be all right. As long as yer 'appy, son.'

Tony bent down and kissed his mother's forehead in a show of love and she patted his head. 'Tell me about the young lady friend,' she said.

'Well, 'er name's Rachel Bradley an' she comes from Bermon'sey,' Tony replied. 'She's a very nice gel, Ma.'

Mary's face suddenly became very serious. 'The Bradleys who've got the cartage business?' she asked.

Tony nodded.

' 'Ave yer told 'er anyfing about bein' a Galloway?' she asked.

'No, but I will when I see 'er,' he answered. 'It's not right ter keep it from 'er, 'specially if we're gonna get serious about each ovver.'

'Don't tell 'er, son. Don't tell 'er yet awhile,' Mary said, a note of pleading in her voice.

'I must, Ma. It wouldn't be right ter keep it from the gel,' he replied.

'I don't want yer ter get 'urt, that's all,' Mary said with a deep sigh.

'Why should I?' he asked.

'The gel's muvver is Carrie Tanner. She married a bloke called Bradley who 'ad a coffee shop in Cotton Lane. Yer lady friend's a Tanner an' you're a Galloway, that's why,' Mary emphasised. 'I told yer about the bad blood between the families, an' it runs deep.'

Tony leaned forward in his chair. 'Did yer tell this woman Lola anyfing about us, about me bein' a Galloway, I mean?' he asked.

Mary nodded. 'Lola's all right, an' I can trust 'er ter keep it secret,' she replied. 'I made 'er swear to it.'

Tony gave his mother a curious look. 'But why tell 'er, Ma?' he asked. 'Yer've just told me not ter tell Rachel.'

Mary's shoulders sagged and she shook her head slowly. 'When I 'ad this last bad turn I thought it was me lot. Lola 'appened ter call round an' she took care o' me till the ambulance came. While we was waitin' we got ter talkin' about you an' 'ow I was worried over yer. It jus' came out. I realised afterwards that I shouldn't 'ave said anyfing an' I made 'er promise ter keep it to 'erself. She will. I know she will.'

The ward sister was coming towards them and Tony got up to go. 'Listen, Ma, I must be off now,' he said. 'You take it easy, d'yer 'ear me?'

Mary gazed lovingly at her son. 'I'll try ter be good,' she said with a smile. 'Be careful what yer say ter yer young lady friend, son. Fink on what I said.'

Tony left the hospital frowning, and walked back through the foggy backstreets to his home off the New Kent Road with a troubled mind.

Fifteen minutes later he put the key in his front door and immediately smelt disinfectant. As he stepped into the house Lola called out to him from the scullery. ' 'Ow's yer Mum?' she asked.

'She's perkin' up, but she's very weak,' he replied, trying to appear relaxed as he walked through.

She motioned him into a chair. 'Yer need a nice cuppa. I've kept the pot warm,' she said with a smile.

Tony undid the buttons of his greatcoat and let it fall open as he looked around the room. Lola had been busy. Fresh washing had been put through the wringer and it stood in a pile on top of the copper. The stone floor had been scrubbed clean and all the dirty crockery washed and replaced on the dresser.

Lola smiled as she eyed him curiously. 'Does it look nice?' she asked.

He nodded. 'I'm very grateful. Muvver told me you was a good friend to 'er.'

Lola smiled again, this time with more meaning in her dark eyes. 'I could be a good friend ter you,' she said quietly. 'If yer'd let me.'

Tony felt embarrassed. 'Mum was tellin' me 'ow yer looked after 'er when she was taken ill,' he said. 'I appreciate what yer did.'

Lola came over to him with the teapot in her hand, standing very close to him as she poured the tea. ' 'Ave yer got a lady friend?' she asked.

He nodded. 'No one special. Just a friend.'

'We all need friends,' she said, in a vaguely mocking voice. 'But we sometimes need more.'

Tony took the proffered cup of tea. 'Fanks. I could do wiv this,' he said, smiling up at her.

'Look, it's a nasty night outside,' she said. 'Why don't I get the fire banked up in the parlour instead o' goin' out. We can sit an' talk fer a while.'

'It sounds good,' he replied, getting up to take off his heavy coat.

Lola hurried out of the room and as Tony rolled up his sleeves he could hear her raking the fire.

'The fire's burnin' up nicely,' she called out.

Tony walked into the room and made himself comfortable in the armchair near the fire. Lola sat opposite him and clasped her hands over her knees in a childlike pose.

'Did yer mum tell yer about what I do fer a livin'?' she asked with an elfish grin playing about her lips.

The young man nodded, his face breaking into a smile. 'She said she wouldn't be the one ter cast the first stone,' he replied. 'It's your business what yer do fer a livin'.'

'Do you approve?' Lola asked him.

'It's not fer me to approve or disapprove,' Tony answered.

'Tell me, Tony. 'Ave yer ever bin wiv a prostitute?' she asked suddenly.

The question took him by surprise and his face coloured slightly.

'Now I've embarrassed yer,' she said grinning.

He composed himself quickly and shook his head. 'No, not yet,' he replied.

'Would yer like to?' she asked.

'I've never given it much thought,' he countered.

'It can be better than fightin' fer it in some draughty doorway,' she told him. 'We know 'ow ter really pleasure a man. It's our business ter give satisfaction.'

Tony stared into the fire for a few seconds and then he looked up at her. 'Tell me somefing,' he said. 'D'yer ever feel the need ter make love, ter let a man love yer fer lovin's sake?'

For an instant Lola's face became hard, then the expression passed. 'Why should I be different from anybody else?' she asked. 'Gels like me feel emotions the same as anyone else. We need a man in our lives. Sellin' our bodies is a different fing entirely. We shut our minds ter such feelin's while we're workin'. Bein' loved an' lovin' somebody is just as important ter street gels as ter the women who work in shops, factories or offices. It might be 'ard fer you men to understand, but I can assure yer it's true.'

'I fink I can understand,' Tony replied.

'Can yer?' she asked.

Tony picked up the poker and moved a large piece of smoking coal into the flames. 'Yer know about me, about who my real farvver was, don't yer?' he said.

Lola nodded. 'Yer mum told me all about yer,' she replied. 'Don't yer worry though, yer secret's safe wiv me. I'm not in the 'abit o' goin' around talkin' about everybody's business. In my game yer gotta be discreet.'

Tony nodded. There was something about the woman he found puzzling. She had befriended his mother and seemed eager to please him. He had always believed that street women were hard-faced and not prone to making friends readily, but Lola was certainly not as he had imagined her sort to be. She was a good few years older than he was but she looked almost childlike as she sat in front of the glowing fire; her eyes were kind and she smiled easily. She was an attractive woman. His mother had her to thank for getting prompt attention when she was taken ill. What had happened to make a woman like Lola take up prostitution? he wondered. She was leaning back now, staring into the flames, and he suddenly felt a strong urge to reach out to her, to hold her close, and he breathed deeply in an effort to control his desire.

'Yer look troubled,' Lola said, sensing that he was uncomfortable. 'Yer mum's gonna be all right, you'll see.'

He nodded, stretching and sighing deeply. 'Look, Lola, I've only got a couple o' days' leave an' I've gotta go down ter Kent early termorrer, ter meet some army pals,' he told her. 'Would yer mind if I turned in now? We could 'ave a drink the next time I get leave.'

Lola looked a little disappointed for an instant, but then she smiled at him. 'You get yer sleep, luv,' she replied. 'It'll be a quiet night ternight while the fog 'olds.'

Tony saw her to the door and suddenly she turned and kissed him on the cheek. 'It's bin nice meetin' yer,' she said. 'I'd like us ter get ter know each ovver much better. I'll look forward ter that drink.'

Tony watched her walk off into the fog and then he bolted the front door, settling himself beside the glowing fire as he thought about the short time he had spent with her. She seemed very friendly, and he worried about how he had suddenly felt aroused by her. He was developing a loving relationship with Rachel, and yet at that particular moment it would have been so easy for him to forget the loyalty he owed her.

The fire was dying and Tony raked at the ashes. What did the future hold for him now that he had an inheritance? he wondered. Would it bring him the unhappiness his mother had warned against? It was all in the unknowable future, he told himself, and there was no point in thinking about it now. These were dangerous times, and there was a war to be fought.

The fog was swirling through the dockland backstreets and along the river it lingered thickly. A tug chugged against the turning tide as it made its way to the brace of barges moored midstream, just downriver from Tower Bridge. No lights shone out and there were no new fires started that night as Wallace leaned his arms on the concrete top of the river wall. It was cold and he shivered. Below him he could hear the lapping of the muddy water against the thick stanchions, and further out in the shrouded darkness he heard the steady throb of the tug's engine as it passed him. He narrowed his eyes as he tried to catch sight of it and then glanced upstream to where the twinkling lights had once been and the lighted bridge that moved up and down. Tonight he saw nothing except the swirling fog and the prow of a moored barge below him to his left. His eyes followed the heavy hawser which went down into the blackness of the hidden river, and after staring down at it for a few moments Wallace straightened up. He would come back tomorrow night when the fog had gone away, he decided. Maybe the lights would be shining tomorrow night; the bridge might go up and down as well. He turned for home, feeling the key round his neck and then slipping his hands deep into his trouser pockets as he shuffled along the quiet cobbled lane.

Chapter Twenty-Eight

Maudie Mycroft hurried back from the market and stopped beside the kneeling figure of Maisie who was whitening her doorstep. 'I just bin talkin' ter Dolly,' she said breathlessly. 'We're 'avin' bunks put in the shelter.'

'Well, that's a Gawdsend,' Maisie replied. 'I don't fink I could stand anuvver night sittin' on those bloody benches. My back's playin' me up somefing terrible.'

Maudie looked up at the grey sky. 'I never thought I'd ever pray fer the fog,' she said. 'Sleepin' between those sheets last night was lovely.'

Sadie was coming along the turning and when she reached her two friends she put down her shopping bag and puffed. 'Those queues are gettin' me down,' she groaned. 'Twenty minutes I queued up at Pearce's an' then when I got ter the counter all the bloody tin loaves 'ad gone. My Daniel can't eat a Vienna. The crust makes 'is gums sore.'

Maisie got up from her knees with a deep sigh. 'I don't know why I bovver wiv this step,' she moaned. 'Look at that rubbish layin' in the gutter. I mean, yer try ter keep up appearances an' there's bloody glass an' stones everywhere. Wouldn't yer fink they'd clean it up a bit more often?'

Sadie grunted. 'That street-sweeper of ours is a bleedin' piss artist. 'E spends all 'is time chattin'. One time they'd send the foreman round ter check the sweepin'. They don't seem ter bovver now.'

'We're gettin' bunks,' Maudie told her.

'Bugs?'

'Bunks,' Maudie repeated. 'In the shelter.'

'Well, it's about time,' Sadie declared. 'Anyfing's better than those benches.'

'D'yer fink they'll be over ternight?' Maisie asked.

'It's a stone certainty, unless the fog comes back,' Sadie replied.

Bert Jolly was making his way towards the women. 'They're puttin' bunks in the shelter,' he said as he came up. 'Yer'll 'ave ter be careful, they 'arbour lice.'

'What yer talkin' about?' Sadie growled at him.

'Lice, that's what I'm talkin' about,' Bert replied. 'They've got 'em in that shelter in Weston Street. I know somebody who goes there. The bunks are made o' sackin' an' it's the worst fing fer lice. Lice breed in sackin'.'

Maudie put her hand up to her mouth and Maisie gave the dapper pensioner a hard look.

Sadie picked up her shopping bag and glared at him. 'You're a proper Jonah's comforter, you are,' she said sharply. 'Ain't yer got anyfing cheerful ter tell us?'

Bert gave her a crooked smile. 'The fog's comin' back ternight,' he said. 'Still, it don't mean ter say we'll get anuvver peaceful night. I was readin' in the paper that the Jerries 'ave got a secret weapon on their planes that sees frew fog. They can prob'ly bomb us any night they want.'

The women watched him walk away and then Sadie turned to a worried-looking Maudie. 'Take no notice o' that ole goat. 'E only does it ter scare us. I've a good mind ter put the fear up 'im,' she growled.

' 'Ow would yer do that?' Maisie asked her.

'I'll fink o' somefink.'

Throughout the blitz, Carrie found herself hard put to keep up with the work that suddenly came her way. The leather firm she had contracted to was badly damaged and all the salvaged stock had to be transferred to another warehouse in Walworth. Carrie sent two of her drivers, Tom Armfield and Tubby Walsh, to the factory and kept Paddy Byrne and Ben Davidson back for the daily deliveries. The phone rang constantly and her drivers found themselves with more jobs than they could handle. They all worked overtime and tiredness and fatigue took their toll. Paddy Byrne drove his lorry with a badly sliced thumb bound up in a bandage, and then Tubby Walsh was taken to hospital with a crushed toe, which meant Carrie was down to three operational lorries until she could find a replacement for Tubby. Just when she had given up hope of getting another driver, Frank Dolan walked into the yard.

'I see yer sign fer a driver, lady,' he said cheerily. 'I've got twenty years be'ind me an' I can 'andle anyfink yer chuck at me. Fodens, Leylands, Bedfords, they're all the same ter me.'

Carried showed him into the office and motioned him into a chair. 'Where was yer last job?' she asked.

'Wilson's,' he replied. 'They got bombed out. Lost all their lorries in the fire.'

Carrie peered at his driving licence and handed it back with a smile. 'This job's only fer a few weeks. We've got a driver off sick,' she told him. 'There might be a permanent job though, if I can get anuvver lorry.'

'Suits me, lady,' Frank replied. 'I got six kids ter fink about.'

'We 'andle all sorts o' goods,' Carrie went on.

'I've done it all,' Frank informed her. 'Barrels, machinery, grain, dock work. You name it, I've done it.'

Carrie breathed a sigh of relief at her good fortune. The driver seemed very confident and eager to start work. 'All right, be 'ere at eight sharp termorrer an' we'll sort the lorry out,' she told him.

As soon as he had left she picked up the phone book and found Wilson's number. Her call was answered by a gruff-sounding voice.

'Yes, that's right. Frank Dolan worked for us for over fifteen years. Can't fault him. Good work record and a very good driver. We're sorry to see him go but we had no option. Our fleet's been destroyed. We're trying to get replacement lorries, but the way things are with the war, it'll be some time. That's all right. Glad to be of assistance.'

Carrie put the phone down and sighed happily. She was back to full strength, for the time being, and she crossed her fingers.

Maurice Salter knocked on Brenda's front door early on Friday evening, quickly adjusting his tie and brushing his hand down the front of his blue serge suit as he waited for her to answer. Things had improved between them lately, and even the old lady seemed less hostile towards him, he thought. It would be nice to take Brenda for a drink before she and her sister Rose packed their mother off to the shelter.

The door opened and Maurice's shoulders sagged when he saw the look on Brenda's face. ' 'Ello, Maurice, I s'pose yer better come in,' she said flatly.

'Well, don't 'urt yerself,' he mumbled as he followed her into the parlour.

Brenda nodded towards the old lady who sat huddled in a chair beside the fire. 'She told me an' Rose she's not budgin' from the fire ternight,' she said. 'You talk to 'er, Maurice.'

'Look, lovey, yer can't stay 'ere ternight,' Maurice said kindly as he knelt down in front of the old woman. 'It's too dangerous.'

'Don't you "lovey" me,' Granny growled. 'I'll please meself what I do. I can't sit on those bleedin' benches any more, not wiv my back.'

'They're gonna put bunks in there soon,' Maurice told her. 'You'll be able ter stretch out an' get a good sleep.'

' 'Ow am I gonna get up on bunks?' Granny asked, glaring at him.

'Yer can 'ave the bottom one,' Maurice said, smiling benignly.

'Well, I don't care if it's top or bottom, I ain't movin' an' that's final,' she growled.

Brenda put her hands on her hips and stood over her recalcitrant mother. 'If you won't move, me an' Rose'll 'ave ter stay wiv yer, an' if we all get killed it'll be your fault,' she said sharply.

Maurice got up from his haunches sighing. 'C'mon, luv, let's go round the Crown fer a drink,' he said to Brenda. 'She'll be all right till we get back. P'raps she'll change 'er mind by then.'

'I can't leave 'er like that,' Brenda replied. 'Rose 'as 'ad ter go 'ome to 'er place ter tidy up. She won't be back yet awhile.'

'Go on, piss orf up the pub,' Granny moaned. 'I'll be all right. If I fell in the fire, I wouldn't be a burden ter yer any more, would I?'

Maurice gave the old lady a blinding look, quickly smiling at her as she glanced up at him. 'I know,' he said, 'why don't yer put yer 'ead back an' 'ave a nice sleep. We'll bring yer a nice carton o' jellied eels back wiv us. Yer like jellied eels.'

'I've gorn orf 'em,' Granny said irritably. 'The last lot turned me stomach.'

Maurice looked at Brenda and shrugged his shoulders. 'What we gonna do, luv?' he sighed.

'Go on, piss orf out, the pair o' yer. I don't want yer makin' a noise roun' me while I'm trying' ter sleep.'

Brenda glanced from her mother to Maurice. 'All right, I'll slip upstairs an' do me face,' she said. 'I won't be a minute.'

Maurice sat down in the chair facing Granny Massey and for a few moments the two stared at each other, then Maurice leaned back and crossed his legs. 'Yer know somefing, luv, I reckon yer very brave wantin' ter stop in the 'ouse wiv all that bombin' goin' on around yer,' he said with a sly smile. 'Specially after what 'appened to ole Mrs Morgan who lived in Bacon Buildin's.'

Granny lifted her head. 'What 'appened to 'er then?' she asked.

'It doesn't matter, really,' Maurice replied. 'It's not a very nice fing ter talk about, not that it'd frighten the likes o' you.'

'What 'appened to 'er?' Granny urged him.

'Well, Mrs Morgan wouldn't go ter the shelter. She 'ad trouble wiv 'er legs, yer see,' he began. 'Anyway, the night they bombed the buildin's, ole Mrs Morgan was takin' a bath in 'er tin tub. When they got to 'er the poor ole gel was stone dead, still sittin' up in 'er bath wivout a stitch on. In fact she was still 'oldin' on ter the scrubbin' brush. The terrible fing was rigor mortis 'ad set in. She was like a block o' stone. They couldn't get 'er out the tub an' they couldn't fit 'er in the ambulance. She went ter the mortuary on the back of a rescue lorry, bathtub an' all.'

'Fer everybody ter see?' Granny cut in.

'No, they covered 'er over wiv a tarpaulin sheet, but the wind blew it off before they could get where they was goin'. Poor old Mrs Morgan. Everybody saw 'er sittin' bolt upright in that tub. She would 'ave died o' shame if she'd known what was goin' to 'appen to 'er.'

'Well, I wasn't plannin' ter take a bath, that's fer sure,' Granny told him.

Maurice uncrossed his legs and leaned forward in the chair. 'Yer sure yer don't want us ter bring yer back any jellied eels, luv?' he asked smiling. ' 'Cos if yer do, I need ter get 'em early. There'll be a run on 'em ternight, 'specially wiv the ding-dong at the shelter.'

248

'Ding-dong? What ding-dong?' the old lady asked.

'They're gonna 'ave a bit of a party fer the pensioners. I don't s'pose it'll amount ter much. A few crates o' Guinness an' jellied eels, pie an' mash an' faggots, an' pease-pudden an' saveloys. Charlie Alcroft's bringin' 'is accordian an' Tom Casey's playin' the bones. I don't fink it'll amount ter much, though. Between me an' you, luv, yer better orf bein' in yer own 'ome sittin' roun' the fire. All that singin' an' dancin' ain't very good for yer, not after all that nosh they're takin' down there.'

Granny looked very thoughtful as Brenda left for the pub holding on to Maurice's arm. Later she eased herself out of her chair and went to the cupboard under the stairs. For a while she rummaged through it and then she straightened up with a sigh of satisfaction. 'These black shoes'll do nicely wiv me new bonnet,' she told herself.

Tony O'Reilly leaned up against the bar and sipped his pint of bitter. The country pub had a low ceiling, and brass and pewter pots hung from the huge black beams. The landlord was a thin man with a walrus moustache and gold-rimmed glasses which he wore halfway down his large nose. At the far end of the carpeted bar two RAF officers talked quietly together and one old man sat resting his gnarled hands on a knobbly walking stick, his eyes never seeming to blink and his glass of beer remaining half full. The only other customers in the bar were two young people who stood very close to each other, the man listening intently for most of the time and the girl occasionally breaking off from her chatter to smile at him in a shy fashion. Tony wondered whether they were lovers and he eyed them slyly, noting the change in the girl's attitude as their conversation went on. Suddenly she turned on her heel and stormed out of the pub, closely followed by the young man, who looked agitated.

Tony glanced up at the ancient clock on the wall behind the counter and studied his drink. It was beginning to feel like a long day. The journey down from London had been slowed by damage to the railway track and he had spent the seemingly endless journey standing in the corridor. Only two trains passed through West Marden that day and he had decided to take the later one, the twelve fifteen to Hastings. He had strolled through the little village in the early afternoon and visited a tea room, where he had sat for some time reading the *Evening News*, drinking cups of tea and chatting to the proprietor, a large, rosy-faced woman who went on endlessly about the war. Later he had strolled through the quiet lanes and gone into the tiny church to look around and rest awhile. It was nearing six thirty when he caught the bus to Claydon. Rachel's letter had explained that the bus stopped at the Plover, a small pub four miles out of the village. She had said that she hoped to get to the pub at seven, but it was now twenty minutes to eight and she had still not arrived.

He finished his pint and ordered another. While the landlord was filling his glass, Tony looked round at the two RAF officers. One was badly scarred about the face and the other looked as though he was bursting out of his uniform. His ginger hair sprouted from each side of his cap and he tended to throw his head back when he laughed. Both officers wore medal ribbons over their breast pockets and seemed to know the landlord quite well.

The door opened and Tony saw Rachel peer in. Her face broke into a huge smile and she hurried over to him.

'I'm sorry, Tony. We got delayed,' she told him, laying her hand on his arm and hinting with her eyes that she could not say more.

'It's all right, Rachel,' he said smiling. 'I knew yer'd come if yer could. What can I get yer?'

'A large gin an' tonic, if they've got any gin,' she replied.

The landlord smiled at them. 'Two bottles left,' he said, reaching down for a glass.

Tony led the way to a corner by the log fire and threw his greatcoat over the back of a spare chair. 'I'm glad yer could get away, especially after that last letter,' he said quietly.

Rachel's face coloured slightly and she gave him a shy smile. 'I was feelin' very lovin' that night,' she replied.

'Well, it was a lovely letter an' I read it twice before I chucked it in the bin,' he said with a serious look on his face.

Rachel looked shocked. 'Yer put it in the dustbin?' she almost cried.

Tony's face relaxed. 'I'm just teasin' yer. I keep it next ter me 'eart,' he replied, touching his breast pocket with his fingertips.

Rachel sipped her drink and looked at him, her pale blue eyes twinkling. 'I'm really glad yer could make it,' she said. ' 'Ow's yer Mum?'

'About the same,' Tony replied. 'She looked very weak.'

Rachel's face became sad. 'I am sorry,' she said softly.

Tony was quiet for a few moments as he stared at the burning log fire, then he looked up at her. 'I got the room,' he said.

'I knew yer would,' Rachel replied. 'I already spoke ter the landlord. 'E reserved it. Is it nice?'

'It's just like 'ome,' Tony laughed. 'No, it's really nice. The ceiling's pretty low though,' he joked, touching the side of his head gingerly.

Rachel looked down at the flames. 'I don't 'ave ter be back ter camp till mornin',' she said in a low voice.

'Will yer stay wiv me?' he asked, his hand going out to touch her arm.

She avoided his urgent gaze for a few moments, toying with her glass. 'I want to, Tony, really I do,' she replied, 'but I can't give meself just yet. I explained why in the letter.'

'It was a lovely letter, Rachel,' he said quietly. 'But yer ferget one fing. We are involved. Us bein' 'ere right now is proof enough. I love yer, an' I want yer. I can't fink o' bein' wivout yer. D'yer understand?'

Rachel sighed deeply. 'I want ter give meself ter yer. Make yer know 'ow much I care fer yer, but I'm frightened. I'm frightened I might lose yer. I couldn't bear it. I'd just die, I know I would.'

Tony leaned forward over the small round table and rested his arms on the hard surface. 'Listen ter me,' he began. 'This war is goin' ter last fer a long while yet. None of us knows if we'll be around ter see the end of it. Very soon our mob's goin' overseas. Rumour 'as it we're goin' ter the Middle East. I don't know fer 'ow long. It could be years. Then there's you. Your airfield's bin attacked. You could 'ave bin killed. None of us know what's in store fer us, Rachel, but I'll tell yer this. As far as I'm concerned, I want ter enjoy every minute, every second that we're tergevver. I want ter love yer an' 'old yer close an' shut the war out. I wanna live fer the moment, an' I want you ter feel the way I do. Just remember that if eivver of us gets killed, then the one who's left will at least 'ave those lovely memories. Fer me it would last ferever, an' it'd be enough.'

Rachel's eyes glistened as she listened to him and she breathed deeply to fight back the tears. 'I love you, Tony,' she whispered.

'Will yer spend the night wiv me?' he asked.

'Do me one fing,' she said.

'What's that?'

'Get me anuvver drink.'

Tony looked serious as he got up from his chair. 'Let's make it a large one,' he said. 'There's somefink I wanna talk ter yer about.'

The evening wore on and the small pub became packed. Smoke rose up to the old oaken beams and laughter filled the bar. Tony and Rachel sat facing each other in the corner, talking quietly and occasionally smiling fondly. His hand enclosed hers, and she sometimes lowered her head bashfully. The clock struck the hour and the landlord rang the old brass bell over the bar. 'Time, gentlemen, please, and ladies,' he called out.

'I should see 'im about the room,' Tony said, stroking his chin.

'There's no worry. Wait until the mornin',' Rachel replied.

'Will 'e mind?' Tony asked.

Rachel gave him a smile. 'My friend Mary Hannen's boy friend used ter stay 'ere sometimes,' she said. 'If Mary could get time off, she'd stay wiv 'im. The landlord always settled wiv them next mornin'. 'E'll do the same fer us. Ole Ben's a nice bloke, an' very understandin'.'

The two young lovers climbed the steep flight of stairs and slipped the latch on the creaking door to the bedroom. Inside, the air smelled of mothballs and lavender and in the light of the small bedside lamp the bed seemed to fill the tiny room. Tony threw his greatcoat on the chair under the window and turned to face Rachel. She closed the door and leaned against it. For a few moments they stood looking at each other

251

then she went to him, her arms open to receive him. Tony wrapped his arms round her slim figure and bent his head down, his lips hovering inches from hers. 'I love yer, Rachel,' he whispered.

Their lips met in a soft, then hard, smouldering kiss. Rachel stood on tiptoe, her arm about his neck. He held her in a tight embrace, his lips moving from her mouth to her neck, brushing her throat. She sighed deeply, her breath beginning to come faster as he caressed her. She could feel his hands stroking her back, down and round to the top of her thigh. Rachel let her body arch backwards, feeling his full length pressing against her. She could feel the urgency of him and he groaned as she stroked him. With a quick movement he picked her up bodily and moved over the bed. Slowly he lowered her down, his breath coming hot against her soft flushed cheek. He was above her now, feeling the roundness of her small firm breasts. He started to undo the buttons of her uniform jacket and suddenly she stopped him. 'Wait, Tony. I need ter freshen up,' she whispered.

He watched her walk out to the adjoining bathroom and then got up from the bed, hot and ready with the promise and excitement. He turned off the lamp before opening the curtains. In the far distance he could see searchlights probing the night sky and knew that London was preparing for another night of bombing. For a while he stared out over the dark hills and then he heard the bathroom door creak open. He drew the curtains shut and turned round. Rachel stood naked before him, her slim body silhouetted against the light behind her. Tony gasped at her beauty. Her legs were long and slender and her waist was narrow above her wide round hips. He gazed at her breasts standing out firmly and glimpsed her small pink nipples in the darkness. Rachel had loosened her hair and it hung down round her shoulders and over one side of her forehead.

'Yer look stunnin',' he gasped.

Very slowly she moved to him, her body seeming to glide across the floor. She put her arms round his neck and her lips parted slightly for his kiss. Tony was suddenly aware of his rough battledress against her bare skin and his kiss was soft and gentle, almost apologetic.

'I gotta undress,' he said in a whisper.

She smiled at him as he moved away. 'Don't be long, lover. I need yer badly.'

Tony came out from the bathroom, turning the light off behind him, and in the blackness he found her aching body. She could feel him trembling as he moved against her on the bed, his lips touching her mouth, her neck, and then her stiffening nipples, licking them with his tongue, softly and slowly, tracing the shape of the tiny mounds. She sighed and wrapped her long slender legs round his thighs, guiding him, urging him into her as he moved up to kiss her open mouth. In that ecstatic moment they became one, as he thrust deep into her, filling her with a delicious sensation she wished would last for ever. He groaned as he pressed faster and deeper and then with a deep sigh and shudder he was spent, his love exploding out of him in waves of quick hot pleasure. He sank down sweating on top of her and they rolled sideways, still locked together in a lingering desire. For a few moments they lay there silently, listening to each other's quick heartbeats and quiet breathlessness. The feelings of frantic excitement were slowly dissolving into gentle sensations of warm satisfaction, and Rachel sighed. 'God, I'm tingling all over,' she whispered in his ear. 'I do love yer, Tony.'

He kissed her lips softly and held her to him, wanting this moment to become etched in his mind for ever. 'I love you too, Rachel,' he said quietly.

Far in the distance the light from raging fires grew wider and higher in the clear night sky. The flash of high explosives made the glow pulsate, a living nightmare that lasted through the long night, searing the saddened eyes of the two young lovers as they sat huddled together in blankets at the small bedroom window.

' 'Ow much more can they take, Tony?' she said, brushing a tear from her eye.

He shook his head. 'They'll take it as long as it goes on, darlin',' he whispered. 'The women'll be standin' in the queues termorrer an' the men'll go ter work. The kids'll be out playin' in the ruins an' collectin' shrapnel.'

Rachel turned her back to the window and went over to the bed. 'Close the curtains, darlin', and hold me. Hold me tight. I'm so frightened.'

'Of that?' he said, nodding toward the distant glow.

'No, fer us. I can see no future fer us while that goes on,' she replied.

Tony went to her, enveloping her in his strong arms. 'We'll survive, Rachel,' he said softly. 'You an' I both.'

Chapter Twenty-Nine

Throughout the bitterly cold December, the air-raid sirens sounded nightly and the blitz continued unabated. Wharves burned, warehouses crumbled in ruins, and tramlines in Jamaica Road were torn out and twisted into knots by the ferocity of one high explosive that landed in the middle of the thoroughfare. Albert Lockwood had the front of his shop blown out, and another bomb landed on the desolation that had once been Bacon Buildings. The little houses in Page Street were still intact, however, apart from missing windowpanes and roof slates. The shelter remained unscathed and folk felt comparatively safe as they sat along its arched length on uncomfortable benches. The promised bunks had still not arrived and Josiah Dawson felt the brunt of the locals' anger.

' 'Ow much longer do they reckon we can sit 'ere?' Sadie grumbled.

'I'll die if I 'ave ter spend anuvver night sittin' up,' Maudie groaned.

'They don't care,' Maisie growled. 'I bet the council people sleep in bunks. They don't 'ave ter sit up every night.'

'We ought ter write ter the papers,' Bert Jolly remarked.

Granny Massey sat silent while the anger boiled around her. She felt that her neighbours were plotting against her and she did not intend to be duped into anything. Her daughter Brenda would not believe her when she said that there should have been a party that night in the shelter and the only reason it did not take place was because she decided to turn up.

'They've all got it in fer me,' she moaned to her long-suffering daughters.

Rose ignored the outburst but Brenda worried, and when she asked her mother where she heard about the intended shelter party, the old lady pointed the finger at Maurice.

'Do me a favour,' Maurice growled. 'Now would I lead the old lady up the garden path like that? She most probably dreamed it.'

Brenda agreed with him. After all, her mother had taken to having arguments with the tailor's dummy recently, and she was getting more and more difficult to manage. She was making it impossible for her and Maurice to have any fun whatsoever.

Early each morning after the raiders had left, Brenda was in the habit of slipping from the shelter to make a jug of tea. Sometimes, when Maurice was not on night shift, she would meet him for a few precious minutes of lovemaking in her quiet house. It was all too brief for Brenda and Maurice's liking, but they were grateful for the chance to be alone together. Granny Massey enjoyed her early-morning cup of tea, however, and was impatient for it to arrive. One morning when all was quiet the old lady decided to leave the shelter on the proffered arm of Maudie, who was leaving unusually early. The sound of bed springs being pounded overhead did not go down very well with Granny Massey, and when Maurice came down the stairs red-faced a few minutes later the old lady became angry. 'I could be dyin' wiv thirst fer all you two care,' she moaned. 'Is that all yer fink of?'

Maurice made a discreet exit while Brenda made the tea, suffering her ageing mother's tirade. ' 'E's no good fer yer,' she went on. 'Too bloody sure of 'imself if yer ask me.'

Brenda did not feel like asking her mother anything just then, and she endured in silence.

'Maurice Salter's gonna make me the laughin' stock o' the street,' Granny continued. 'Those daughters of 'is are all no-good little cows. The blokes they bring 'ome. 'E'll make you as bad, mark my words.'

Brenda had heard enough. 'Shut up, Muvver, fer Gawd's sake,' she said sharply.

'That's right, shut me up. Don't let me get a word in edgeways,' Granny raved, dabbing at her eyes with a handkerchief. 'Yer'll be sorry when I've gorn.'

The old lady finally calmed down, but after that day it was very rare for Brenda to get the chance of an early-morning romp with Maurice, except for the few times she managed to creep out from the shelter while Granny was snoring.

During the week before Christmas, Josiah Dawson, acting in his official capacity as street and shelter warden, and without any prompting from Maurice Salter, decided to organise a Christmas Eve party for his charges. Dolly hugged him and told him how proud she was of him for being so concerned for everybody, and immediately took over arranging things. A meeting was called in her parlour and endless tea was served.

'We could all do a bit o' bakin',' Maisie suggested. 'I'll do rock cakes.'

'I'll make jellies,' Maudie offered.

'I'll do chocolate sweets out o' cocoa an' marzipan,' Sadie said.

'My relation works at the custard powder factory, she'll be able ter get us a large tin o' custard powder fer next ter nuffink,' Dolly piped in.

Nellie Tanner got to hear of the planned party, and although she did not use the shelter herself, she wanted to help her old friends. 'I'll do the lemonade,' she volunteered. 'I've got time on me 'ands.'

Nellie carried the news of the party to her daughter, and Carrie felt that it would be a good idea to go along and see Corned-beef Sam at the cafe in Cotton Lane. Sam was an old friend and Carrie had been meaning to call in on him for some time. She hoped that he would be able to bake her a batch of fancy cakes and mince pies if she approached him nicely. He had bought his business from her and her first husband Fred some years previously and had quickly established himself as a firm favourite among the working population of Bermondsey. Carmen and dockworkers packed into his establishment and he had become something of an institution.

' 'Ello, luv,' he beamed when he saw Carrie. ' 'Ow the bleedin' 'ell are yer? I thought yer'd fergot yer ole pal.'

Carrie laughed and planted a kiss on his cheek. 'I know it's bin some time, Sam, but I've bin so busy,' she told him.

He waved his hand at her. 'Don't I know it,' he replied in his camp voice. 'I bin so busy meself these past few weeks I don't know whether I'm punched or bored. I got me winders blown out last week. Mind you, I was miles away at the time. I got a friend down at Bromley. I stay wiv 'im most nights. I couldn't stay round 'ere, luv, it's much too dangerous fer me. I like the quiet life.'

Carrie sat chatting with him for some time in his back kitchen and when she finally told him about the proposed shelter party for her old Page Street neighbours, Sam was supportive. 'I've got a large tin o' corned beef they could 'ave, but don't ask me where I got it from, luv, 'cos if I tell yer, a certain docker's gonna scratch me eyes out,' he joked.

Carrie touched his arm in a fond gesture. 'What we need is some mince pies and fancy cakes. Of course I'll pay yer what yer want.'

'Leave it ter me, sweetness,' he replied, giving her a large wink. 'I'll 'ave 'em all ready for yer on Tuesday night. Tell yer what, I'll bring 'em round the yard on me way ter the station. It'll be early, mind. I couldn't stand bein' caught out in a raid. I'd die, really I would.'

Carrie laughed aloud at his comical expression as she got up to leave. 'I'll be waitin', Sam,' she told him.

Sam waved her goodbye from the front of his shop and as she walked away along Cotton Lane, she heard him call out, 'If yer can't be good, be careful, an' if yer can't be careful, remember the date.'

It always felt strange when she went back to the cafe, Carrie thought. The early days had been spent behind that counter, serving the carmen and dockers, joking with the men. Fred would be working hard in the little back kitchen, wary of her chatting with the customers. Fred was gone now, and she had moved on and made a success of her transport business. How the time had passed. It had been hard work but they were happy years for most of the time, she recalled. Now the country was at war and the surroundings she had grown up in were slowly being pounded into dust by the heavy nightly bombing. It would never be the same, she realised. One day the little streets would be no more. The little homes would go. What buildings would come to replace them then? she wondered. Would the wharves and docks rise again from the ashes? What sort of people would come to live by the river? Carrie sighed deeply, feeling suddenly depressed as she walked back to the transport yard in Salmon Lane through the gathering gloom.

The Christmas Eve festivities started early in the shelter. Food was laid out on kitchen tables, trestle tables, planks of wood and along the benches. Children wore paper hats and ate their fill from a fare of mince pies, fancy cakes, custards and jellies, as well as chocolate sweets. There was lemonade in abundance, and ginger beer which Sam had supplied, along with his cakes and pies, and would take no money for. The kind and generous cafe owner's standing rose even higher on that wartime Christmas Eve.

Most people had expected a respite from the nightly bombing over Christmas, and they were right. The night of the 24th remained quiet, and when the children settled down, beer was passed round. Laughter and the sound of carols carried out on the cold night air, and during the excitement one lone figure decided to seize the opportunity and slipped away into the darkness, making his way down to the river.

On 29 December, the blitz resumed with a vengeance. The City of London was fire-bombed and the flames roared skyward, fanned by a strong wind and made even more dangerous by the unusually low tide. Fire crews struggled to pump water from the river, and reserve fire engines from neighbouring counties were rushed to the metropolis. All through the night the fires raged and rescue squads were kept working until they were totally exhausted.

Billy Sullivan had spent Christmas with his family in Gloucester, and now as he held on grimly while his lorry rushed through the glass-strewn streets, he fingered the little medallion he wore round his neck. It was a gift from Annie; she had had it blessed by the priest.

'Take it, darling, and wear it always,' she told him. 'It comes with our love, mine and the children's.'

It had been an idyllic two days, and over all too soon. There was no time to remember it now, though. People were lying trapped beneath a block of buildings which had taken a direct hit and before the dust had settled Billy and his team were already hard at work.

In Tyburn Square, the Botleys were worried as they sat together in their reinforced cellar. 'I'm sure that young Mr Galloway thinks it's our fault his father doesn't use our shelter,' Beryl remarked, touching the side of her head with her fingertips.

'Well, we can only suggest to him that he comes here, dear,' Cyril replied. 'We can't force the man.'

'Oh, dear, it's such a worry,' Beryl went on. 'Maybe you should go and talk to him, make him see sense.'

'Look, dearest, we've tried more than once,' her husband reminded her. 'There's no use you worrying too much, you know how it brings on those migraines.'

Beryl sighed. It was not so long ago that she had forbidden her husband to have the old man in the house, but things had changed. The bombing had become heavy, and she felt guilty for her unfeeling attitude towards him, even though the old man acted like a pig. If anything happened to him, she would blame herself. Maybe she should go and remonstrate with him. She might be able to make him see sense.

'Everything all right, dear?' Cyril enquired as he poured himself a stiff drink.

Beryl nodded. How things change, she thought. At one time Cyril's drinking habits would have irked her and she would have nagged him mercilessly. Now it didn't matter any more. Only survival mattered, survival and caring for one's fellow creature.

Some time later Beryl felt positively at ease with herself as she climbed the stairs from the cellar and took her coat down from the hall stand. She heard her husband call out to her not to be long and to be careful, but Beryl was on a mission of mercy. She would encourage the old man down into the safety of the cellar even if it was the last thing she ever did.

George Galloway heard the knock on his front door and stirred in his chair. The second, louder knock made him sit up straight and he brushed a gnarled hand over his forehead. 'Who the bloody 'ell can that be?' he said aloud as he struggled to his feet, taking up his walking cane and hobbling out into the hall.

'Are you there?' a voice called out to him.

'Yes, woman, I'm bloody well 'ere,' he growled as he reached for the front-door catch.

Beryl smiled sweetly at him as he stared moodily at her. 'We're expecting an air raid tonight, Mr Galloway,' she began.

'Who told yer?' George asked sarcastically.

Normally Beryl would have taken umbrage and scurried back into her house but tonight she was feeling very forthright. 'Now listen, Mr Galloway. Cyril and I promised your son faithfully that we would make sure you were safe,' she said firmly. 'If the air raid starts, you won't be very safe sitting in this house of yours. Cyril and I insist that you join us in our cellar. We have a drink or two for you. I assure you you'll be quite comfortable.'

George nodded. 'Look, I'm just goin' ter smarten meself up a bit. I'll give yer a knock if the siren goes orf,' he said grudgingly.

'Well, see you do,' Beryl told him, amazed at her new-found courage.

George went back into his front room and slumped down in his leatherbound chair. 'The woman's a bloody nuisance, they both are,' he said aloud to himself. 'Why can't the pair of 'em leave me alone?' Still, maybe he'd better make use of their cellar, he thought. He didn't like to admit it, but the nightly bombing was beginning to unnerve him.

Two large Scotches later the air-raid siren wailed out and George eased himself out of the chair. He was still wearing his grubby shirt and creased trousers and his thinning white hair was in disarray, though he had splashed cold water on his face in a half-hearted attempt to freshen up. He made for the door and slipped on his suit coat, going back to drain the contents of his glass before leaving the house.

Cyril answered his knock. 'Well done, Mr Galloway,' he said smiling. 'It's better being here with us than sitting alone in that house of yours. Do come in.'

George made to cross the threshold when he suddenly stopped. 'Sod it, I've left me watch an' chain back there,' he said irritably.

'Never mind that, come in quick,' Cyril urged him.

'I can't leave me watch an' chain be'ind,' George told him. 'I've 'ad that piece fer donkey's years. It goes everywhere wiv me.'

Cyril sighed in resignation as he watched the old man go back up the steps. 'Don't be long,' he called out. 'I can hear the planes coming.'

George made his way back into the house and stroked his chin thoughtfully. 'Now where did I put that watch an' chain?' he said aloud.

A search of the front room failed to find it, and the old man slumped down in the chair. Suddenly he slapped his thigh. He got up and climbed the flight of stairs to the first-floor bathroom. A loud explosion startled him and he swore under his breath. Another, louder crash rocked the room and George staggered against the bathroom door. He could see the watch and chain hanging from the open door of the wall cabinet where he had placed it while he washed. He picked it up and let his fingers move gently over the small gold medallion which hung from the chain. Just then there was a loud clattering. George was startled as he gripped the medallion tightly in his fist, and at that moment the whole house collapsed around him. He felt himself falling, seemingly for ages, and then a searing pain tore through both his legs.

It was hard to breathe in the rising heat and he cried out in agony. Slowly he moved his hands up to his chest and realised that he was pinned down by a heavy object. He could not feel his legs now, only the tightness across his chest and the heat on his face. Overhead he could see the night sky, and just like when he was a young waif, sleeping out rough on the streets with William Tanner, there were stars twinkling in the darkness.

The explosion had knocked the Botleys off their feet and Cyril groaned as he rolled onto his side in the sudden blackness. 'Are you all right, dear?' he called out anxiously.

Beryl spat out a mouthful of dust. 'Yes, I'm all right,' she answered. As soon as he got his wife to her feet, Cyril felt his way to the cupboard and took out a kerosene lamp. Once he had managed to light it, he held it up and looked around. The ceiling had held, although most of the plaster had fallen down, exposing the wooden laths. Beryl looked badly shaken and he could see that she was trembling violently. 'There, there, it's all right,' he said encouragingly. 'You'll soon be all right.'

Beryl grabbed his arm suddenly. 'Mr Galloway!'

'I'll go and see if he's all right,' Cyril told her.

'Don't leave me alone!' Beryl cried out.

The Botleys climbed the stairs to the ground floor and immediately felt the heat. Smoke was starting to pour along the passage, and then there was a loud crash that sent the two of them sprawling. Cyril regained his feet and led his terrified wife to the front door. The blast had jammed it tight and try as he might he could not move it. Smoke was filling the passageway and there were flames licking at the door. 'Quick! The back way out!' he shouted.

The two of them hurried to the back of the house and Cyril slid the bolt. The door creaked open and as they stepped out into the brightly lit yard, the house began to fall behind them.

As dawn light filtered down over a battered London, still the smoke from the fires drifted up into the angry sky. Everywhere people were emerging from their shelters and places of safety to stand mesmerised by the carnage wrought. In Tyburn Square rescue teams stood by while firemen battled to put out the fire which had destroyed two adjoining houses. Opposite, a small group of shocked onlookers waited and wondered.

'I didn't know the old boy very well, but I know he had a business of sorts,' one remarked.

'He was a nice old chap,' Cyril Botley said, his arm round his distraught wife Beryl.

'Yes, he was a very nice old man,' Beryl said, her voice breaking.

Throughout the morning a rescue team worked at the ruined houses, and at midday they recovered the charred body of George Galloway.

Across London, in a quiet suburb, Gloria Simpson was making breakfast. She answered the knock on the door and then hurried upstairs to rouse Frank Galloway. 'There's a policeman at the door,' she said falteringly. ' 'E's askin' fer you.'

An hour later Frank was on his way to the makeshift mortuary at a school behind the Jamaica Road. When he arrived he was met by a very weary-looking policeman whose uniform was caked in dust.

'Yer better prepare yerself,' he said. 'There was a fire.'

Frank followed the officer into the school buildings. Bodies shrouded in white sheets filled the hall, and when the officer stopped at the end of a row, Frank was already feeling ill. A mortuary attendant gently lifted the sheet and Frank retched. The burnt face was unrecognisable.

The policeman laid a hand on Frank's shoulder. 'Come out in the air,' he said kindly.

Frank followed him out into the school playground and leaned against the wall as he tried to recover his composure.

'It's never a pretty sight,' the policeman said.

'I can't tell if it's him,' Frank gasped hoarsely.

'This might 'elp the identification,' the officer said, opening his fist. 'It was found clenched in the 'and o' the body. A Mr an' Mrs Botley who lived next door ter yer farvver said he went back inter the 'ouse fer 'is watch an' chain jus' as the bomb dropped.'

Frank looked down and saw the gold medallion resting on the policeman's open palm. 'Yes, that was my father's,' he said in a flat voice.

'You'll be able ter claim it after the formal identification,' the officer told him.

'The times I willed him to get rid of it,' Frank muttered.

'I don't understand, sir.'

'I don't expect you to.'

'You won't be wantin' it then?'

'As far as I'm concerned, that medallion belongs at the bottom of the river,' Frank said as he turned on his heel and walked away.

Chapter Thirty

On the second day of January 1941, the local papers printed the news of George Galloway's death. Mention was made of the fire bomb on Tyburn Square which claimed the life of the well-known and respected businessman. By that time nearly everyone in the dockland community had heard of his demise. The information was carried back from the market by Mrs Watson and passed via Mrs Haggerty to the rest of Page Street. When Maisie Dougall heard the news, she made a special trip to Salmon Lane to tell Nellie Tanner.

Later that day Carrie got back from a meeting with the leather firm feeling happy. She had negotiated a new contract which would run until the summer with an option to agree a more permanent arrangement. It was the most she could have hoped for and it meant that there was now regular work for at least one of her lorries.

Joe met her as she came into the yard with a serious look on his face. 'Yer better go up ter yer mum, luv, she's bin actin' a bit strange,' he told her.

Carrie threw her coat over the back of a chair and hurried up to the back bedroom. Nellie was sitting by the window looking out at the ruins of the pickle factory, her chin resting on her hand, and she ignored her daughter's greeting. Carrie went to her and as she knelt down beside her, she could see that she had been crying.

'What is it, Mum? Are yer feelin' ill?' she asked gently.

Nellie continued to stare out of the window. 'George Galloway's dead,' she said simply.

'Dead?' Carrie repeated.

' 'E was killed in that big air raid last Sunday night,' Nellie said in a low voice. 'Maisie came round ter tell me.'

Carrie sat back on her haunches and stared at her mother's pale face, feeling suddenly drained. She could feel no emotion, nothing inside. All her life, from when she was just a young child, she had felt contempt for the man. His treatment of her father and indeed the whole family had made her bitter and vengeful, and she had vowed to get back at him somehow. Her love for Joe had been her saving grace. He had been, and still was, a restraining influence on her, but deep down nothing had changed. Her hatred for the Galloways had still been smouldering

262

inside her, and now that George Galloway was dead, there was no elation, no satisfaction, only an emptiness.

She laid her hand on her mother's arm.

'I've got no reason ter feel sad about the man's passin',' Nellie said in a voice that sounded weary. ' 'E did me wrong, did us all wrong, but I can't feel glad that 'e's dead.'

Carrie nodded slowly. 'I never wished 'im dead, Mum,' she replied. 'My aim was ter ruin 'im in business, jus' like 'e nearly ruined our family. God ferbid, I never wished 'im dead.'

Nellie turned to face her daughter. 'I know, dear,' she said softly. 'Us Tanners don't 'ave that blackness in our souls. I remember well the day George Galloway came into our 'ouse next ter the stable. Yer farvver was laid up wiv busted ribs an' Galloway told 'im 'e was sacked. I could 'ave done murder then, but yer farvver just took it calmly. There was never any blackness in my Will's soul, Carrie.'

'I know that, Mum,' she replied.

Nellie turned back towards the window. 'They say the Lord moves in mysterious ways,' she said, her voice faltering. 'If I wished the man dead, I could be bringin' the wrath down on my Charlie's 'ead. Gawd, I miss that boy. I jus' pray ter the Lord ter let me see 'im jus' once before I die.'

Carrie's arm went round her mother's shoulders as Nellie bowed her head and sobbed.

During the early days of January, raids on London became more sporadic. There were quiet nights, when the Luftwaffe were concentrating their efforts on other major cities. Many Bermondsey folk forsook the shelter for their beds, but they were often rudely awoken by the dreaded wail of the siren, and they would hurry from their warm beds through the icy streets and sit huddled together until the all-clear sounded. Others continued to go to the shelter every night and they managed to get some sleep, however fitful, now that bunks had at last been installed.

Throughout the early days and nights of January, Rachel spent long, tiring hours in the plotting room at West Marden. Every raider crossing the south coast was marked and observed on the huge map at the operations centre, and whenever a large enemy formation was picked up on the radar, Rachel was filled with fear and concern for her loved ones back in London. But there was no time to dwell on things. Important information flowed to and fro and had to be processed, and it was only during the brief respites that she was able to think about her family, and the young man she had given her heart to, Tony O'Reilly.

On one such evening Rachel lay on top of her bed in the quiet dormitory, her hands clasped behind her head as she stared up at the high rafters. She had received another letter from him that very morning and delicious thoughts of love filled her mind. Tony had shocked her by what he had told her that evening at the Plover Inn. He had wanted to set the record straight, fearing that it might alter her feelings towards him but convinced that she had to know the truth. He need not have worried, she reflected. Love for him burned brightly inside her and it mattered for nothing that the man she was sleeping with had been sired by a Galloway. The long-standing feud between her mother and the Galloways was not of her making, or Tony's. He would be going off to fight very soon and her only concern was that he survive and return safely to her.

Rachel turned onto her side and took out Tony's letter from her breast pocket. Her face felt hot as she reread his words of love and his memories of that wonderful night of passion. She ached for him and needed him and she sighed deeply. There was so little time for them to be together, to share their thoughts, and their love.

Rachel put the letter back in her tunic pocket and turned onto her back once more. She would have to tell her mother the truth about Tony, she knew. What would her reaction be? Would she forbid her to see him ever again? Thoughts and fears crowded her mind and Rachel closed her eyes. She saw the angry face of her mother standing before her. Tony was waving to her as he went away, and when she tried to reach him her legs felt as though they were set in concrete and she cried out in her anguish. Arms were pulling her back and she struggled.

'C'mon, Bradley, pull yourself together. There's a flap on!'

Rachel woke up with a start to see the florid face of the duty sergeant standing over her and she quickly sat up and slipped her legs over the edge of the bed.

'You've got five minutes to wake yourself up, then it's the ops room, all right?'

Rachel nodded dumbly at the sergeant and buttoned up her collar. A few minutes later she took her place at the plotting table.

'Glad you could make it, Bradley,' the controller said sarcastically. 'It looks like another big 'un.'

The new year was only days old when Gloria Simpson made the journey across London cursing Bella Galloway as she sat on the rattling, swaying Tube train. The dark swelling beneath her right eye showed up vividly against her pale skin and there was blood on her lower lip. Why did the woman have to get in touch with Frank at this particular time? she fumed. For months now her lover had had no word from her, then out of the blue he had got a letter saying she wanted to meet him in Norwich. Why didn't she have the decency to come back to London instead of expecting him to travel up to Norwich? He had been a changed man when he returned and the argument that followed showed him up for what he really was.

The train pulled into Charing Cross Station and a group of servicemen came into the carriage. Gloria gave them little more than a passing glance. Normally she would have used her guile to attract their attention, for she was used to picking up trade wherever she could, but today she had no desire to show her face to them, and besides she was preoccupied with other problems. Was that bitch Bella after working her way back into the fold, or was she merely seeking something from Frank? Of course she might have heard of his father's death and wanted to learn something to her advantage. He would be a fool to give her anything, Gloria thought, after what he had said about her and that little brat Caroline.

Gloria felt the swelling inside her lip with the tip of her tongue and winced at the recollection. She had been furious when Frank told her that Bella was coming back to the Ilford house to live, after all he had said to the contrary. He had used the back of his hand on her when she questioned his manhood and had thrown her bodily from the house. Perhaps she should be grateful to Bella for exposing the true Frank Galloway, she thought bitterly.

The train sped under the river to Waterloo. When it pulled into the Elephant and Castle, Gloria stepped out of the carriage and walked along the platform with her hips swaying, to the amusement of the soldiers. Once out in the cold morning air, she hurried along the New Kent Road and turned into the backstreets. It was nearing noon and she had promised to meet Lola at the Bunch of Grapes, a little pub which her friend often used.

Lola was sitting alone and she stood up as she spotted her friend walk into the bar.

'You're lookin' a bit the worse fer wear, Gloria,' she said, wincing. 'Who done that ter yer?'

Gloria gave her friend a hard look. 'Yer don't look all that good yerself,' she growled.

Lola forced a smile. Gloria never changed, she thought. Her tongue was as sharp as ever. 'I was surprised to 'ear from yer so soon. Is everyfing all right?' she asked.

Gloria nodded to the bored-looking barman. 'We'll 'ave two o' what she's drinkin',' she told him, turning to Lola with a smile. 'Yeah, everyfing's fine. I've bin beatin' meself up fer kicks.'

Lola looked a little chastened as she followed Gloria to the table. 'Was t Frank?' she asked with concern.

Gloria nodded. 'I've finished wiv the whoreson,' she said disgustedly. I need ter talk ter yer.'

Once they were seated at a corner table with their gin and limes, Gloria's face became serious. 'Frank Galloway's farvver's bin killed in n air raid,' she said quietly.

Lola pulled a face. ' 'Ow terrible.'

'I'm worried, Lola,' Gloria said, reaching into her handbag for a cigarette. 'I was gettin' inter this business over me 'ead.'

'What d'yer mean?' Lola asked, a puzzled look on her painted face.

Gloria lit a match and puffed on her cigarette. 'Yer remember when I asked yer ter find out about the O'Reilly woman? Well, as far as I knew, Frank wanted the information out o' curiosity. 'E told me at the outset 'e was worried over 'is farvver bein' took on by this woman, but it wasn't true. It goes deeper.'

'Well, I can see that,' Lola answered. 'The O'Reilly boy is Galloway kin, which means your fella's quite likely to 'ave 'is nose put out o' joint as far as the ole man's money goes.'

Gloria nodded. 'I didn't dare tell 'im what yer told me, I was too scared of what 'e might do,' she said.

'Is that why 'e bashed yer, 'cos yer didn't tell 'im anyfing?' Lola asked.

Gloria shook her head. 'Nah, it was over that prat of a wife of 'is. She's comin' back to 'im.'

'Jus' like men,' Lola said, shaking her head slowly. 'They ain't werf a carrot, none of 'em.'

Gloria drew on her cigarette and stared down at her drink. 'It was 'is eyes that frightened me,' she said quietly. 'I've never seen that look before. I fink 'e could 'ave cheerfully killed me.'

Lola took a small sip of her drink. 'Yer know somefink, Gloria. I'm glad yer didn't say anyfink about the O'Reilly boy comin' inter that money,' she said in a low voice. 'It's bin worryin' me. I've got ter like that old lady, an' the boy too. 'E's a smasher.'

Gloria picked up her glass and gazed at it. 'That Frank's capable of anyfing. I found that out soon enough,' she sighed. 'There's somefink stewin' inside 'im. 'E's changed, Lola. 'E's like a different person now, an' when 'e 'eard about 'is farvver gettin' killed in that air raid 'e went all quiet. I don't like it.'

' 'E certainly took it out on you,' Lola replied, glancing at the angry lump under her friend's eye.

'I'm scared o' what 'e might do when 'e finds out about the boy bein' a Galloway,' Gloria said.

'Yer mean 'e might try ter do the boy some 'arm?' Lola asked incredulously. 'Surely not? 'E'd get found out.'

Gloria shrugged her shoulders. 'It depends 'ow desperate 'e was,' she replied. 'Accordin' ter what Mary O'Reilly told yer, the boy was gonna be well set up when the old man died.'

'I wouldn't fink 'e'd go that far,' Lola said, sipping her drink. 'If Frank does away wiv the boy, 'e's gonna be the prime suspect, it stands ter reason. The rozzers are gonna be on 'im straightaway.'

Gloria pulled a face. 'After they read the will, 'e would be, but don't ferget 'e's not s'posed ter know anyfing about the boy bein' a Galloway.

If 'e done it before the will's read, 'e wouldn't be suspected, an' yer gotta remember that people are gettin' killed every night. Jus' s'posin' the O'Reilly boy was found dead in the gutter after an air raid wiv 'is 'ead caved in. It'd be put down ter the bombin'. Who's ter say ovverwise?'

Lola was quiet for a few moments. 'I see what yer mean,' she replied. 'Anyway, Galloway can't do anyfing until the lad comes 'ome on leave again.'

Gloria lit another cigarette and puffed at it nervously. 'If Frank Galloway did do anyfink stupid, I'd be an accomplice,' she whispered. 'After all, it was me what got 'im the information.'

'Yeah, frew me,' Lola grated. 'I don't want ter be involved. I ain't plannin' ter swing fer no man, least of all that ponce Galloway.'

Gloria patted her friend's hand. 'No one's gonna implicate you. Me an' you 'ave gotta stick tergevver. Between us we can watch out fer the O'Reillys. Yer've wormed yer way inter the old lady's good books. She trusts yer. Stay friendly wiv 'er, an' make sure yer find out when 'er boy's comin' 'ome on leave an' let me know as soon as yer find out. One fing though. On no account let on to 'er that there's any danger to 'er boy, 'cos if yer do yer gonna implicate yerself, an' me. Understand?'

Lola toyed with her drink. 'S'posin' the boy don't get any more leave till after the will's read, it'll be too late fer your bloke ter do anyfink then I should fink.'

'We can't bank on that,' Gloria replied. 'Mary O'Reilly could kick the bucket any time, the way she is, an' anyway it might be a few weeks till they sort Galloway's will out. We gotta be prepared fer the worst.'

'Yeah, yer right,' Lola said nodding. 'Are yer back at yer own flat?'

Gloria shook her head. 'I'm in the same block but a different flat,' she told her. 'If yer need ter get in touch wiv me, phone Sammy McCarthy same as usual. Now let's 'ave anuvver drink.'

The funeral of George Galloway was a quiet affair. Only one carriage followed the hearse and it was occupied by Frank Galloway, George's good friend John Hargreaves, and Mrs Duffin the housekeeper. The hearse was bedecked with wreaths, one of which bore no name of sender, merely the inscription, 'With Gratitude'.

Frank sat with his chin resting on his hand, staring out through the purple blinds. Bella had cried off, saying she could not get away from her travelling troupe, and his daughter Caroline had sent her sympathies and asked him to buy a spray of flowers for her. It was typical of them, he thought disdainfully. Only John Hargreaves showed any real emotion. Mrs Duffin had made the journey out of a sense of duty and she sat upright in her seat facing him with a blank look on her thin face.

Frank considered his own feelings. He would miss the old boy, but he had been a very hard man who had shown little love to his family during his lifetime. Only Geoffrey had managed to elicit any sort of real feeling from him. His death in action had made the old man even more morose and bitter and he had never really recovered from the loss. The old man would have preferred Geoffrey to run the business, but the fact that Frank had stepped into the gap and been a dutiful son did not seem to have endeared him to his father in any way. Soon the will would be read and then he would finally learn just how much he had been valued, and loved.

Rachel had arrived home on a weekend pass and she sat talking to her mother in the cosy parlour. A fire was burning brightly and the curtains were drawn against the inclement weather. Carrie noticed how tired and jaded her daughter looked, and she waited until her mother had gone up to her room and Joe had gone off to bed before drawing her daughter into an intimate conversation.

'It must be a very important job, an' frightenin' too,' she remarked. 'Especially when there's a big raid comin' up.'

Rachel nodded. 'The worst time is when we can see the direction they're 'eadin',' she replied. 'Every time it's London I get a tight feelin' in me stomach. I fink about you an' Joe, an' Gran. When we get a break, I go outside and stand lookin' towards London. I can see the flashes, an' the glow in the skies. It's terrible. I feel so sick inside.'

'Never mind, luv. We've got yer fer two 'ole days,' Carrie said smiling. 'Yer can stretch out ternight in those nice clean sheets I've put on yer bed, an' if we're lucky we'll get a quiet night.'

Rachel stretched her stockinged feet towards the fire and yawned. 'I feel so exhausted,' she sighed. 'I fink I'd sleep right frew a raid.'

Carrie's eyes were serious. 'We'll 'ave ter wake yer if the siren goes, luv,' she told her. 'It's safer in the cellar.'

Rachel smiled. 'If yer can,' she joked.

Carrie sat staring into the fire for a few moments and then she looked up at Rachel. 'Does Tony still write ter yer regularly?' she asked.

Rachel nodded. 'All the time. We're very close, Mum,' she replied.

'Is it serious?' Carrie asked.

'I love 'im, Mum,' she said quietly, without embarrassment.

'I didn't need to ask, really,' Carrie replied. 'It's in yer eyes, in the way you act. I could tell right away. But is it the same fer Tony?'

Rachel nodded, staring at the flaring coals with a distant look in her pale blue eyes.

Carrie gazed at her daughter with concern. 'I can imagine what it must be like, the way the war's goin',' she said quietly. 'The future's so uncertain. Just be sensible, luv, an' try not ter let yer 'eart rule yer 'ead. At least yer both young. One day yer'll be tergevver fer always, please Gawd, if yer still keep yer love alive.'

Rachel met her mother's eyes, feeling suddenly frightened inside. Now was the moment to tell her. There could be no wavering. It had to be now. She took a deep breath as she leaned forward in her chair.

'Mum, there's somefink yer gotta know,' she began.

'Yer not got yerself pregnant, 'ave yer?' Carrie asked quickly.

Rachel shook her head with a brief smile. 'No, it's about me an' Tony,' she replied.

'What is it?' Carrie pressed her.

'Well, yer see, Tony never knew who 'is farvver was, not until recently, that is,' she said. 'Then when 'is muvver got seriously ill an' knew she could die, she told 'im. Yer gonna be shocked, Mum. Tony's farvver was Geoffrey Galloway.'

Carrie stared at her daughter for a few moments, trying to take in what she had just heard. 'Geoffrey Galloway?' she repeated. 'Your Tony, a Galloway?'

Rachel nodded, her heart sinking as she saw the horrified look on her mother's face.

'There's no end to it,' Carrie gasped. 'That family seems to 'aunt us. Of all the boys yer could 'ave fell in love wiv, it 'ad ter be a Galloway. Why, Rachel, why?'

Rachel shook her head slowly. 'I don't know about the workin's o' fate, Mum,' she replied. 'I don't know why. All I know is that I love Tony, an' 'e loves me. That's enough fer us. We just met an' fell in love. This fing between the families shouldn't affect our love fer each ovver. I won't let it.'

Carrie felt sick inside. It was as though the ghost of George Galloway had come to haunt the Tanners, and he was hardly cold. It was as though he was laughing at her from beyond the grave.

'Did George Galloway know about Tony?' she asked in a flat voice.

'Tony's muvver went ter see 'im some time ago,' Rachel said, looking down at the flames among the coals. 'It was when she realised 'ow ill she was. She wanted what was best fer 'er son.'

'What was the ole man's reaction?' Carrie asked.

' 'E was angry at not bein' told years ago, but 'e was very 'appy ter know that 'e 'ad a gran'son, an' 'e said 'e was gonna provide fer Tony in the will,' Rachel told her.

'When's the will bein' read?' Carrie asked.

'I don't know,' Rachel replied. 'Pretty soon I should imagine.'

Carrie fell silent, trying to calm the anger growing inside her. The love she had for her daughter stayed her from speaking her mind. She could see nothing but heartbreak in store for Rachel in being involved with a Galloway. The whole family seemed fated. Geoffrey had been killed in the First World War, Josephine had taken her own life, and the patriarch of the family had died violently. Frank Galloway was very much alive, though, and he had been instrumental in perpetuating the

269

bad blood between the families. What new devils would come of Rachel's involvement with the Galloway grandson?

'I 'ad ter tell yer, Mum,' Rachel said quietly, breaking into her thoughts. 'It'd come out soon enough anyway.'

Carrie nodded. 'I'm glad yer told me,' she replied, 'but I can't pretend ter feel 'appy for yer, because I don't. The bad blood between the families runs too deep fer that.'

'It can't go on ferever, Mum,' Rachel said. 'Some day it's gotta end.'

'It might in your lifetime, but it certainly won't in mine,' Carrie retorted bitterly. 'After all that's 'appened, ter fink that a daughter o' mine would fall in love wiv a Galloway.'

'We can't pick an' choose the families o' the fellas we fall in love wiv,' Rachel said angrily. 'Love's not like that, you should know as well as anybody.'

'What d'yer mean by that?' Carrie asked sharply.

Rachel met her mother's hard gaze. 'Look at you an' Joe. What 'appened to 'is family 'ad a bearin' on what 'appened between you two. Joe went ter prison over a vendetta, and you 'ad ter suffer because of it. I watched yer suffer, remember? I saw what prison did ter Joe, an' 'ow it affected you. I suffered wiv yer, Mum. Don't ferget I love Joe too. You stuck by 'im. Yer never stopped lovin' 'im, even when 'e walked out on yer, an' yer won in the end. That's 'ow it's gonna be wiv Tony an' me. I won't let the sins o' the farvver make any difference ter the way I feel. I love Tony an' I won't give 'im up, no matter what.'

How alike they were, Carrie thought helplessly. Rachel had the same dogged determination, the same single-mindedness. She would not be moved, and suddenly Carrie was reminded of Josephine Galloway. What agonies the poor child must have suffered to make her take her own life. It must never happen to Rachel, she vowed. She must always feel the love and security of her family around her, and know that they cherished and accepted her, no matter what. Her arms went out to her daughter and she pulled her close, her tears falling as Rachel hugged her tight, gently patting her mother's back.

'It'll work out, Mum, you'll see,' she said tenderly.

Chapter Thirty-One

Frank Galloway sat reading the *Evening Standard* and he glanced up as Bella flounced into the room. Only that morning she had told him that her touring days were over and she would be with him in his hour of need, as she put it. The thought filled him with loathing for her. It was more likely that her latest fancy man was away and she needed a place to stay for the time being. She would not miss being present at the reading of the will and would no doubt act the sorrowful daughter-in-law for the benefit of those present.

Frank eyed Bella over the top of the paper as she busied herself at the drinks cabinet and noticed that she had piled on quite a bit of weight round her hips and waist. Not so long ago she would have gone into hysterics over half an inch, but now she seemed to have mellowed. Not so their daughter Caroline. She had adopted most of her mother's habits and mannerisms and, worse still, she had threatened to move back into the family house, now that she had broken with her current young beau.

Frank hid his anger and tried to smile as he took the glass of whisky from Bella. He would have to be very careful how he handled things, he realised. His mistress had been sent packing only the day before Bella arrived back, though not without him having to resort to a backhander or two. Now he had to settle down to being the dutiful husband if he was to keep Bella from slipping back into her usual detestable ways while he sorted himself out.

There had been an unfortunate delay in the reading of the will. John Hargreaves had been taken ill at the graveside of his old friend and had been rushed to hospital. His firm of solicitors had managed to obtain an agreement to delay the reading until the doctor's report on Hargreaves' medical condition had been received. The elderly solicitor had been diagnosed as suffering from exhaustion and after a short rest he returned to the office. Things were now beginning to move. A date had finally been set for the reading of the will. There was also the new Bristol contract to be discussed, and Allan Wichello the bookmaker was getting impatient for his account to be settled.

'It's been a pig of a day,' he sighed as he sipped his watered-down Scotch with distaste.

'Poor dear. Never mind, you just relax an' I'll get you something to

271

eat. You must be starved,' Bella replied, not bothering to get up from the divan.

Frank put down the paper and loosened his tie. As soon as the reading of the will was over, he would know for sure what to do. The properties alone would give him the collateral he needed to set up an accountancy business. It was what he was trained for and it was certainly a more civilised profession than the transport business, he told himself.

On a cold Monday morning the Galloway family's solicitor walked into his office feeling rather tired. The air raid had not been too heavy but it had lasted for most of the night and he had had little sleep. John Hargreaves had always prided himself on his efficiency and professionalism, and as he waited for everyone to arrive he awarded himself a large Scotch. Getting permission for Trooper O'Reilly to attend the reading of the will had proved to be no problem. The lad's commanding officer had been very accommodating, and he sounded very pleasant on the phone. His other task had been harder. It had been difficult to locate the old lady, and making arrangements with the church welfare people to get her to the reading had taken up a lot of his time. But all was now ready and Hargreaves poured himself another Scotch.

First to arrive was Mrs Duffin, whose face was impassive as she was shown into the waiting room and sat down on the hard leather bench staring ahead. Next came Frank and Bella Galloway, he with his grey hair well groomed and wearing a blue serge suit over an immaculate white shirt and grey tie. Bella came in holding on to Frank's arm. She had been well schooled in the art of presentation, and for her the occasion warranted something demure. Her two-piece suit was in grey, worn over a high-collared blouse which was buttoned to the neck. Her shoes were plain black and she carried a black leather handbag. She had not been lavish with her make-up that morning and she looked positively reverent as she seated herself next to Mrs Duffin without acknowledging her.

A few minutes later Tony O'Reilly walked into the outer office. He was in uniform and still looked tired after his long night journey from Yorkshire. He glanced quickly around at the gathering and then sat down next to Frank Galloway, who gave him a puzzled look.

Soon John Hargreaves came out from the inner office and smiled benignly at the assembly. 'We're just waiting for one more. Would you all like to come in?' he said with an inviting sweep of his hand.

Chairs were set out facing the large carved oak desk, and as the visitors made themselves comfortable the young secretary put her head in the door. 'The car's here,' she said quickly.

Hargreaves left the room and returned after a short while pushing a wheelchair. The occupant, an old lady, sat bowed, a tartan blanket wrapped round her shoulders. Her white hair was set in waves and her surprisingly lively dark eyes darted from one person to the other as the solicitor positioned the wheelchair next to Mrs Duffin.

Frank suddenly rose from his seat. 'Well, I'll be blowed. If it isn't Nora Flynne,' he said, going over and taking her hand in his.

Nora gave him a weak smile. 'Hello, young Frank,' she replied in a quiet voice. 'Yer've filled out a lot.'

'How are you, Nora?' he asked.

'It's me legs, but I mustn't grumble.'

John Hargreaves seated himself at the desk and when Frank had resumed his place, he looked round at the gathering. 'As you all know, we are here for the reading of the will of George Galloway, and I would like to proceed forthwith,' he said in his gruff voice.

There was complete silence as he opened an envelope and removed a single sheet of paper which he set down in front of him. For a few moments he stared down at it, then he adjusted his tortoiseshell spectacles, cleared his throat and began reading.

> I, George Galloway, of 24, Tyburn Square, Bermondsey, London, being of sound mind and body, declare that this is my last will and testament. I revoke all former wills and testamentary dispositions made by me. I appoint John Hargreaves, solicitor, to be the sole executor of my will, but if he does not survive me then I appoint any partner of the same firm to act as executor.

Frank Galloway's jaw was set firm as he waited and his eyes stared unblinking at the elderly solicitor.

> I give and bequeath my transport business, namely, George Galloway and Son, cartage contractor, to my son Frank, with the hope that the business will continue to trade under the family name. To my old and valued housekeeper Mrs Nora Flynne I bequeath the sum of one hundred pounds. To my present housekeeper Mrs Ada Duffin I bequeath the sum of fifty pounds. To my grandson, Tony, I give and bequeath the residue of my estate including my properties in Page Street, Bermondsey, Wilson Street, Bermondsey, and Allen Street, Rotherhithe, the aforesaid properties as defined in the deeds of ownership. With this goes my earnest hope that my grandson Tony will use the properties to raise the necessary capital for the establishment of his business, which would trade under the family name.

Frank Galloway's face had become ashen and his jaw muscles

273

tightened. Hargreaves continued reading.

> Should my grandson fail to produce an heir and fail to survive my son Frank, then the residue of my estate will pass to my only surviving son. In witness whereof I have hereunto set my hand this 3rd day of December 1939.

Bella Galloway gave her husband a hard look as they made their way to Broad Street Station by taxi. 'I just can't believe it,' she said for the hundredth time. 'For years you've struggled in that damned business, and for what? The old man must have been senile. Fancy giving all that property to a grandson he hardly knew. It was yours by right. He had no reason to leave you almost penniless.'

Frank Galloway's face mirrored his shock and anger but he made no immediate reply. If that bitch Gloria had done her job properly instead of relying on her friends he might have been able to have done something about it, but it was too late now, he thought. At least he had finally rid himself of her and her constant excuses. There was nothing he could do now about the situation which seemed so unreal, but was in fact only too real. Hargreaves had explained it all. There was no question of the old man being of unsound mind, and no possibility of there being a mistake in the identification of Tony O'Reilly's father. There had been letters, and the birth certificate. Yes, Hargreaves had spelt it all out. The old man had got his earnest wish, a grandson to carry on the family name. It felt as though Geoffrey was laughing at everyone from beyond the grave, and Frank suddenly shivered violently. 'At least I've still got the business,' he said finally, and in a flat voice.

'The business,' she almost choked. 'I shouldn't think for a minute you'll be able to sell it, not while there's a war on. Nothing's changed, you're no better off now than when you're father was still alive. No, it's damned unfair, it really is.'

Frank sat silently fuming as the taxi drove over Tower Bridge. His mind went back to his wedding day. He recalled the young woman who was so absorbed with Geoffrey at the reception, and he wondered whether she was the one who had become the mother of his child. It was just like Geoffrey to be so secretive. Why hadn't he brought the girl home, or made an honest woman of her? Perhaps that had been his intention, Frank thought. Well, there would be no accountancy business now, unless he could sell the transport business, and as Bella had said, that was very unlikely at the present time. Maybe fate would intervene. Tony O'Reilly might get killed in action, but then again he might be wounded and invalided out of the service, or he might survive without a scratch. Then he would have his newfound wealth with which to set himself up in business, though he would probably fail and lose it all. As like as not he would squander the money.

As the taxi turned into the narrow streets of the City of London, Frank felt a black depression descending over him and he turned to Bella, hoping for a glimmer of support. She was gazing out of the window, her face set firm, and he knew that the very brief truce in their agonising marriage had ended.

Nora Flynne sat talking to Tony as she waited for a car to take her back to the church home for elderly ladies. 'We were good friends once, yer muvver an' I,' she told him. 'We lost contact after I went inter the 'ome. I'm sorry she's so poorly. Yer will give 'er my love, won't yer?'

Tony nodded. 'Maybe she'll come an' visit when she's feelin' better,' he said.

'That'll be very nice,' Nora replied. 'You must come too, if yer not overseas.'

'I certainly will,' the young soldier said smiling at her.

Nora studied him for a few moments and then reached out a bony hand and laid it on his. 'Yer've just come into a lot o' money, young man,' she said with a deep look. 'Use it well. Money can't always bring yer 'appiness. It didn't bring George Galloway much 'appiness.'

Tony gave her a big grin. 'I won't let it taint me,' he replied. 'When the war's over, I'm gettin' married. I'll make it work fer us.'

Nora nodded slowly, her tired eyes blinking rapidly. 'Yer got a young lady then? Is she from round 'ere?'

'She comes from Salmon Lane. 'Er name's Rachel an' she's a Tanner gel,' Tony informed her, waiting for the old lady's reaction.

She looked shocked and sighed deeply. 'I knew the family. A Galloway marryin' a Tanner, now that will be somefink,' she said, nodding her head.

Tony smiled at her again. 'Rachel an' me know all about the bad blood between the families, but it don't worry us,' he said lightly. 'It's no concern of ours.'

'Oh, but it is,' Nora replied, her eyes widening as she looked at him. 'Make no mistake about it, young man. Yer gotta remember, I was 'ousekeeper ter George Galloway fer many years an' I know. I could tell yer fings, fings that'd surprise yer. The bad blood between the Tanners and the Galloways runs deep. The minglin' o' blood 'appened once an' the result was somefing I don't care ter talk about. You must ask yer muvver about it. She'll tell yer.'

Tony could feel the passion in the old lady's words. 'She 'as told me about certain fings,' he said. 'She told me about Josephine Galloway.'

Nora's eyes clouded as she mumbled the name. 'Josephine. I loved that girl like she was me own,' she told him. 'The poor dear's end was so tragic. There was nuffink I could do ter prevent it. Nuffink anybody could do. The damage was done the day she was conceived.'

Hargreaves' secretary looked into the room. 'The car has arrived, Mrs Flynne,' she informed her.

Tony got up to leave and Nora beckoned him to bend down to her. 'There's somefink I wanna say before yer go, young man,' she said in her frail voice. 'Don't ferget ter give my love ter yer muvver, an' tell 'er ter come an' see me soon as she's able. Now this is important, an' I want yer ter promise me yer'll remember what I'm gonna say.'

Tony nodded. 'I promise.'

Nora fixed him with her dark eyes. 'If yer ever find the bad blood between the two families starts ter mar yer 'appiness, or that of yer young lady, or if ever the Galloway money troubles yer for any reason, then yer must come ter see me. It's very important. D'yer understand?'

'I understand, Nora. I won't ferget,' Tony said, patting her hand.

The driver arrived and he made sure that the old lady was tucked snugly in the blanket before he wheeled her from the room, and as he spun the chair round to face the door, Nora nodded sternly at Tony. 'Remember yer promise,' she reminded him.

All through the bitter winter the nightly bombing went on. Sometimes the weather deteriorated enough to prevent an air raid but as soon as it improved, the raiders were back. Other cities were being targeted as well and on some nights London was spared. During February, more and more people began to sleep in their own beds, only going to the shelter when the air-raid siren sounded. On some nights the bombing was light and some folk ignored the air-raid warnings altogether.

Maurice Salter worked a tiring shift system and whenever he was able to, he slept in his own bed, ignoring the siren and pulling the bedclothes over his head as he went back to sleep. Maurice's three daughters preferred to hurry down to the shelter when the siren went, however, and one night when he was snoring loudly through an air raid he was shaken awake by a very agitated Brenda Massey.

'Maurice. Maurice! Maurice!' she cried. 'Mum's 'ad a fall.'

The sleepy man roused himself and yawned as he looked up at Brenda. 'A fall, yer say? Where is she?'

'She's layin' at the foot o' the stairs groanin'. I fink she's broken somefink!' Brenda gasped.

' 'Ow did yer get in?' Maurice asked as he slipped his legs over the edge of the bed and reached for his trousers.

'Yer door was left ajar,' she told him.

'It's those bleedin' gels o' mine. I could 'ave bin ransacked,' he growled. 'Not that there's anyfink werf takin' in this 'ouse.'

Brenda was getting impatient. 'Never mind that. Mum might be badly 'urt,' she said anxiously.

Maurice slipped his bare feet into his shoes and hurried down the stairs behind Brenda. Outside, there was a full moon and flashes of gunfire raked the clear sky. A dull drone of aircraft sounded in the distance as the two hurried along Page Street to Brenda's house. The door was open and as Maurice stepped into the passageway he saw the old lady lying on her back with her feet resting on the bottom stairs. Her long dress was smoothed down over her thin legs and her hands were clasped together, as though she had lain down to sleep.

'I'm done for,' she groaned as Maurice bent over her.

'Where's the pain, luv?' he asked.

'Me legs. It's me legs,' she moaned.

Maurice very gently ran his fingers over the old lady's shins and ankles and could find nothing unusual. 'Top part or bottom part?' he asked her.

'All over,' Granny said, looking up at Brenda with a wicked glint in her eye.

Maurice leaned back on his haunches. 'I can't go touchin' the top of 'er legs. You'll 'ave ter do it,' he told Brenda.

Granny winced as Brenda slid her fingers down her thin thighs.

'I can't feel anyfing wrong,' Brenda said.

Maurice noticed the sly grin that hovered for an instant on the old lady's face and he decided that she had been up to one of her antics. 'If yer ask me, she's laid down there on purpose,' he whispered to Brenda. 'If she'd 'ave fallen down the stairs 'er clothes would 'ave bin round 'er neck.'

Brenda had to agree with him. 'What we gonna do?' she asked him.

'Fetch an ambulance,' the old lady groaned. 'I could be dyin'.'

'They're all busy,' Maurice replied gruffly, turning to Brenda. 'Don't worry though, I know what ter do. I'll run round ter Billy Bennett's place. 'E's got a barrer. We could tie yer mum on it an' run 'er up ter the 'ospital. While I'm gone, though, yer'd better tuck 'er up in a blanket. We don't want the mice runnin' up 'er dress while she's layin' there.'

Maurice winked at Brenda as he went out of the door, ignoring the old lady's protestations. 'Don't worry, I'll be back in a minute,' he called out.

He went back to his house and put the kettle on. Ten minutes later he walked back into the Massey house to find Granny sitting comfortably in her favourite chair. ' 'Ow are yer, Gran?' he asked pleasantly.

'None the better fer yer askin',' she growled at him. 'Barrer indeed. I'd never live the shame down.'

'C'mon, luv, don't be obstinate,' Maurice said blithely. 'Billy's bringin' the barrer round in a few minutes. Let the 'ospital give yer the once over. It won't take long.'

'Poke the bleedin' barrer up yer arse,' Granny shouted. 'I told yer once, I ain't gettin' on no bloody barrer.'

The sound of the all-clear drowned Granny's further comment and Maurice sighed. 'Well, I'm goin' back ter bed. Brenda, can you go an' tell Billy Bennett we don't need the barrer after all?' he asked.

Brenda hid her smile. 'All right,' she replied, following Maurice out of the house.

Five minutes later, after a quick cup of tea, Maurice and Brenda were tucked up beneath the sheets. 'D'yer fink we're wicked?' Brenda asked him.

'Yeah,' Maurice replied, turning towards her.

Carrie sat with Joe discussing her most recent employee.

'It's not as though Frank Dolan's incompetent,' she remarked. 'It's just the way 'e acts sometimes.'

Joe scratched his head thoughtfully. 'I know what yer mean,' he replied. 'The ovver night 'e didn't seem as though 'e wanted ter go 'ome. 'E was talkin' ter me fer ages after 'e'd parked 'is lorry up. Bundle o' nerves 'e is, too.'

Carrie shook her head. 'I was askin' Paddy Byrne about 'im an' 'e said Frank Dolan was tellin' 'im that 'e 'ad seven kids. 'E told me 'e 'ad six. Paddy reckons 'e's a bit strange.'

'Well, as long as 'e does 'is work satisfactory there's nuffink ter worry about,' Joe said.

'I s'pose yer right,' Carrie answered, getting up to turn on the wireless for the news broadcast. 'It's just a bit strange. Fer a start, 'e don't look nowhere near fifty, an' then there's that bag 'e always carries about wiv 'im. I was wonderin' if 'e's sleepin' rough or in lodgin' 'ouses.'

The newsreader's deep voice interrupted their conversation to say that the call-up had been extended once more, and all men born in 1903 would be required to register within the next few days.

Joe grinned as he listened. 'They'll be comin' fer Frank Dolan next,' he joked.

Joe's words proved to be prophetic, for two weeks later the police called at the Salmon Lane yard.

'We understand that you've got a Frank Dolan working here as a driver,' the policeman said.

Carrie nodded. 'Yes, that's right. Why, what's 'e done?'

'What time is he due back?' the policeman asked, ignoring her question.

' 'E's on the food contract an' it's all local work. 'E'll be back in the yard inside the hour, I would say,' Carrie answered.

The two policemen nodded and left.

'What's that all about?' Joe asked as he came over from the lorry shed.

'They was askin' about Frank Dolan,' Carrie told him. 'I 'ope 'e's not in any trouble.'

At twenty minutes past four Frank Dolan drove into the yard and climbed down from the lorry. 'Shall I park it up, Joe?' he called out.

Carrie came out from the office and beckoned him over. 'Frank, I've 'ad the police in a short while ago,' she said. 'They was askin' for yer.'

'Oh my Gawd!' he gasped, grabbing his large canvas bag.

Just then the yard seemed to be filled with policemen, some of them in plain clothes. Two jumped from a police car but were not quick enough as Frank threw his bag in their path and scampered to the rear of the yard. As they regained their footing, others were running into the yard and giving chase. Frank Dolan climbed on top of the shed and clambered across the roof which backed onto an alley. As he was about to jump down, he saw two policemen in the alley waiting. His escape route was blocked. He jumped back down into the yard and was immediately pounced on by the policemen. For a short while he struggled violently, but when he realised that it was useless he let himself be handcuffed and bundled into a police car. As the car drew out of the yard, he nodded to Carrie and Joe who were standing by the office.

'What's 'e wanted for?' Joe asked a detective who seemed to be in charge of the operation.

'He's a deserter, for a start,' the detective replied.

'But I registered 'im at the labour exchange an' I phoned up 'is last employer fer a reference,' Carrie said looking puzzled. 'They told me 'e was put off because the firm lost all their lorries in the bombin'.'

'Yeah, that's right,' the policeman replied. 'Frank Dolan was put off in November, but that fella wasn't Frank Dolan. We found the real Frank Dolan a few weeks ago. He was lying in a back alley off the Old Kent Road with his head caved in. The man we just arrested was Arthur Threadgold. He's wanted in Liverpool, Manchester and Bristol, and God knows where else. You've been lucky. Arthur Threadgold's a very dangerous man.'

'Tell me, as a matter of interest. Why did it take yer so long ter get onter this Threadgold character?' Joe asked. 'If 'e killed Frank Dolan an' assumed the man's identity, yer should've been able ter find 'im when 'e was registered fer work at the labour exchange. 'E's bin wiv us fer some time now. An' anuvver fing. 'Ow comes 'e knew where Frank Dolan last worked?'

The detective buttoned up his coat and dusted a sleeve with the palm of his hand. 'Dolan, Threadgold and another character by the name of Thomas Westlake all lodged at the same working men's hostel in Tooley Street and the three of them got pally,' he began. 'Threadgold borrowed Dolan's driving licence and identity card to get the job with you and then he returned them to him. Dolan knew that Threadgold was a deserter, but he wasn't worried. He intended to go up north to work in munitions. Anyway, one night Dolan and Westlake were playing cards at a pub in the Old Kent Road and they fell out over the stakes. Westlake followed Dolan outside and hit him over the head with a brick. He dragged the body round into an alley nearby and then took Dolan's wallet and money. There was nothing on the body when it was discovered, which made the identification difficult. Dolan wasn't working at the time he was killed and he apparently had no dependants.'

'So nobody reported 'im missin',' Joe cut in.

The detective nodded. 'Exactly. All we had to go on was the victim's blood group. Anyway, last week we arrested Westlake for being drunk and disorderly and as is usual we logged the man's possessions. He had a leather wallet on him with the initials "F.D." embossed in gold leaf on the front. When we asked Westlake about it he told us that he'd found the wallet in the street. Fortunately for us our desk sergeant noticed a small dark stain on the outside of the wallet and he suggested it might be blood, so we sent it away and the results proved him right. What the test also told us was that the blood was group O, and that there was a thumb print in the stain. The thumb print belonged to Westlake, but his blood group was AB. He must have handled the wallet before the blood dried on it.

'We were aware that we had an unidentified murder victim in cold storage and when we checked the files we found that that man's blood group was O. Anyway, when we confronted Westlake with the evidence we had, he admitted everything. He also told us about the deal Threadgold did with Dolan. Maybe he was hoping that the judge would take that into consideration. The rest was easy. We checked with the local labour exchanges and found that a Frank Dolan was registered as working with your firm.'

Joe shook his head slowly. 'If this Westlake bloke 'adn't bin picked up on a minor offence, you'd still be in the dark, and Threadgold would still be workin' fer us,' he said.

The detective smiled. 'Maybe, maybe not. Arthur Threadgold is a murderer,' he said calmly. 'He's wanted in Manchester for killing a grocer, in Liverpool for the murder of a coalman, and in Bristol for the killing of a linen draper. All those victims had one thing in common.'

'What was that?' Joe asked, intrigued.

'They all employed him.'

Chapter Thirty-Two

Gloria Simpson's top-floor flat was very much the same as her previous one. It had two rooms, with a tiny scullery and toilet leading off the small sitting room. Her old flat on the floor below had been taken over by another street girl whom she knew as Muriel. She worked the same pubs along the riverfront in Rotherhithe, where they had solicited clients from among the Scandinavian and Russian seamen when the timber ships sailed into the Surrey Docks. The destruction of the Rotherhithe docks had forced some of the local street girls to move away, but the options for older women such as Gloria and Muriel were limited. Both women rented their flats from Sammy MacCarthy, who was the caretaker and handyman of a row of three-storeyed Victorian houses in Norwegian Street. Sammy was a stockily built, bushy-haired man in his mid-forties. He was known locally to be a hard, no-nonsense character and he supplemented his income by poncing for the local street women, making introductions, warning off the undesirables, and taking his cut from the proceeds.

Sammy was fixing a new sash cord into a downstairs window when Gloria came walking along the narrow street which backed onto the dock wall. ' 'Ow yer doin', Sammy?' she called out to him.

The large man slipped the claw hammer into his wide leather belt and jerked his thumb towards the house as he turned towards Gloria. 'I'll be 'appier when this family move out,' he growled. 'They're on notice ter quit.'

Gloria sighed and shook her head. She knew of the couple, who seemed to spend most of their lives fighting each other round a tribe of unruly children every time they came back from the pub. Sammy had had to replace at least two windows recently, and she could understand his irritation.

'Anyfing doin'?' she asked him.

'There's a big do at the Norwwegian Club by the tunnel on Saturday evenin',' he replied, scratching the back of his hand. 'I'll see if I can get yer an invite.'

Gloria slipped her hands into her long flared coat. 'I'd appreciate it, Sammy,' she said, starting to walk on.

'By the way, someone called round ter see yer this mornin',' he told her. 'She said 'er name was Lola.'

'Did she leave any message?' Gloria asked him.

'She said she'd come back later, that's all,' Sammy replied, going bac
to his task.

Gloria hurried up the short flight of stone steps to her front door an
let herself into the house. The place smelt of mildew and boiled cabbag
as she climbed the three flights of stairs to her small flat. How differen
it was from the house she had grown accustomed to in Ilford. Sh
sighed sadly as she took out her door key.

The late evening sun was dipping down behind the rooftops as Glori
sat drinking tea and staring out over the ravaged Surrey Docks and th
quiet river. She had not seen Lola since the day she was thrown out o
Frank Galloway's house. What did Lola want her for? Gloria wondere
as she sipped her tea. Maybe she had got too worked up about the whol
thing. Maybe she had been wrong in suspecting that Frank would d
any harm to the O'Reilly boy. After all, Frank Galloway was a respecte
businessman with everything to lose. He would probably have expecte
his father to take care of the grandson anyway.

An hour later Lola called again and she had news. 'The O'Reill
boy's got most o' the money. All your ex-fella got was the transpor
business,' she said, still puffing from the long climb up the stairs. 'Mar
O'Reilly told me yesterday when I called round ter see 'er.'

'She's out of 'ospital, then?'

'She came out the day before yesterday.'

' 'Ow is she?'

'The woman still looks very ill.'

Gloria stroked her chin thoughtfully. 'Did Tony go ter the readin' o
the will?' she asked.

Lola nodded. 'They gave 'im leave but 'e 'ad ter go straight back, by
all accounts.'

'Well, at least 'e's safe while 'e's away,' Gloria remarked.

'Yer still don't fink 'e'll come to any 'arm, do yer?' Lola asked.

Gloria shrugged her shoulders. 'I dunno. I wouldn't trust Fran
Galloway as far as I could see 'im, not after the way 'e beat me up.'

Lola sipped her tea. 'I shouldn't worry too much, luv,' she said
'Don't ferget the O'Reilly boy's in the army. 'E won't be able ter touc
the money yet awhile. Frank Galloway knows that. 'E'll be 'opin' th
lad gets killed, I should fink.'

Gloria nodded. 'Yer prob'ly right,' she replied. 'Anyway, we're wel
out of it. What Galloway does now is no concern of ours.'

'That's right,' Lola said, passing over a packet of Woodbines. 'Jus
fink on the bright side. At least you didn't tell that ponce about Ton
bein' a Galloway. If yer 'ad 'a' done, it could 'ave caused trouble fer u
later.'

Gloria puffed on her cigarette. 'Anyway, 'ow's business?' she asked

282

Lola waved her hand in a theatrical gesture. 'Don't ask,' she smiled. 'I'm stuck wiv me ole regulars, an' they won't make me rich. What about you?'

Gloria shrugged. 'The trade's dead round 'ere since the docks copped it. I'm seriously finkin' o' turnin' it in. I'd be better orf workin' in a factory.'

'Yer could do it part-time,' Lola joked. 'Jus' fink o' the fellas yer could 'ave be'ind the boxes.'

The two women sat chatting for a while, then as the evening darkened, Gloria drew the blinds. 'C'mon, Lola,' she said, 'let's go up the Samson. We might get lucky all of a sudden.'

As the spring days became warmer, Bermondsey folk began to feel optimistic. The invasion scare had all but abated and the nights were less dangerous. Occasionally the raiders returned, but the damage was less severe, and the casualty rate was lower. Other cities were being bombed, however, and when people gathered in pubs or at the markets they sympathised with the plight of their fellow Britons.

'Those poor sods in Plymouth copped it last night, I see,' the greengrocer said to Maisie.

'Yeah, I 'eard it on the news,' she replied. 'Gawd 'elp 'em.'

'Bristol got it last night,' the butcher told Sadie Sullivan while he was chopping the meat.

Sadie winced as the cleaver whistled down dangerously near the butcher's fingers. 'You mind what yer doin',' she told him.

'Yus, they're all gettin' it,' the butcher went on regardless. 'Glasgow, Liverpool, Birmingham. We know what it's like fer 'em, don't we, luv?'

Sadie picked up the wrapped meat and made her way back home. The May sunshine was pleasant and she felt happy. She had saved her meat ration for the weekly gathering of her clan. Her boys would be coming round with their families that evening and Billy would be there too. It would be a rare get-together and Sadie was planning a feast.

Maudie Mycroft returned home from the market feeling anything but happy that morning. She had been informed by her husband Ernest that from now on he was going to sleep at home in his own bed. They had been spending their nights sleeping on the uncomfortable shelter bunks, Ernest taking his turn outside with the other men, but now he was adamant.

'I'm sure these are bug bites,' he had told Maudie.

'It's just a spring rash,' she replied.

'Spring rash me arse. They're bites,' he growled. 'You can sleep down the shelter if yer like, but I'm takin' a chance in me own bed from now on. Let's face it, we don't get a raid every night, an' besides, we can always pop over the shelter if it does get too bad.'

Maudie sighed in irritation as she hurried home. The way he had talked, it was as though he considered popping over to the shelter through the bombs and shrapnel the same as taking a stroll down the market. Ernest seemed to be getting very dopey in his old age. The marks on his arms did not resemble a spring rash, though, she had to admit, resigning herself to being dug out from the wreckage of her home one night soon.

Frank Galloway walked through the spring sunshine with his face set firm as he turned into Ferris Street, a little backwater off the New Kent Road. The twin rows of terraced houses showed the scars of the blitz and most of them had their windows boarded up. Slates were missing from the roofs and there were workmen replacing some front doors further along the turning. Frank stopped at a corner house where the street was bisected by another little road and he glanced up at the number before knocking.

'Mrs O'Reilly?' he asked as the frail figure opened the door.

'That's right,' she replied, eyeing him suspiciously.

Frank smiled disarmingly at her. 'My name's Frank Galloway, Geoffrey's brother.'

For a few moments Mary O'Reilly looked at him closely, and then her eyes showed a glimmer of recognition. 'It's bin a few years, but I remember yer face,' she said, her fingertips held up to her mouth. 'Would yer like ter come in?'

Frank followed her through the dark passageway and into the small parlour. He noticed the row of medicine bottles standing on the untidy dresser and he could smell chloroform. Grey ashes from the previous night's fire still filled the grate and there was a grubby blanket thrown over the one easy chair by the hearth.

Mary turned to him and motioned to an upright chair beside the bare wooden table. 'Yer must excuse the place,' she said in a tired voice. 'I'm waitin' fer me friend ter call. She does a bit o' cleanin' fer me, I'm too ill ter do it meself, yer see.'

Frank sat down and watched as Mary lowered herself painfully into the easy chair. 'I remember you too,' he said with a smile. 'You were with Geoffrey at my wedding. I remember you dancing with him.'

Mary nodded slowly. 'That was a long time ago,' she replied. 'We all get older.'

Frank reached into the inside of his coat and took out a large envelope which he laid down on the table. 'Geoffrey and I were very close, you know,' he began. 'It came as a big shock to find out that Geoffrey had a son. There's a few things here that belonged to my brother. I thought you and your son might like them.'

Mary watched as he pulled a batch of photographs and papers from the envelope. 'These were taken when we were very young. There's the

284

letter we got from Geoffrey's commanding officer and another from his platoon officer,' he went on. 'This is the last photo he had taken. It was his platoon, just before his last action.'

Mary took the proffered photographs and letters, her eyes squinting in the dull light as she studied them. Frank watched her closely. She hardly seemed to show any emotion at all. While she read the letters, he glanced around the room. There was a framed photograph of her soldier son standing on one side of the high mantelshelf and another of him in civilian clothes at the opposite end. Behind her was a sepia photograph of Geoffrey in uniform set in an ebony frame, and Frank recognised it as the one that had once stood in the large front room at Tyburn Square.

'Yer farvver gave that ter me,' Mary said, noting that he was staring hard at the picture.

'I thought I recognised it,' Frank replied. 'My father treasured that photo.'

'It must 'ave bin 'ard fer 'im ter part wiv it,' Mary said, turning in her chair to look up at it.

Frank nodded. 'Well, at least he realised his big ambition of having a male heir,' he said, looking into the ashes in the grate.

'It must 'ave come as a big shock ter you,' Mary said, eyeing him closely. 'What wiv my boy gettin' the properties an' all.'

Frank's face looked stoic as he shrugged. 'I got the business, which I expected. As for the properties, well, it was the old boy's wish that they should be used for your son to get on his feet. Good luck to him. I hope he succeeds. It was what my father wanted.'

Mary looked hard at him, trying to see some hidden resentment there, but his face did not betray any trace of malice. 'Yer don't 'ave any ill feelin's terwards my boy?' she asked.

'Good gracious, no,' Frank replied, his face breaking into a smile. 'Those properties have to be managed. I'm quite content to take on the business. It's a thriving concern and quite enough for me to handle.'

Mary eased herself forward in her chair. 'I'm very sorry, I 'aven't offered you a cuppa. Would yer care fer one?' she asked.

Frank waved her back. 'No, it's quite all right,' he replied quickly. 'I just called round to give you those mementoes. I'm sure your son will be pleased with them. Will you send them to him?'

'No, I'll wait till 'e gets 'ome. 'E's comin' 'ome on embarkation leave termorrer,' she replied, suddenly caught by a fit of coughing.

Frank waited until she had regained her composure and then made to leave. 'Well, it's been nice meeting you again, Mrs O'Reilly,' he said, holding out his hand to her. 'I wish you well.'

Mary clasped his hand. 'I'm very glad to 'ave seen yer,' she replied. 'It's good ter know that there's no ill feelin' on your part. I wouldn't like ter die knowin' that Tony's made any enemies.'

'There's no ill feeling, none whatsoever,' Frank replied quickly. 'Well, take care. I hope sleeping in the shelter doesn't affect you too much.'

'I never use the shetler,' Mary told him as she showed him to the front door. 'I couldn't stand it wiv my complaint. I take me chances 'ere.'

'You don't sleep upstairs, do you?' Frank asked.

Mary shook her head. 'I sleep in the back room. I've got the winders boarded up an' I sleep comfortable.'

As Frank was about to step out into the street, Mary touched his arm. 'My Tony's found 'imself a young lady,' she said. 'She's Carrie Tanner's daughter, Rachel. I fink yer've a right ter know. After all, you are family.'

For an instant Frank Galloway's face changed as he looked wide-eyed at the frail woman, then he smiled briefly. 'Is it serious?' he asked.

Mary nodded. 'It looks like it. I 'ope so anyway. Maybe it's the best fing, fer both families, if they do decide ter wed,' she remarked. 'Life's too short ter bear malice. I pray the two families can come tergevver.'

Frank walked away along the street cursing Mary O'Reilly. Her revelation had been a big shock, and a dark anger rose up within him. He had been compelled to go to see her. Since the reading of the will he had not been able to sleep; his head ached constantly, and the pain was getting worse. All he had been able to think about was the injustice of it all and revenge against the woman who had borne the bastard son, the grandson who gained almost everything. He had been keen to see the woman, to find out more about her, her habits, friends, and the lay-out of the house so that he could finalise his plans to get rid of her and her son without the finger of suspicion pointing in his direction.

Now, as he walked along the narrow turning his head was pounding and all he could think about was the Tanner family. They were laughing at him, deriding him as they opened their arms to welcome the bastard grandchild, and the Galloway wealth into the fold. He could not allow it to happen. He would sooner die than let it happen.

The knowledge Frank had gained just a few short minutes ago was enough to push him over the thin line of reasoning, and his thoughts became maniacal.

Rachel sat at the plotting table on Saturday evening, and as she stared down at the blank expanse of map, her thoughts were with Tony. His letter had filled her with both joy and sadness. They would be together for a whole week, and then would come the parting. He had said nothing in the letter about his destination, but he had told her before that it would most likely be the Middle East. The separation would probably be a long one and Rachel was determined to make their brief time together something that she would remember and cherish until he returned, and he would come back to her, she knew in her heart. She felt sure that it was meant to be.

The loud ringing of the phone roused her from her reverie and she sat up straight in her chair, waiting for the alert.

The controller smiled as he put down the phone. 'Heavy cloud over the Channel,' he said. 'No sign of activity.'

The plotters relaxed once more, each engrossed in their own thoughts.

The plotter next to Rachel removed her headphones and rubbed her aching neck. 'I envy you, Rachel,' she said with a sigh. 'A whole week away from this. I bet you'll come back pregnant.'

Rachel held up her crossed fingers. 'Don't wish a baby on me, Carol,' she replied with a grin. 'Tony's on embarkation leave.'

'How did you fiddle it?' Carol asked.

'Friends in the right places,' Rachel answered with a straight face.

'You must have,' Carol replied. 'I couldn't get leave when my fella was home.'

'Luck o' the draw,' Rachel replied with a sly smile.

'When's your fella get home?' Carol asked, toying with her headset.

' 'E should be 'ome by now, an' I'll be there wiv 'im termorrer,' Rachel told her, her eyes flashing.

Suddenly the phone rang and this time the controller's face took on a serious look. 'Alert!' he shouted as he banged down the phone.

The expanse of map was no longer blank and in the balcony above the room anxious officers watched the build-up of enemy aircraft. As the plotters pushed and pulled the counters over the large map it became evident that formations of aircraft were converging to form an armada, and the destination soon became clear: London.

'God help 'em,' the senior officer said quietly to his subordinate as he watched the build-up. 'This is the biggest yet.'

Rachel felt the familiar sickness in the pit of her stomach. Tonight her family would face the heaviest air raid so far, and Tony was there too.

Chapter Thirty-Three

Billy Sullivan had found time to write to Annie during the few quiet nights and he yawned as he kicked off his boots and put his feet up onto the chair facing him. He had finished his tea and looked forward to a short nap before going off to the Bargee for a pint with Danny.

The loud knock on the front door startled him. He quickly opened it to see a young messenger standing there holding on to the handles of his bicycle.

'There's a red alert!' he said breathlessly.

Billy nodded, his face set firm. 'Tell 'em I'll be there in fifteen minutes,' he said quickly.

The messenger hurried off to warn the street warden and Billy went out into the scullery and splashed his face with cold water. He felt a strange sense of impending danger as he got ready to leave. The letter he had only just posted off to Annie told her he was well and that he hoped that the worst of the bombing was now over. He had assured her in the letter that he would take no undue risks, and said how he was dying to hold her in his arms once more. Now he was readying himself to go about the dangerous task of rescuing the trapped, some of whom would be badly maimed, and recovering the bodies of the dead that would be lying crushed beneath the rubble.

Billy grabbed his steel helmet and gas-mask case, and then before leaving he glanced up at the crucifix over the mantelshelf, his lips moving in a silent prayer.

Danny Tanner sat waiting for Billy in the Bargee, and as he picked up his pint he glanced up at the large clock on the wall behind the counter. Billy was late, he thought. It was unlike him to be late for a drink. Perhaps he had fallen asleep or there might be an alert.

The publican voiced Danny's fears. 'There's a full moon ternight,' he said as he pulled on the beer pump. 'The tide's runnin' fast, too.'

Danny knew just what the publican meant. It would be an unusually low tide tonight, and with the bright moon lighting up London, it was very probable that the lull in the bombing would come to an end. The low tide would be in the raiders' favour, making it difficult for the firefighters to pump water from the Thames.

Danny realised that Billy was not going to show up and he finished his pint. 'I'll be seein' yer, Charlie,' he called out to the publican as he made for the door.

'Are yer workin', Danny?' Charlie asked.

The lighterman nodded. 'We're takin' some barges out on the tide,' he replied.

He heard the words 'Good luck' called out to him as he pulled the collar of his seaman's coat up round his ears. Even on a mild peaceful night Danny knew that the river could be cold and treacherous.

Josiah Dawson had had a hard day at work, and after tea he dozed off in his favourite chair. An hour later he stirred and grunted as his shoulder was shaken roughly. 'Whassa matter?' he growled.

'It's the messenger boy. There's a red alert!' Dolly told him urgently.

Josiah sat up straight and rubbed his eyes. 'Right. Get the kids ready fer the shelter,' he said quickly. 'There's a full moon ternight. We can expect the worst.'

Dolly watched as her husband threw on his coat and grabbed his steel helmet. 'Mind 'ow yer go, luv,' she called out as he hurried from the house.

Dolly's daughter Joyce was already putting her coat on. Although only seven years old, she knew that the bombs would soon be falling and she wanted to get to the safety of the air-raid shelter. The boys answered their mother's loud cry and they hurried down the stairs clutching their coats.

'Where's Wallace?' Dolly asked Dennis, the elder of the two.

' 'E's gone out, Mum,' Dennis answered.

Dolly sighed deeply. 'That boy's gonna be the death o' me,' she groaned. 'Well, we can't wait. Dennis, take that bundle o' beddin'. Leslie, grab that bag.'

The two lads did as they were told and Dolly quickly turned off the gas and electricity before leading the three children out into the bright moonlight.

The siren began to wail as the Dawsons hurried along Page Street, being joined by their neighbours. Iris Tanner was hurrying along with her three boys and Maudie was holding on to her husband's arm, grateful that the siren had sounded before they got into bed.

'I told yer, didn't I?' she was moaning to Ernest. 'I'd sooner be bitten by bugs than bombed in me bed.'

'Shut yer noise, woman,' Ernest reproached her. 'People are gonna fink we got bugs indoors.'

Dolly's daughter was whimpering in fear and Leslie put his arm round her as they reached the shelter entrance. 'You'll be all right,' he said, trying to be grown-up.

The three Salter girls came running along the street, ' 'E makes me so mad,' Brenda puffed. ' 'E's so bloody obstinate.'

'Well, it's up to 'im. If 'e wants ter stay in the 'ouse, it's 'is look-out,' Lily gasped.

Sadie and Maisie hurried along the turning behind Mrs Watson, Mrs Green and the elderly Mrs Haggerty. 'Don't sit near those three wise monkeys,' Sadie said sharply to her friend. 'They'll give us an earache wiv their bloody nonstop chatterin'.'

Josiah was ushering everyone into the safety of the concrete caverns. When he caught sight of Dolly with the children he pulled her to one side. 'Where's Wallace?' he growled.

'He went out earlier. Gawd knows where 'e's got to,' Dolly groaned.

Josiah swore under his breath. 'Get the kids inside an' soon as I get a chance I'll go an' look fer 'im,' he told her.

Danny glanced up at the large bright moon in the night sky as he walked swiftly along the cobbled lane that led down to the Cherry Garden steps. The cutter was waiting and as he climbed aboard he heard the wail of the siren. Already the roar of aircraft was becoming louder and suddenly the guns in nearby Southwark Park opened up. Amid the deafening noise, the cutter made its way midstream on the ebbing tide and manoeuvred into position beside the brace of laden barges. Danny clambered aboard the first one and began working away at the mooring rope, ready for the approaching tug which he could see clearly by the light of the full moon.

Suddenly there was a loud roar and a nearby wharf erupted in flames. Danny almost lost his footing in the blast, steadying himself quickly as the tug was manoeuvring to come alongside. He heard a shout and saw the tug's skipper pointing upriver, his urgent warning lost in the din. Danny glanced over to Tower Bridge and saw the dark object coming towards them, flying low above the twin towers. He threw himself prone on the deck of the barge, his hands over his ears. The next instant he was lifted bodily from the deck as the first bomb fell. He had the sensation of floating in mid-air, then suddenly the cold water shocked him back to stark reality.

When Danny broke surface he saw the burning wharves and the smoking remains of the tug. One of the barges was lying on its side slowly sinking in the muddy water and the other was drifting downstream. His heavy coat was waterlogged and badly hampering his movement. As he fought to undo the buttons, he was gripped by an agonising pain in his left arm and he gulped a deep breath as the water closed over him. He struggled back to the surface, somehow managing with tormenting pain to twist himself out of his coat. He realised that the tide was carrying him downstream. He knew that once he got into the swirling eddies, he would surely drown. He struck out for the quayside but his left arm was useless, torturing him with pain. He tried a side stroke but he could not make any headway. He could feel the undertow pulling him down and he knew that his life was coming to an end. He thought of Iris in that instant, and of the children. Were they safe in the shelter?

Something brushed past him and he saw that it was a length of timber. With a last despairing effort he reached out and with his good arm he managed to cling to it, desperately trying to straddle it as he felt his strength fading fast.

Wallace sat by the river, watching the distorted reflection of the moon in the muddy waters. He listened to the gurgling, sucking noise as the tide ebbed and he felt at peace. There had been no racket of war for the past few nights and he hoped that there would be no more bombs falling and no more guns roaring ever again. He wanted the lights to come on upriver and to see the gentle glow in the night sky. There were no lights tonight, but at least the moon was shining brightly.

The scream of the air-raid siren made Wallace jump down from his perch on the river wall. For a time he stood rooted to the spot, and then he decided to hurry back home before the other noises started. The sudden swish and violent explosion along the turning rocked him on his feet and he crouched down against the wall, pressing his hands over his ears. The street in front of him was full of flames and he realised he could not get back that way. Another explosion came from the direction of the river and a spray of water fell on him, wetting him through. He became desperate. He wanted to run, but he dare not rise from his meagre shelter. Overhead, shells burst brightly in the sky and he could feel the rumbling earth beneath him. Slowly, trembling, he raised himself up and peered over the wall at the river. He could see a ship burning and a smouldering barge drifting downriver. Along the quayside, fires were raging, and just then Wallace spotted the floating plank of wood. It seemed to be swirling round in the water, caught in an eddy, and he saw what looked like someone clinging to it.

He remembered hearing that falling in the Thames was very dangerous and the currents would surely carry a person away. That man was going to be drowned, Wallace thought. What could he do to stop it happening?

There was nothing he could do. He peered over the wall, wide-eyed with fear and dread for the man clinging to the plank. He watched helplessly as it swirled, and then he saw it move towards the mud a little way downstream. The man was going to be all right, he thought, he was pulling himself out of the water. Wallace became agitated as the man stumbled and fell. He was not moving now, and above him the flaming wharf was shedding burning debris. It was falling near him and still the man did not move.

Wallace slumped down on the wet cobblestones, his back pressed against the wall. He bit on his fingertips in his anxiety, hardly able to think. Suddenly he jumped up, wincing at the noise of the guns. Maybe he could go down the steps and pull the man away from the burning wharf. He hurried along, bent double, terrified by the gunfire. He reached the slippery steps and gingerly made his way down to the bottom. The tide was going out fast and as he put his foot onto the slimy mud it sank up to his knee. Wallace cried out in fear as he struggled back onto the steps. It was no use. He could never reach the man this way. What could he do? He must get help. His father would know what to do.

Josiah was standing in the shelter entrance talking to a group of men when he saw Wallace hurrying down the slope towards him. He could see the wet mud on the lad's trousers and with an angry roar he reached out for him, cuffing him round the head. Wallace put up his hands to protect himself and Tom Casey stepped up to the street warden.

'Leave 'im alone, mate, fer Gawd's sake,' he shouted.

'I'll murder the little git if 'e slopes orf again,' Josiah growled, pushing his son towards the shelter door.

Wallace stood where he was, his eyes filled with angry tears. 'Man's in the river,' he gulped, pointing away up the slope.

'Get in that shelter,' Josiah snarled at him.

Still Wallace stood his ground, his eyes wide in agitation. 'Man in the river. Burnin' all round 'im,' he cried out.

'What's 'e on about?' Tom Casey asked.

Suddenly Wallace ducked under his father's arm and rushed up the slope towards the street, stopping to wave the men after him.

Josiah glanced quickly at Tom, and without a word between them they hurried after him, belatedly recognising the lad's urgent plea for help.

Through the backstreets they hurried, following Wallace and urging him on every time he turned to see if they were still with him. At the Cherry Garden steps, he stopped and pointed. 'Man down there,' he cried.

Tom was first down the slippery steps, closely followed by Josiah. Tom pointed to the right where the still figure was lying face down on the length of timber, surrounded by burning chunks of wood from the blazing wharf.

'We'll need some planks,' Josiah shouted as he ran back up the steps.

Wallace pulled on his father's arm and Josiah allowed himself to be led along the lane. Wallace pointed excitedly to the timber lying scattered across the ruins of a warehouse and soon the three were back at the steps, each carrying a plank. Twice they made the journey before they were able to reach the unconscious lighterman. More burning debris fell around them as they gingerly eased Danny back, dragging him by his shoulders till they reached the safety of the steps.

'Mind 'ow yer carry 'im, Tom, 'e's got a broken arm by the looks of it,' Josiah told him.

At the top of the steps they laid Danny on his back with Josiah's coat under his head. Josiah bent over him and tapped his face gently. Suddenly Danny groaned and opened his eyes.

'Yer all right, mate, fanks ter me boy. 'E spotted yer an' 'e come fer us,' Josiah said proudly, looking up quickly at Wallace.

Tom went off to find a stretcher-bearer, and when the car finally arrived, Danny was strapped into the stretcher and placed on the roof. As the car drove out of the riverside lane, Josiah turned to Wallace and threw his arms round him. 'I'm sorry, son. I didn't know what yer were tryin' ter tell me,' he said gently. 'I'll never lay a finger on yer ever again, Gawd strike me dead if I do.'

Tom swallowed hard as he walked away along the cobbled lane. At the end of the road he turned to see Josiah setting off, his arm round Wallace's shoulders. The night smelt of cordite and burning wood, and the reek of danger was thick in the air. Tom hurried on, gently wanting to get back to what safety there was at the shelter, and his family.

Billy Sullivan had just reached the rescue squad's depot in Abbey Street when the first request came in by phone. A factory in Long Lane had been hit and there was a nightwatchman buried under the rubble. Billy gritted his teeth as the vehicle drove quickly but carefully over the debris-filled street and as it squealed to a halt he was running with the rest of the crew. Time was paramount if the man was to have any chance of survival. The local policeman showed them the watchman's likely whereabouts, and Jim Davis organised his men to begin digging.

For a time they worked without speaking, deafened by the din of war raging overhead. When they had made enough progress, Billy squeezed himself into the makeshift tunnel, dragging a heavy steel prop behind him. Other men removed timbers and manhandled huge chunks of masonry to lengthen the tunnel into the heart of the ruined factory.

Jim Davis was working at the head of the tunnel along with another of his squad when they heard a faint whimpering.

'Listen, Jim, it's comin' from below us,' the rescuer said, spitting out a mouthful of brick dust.

'It sounds like a dog,' Jim replied, reaching his hand down into a narrow gap in the rubble. 'I can't feel anyfing. We must be over the roof o' the offices.'

The two dug downwards, followed by Billy who passed the pieces of timber and brick back to the team man behind him. Suddenly Jim Davis disappeared through the hole and the men heard him cursing.

'You all right, Jim?' Billy shouted.

'Yeah, just about. I landed on the bloody table, head first,' he growled.

'What's the score?' the other rescuer called down into the hole.

'No sign o' the watchman. There's a mutt 'ere though,' he called out. 'Poor little fing's terrified, but it looks all right.'

The trembling mongrel was passed up to Billy who cuddled it to him as he eased himself backwards out of the hole. In the cool night air, with the noise all around, the dog started whining and Billy patted its head reassuringly. 'Where's yer owner, little fella?' he said quietly. 'Is 'e down there somewhere?'

The mongrel started to struggle and Billy gripped him tighter. 'It's all right, yer safe,' he said.

An old man scrambled over the rubble of the factory towards Billy. 'Gawd bless yer, son,' he cried, holding out his hands to the dog.

The mongrel whimpered as it scrabbled into the old man's arms and Billy's blackened face broke into a wide grin.

'I see 'e's yours,' he said. 'Are you the nightwatchman?'

The old man nodded. 'I went out ter the pub fer an Arrowroot biscuit an' a bottle o' beer an' I saw the 'ole place fall in,' he puffed. 'It was terrifyin'. I never thought I'd see Mitzi again, not alive anyway.'

Billy patted the dog's head. 'Well, yer can enjoy yer beer now,' he said, still grinning.

'This ain't mine,' the old man said indignantly. 'I never touch the stuff. It's fer Mitzi. She likes 'er Arrowroot an' a bottle o' stout, don't yer, gel?'

Billy heard Jim's voice coming from underground and he became serious. 'If I were you I'd make meself scarce. Our guv'nor's bin searchin' the ruins fer yer,' he said quickly.

The old man slapped Billy on the back and hurried away, just as Jim reappeared, cursing loudly. 'No nightwatchman there,' he said. 'Prob'ly pissed orf down the pub, wiv a bit o' luck. I'll 'ave ter get cleaned up now. I'm covered in bloody dog shit.'

The driver came hurrying over. 'We got anuvver one an' it's bad!' he shouted above the gunfire. 'Block o' flats in Garner Place. A direct 'it an' there's a shelter in the basement!'

Jim called his men together. 'C'mon, let's go,' he shouted. 'Who wants ter sit next ter me?'

As the blitz raged, Carrie sat with Joe and Nellie in the cellar of their house.

'This sounds like the worst one yet,' Nellie remarked, constantly wincing as loud explosions shook the house. 'Gawd 'elp us all. 'Ow much more 'ave we gotta take?'

Carrie patted her mother's arm reassuringly. 'We'll be all right, Mum,' she said quietly.

Joe got up and stretched. 'I fink I'll go up an' make a pot o' tea,' he said, 'That's if the gas is still on.'

'You stay where you are,' Carried ordered him. 'Wait till it quietens down a bit.'

'Carrie's right,' Nellie said. 'We got enough problems, wivout worryin' about you gettin' yer 'ead blown orf.'

Joe smiled as he eased himself back down into the chair. 'I bet Rachel's worried,' he remarked. 'She was prob'ly on duty ternight.'

Carrie nodded without replying. She had been thinking about Rachel at that moment, and about the conversation they had had when she was last at home. The news about Tony O'Reilly being Galloway's grandson had shaken her. The Jamie Robins affair had steeled her to go on fighting the Galloways, and now that George Galloway was dead there was only one man left to deal with. Frank Galloway would pay for what he did to Jamie, she had sworn. Now, out of the blue, she was suddenly faced with the prospect of her only child being married to a Galloway. From what Rachel had told her Tony seemed a nice lad, and it was obvious that her daughter was madly in love with him, but he was still a Galloway. He had their blood. Had he inherited the ruthless streak which made them so hard and insensitive, made them use people and destroy their lives? she wondered. True, Geoffrey Galloway had not been as hard as his father and brother, but it was all the same blood.

Carrie sighed and looked over at her mother who was trying to get on with a piece of needlework. She looked at Joe and realised that he had been staring at her.

'Rachel?' he asked.

Carrie nodded with a brief smile. Joe had become very perceptive lately. He seemed to have acquired the knack of reading her mind.

'I was jus' finkin' about 'er an' Tony,' she replied. 'I wanted ter scream an' shout at 'er when she told me about 'im. I couldn't though. I wanted ter warn 'er too, but I couldn't even do that. It took me by surprise.'

Nellie looked up from her sewing. 'Yer did right, Carrie,' she said quietly. 'Yer couldn't say anyfing ter drive a wedge between yer, an' it would 'ave done, mark my words. That gel finks the world of 'im. She would've bin torn between the boy an' 'er family. All yer 'ave ter remember is what 'appened ter young Josephine. If George Galloway 'ad've bin open wiv the gel right from the start, 'e might 'ave prevented 'er doin' what she did. By the time 'e did tell 'er the trufe, it was too late.'

Carrie nodded. 'That's exactly why I couldn't say what I was feelin', Mum,' she replied. 'I'm worried, though.'

Joe leaned back in his chair and brushed a hand over his head. 'It's early days yet,' he said. 'Rachel an' the lad are gonna be tergevver fer a few days an' then 'e's goin' off ter the front. Anyfink could 'appen. God ferbid, the lad might never come back. Yer must allow 'em a bit of 'appiness while they've got the chance.'

Carrie sighed. 'Rachel's a sensible gel, an' the lad too. It's just the thought of 'im bein' a Galloway. I've just got this terrible feelin' that nuffin' good'll come of it.'

Nellie looked up again, briefly sucking her pricked thumb. 'I always felt that the Galloway family was ill fated,' she said. 'Their money never brought 'em much 'appiness over the years. But we all get older, an' when we do, we come ter see fings in a different light. This might be what's needed ter break the chain. Yer gotta give 'em the chance. Besides, it's right what Joe said jus' now. Anyfing could 'appen. Just give 'em yer blessin', Carrie. Give 'em the start they need. The Lord Almighty'll do the rest.'

Maurice Salter had decided that come hell or high water he would spend the night in his own bed. He had done his share of double shifts recently and he was feeling exhausted. When the siren screamed out and his daughters tried to rouse him from the armchair, he had waved them away impatiently. He was enjoying his nap, and after a bit of supper he was looking forward to his comfortable bed. Now, as the house rocked and shook, he was snoring loudly. He did not hear the sudden swishing noise or the bang that followed it, but he woke up when a large piece of chimneypot dropped through the ceiling onto his bed, missing him by inches.

'What the bloody 'ell's goin' on?' Maurice shouted aloud as he saw the chunk of chimney lying on the pillow beside him. He turned onto his back and blinked a few times at the large hole in the ceiling, then scrambled frantically out of bed.

Ten minutes later he was sitting downstairs in the parlour watching the kettle begin to steam on the low fire. There was nothing he could do until the raid was over, he told himself. Then he would have to report the damage and get the workmen to put a piece of tarpaulin over the hole in the roof for the time being. Trouble was it might rain in the meantime, and then what? The bedclothes would be soaked, the ceiling plaster would fall in and the whole house would become damp and musty. Perhaps it would be better if he did the repair himself. There was an old tarpaulin sheet rolled up on the lavatory roof out in the back yard, and he could borrow a ladder easily enough.

He sat sipping his tea. The air raid seemed to have died down, and the gunfire had abated too. It was still only three in the morning and he knew from experience that the second wave of bombers would not be very long in coming. Better to get that tarpaulin sorted out now, he thought, putting his cup down. He put his overcoat on over his nightshirt and went out into the back yard.

'Oh my good Gawd!' he cried aloud as he stood looking at the dark object which had half buried itself in the yard. 'It's an unexploded bomb!'

The tarpaulin was forgotten as he gingerly took off his overcoat and crept up the stairs, frightened of making any noise. That thing might go off at any second, he thought. I'll have to report it to the police, and the street will have to be cleared.

Maurice threw the piece of chimneypot in the corner, wincing as he remembered to be quiet, and then sat down on the edge of his bed, trying to stay calm. If he was careful not to do anything silly, he would be all right, he told himself. First things first. Where's my trousers? he thought, looking round the bedroom. Then he remembered that he had undressed downstairs, being alone in the house. Carefully he got up and looked briefly over his shoulder at the window, as though expecting the bomb down below to explode at any second. Suddenly he heard a creak on the stairs and a gentle tap on his bedroom door.

'Are you awake, luv?'

'Oh my Gawd! It's Brenda!' he said aloud.

Brenda Massey pushed open the door and Maurice saw that she was wearing an overcoat over her long nightdress.

'Brenda,' he began hesitantly, wondering how he was going to explain about the unexploded bomb without putting her into a panic.

'Maurice, darlin'. I couldn't bear bein' alone ternight,' she said. 'Mum's gone ter stay wiv Rose an' I was sittin' in the shelter finkin' o' you. I 'ad ter come.'

'But, Brenda. It's a bit awkward ternight,' he said falteringly.

'Awkward nuffink,' she replied in a husky voice. 'Yer never let anyfing come between us an' our lovin'. I want yer, Maurice.'

Maurice winced as she sat down heavily on the bed beside him and started stroking his thigh. 'But it's dangerous up 'ere,' he told her in a weak voice.

'There's danger all around us, but we are two people in love. Nuffink else matters in the 'ole world,' Brenda went on, using the words from a film she had seen only a couple of days ago.

Maurice slipped his arm round her shoulders. 'Listen, luv,' he began. 'I love yer, an' you love me, right?'

Brenda fluttered her eyelashes and smiled sweetly at him.

'Well, yer must trust me. I wouldn't let anyfink 'appen ter yer,' he went on.

' 'Course yer wouldn't, darlin',' she sighed, rubbing his other leg.

'Well then, let's go downstairs an' I'll get dressed, then I'll take yer ter the shelter.'

Brenda turned towards him and wrapped her arms round him, pushing him back onto the bed. 'Darlin', I can't live wivout yer,' she breathed huskily. 'I need yer, need yer passionately. Tell me yer need me too.'

Maurice gulped as he fought to get out from under her. 'Yer don't understand,' he gasped. 'Your life, everybody's life depends on me. I must get dressed.'

Brenda was pleased with his performance so far, he was so straight-faced, but she had no intention of waiting all night for him to ravish her. In the film the hero succumbed very quickly, and if Maurice had seen it he would have known. 'Darlin'. Love me. Love me now,' she pleaded.

'I can't,' he gasped, squeezing from beneath her.

Brenda finally lost her patience. 'What's the matter wiv yer?' she said in a loud voice. ' 'Ave yer gone impotent or somefink?'

Maurice pointed to the ceiling as Brenda rolled over onto her back. 'Look at that,' he said.

'Never mind that. We can see the stars as we make love,' she drooled.

'I can't,' Maurice groaned.

'But why?'

' 'Cos there's a bloody great unexploded bomb in the back yard, that's why,' he shouted.

Chapter Thirty-Four

Tony O'Reilly stepped from the number 63 bus and hoisted his rifle over his shoulder as he set off through the backstreets to his house in Ferris Street. He was wearing a full pack and the thick canvas straps felt uncomfortable as he walked along, his studded boots sounding loudly on the pavement. A few people were standing around at their front doors and they gave him little more than a passing glance. The sight of a soldier in full service pack was quite usual now and only a few small children showed any interest.

Tony finally reached his corner house and knocked on the front door. His heart missed a beat when the door opened and he saw Lola standing there, a serious look on her flushed face.

'I'm glad yer 'ere, Tony. It's yer mum. She's took a turn fer the worse this mornin',' she said gravely.

He stood his rifle against the wall in the passageway and struggled quickly out of his packs.

'She's bin askin' for yer,' Lola told him, following on as he hurried into the back bedroom.

The room was stuffy and there was a strong smell of disinfectant.

' 'Ello, Ma. 'Ow yer feelin'?' Tony asked in a soft voice as he bent over the bed.

Mary's eyes opened briefly and a ghost of a smile touched her white lips. 'I bin waitin' for yer, boy,' she uttered in little more than a dry whisper.

Tony glanced up anxiously at Lola who was standing by the door. She nodded her head slowly. 'Stay there wiv yer mum, Tony, I'll make yer a nice cuppa,' she said kindly.

Mary's eyes flickered as she lifted a bony hand up off the covers and her lips moved. Tony bent over her, his ear to her mouth.

'Are yer all right, boy?' she whispered.

Tony stroked her cold hand. 'I'm fine, Ma,' he answered.

Mary held on to his hand. 'I've bin worryin' about yer,' she said, her eyes struggling to focus on him. 'Yer'll be goin' orf ter fight soon an' I want yer ter know I've said a prayer fer yer.'

The young soldier's eyes filled with tears as he bent over his dying mother. 'I'm gonna be all right, Ma,' he said. 'You'll still be 'ere when I get back.'

Mary forced a smile. 'I've seen me time out, Tony,' she whispered. 'I've come ter terms wiv it. I jus' want yer ter know I 'ad ter do what I did fer your sake. I wanted ter see yer on yer feet before I went.' She paused for a moment. 'Jus' be careful wiv the money, son,' she whispered. 'Don't ferget yer own. Jus' remember that money can bring yer 'appiness or misery. It's up ter you.'

Tony held his mother's hand in his. 'There's no need fer yer ter worry yerself, Ma,' he whispered in her ear. 'I'll never ferget me own, or where I come from.'

Mary smiled and then her face became rigid as her eyes closed. Tony gently placed her hand back on top of the covers and leaned back in his chair. He could see clearly that she was fading away, and when Lola came back into the bedroom carrying a cup of tea, he glanced up anxiously at her.

Lola put the cup down on the chair beside the bed and bent over Mary. 'She's asleep, luv,' she whispered. 'Ole Dr Kelly's bin round an' 'e said ter send fer 'im if we need to. Anyway, I'll leave yer alone fer a while. I'll come back later.'

Tony sat looking down at the ashen face of his dying mother. He could see the weak pulse beating in her neck and the occasional slight movement of her lips, as though she was trying to form words. She had told him before about her fears over his inheriting the Galloway money, and now in her last few hours she was talking about it again. Rachel had told him in her last letter of her own mother's concern, and he rested his chin on his hand as he stared down at the sleeping figure of his mother. He had vowed that he would not let the money change him in any way, if he could possibly help it. But would it change him in Rachel's eyes? he wondered. What was it that old Nora Flynne had said when he spoke to her after the reading of the will? That he should go and see her if he was troubled by the money. Why was she so adamant about it? What was it that made everyone so concerned?

Tony sipped his tea slowly and watched his ailing mother as she slept. It had been very hard for her over the years, he realised. From the very beginning she had vowed to stay independent of any help from the Galloway family, and it must have been difficult for her to make the initial approach to the old man. Knowing that her health was failing, she would have felt driven to provide for his future, but he knew that she must have agonised over whether it was the right thing to do, judging by her warnings to him about the way he handled his inheritance.

His mother seemed to be sleeping peacefully and Tony took the opportunity to go to the scullery and boil the kettle. He washed and shaved, and then changed into his civilian clothes, putting on a clean shirt and grey trousers which he found in his wardrobe. All of his clothes had been washed and ironed and he knew that it was something his mother had not been well enough to do. The whole house looked clean and tidy and Tony realised that it must have been Lola who had made it so. He must thank her for her help, and for the way she always seemed to be there when his mother was poorly.

The evening felt chilly and he lit the fire, banking it up with a large piece of coal. He had just boiled the kettle again and was making tea when Lola returned. She laid a paper parcel down on the table and unwrapped it.

'I just bin up ter Kellerman's. They stay open late on Saturdays,' she told him. 'I got some brawn. Yer mum said yer like brawn.'

Tony smiled at her and nodded. 'I 'adn't thought about eatin',' he replied. 'That looks good.'

Lola took a loaf of bread from the cupboard and proceeded to cut thick slices, coating them liberally with margarine. She spread the thin slivers of brawn between the bread and handed Tony his sandwich on a plate. 'I've not 'ad a chance to eat meself,' she said, taking a bite from hers.

Tony poured the tea and handed Lola a cup. 'I'm sorry but I should 'ave fanked yer fer takin' care o' me mum,' he said, 'an' fer doin' all me washin' an' ironin'.'

Lola waved his thanks away. 'It's no trouble,' she replied. 'She insisted on payin' me but I wouldn't let 'er give me too much. I've got quite fond o' yer mum. She was good ter me when I needed 'elp.'

Tony's raised eyebrows prompted her to go on. 'Yer know what I do fer a livin',' she reminded him. 'About a month ago I got a wrong 'un. D'yer know what I mean by a wrong 'un?'

Tony nodded. 'I fink so.'

'No, yer don't,' Lola replied smiling at him. 'One night I took a client back 'ome an' 'e turned nasty. 'E wanted more than I was prepared to give. Anyway, I tried ter get rid of 'im an' 'e beat me up. I couldn't work fer a week an' I was feelin' very sorry fer meself. It was yer mum who come ter me aid. She paid me rent an' 'elped me out wiv food. I couldn't 'ave managed wivout 'er 'elp. Not once 'as she criticised me or tried ter preach ter me. I appreciated that. Anyway, I managed ter pay the money back I borrered from 'er, an' I might tell yer I 'ad a terrible job makin' 'er take it, so now I'm repayin' a bit of 'er kindness, though like I say, she insists on payin' me fer the washin' an' ironin'.'

'Don't yer 'ave somebody ter watch out fer yer when yer workin'?' Tony asked her.

Lola smiled. 'A ponce, yer mean?'

He shrugged his shoulders. 'I would 'ave thought it was necessary to 'ave somebody watchin' out fer yer,' he said.

The street woman snorted dismissively. 'I did 'ave somebody lookin' out fer me at one time,' she replied. 'It was my ole man. 'E was as useless as they come, an' as thick as two short planks. 'E used ter wait on my earnin's ter go out an' get pissed, an' then 'e'd be wantin' to 'ave 'is way wiv me when 'e got 'ome. I stood it fer as long as I could an' then I chucked 'im out. It was the best day's work I ever did. I can look after meself.'

Tony ate his sandwiches without saying anything, and when Lola lapsed into silence he studied her face as she stared down at the glowing coals. He felt compassion for the warm-hearted prostitute and after a few minutes he leaned back in his chair and rubbed his hand round the back of his neck.

'When the war's over I'll be goin' inter business I expect,' he announced suddenly. 'Maybe I could give yer a job.'

'Workin' fer you?' Lola said, her eyes sparkling. 'An' what would I do, look after yer clients' needs?'

Tony grinned. 'I s'pose yer could make me tea an' keep me place clean, or yer could do me books,' he added quickly, noting the look in her eye.

Lola kicked off her shoes and wiggled her stockinged feet at the flames. 'Let's wait till the war's over,' she told him.

The sound of coughing coming from the back bedroom startled them and they hurried to tend to Mary. Tony eased his mother upright while Lola dabbed at her red-flecked lips.

'Yer gotta understand it's quite probable yer mum won't last the night out,' she said quietly, trying to be kind. 'All we can do is keep an eye on 'er.'

'We?' Tony queried. 'There's a full moon ternight. I should fink we're gonna be in fer an air raid. Yer should get yerself off ter the shelter soon,' he told her.

Lola shook her head. 'I couldn't leave 'er,' she replied. 'If there is a raid, I'll take me chances 'ere. What's ter be will be.'

Back in the parlour Tony drained his cup and reached for the teapot, feeling grateful that Lola had decided to stay. 'I s'pose yer'll be wantin' anuvver cuppa now,' he said smiling.

When they'd finished their tea Lola went out to the sink and rinsed out the two teacups and Tony sat watching her through the doorway. She was in her early forties, he guessed. She was dark in complexion and her large brown eyes were warm and friendly, in a round face that inclined to be chubby, with narrow lips and a dimpled chin. Her hips were large and she was full-busted, though her legs were slim and she had slender ankles. She must have been a beautiful woman in her youth, he thought. But the life she led had taken its toll. There were red patches on her face and her hair looked coarse and wispy. There were bulges under her eyes and her fingernails looked like they were constantly being bitten.

302

Lola dried the cups and set them down on the table. 'I'll go an' take anuvver peep at yer mum,' she said.

Tony leaned back in his chair and stared at the fire. The prospect of seeing Rachel again filled him with excitement and he thought about the few days they would spend together. It would be the last time for a lengthy period, he knew, though his regiment's destination had not yet been divulged. The tanks and armoured cars had been getting a treatment of sand-coloured paint and camouflage, and the troops were being issued with tropical clothing. The strong rumour was that they were bound for North Africa, though one wag had said that it was a subterfuge and they were really going down to guard the south coast against an invasion. There was also speculation that the regiment was bound for India.

Lola came back into the room and sat down beside the fire, facing him. 'She's sleepin' peacefully,' she said.

Tony nodded, his eyes getting heavy as he stared into the fire. 'Are yer sure yer feel all right about stoppin' 'ere?' he asked. 'It could be an 'eavy raid wiv that full moon.'

Lola nodded her head, frowning at him. 'I'm all right,' she replied. 'I've got a big man ter protect me.' Tony blushed slightly and she smiled. 'Yer mum told me about yer young lady,' she said. 'I understand it's serious.'

'Yeah, it is, but it'll be some time before I get the chance ter see 'er after this leave,' he replied. 'We're goin' overseas very soon.'

'D'yer know where?' Lola asked.

Tony shook his head. 'It might be the Middle East,' he told her.

They were quiet for a while, each staring into the burning coals, and it was Lola who broke the silence. 'D'yer fink yer young lady will wait fer yer?' she asked suddenly.

Tony looked up, surprise showing on his open face. 'Of course she will,' he replied, sounding a little sharp.

Lola shrugged her shoulders. 'Some don't,' she said. 'But then that sort are not werf considerin' in the first place,' she added, seeing the concern on his face. 'No, I'm sure yer young lady'll stay true. She's a lucky gel. If you were footloose an' fancy free I'd be askin' yer ter put yer shoes under my bed, an' there'd be no charge.'

Tony laughed loudly, trying to hide his embarrassment, and just at that moment the air-raid siren sounded.

They got up and went out into the back bedroom, both concerned about the effect of the wail on the sick woman. As Tony leant over the bed, he could see that his mother had not heard it. Her breath was slow and shallow, and the pulse in her thin neck was steady but faint.

The two left the room and went back into the warm parlour, Lola wincing noticeably as the anti-aircraft guns opened up. For a while they sat without speaking, then as the first explosion sounded Lola pointed to the bedroom. 'I fink we'd better sit wiv yer mum, Tony,' she said.

The house shook and they heard the sound of breaking glass and the clatter of roof tiles falling on cobblestones. Plaster dust fell on the counterpane and Tony instinctively bent over his mother. She had still not woken up and he glanced at Lola.

'She's in a coma,' she said quietly. 'She won't 'ear anyfing.'

The noise became louder and the house shook violently as a bomb fell nearby. Guns constantly roared out deafeningly and the crash of exploding bombs sounded every few seconds, but time seemed to be standing still in the room as the blitz raged angrily around them. Lola crossed herself as she looked up at the ceiling. 'This is the worst one yet, by the sound of it,' she said in a voice edged with fear.

Tony nodded, leaning forward over the sleeping form of his mother. Suddenly Mary jumped in her sleep and began to fidget. She started mumbling and her hands were moving as though trying to come up and cover her ears.

Lola touched Tony's arm. 'I fink yer should go fer the doctor, luv. I don't fink it'll be long now,' she said quietly.

Tony looked at her anxiously. 'Will yer be all right 'ere?' he asked.

Lola nodded. 'Go an' fetch 'im, luv,' she said.

Tony slipped on his coat and hurried out of the house. The street was as bright as day and the red glow of destruction in the sky reflected back down onto the grey cobblestones. Gunflashes and black smoke pouring towards the heavens reminded Tony of his time on the beaches at Dunkirk and his face was set firm as he hurried along towards the New Kent Road where the elderly Dr Kelly lived. He saw a large fire burning up ahead and a fire tender drove past as he hunched his shoulders and bent his head against the shrapnel.

At last he reached the doctor's house sandwiched between two shuttered shops. His loud knock was answered by a grey-haired lady whom he recognised as the doctor's wife.

'It's Mrs O'Reilly. She needs the doctor,' he said breathlessly.

The woman nodded. 'The doctor was expecting you,' she told him. 'He's out on call. I'll get him to come round as soon as possible.'

Tony thanked her and hurried back towards Ferris Street. Above in the angry night sky the moon seemed as serene as ever, as if it were smiling down on the scenes of carnage and destruction. When he turned the corner into Ferris Street, Tony suddenly gasped and started running. His house was ablaze. Smoke poured from the windows and he could hear the crackle of flames eating away at the inside. He stood back from the front door for an instant then charged forward, using his shoulder to barge in. As he broke in he fell over Lola who was lying beside the front door groaning. Smoke filled the passageway and he coughed loudly as he dragged her out into the street. He turned to go into the flames for his mother but suddenly the house was engulfed.

The heat beat him back and he fell down on the pavement scorched and blackened.

Lola was stirring painfully, and as he crawled to her she rolled onto her side and her eyes flickered.

'Yer mum died just as yer left,' she managed to gasp out.

Tony looked down at her. She was badly burned; all the hair had been seared from her head and her face was blistered and swollen. She tugged on his arm and he bent over her, cradling her head in his arms. He could see there was nothing that could be done for her and he raised his eyes helplessly towards the smoke-filled sky as she tried desperately to speak.

She coughed suddenly and cried out in pain. 'Tell Gloria,' she muttered. 'Tell Gloria she was right . . . 'E did . . .'

Her voice trailed off and Tony felt her go limp in his arms.

He was still cradling Lola's head when Dr Kelly arrived in his ancient Vauxhall. He bent down over the still figure and took off his steel helmet as he made a brief examination, then he glanced at Tony, shaking his head.

The young man jerked his head towards the flaming house. 'This lady was wiv me mum,' he said. 'She told me she died just as I left ter fetch yer.'

Old Dr Kelly brushed a hand over his snow-white hair and replaced his steel helmet. 'That was a blessing, son,' he replied quietly.

Tony nodded. 'It must 'ave bin an incendiary bomb. I couldn't get back in there fer 'er.'

Dr Kelly stared at the burning house. 'Were your army clothes in there?' he asked.

Tony nodded. 'Me rifle an' full pack as well,' he replied.

'Don't worry, come and see me before your leave's up. I'll give you a letter to take back to camp with you,' the doctor told him. 'It should do. Now you'd better get off the street, it's getting worse. Don't worry, I'll deal with everything,' he added quietly, nodding towards Lola's badly burned body.

Tony got up reluctantly and made his way to the nearby shelter, a brick-built, reinforced surface shelter that had been erected in a cul-de-sac off Ferris Street. In the covered doorway he saw a few faces he recognised among the men who were standing on guard, helpless as the fires raged and bombs fell. They were huddled together and one elderly man reached out towards him. 'Are you all right, Tony boy?' he asked with concern as he grabbed the young soldier's arm and pulled him under the concrete canopy.

Tony gazed back out into the street. 'The 'ouse is gone. I couldn't get ter me muvver, the fire was too fierce,' he replied.

The men all stared at him, not knowing what to say, and the elderly man looked down at his wet, sticky hand. 'Yer bleedin' son,' he said.

Tony saw the large patch of blood on his coat sleeve and he realised it had come from Lola as he cradled her in the crook of his arm. 'I'm all right,' he replied.

'I'm very sorry about yer muvver, son,' the old man said. 'She was a very nice lady. I knew 'er well.'

Tony gave him a brief smile. 'She died before the fire started,' he told him. 'I would 'ave bin dead too if I 'adn't gone fer the doctor. Me mum's friend was wiv 'er at the time. She's dead too.'

The old man shook his head sadly. 'Poor Lola. She was very good ter yer muvver.'

'Yer knew 'er then?' Tony asked him.

The elderly man nodded. 'We all did round 'ere. I can't believe she's gorn,' he said miserably.

Lola's last words came into Tony's mind and he looked intently at the old man. 'D'yer 'appen ter know who Gloria is?' he asked.

A loud explosion shook the shelter and the men huddled down to escape the flying debris. The old man cursed aloud and dusted his coat with a gnarled hand. 'Yer was askin' me about a Gloria,' he said.

Tony nodded. 'Lola mumbled the name Gloria just before she died.'

'I'm sorry but I don't know anybody by that moniker,' the old man said, scratching his bald head. 'Any o' you lads 'eard of a Gloria?'

The men all shook their heads. 'Could be one o' the street gels,' one said.

Throughout the rest of the night, bombs continued to fall and many backstreets were hit and destroyed. Wharves, factories and warehouses burned out of control as the fire crews struggled to pump water from the middle of the river. The tide was at its lowest for years on that particular night. Medical staff worked tirelessly through the night as casualties filled the local hospitals; even the boiler room at one hospital was used to house the less severely injured patients.

As the dawn light filtered into the smoke-filled sky, Tony left the shelter and walked through the devastated streets. No buses or trams were running and everywhere he looked he saw grey-faced people standing around in a state of shock. The by now familiar smell of cordite and smouldering timbers filled the air, and as he made his way towards Rachel's home in Salmon Lane, he shivered uncontrollably, although the morning was warm.

Chapter Thirty-Five

Page Street was deathly quiet as the bomb disposal team worked on the unexploded bomb in the Salters' back yard. All the inhabitants of the little backstreet had been sent to a nearby rest centre and Maurice Salter found himself the centre of attraction.

'Gawd, it must 'ave bin terrifyin',' Maisie remarked to him.

Maurice shrugged his shoulders. 'I took a good look at it an' I could see the nuts an' bolts on the side of it,' he replied. 'So I put me ear to it ter find out if it was tickin'.'

'Was it?' Maisie asked, her eyes open wide.

'Nah, there was a funny whirrin' noise though,' he told her. 'I guessed it was the auto-gyro goin' round so I decided I'd better sort it out.'

'Go on.'

'Well, I made meself a cuppa an' I thought about it while I was drinkin' me tea.'

'What then?'

'I got me tools out to 'ave a go at it while yer were still in the shelter but I thought better of it. I wasn't worried fer meself, yer understand, but it could 'ave done untold damage ter the street if it 'ad 'ave gone up.'

Maudie was equally eager to talk to Maurice. 'I bet yer won't be sleepin' in yer own bed from now on,' she said, thinking of what her husband had promised her.

Maurice shrugged again. 'It don't worry me, luv,' he said. 'I get a better sleep in me own bed. It's more private, too.'

Brenda Massey was standing beside him and she stifled a grin. Maudie, however, looked horrified at his bravado. 'Didn't yer feel a bit scared when yer see that 'orrible fing stickin' up in the yard?' she asked him.

'Nah. Like I said, I understand about mechanics,' he replied. 'Yer gotta know about such fings when yer work at the gasworks. As a matter o' fact I wanted ter give the bomb disposal chaps an 'and but the sergeant in charge said they could manage quite well. 'E promised ter give me a shout if they do need any 'elp though.'

'Cor, ain't yer brave,' Maudie told him. 'My Ernest would 'ave run a mile, wouldn't yer, luv.'

Ernest growled an unintelligible reply and dragged his wife away.

Sadie meanwhile, had been talking to Maurice's daughters and she was of the opinion that their father was a raving idiot.

'What possessed 'im ter stay in the 'ouse last night?' she asked Lily.

' 'E's so bleedin' obstinate at times,' the young woman replied. 'We kept tellin' 'im that one night somefing would 'appen. Who'd 'ave thought it'd be an unexploded bomb though? Jus' fancy, 'e could 'ave bin blown sky 'igh.'

' 'E would 'ave bin, an' the 'ole bleedin' lot of us too if 'e'd started fiddlin' about wiv the bloody fing,' Sadie told her.

'I don't fink 'e would 'ave touched it,' Lily said smiling. 'Our dad looks all cool, calm an' collected but it's all swagger. 'E's bin shakin' like a leaf ever since 'e first discovered it.'

Brenda and Barbara Salter both looked a little embarrassed as they listened to their father going on about the unexploded bomb and Barbara was moved to interrupt the conversation he had started with Bert Jolly and the three wise ones, the Mrs Green, Haggerty and Watson.

'Why don't yer sit down an' rest, Dad?' she said, giving him a wicked look. 'Yer look tired.'

Maurice scoffed at the idea. 'I was just tellin' the ladies, I might be called ter give the bomb disposal fellas an 'and,' he said. 'I know the layout o' the place, yer see. There's the gas pipes an' water supply. Yer gotta know where all those fings are.'

'Why's that?' Mrs Green asked.

'Well, yer see, if the bomb did go orf an' they 'adn't shut the gas orf, then there'd be a sort of chain reaction,' he told her, hooking his thumbs through his braces.

'Oh yeah,' Mrs Green replied, not knowing what he was talking about.

' 'Alf o' Bermon'sey could go up if they never shut the gas orf,' Maurice told her.

'Yer mean ter tell me the bomb disposal blokes wouldn't know 'ow ter shut the gas orf?' Bert queried.

'Not in our 'ouse, they wouldn't,' Maurice informed him. 'Yer see, I boxed all the pipes in when I done a bit o' decoratin'. They wouldn't know where ter look. Mind you, I'm not sayin' I wouldn't be a bit scared ter go back in the 'ouse wiv that bloody great bomb sittin' in me back yard, but at times like these yer ferget yer fears, don't yer?'

Bert nodded. 'If they call yer back ter give 'em a bit of 'elp, yer could be in fer a medal, yer know. Yer could even get the George medal.'

'They'll more likely put 'im up fer the VD an' scar, lavatory ball an' chain,' Tom Casey growled to his wife.

'Don't you start,' she told him sharply. 'One joker's about all I can stand, fank you very much.'

By midday the bomb was disarmed and the Page Street folk returned home. Granny Massey had the final word on the subject.

'Trust that clown ter be different,' she growled. 'If it 'ad landed anywhere else, it would 'ave gorn orf.'

'Well, it wasn't Maurice's fault it didn't go orf,' Brenda said sharply.

'Pity it didn't. Did you 'ear the silly git goin' on about what 'e was gonna do? Take 'is tools to it indeed,' Granny said scathingly. 'There's only two tools 'e know 'ow ter use an' one's an 'ammer.'

Bella Galloway was not too sure any more whether returning to her home in Ilford had been a wise move. The reading of the will had been a bombshell but Frank had taken it all so calmly. She had expected him to rant and rave about it all and she would have understood. If it had been her father, she would have contested the will but Frank had said that it was not worth the expense.

Bella cursed to herself as she sat in front of her dressing-table mirror and brushed her unruly hair. It used to be so manageable, she thought. Her face was looking blotchy, too, and there were pouches forming beneath her eyes. Thank goodness her talent had not deserted her. Graham Cunningham had been at pains to say that she would be his first choice when he put his new show together. There might be a part in it for Caroline too, he had said. Caroline was doing well at drama school and she had been in a few student revues to entertain the forces recently. A chip off the old block, Graham had said, though Bella recalled admonishing him about the word 'old'. She would have to keep an eye on Caroline, she realised. Graham was a lecher, and she had learned through experience that he enjoyed seducing his female cast. She had been in that position herself long ago, though she could not really consider herself to have been seduced. It was more a case of vamping her director.

Caroline came into the bedroom and flopped down on the bed. 'He's still snoring, Mummy,' she said disdainfully.

'We'll let him sleep,' Bella replied with a false smile. 'Daddy was at the yard all through last night's raid.'

'Why did he have to be there?' Caroline asked, looking over her mother's shoulder at her profile. 'Surely the manager could have sorted things out?'

Bella shrugged her shoulders. 'You know how Daddy has to supervise everything,' she sighed, 'and that manager is a complete nincompoop, from what I've heard. It's been a week now and the front gates are still not repaired. Then there were the files and books to salvage from the office fire. I think it's all been too much for the poor dear. When he came home this morning he was absolutely all in. I made him go to bed immediately. I can't stand him around me when he's tetchy, and you know what he's like when he gets tired, especially since that business of the will.'

Caroline pulled a face. 'Yes, but he's not being fair to you, Mummy. After all you've done to support him. I mean to say, how many in your position would have given up a marvellous career for a grumpy husband?'

Bella smiled benignly at her daughter. She would not have described her career as all that marvellous over the past year, though Graham seemed to think that she had been a wonderful trouper. But then Graham had said that one night when he had had too much to drink and was trying to atone for his inadequacy between the sheets.

'We must make allowances,' Bella said with forced gravity.

'Will you stay here or go back to the show now that Daddy's got to carry on with the business?' Caroline asked.

Bella sighed and put down the brush, feeling that she was wasting her time on her hair. 'I'll wait and see. It all depends on Graham Cunningham,' she replied with a sly smile. 'He's promised me a lead in the new show.'

Caroline hid her displeasure. Graham had told her that he was looking for a new, fresh face, someone with exceptional talent who would take the audience by the scruff of the neck, captivate them by sheer presence. He had intimated that she was in the running for the starring role, and Caroline was more than willing to make the necessary sacrifices for stardom.

In Salmon Lane, Carrie and Joe were still clearing up after the raid. The yard was strewn with rubble from a nearby explosion and one of the lorries had had all its windows blown out. The gate was hanging from its hinges and neither the water nor the gas was working. Worse still was the news that Paddy Byrne had been bombed out and was going to be off for a few days while he sorted things out. Rachel was due home that day and Carrie was worried about how she was going to get to London. The local policeman had told her that all the nearby stations were closed due to extensive damage and the regular routes throughout the borough had been disrupted. The transport manager of the leather factory she was contracted to had been on the phone to say that the warehouse had been badly damaged during the raid and they would be unable to trade for at least a week or two.

Joe was whistling as he swept up the yard, trying to remain cheerful in spite of all the dislocation, but Nellie was very pessimistic about their chances for survival if they had to face another air raid.

'I was listenin' ter the news earlier,' she told her daughter. 'They reckon it's the worst raid we've 'ad in London. We can't stand much more of it. I saw Mrs Black come past the gate early this mornin' an' she got talkin'. D'yer know that they've gotta let the fires burn themselves out? The Thames was almost dry last night. 'Er 'usband's in the fire brigade an' 'e told 'er that it was the worst night they've ever 'ad ter face. Gawd knows what's ter become of us.'

Carrie went out to help Joe in the yard, and suddenly she looked up to see a young man standing by the gate. He was ashen-faced and dishevelled and his clothes were creased and blackened. She quickly went over to him, shocked by the state he was in.

'Whatever's wrong?' she asked him anxiously.

'I didn't know where else ter go,' he said in little more than a whisper.

'You're – you're Tony O'Reilly,' Carrie said suddenly, looking into his frightened eyes.

The young man nodded slowly and Carrie felt his eyes searching her for some reaction.

'I'm Rachel's mum,' she said quickly. 'Whatever's 'appened?'

Tony's head drooped and he shuddered noticably. 'My mum died last night, in the air raid. The 'ouse was bombed.'

Carrie had often wondered how she would receive the young man who had captured her daughter's heart. Would her feelings against the Galloways erupt into anger or would she feel a coldness towards him? None of that mattered now as she stood at the gate facing the distressed young soldier. Her warm heart went out to him and she wanted to hold him tight against the tragedy he had experienced. She slipped her arm around his shoulders and led him into the yard.

Joe hurried over. 'What's wrong?' he asked sharply.

'This is Tony, our Rachel's Tony, an' 'e's out on 'is feet,' Carrie said, her eyes wide with concern. 'Tony lost 'is mum last night. Their 'ouse was bombed.'

Joe led the young man into the house.

' 'E's in a state o' shock,' he whispered to Nellie as Tony slumped down into the armchair.

Carrie took the steaming kettle from the fire and made a pot of tea while Joe went into the yard to throw some more wood onto the large brazier they were using to heat up buckets of water.

Tony sat sipping his tea, slowly telling them what had happened. 'I didn't know where ter go after the raid ended,' he said in a hushed voice. 'I started out ter come 'ere but I suddenly felt so tired. Me legs were givin' out an' I sat in the churchyard fer a while. I must 'ave fallen asleep an' I woke up shiverin'.'

'Well, we're glad yer 'ere now. We'll fill the bathtub an' yer can 'ave a nice soak, then it's bed fer you, me lad,' Carrie told him firmly.

Tony started to protest but she silenced him with a wave of her hand. 'Rachel's gonna be 'ome terday, please Gawd, an' yer wouldn't want 'er ter see yer lookin' all tired and worn out, now would yer?' she reminded him.

Joe had been busy filling up the bathtub, and as he was putting fresh buckets of water on the brazier, he saw Danny's wife Iris hurrying into the yard.

'Danny's bin 'urt,' she said, her voice almost breaking. 'I've just come from Guy's.'

' 'Ow bad is 'e?' Joe asked, taking hold of her arm and leading her towards the house.

'It's 'is arm. It's broken, an' 'e's swallered a lot o' water,' Iris told him, her hand going up to her mouth.

Carrie and Nellie listened with grim faces to her account of Danny's accident. 'It was Dolly's lad Wallace who spotted Danny in the river,' she told them. 'If it wasn't fer 'im 'e'd 'ave bin dead now.'

'Wallace spotted him?' Carrie said.

Iris nodded. 'God knows what 'e was doin' by the river durin' the raid, but it was providence 'e was there. 'E run fer Josiah an' 'im an' Tom Casey an' Wallace pulled Danny out. It was a miracle 'e survived, accordin' ter Josiah. There was bits o' burnin' debris fallin' all round 'im when they got to 'im. 'E was lyin' in the mud by the river wall.'

'Thank Gawd for Wallace,' Nellie said and stiffly got to her feet. 'I fink I'll go an' 'ave a lie-down now. Anuvver night like last night an' I'll be sleepin' on me feet.'

Carrie sat comforting Iris for a while and then they left together to visit Danny at Guy's Hospital. Tony was soaking in the bathtub and Joe took the opportunity to finish clearing the yard. It was true that the last night's raid had been the heaviest yet. All the services were cut, transport was not moving and even the fires were being left to burn themselves out. Joe felt suddenly depressed. They couldn't be expected to carry on like this.

It was then that he felt the strong desire to take a drink. At first he dismissed the feeling, but on this occasion he found it very difficult to ignore. He had a nagging urge to go to the cupboard in the parlour; there was a bottle of brandy there, kept for Nellie when she had one of her bad turns.

For a while he tried to forget it, but later, when the tidying up was finished, he went into the parlour and stared for a time at the cupboard. Tony had finished his bath and gone to bed as Carrie had told him to. For years now he had resisted all temptations to take a drink. Never had he gone near a pub since his pledge to Carrie, but the urge now was stronger than he had ever known it. Slowly his hand reached out for the bottle and quickly he pulled back. It would be a betrayal, he knew, even to take the smallest sip. Just one little sip would be the starting. He lowered his head and gripped his hands into tight fists, fighting his desire. Just one little sip, he heard himself say. Just one little sip.

'Don't do it, Joebo,' he heard a voice say, and turned quickly to see Rachel standing in the doorway.

Joe spread his arms and immediately Rachel went to him, hugging him tightly.

312

'I've bin worried sick in case I found the place gone when I got 'ome,' she said shuddering.

Joe placed his hands on her shoulders and eased her away from him, and there was a serious look on his face. 'Yer know yer just saved my life,' he told her. 'I came so close just then. Let me look at yer. Gawd, yer look beautiful. Young Tony's a lucky lad.'

Rachel's eyes searched his. '' 'As it bin bad lately, Joe?' she asked. 'The urge fer a drink, I mean?'

He shook his head vigorously. 'No, it must 'ave bin the effects o' last night. It was terrible,' he said quietly.

Rachel sat down heavily in the chair and undid the buttons of her tunic. 'I was lucky ter get 'ome,' she said. 'There's no trains runnin' from Kent, but I managed ter scrounge a lift from one o' the drivers. I got ter Sidcup, then I got a bus as far as Black'eath. I walked from there. I've never seen anyfing like it. There's 'ole streets all in ruins, an' there's fires still burnin' out o' control.'

He shook his head sadly and gave a deep sigh. 'It was very bad,' he replied.

Rachel looked around. 'Where's Mum? I was expectin' 'er ter come boundin' in. And Gran?'

'Nellie's upstairs, restin'. Yer mum's gone ter see yer Uncle Danny. 'E's in Guy's. It was while 'e was workin' last night, luv,' he said calmly. '' 'E's got a broken arm. They fished 'im from the river an' they say it's a miracle 'e's still alive.'

Rachel stood up and started to button up her tunic. 'I'll go an' see 'im right away,' she said quickly.

Joe went to her and gripped her arms. 'Now look, young lady, yer've jus' got 'ome,' he said firmly. 'Besides, they won't let too many round the bed at one time. Yer Uncle Danny's gonna be all right. Now kick yer shoes off while I make some tea.'

Rachel watched while Joe spooned tea leaves into the large china teapot and after a moment or two he deliberately met her gaze.

'There's somefing else,' he said quietly. 'Young Tony's muvver died last night.'

Rachel dropped her head. 'I'm so sorry. Tony worshipped 'is mum. It'll be a terrible loss. I must get round ter see 'im soon as I've 'ad me tea.'

'There's no need. 'E's 'ere,' Joe told her.

'' 'Ere?'

'Tony's asleep in our room.'

Rachel was puzzled and Joe proceeded to tell her all he and Carrie had learned from Tony. By the time he had finished, Rachel was filled with an intense yearning for her young man. She wanted to go to him, hold him close and comfort him, but she knew that at the moment he needed sleep most of all. There would be time. Five days of being together. Five whole days in which she would comfort him, make him feel good and love him, and he would love her.

1944

Chapter Thirty-Six

A bright sun shimmered over the still waters of the River Thames as the two old friends took their Saturday afternoon walk along its quiet industrial reaches. The tall cranes were still, arched down towards the patched-up wharves and the blackened gaps where the quayside had been blasted beyond renovation. Laden barges lay at anchor in midstream, and a little way upriver, Tower Bridge loomed, its twin towers guarding the inner pool of London like sentinels.

The two friends walked slowly, hands in pockets, their hair greying, their gait less confident now. Billy Sullivan's shoulders still rolled, though not so noticeably, and Danny Tanner did not hold himself quite so upright any more.

'That's where I went in,' Danny said, almost to himself.

Billy heard his friend say that every Saturday afternoon but he still nodded and followed the direction of Danny's pointing finger, and he still made the same observation. 'You was lucky that night, Danny boy.'

Danny nodded and almost without thinking rubbed at his slightly shortened arm which he had not been able to use properly ever since. 'That finished me as a lighterman, but I'm not sorry,' he went on. 'A lighterman's game is more suited ter the young man as long as 'e's got the strength.'

Billy felt a sadness for his old friend. The river was Danny's life, and he had never been more happy than when he was jumping between moving barges and fighting to get them in position, whether for the trip downstream or into their Bermondsey moorings. Now he was reduced to working as a checking clerk, still on the quayside, but he held a pencil and clipboard in his rough, weatherbeaten hands instead of a thick hawser.

They turned away from the river, still tasting the tangy air and the beer they had drunk that lunchtime at the Bargee. They passed by the boarded-up ruins of Bacon Buildings and Billy ran his fingers along the corrugated sheeting that was bowing out from the movement of the soil. 'The ole place 'as changed over the past couple o' years,' he remarked.

Danny's memories of the buildings were mixed. On the one hand he remembered his mother and father discussing Carrie's new venture, his mother voicing her reservations and his father full of excitement at the prospect of working with his beloved horses once more, and on the other hand he recalled the hard times, the flickering gas jets casting gloomy shadows, the peeling paintwork, the ripe smell of the communal bins and the creaking, freshly scrubbed wooden stairways. He recalled the tragedy too: the sad woman who had walked from the buildings one night, out through the snow to end it all in the freezing river. She had almost cost him his own life when he went in the water to save her, and all it did in the end was put back the day when she finally killed herself.

Billy's shoulder touched Danny's as he moved to cross the street, and Danny grinned to himself. It was always the same. No words were exchanged, there was no need to discuss where the walk should take them. Going back home without first going to Wilson Street would be sacrilege as far as Billy Sullivan was concerned and Danny understood. They walked on silently, Billy humming to himself and Danny burping from the last pint which he had needed to gulp quickly before the pub closed.

Billy shook his head as they stood looking at the ruins of Murphy's Gymnasium. 'They said they was goin' ter get that memorial stone out,' he grumbled. 'I'll 'ave ter see the farvver again. It's a bloody disgrace.'

Danny nodded as he looked over the low fencing at the one wall left standing. His own brother's name was on that sandstone tablet, along with two of Billy's brothers, and the other lads they had grown up with who had fallen in the first war. Their names were all there on that stone, battered by the elements and abandoned, it seemed, to crumble into dust. The gymnasium had stood its ground throughout the blitz, until the last night that bombs rained down on London. Then it had received a direct hit.

'Yer know the score, Danny,' his friend said with feeling. 'Yer know 'ow much it meant ter me ter get that place built. Now they can't even recover that memorial stone. Well, I tell yer now. If it's not done soon I'm gonna take the law inter me own 'ands an' get it meself. Strike me dead if I don't.'

Danny put his arm round Billy's shoulders and pulled him away from the ruined gym. They had both spent many happy hours inside the building coaching and working with the kids; it had been a fight against apathy and mistrust just to get the place built, let alone encourage people to come. They had won through though, until in the end it became the only place to send the sons to learn the noble art. There were so many stories attached to that place, Danny thought. One day he would tell his children, as no doubt would his old friend Billy.

'Crikey, I feel tired,' Billy said as they turned back into Page Street. 'Mind you, it's lovely 'avin' my Annie and the kids 'ome. I'll 'ave a nap I fink, an' then Annie'll wake us wiv a nice cuppa. I gotta be up sharp, I'm takin' 'er ter the pictures ternight.'

* * *

Josiah Dawson had stood down from his post as street warden. Through the blitz he had gained the local folk's respect and gratitude, as well as the special thanks of neighbours like the Tanners. Danny owed his life to the Dawsons, father and son, as well as to Tom Casey. The Gordons, too, had reason to thank Josiah. He had undoubtedly saved both their lives when they were threatened by the Scots villain from the Elephant and Castle, Dougal McKenzie.

Terry and Patricia Gordon often found time to remember the rough, no-nonsense character during their hectic days stewarding an exclusive golf club in Suffolk, and for the last couple of years Josiah and Dolly had received a Christmas card from them. Josiah now confined his labours to his daily job of renovating bombed houses for a local builder.

The tide of war had turned some time ago. It was not long after the terrible Saturday night air raid in May that it had begun to change, and Sadie was adamant that she had known all along.

'Let's face it,' she said. 'That air raid was the last one we got. All right, they bombed Birmingham the next night, but it was the beginnin' o' the end as far as the Jerries were concerned. When they invaded Russia they bit orf more than they could chew. Now we all know there's gonna be an invasion soon, but it won't be us what's gotta worry this time.'

Sadie's old and trusted friend Maisie nodded her head vigorously. 'I make 'er right,' she said to the assembled·company in her parlour. 'Look at all those Yanks walkin' about over 'ere. My Fred said 'e 'eard that they've shut Brighton an' Eastbourne right up. Full o' troops, they are. Fred said 'e reckons there'll be an invasion any day now.'

Maudie nodded too. 'My Ernest said 'is mate told 'im that every night there's troop trains an' ammunition trains goin' down ter the coast. They travel in the middle o' the night fer secrecy.'

Dolly was eager to put her point of view to the others. 'It'll be sometime in June, mark my words,' she said mysteriously.

' 'Ow come?' Sadie asked.

Dolly looked over her shoulder as though some outside person might be listening through the wall. 'Maurice Salter told me.'

The gathering tittered, but Dolly was unfazed. 'Now listen a minute,' she said. 'Maurice's daughters are all goin' out wiv Yanks. They met 'em at the Palace Dance 'All up West. Anyway, Maurice told me that all their fellas are movin' out next week. Nuffink definite's bin said, mind you, but the Yanks are sure it won't be long now. They reckon early June.'

Maisie was nodding her head again, as though she had suddenly been struck by a revelation, and everyone started to look at her.

'So that's it. I wondered 'ow come 'e could get such fings,' she said.

'What fings?' Sadie asked.

'Silk stockin's an' chewin' gum,' Maisie replied. 'Maurice 'as bin knockin' stocking's out at five shillin's a pair. 'E's bin givin' all the kids chewin' gum too.'

'My Wallace came in the ovver night chewin' 'is 'ead orf,' Dolly piped in. 'My Josiah didn't 'alf ruck 'im, 'specially when Wallace stuck it in the saucer while 'e ate 'is tea.'

Sadie was curious. 'What you doin' wiv silk stockin's, Mais?' she asked. 'I thought lisle was all yer'd wear.'

'P'raps she's got a man friend,' Dolly said smiling.

Maisie was a little put out. 'An' what's wrong wiv me tryin' ter make meself look nice?' she growled. 'I ain't got bad legs fer me age.'

Maudie showed a rare spark of daring, turning to Maisie and saying, 'If yer get any spare ones, I'll 'ave a pair. My Ernest said I ain't got such bad legs fer me age eivver.'

'Yer'll all be wearin' silk knickers next,' Sadie said with sarcasm.

'I never wear anyfing else,' Dolly cut in, guffawing loudly as she nudged Maudie.

Carrie was enjoying a very busy time. Her business had been spared, and although she had lost most of her regular customers during the blitz, she had managed to keep all her drivers. She had recently secured a regular contract with the large food factory in Dockhead, which was worked by Paddy Byrne and Tubby Walsh. They were totally reliable, with regular bonus earnings giving them an added incentive. Ben Davidson and Tom Armfield worked the casual contracts and they too were included in the bonus arrangements.

Carrie had been making plans and she was looking towards moving to a larger yard locally, once she had obtained a Government permit to increase her fleet. She had found that heavy commercial vehicles were hard to come by unless they could be guaranteed to operate on regular food contracts. The deal she had just negotiated with the Dockhead factory, if renewed after six months, would allow her to apply for the necessary permit. There was another very important contract in the offing: the local brewers had put their hop supply out to tender and it would be a long-term arrangement. The contract was currently with the Galloway firm and for Carrie it was the perfect prize. Her tender had been submitted and she was waiting impatiently for news. Meanwhile there were other decisions to be taken. Joe had been pressing her to promote one of the drivers to transport foreman, which would allow her more time away from the office. Tom Armfield was their mutual choice. He was a quiet, intelligent man who knew the business and had been with her from the beginning. He was liked and respected by the other drivers and seemed to be the obvious choice.

Rachel had been transferred from West Marden to a bomber base in Lincoln and her duties were quite different. She now plotted the outward-bound squadrons of bombers and talked home the returning planes. She found the work very demanding, and on more than one occasion she had to deal with a badly damaged plane struggling home on two engines with a wounded crew aboard. The first time it happened it left her physically sick as the plane skidded to a halt on the runway only yards from the control tower. The sight of the crew being taken from the stricken aircraft, their flak jackets soaked with blood, was too much for her and she broke down in tears. She had been ready to ask for a transfer, until an understanding wing commander talked to her. He had made her see that there was no disgrace in shedding tears, only in running away from the responsibilities she faced. Rachel knew in her heart that she must never do that, and from then on she worked confidently and calmly as the bombers returned.

The days at Lincoln were heady ones. Each night squadrons of Lancasters left the base for targets in Germany, and as they returned American squadrons of Flying Fortresses left on daylight bombing missions. Germany was suffering raids round the clock and there was a clamour to invade Europe now. Amid all the excitement and activity Rachel managed to find only a few quiet moments, and when she did she would think about Tony. They had pledged their love before he left for the Middle East, and there had been regular letters. She carried his photograph in her handbag, and she had his token of love which he had given her the night before he left. It was a small gold heart on a tiny chain which she wore round her neck. On the back of the locket he had had the words 'I Love You' inscribed, and every night Rachel put the locket to her lips and prayed for his safety before she went to sleep.

It had been three years now since Tony had left and Rachel had followed the news from the Middle East anxiously. At first there were victories, but setbacks had continued throughout the first year. It was not until early in '43 that news came over the wireless of the British Eighth Army's drive to Tripoli. Rachel had been filled with excitement just after her move to Lincoln in May '43, when it was announced on the news that all Axis resistance in the Middle East had ceased. Surely now Tony would come home, she thought.

It was not to be, for a few weeks later the Eighth Army invaded Sicily. The war was moving into a decisive phase and she despaired of seeing him again until the final victory. It was wrong and so unfair, she thought. He had been at Dunkirk, and had served for three years in the Western Desert, and now he was fighting in Sicily.

Rachel had little time to dwell on her sad thoughts. The bombing raids were stepped up and every night the locally based squadron went out to join the gathering air armada for the thousand-bomber raids on the heart of Germany's industrial region. Everyone seemed to be living on a knife-edge with the tension, and when bad weather grounded the planes the anti-climax was tangible.

On one foggy and damp Saturday night, a camp dance was held. Many of the aircrews were present and the atmosphere became electric. Young men, many in their early twenties, took the opportunity of a rest from flying to have a good time. They drank heavily, sought out the women, and one or two skirmishes started.

Rachel had not intended to go to the dance but her best friend, a young girl from Liverpool, persuaded her. Connie Ransome was keen on one of the young fliers and she wanted Rachel to make up a foursome.

'Look, I know you're spoken for, love, but it's not like you're being unfaithful,' she said encouragingly. 'You need the break, we all do. It's been like this for weeks now and if you don't let your hair down once in a while you're not going to be any good to that young man of yours. You'll be a mental and physical wreck by the time he does get home.'

Rachel felt that Connie had a point and she reluctantly agreed to accompany her to the dance.

At first it seemed quite a normal camp affair. Young men asked Rachel to dance and she obliged. There was the usual close contact and the groping hands, which she dealt with confidently, but then she was approached by an older man whom she recognised as one of the civilians working on resurfacing the emergency runway. He could hardly stand, and when she declined his invitation to dance he became abusive. The young airman who had made up the foursome was getting the drinks and when he came back he remonstrated with him.

'Why, you young pup,' the man slurred. 'I'll knock your block off.'

His punch was slow and clumsily thrown, giving the young airman plenty of time to dodge it. The drunk kept coming forward and tumbled over the airman's outstretched foot. He crashed down face first but he was still not finished, rolling over onto his back and glaring up at his opponent. With a growl he scrambled to his feet and squared up with his fists, only to be quickly bundled away by his civilian friends.

'I'm sorry,' the young man said smiling. 'I shouldn't have left you.'

'I need this,' Rachel answered, taking the proffered gin and lime.

The young airman watched her down the drink with some amusement. He sipped his, pulling a face.

'What is it?' Rachel asked him.

'It's Irish whiskey. That's all they had,' he said with a serious expression on his smooth face.

He had been introduced to her as Matt Williams but as yet Rachel had not used his first name. He, too, seemed to be reluctant to call her by name, and it remained awkward until Matt took another sip of the whiskey and coughed violently.

'I bet yer never drunk that stuff before, Matt,' Rachel remarked.

For an instant the young man looked peeved, then he relaxed into a wide grin and nodded. 'How did you guess, Rachel?' he spluttered.

'I bet you don't dance neivver, do yer?' Rachel pressed him.

He shook his head. 'I know I'm a sorry sort of date, but I didn't want to disappoint my pal Charlie,' he replied. 'He and Connie seem to be enjoying themselves, at any rate.'

Rachel gave him a smile, warming to his honesty. 'Well, if we're not goin' ter dance, we'd better chat,' she grinned. 'Tell me about yerself.'

Matt scratched his head. 'Well now, my parents were in the foreign service and I was born in India. I went to boarding school and then my parents were killed in a flying accident out in Africa. I was taken under my aunt's wing and I lived in Norfolk until I volunteered. I was at a grammar school and they accepted me for flying training. I went to gunnery school and here I am, rear gunner of O for Oliver, the best Lancaster and best crew on the base.'

Rachel had been gazing at the young crewman while he spoke. He was fair-haired, with the most intense grey eyes. His face was smooth as if it hardly needed a razor. He was slight of build, but athletic-looking. His most endearing feature, she felt, was his mouth. It was full of expression, and his crooked smile gave promise of a cavalier attitude to life.

' 'Ow old are yer, Matt?' she asked bluntly.

'I'm nearly twenty,' he told her.

' 'Ow many ops 'ave yer done?'

'Nearly twenty.'

'One fer each yer of yer life.'

'You could say that.'

'Are yer scared?'

'As you breathe,' he said smiling.

'What made yer volunteer fer aircrew, 'specially after yer parents were killed in an air crash?' Rachel asked, intrigued.

The young man shrugged his shoulders. 'It just seemed the thing to do. Call it bravado, idiocy, anything you like. I like to think it was a worthwhile thing to do.'

'At nineteen?' Rachel asked, feeling suddenly tearful.

'I was eighteen at the time,' he corrected her.

'Tell me. Was—'

'Woah. That's enough about me,' he cut in. 'Let's hear a bit about you. But first another drink.'

'Yer not gettin' yerself anuvver whiskey, are yer?' Rachel said quickly.

He grinned lopsidedly. 'Now I've been found out I'll get myself a lemonade. Same for you?'

She nodded and watched him walk to the bar. He had the swagger of a young man, and the innocence, but there was something about him that fascinated her. His mind seemed much older, much more mature than other young men of his age she had met. He was so young to be flying on bombing missions. So young and so lonely, no doubt. Just that one aunt to return to and no regular girl friend. Perhaps there was someone, but she doubted it.

Matt returned and put the drinks down on the table. The band was playing a quickstep and the dancers moved across the floor beneath the spotlights. The air was warm and smelt of smoke, blue wreaths hanging in the air.

'Would yer mind tellin' me one fing?' Rachel asked him.

'Fire away,' he said lightly.

'Is there somebody special?'

'My aunt's special,' he grinned.

'Yer know what I mean,' Rachel said quickly.

Matt's face became serious and he shook his head. 'No, there's no one special. There was once, but she went off with someone else.'

'All I can say is, yer well rid of 'er,' Rachel told him with feeling.

'Well, thank you, kind lady,' he replied. 'Now what about your life story?'

Rachel told him of her early days, her parents and her first love who had died early in the war, and the man in her life now. All the while Matt sat staring at her and when she finished he sighed. 'I wish I'd met you before the others. I would have made you love me,' he said without any embarrassment.

Rachel smiled at him. 'I bet yer would 'ave,' she said.

The band struck up with a waltz and Rachel suddenly took him by the arm. 'C'mon. I'm gonna show yer 'ow ter waltz,' she said quickly.

'I can't,' he protested, pulling away from her grasp.

'Look, it's quite easy,' she persisted. 'Jus' foller me an' you'll be fine.'

Matt stepped onto the dance floor and allowed himself to be guided into the swaying, slow-stepping dancers. He could feel her body against his, her hips and thighs pressing against him, urging him round, and he began to relax.

He was a natural mover and not once did he step on her toes. She could smell the cologne that he wore, and she let her face nestle onto his shoulder as they began to move more confidently. He held her tight, yet not too tight, his hands clasping hers comfortably, and Rachel was suddenly shocked by her secret thoughts. He could be a very good lover, she decided, he had that gentle but firm touch. She breathed deeply in an effort to control her dangerous feelings. She had been parted from Tony for too long. She needed him, the feel of him caressing her, the warmth of his body next to hers, the closeness and fulfilment of union. But Matt was the man who was with her, a young desirable man whom she could enjoy, who would sate her appetite. No, it was wrong, she told herself. It was so wrong to lead him on and encourage him, betraying the trust of her one love, so far away and in so much mortal danger.

The dance ended and Matt led her from the floor. He smiled as he looked at her and his eyes widened. 'That wasn't as bad as I thought it would be,' he said.

They finished their drinks and at the other side of the hall another skirmish started. Matt glanced shyly at Rachel. 'Do you fancy taking a breath of air?' he asked.

Rachel nodded, suddenly feeling excited. Outside, the night was damp and the darkness was all around them. No lights shone and the stars were covered by a lingering fog. Matt turned to Rachel and as he took her by the hand he reached into his tunic pocket and took out a flat torch. Rachel found herself being led along a narrow path; Matt obviously knew where he was making for. It did not matter. Nothing mattered at that moment, except that she was with him, holding his hand and allowing herself to be led along by the dim light of his pocket torch.

They reached a stiled gate and Matt helped her over. No words were spoken until they reached a large corrugated shed, then Matt gave a grunt of satisfaction. 'It's not locked,' he whispered.

Rachel heard the lowing of cattle and smelt the fresh, sweet hay as she followed him inside. She remembered seeing the shed in the daylight, and as she tried to focus her eyes on the black interior, the young airman pulled her down into the hay. It felt soft and warm, and she did not resist when he slipped his arm round her and leaned over her. She felt his breath coming fast as his lips found hers and she did not resist his kiss. It was soft and gentle at first, then his passion grew. He became ever more urgent, his hands groping her, his body pressed against her. Rachel moved her head sideways and felt his open mouth on her slim neck.

'Steady, Matt,' she whispered.

'I want you, Rachel,' he gasped.

She eased herself down and let her skirt ride up round her slim thighs. His hands were rubbing upwards over her stockings until he reached the soft flesh of her haunches.

She was suddenly afraid of her own desires and she stiffened. 'No, Matt, no,' she told him firmly.

The young airman did not heed her and with difficulty Rachel slid from under him, turning to face him in the sweet-smelling hay as he rolled onto his side.

'I can't. It's wrong,' she said quietly, her fingers clutching the locket around her neck.

Matt smiled in resignation and as he attempted to reassure her by touching her upper arm she brushed his hand away fiercely.

'I shouldn't 'ave come 'ere wiv yer. I was wrong,' Rachel said quickly, her voice choked with emotion.

325

The young man sat up and leaned forward, his arms resting on his drawn-up legs. 'I know, you're spoken for,' he replied. 'It's all right, understand.'

Rachel stood up and brushed the hay from her uniform. 'I really am sorry, Matt,' she told him kindly. 'I shouldn't 'ave led yer on.'

He stood up and faced her, his face still flushed. 'It doesn't matter. We'll just put it down to the war, shall we?'

They left the barn and walked back through the night towards the sound of music, Rachel holding onto his arm. At the entrance to the hall Rachel turned to him. 'If I could 'ave loved yer I would 'ave done, Matt,' she said softly.

He merely nodded and as they walked into the bright light he turned and smiled as the band struck up with 'We'll Meet Again'.

'Let's drink to that,' he said.

Chapter Thirty-Seven

Bella Galloway walked unsteadily into the untidy room and slumped down in an armchair. The screwed-up cushion pressed awkwardly into the small of her back. She grunted as she moved forward and straightened it, leaning over to pick up an old copy of the *Illustrated News* which she flicked through quickly. The room was stale and the curtains were still drawn, although the sun was shining brightly outside. Bella was recovering from her most recent bout with the bottle and she could feel her raw throat and the tightness in her chest from the packet of Chesterfield she had smoked. Her head was pounding and her mouth was dry. She desperately needed a drink, but she dare not, not this early. She had only just got up.

For a while she sat staring down at the cluttered coffee table as the events of the previous night slowly came back to her. The argument had been over the usual thing, but on this particular occasion it had become nasty. Frank had threatened her with violence, grabbing her and throwing her roughy down onto the bed before storming out of the house. He had been drinking too, she recalled. His breath smelt of whisky and he was in a violent temper. He had accused her of being a slut, a money-grabbing whore who was not even a pathetic excuse for a wife, and unless she mended her ways and started to keep the house clean, he would beat her.

It all came back now, and Bella sat in the darkened room brooding on her change of fortune. Once she had been the toast of the theatre world, a young star with a good singing voice and acting ability. They had all told her so. Even the top impresarios had come to see her perform. The damn war had been the start of her decline, she groaned to herself, that and marrying Frank Galloway. He had never been any good to her. In fact he had speeded her downfall by his bad manners and his uncultured behaviour in front of her influential friends. He had a lot to answer for. If he had been a more strict father perhaps Caroline would have turned out to be a more loving, loyal daughter. Perhaps then she wouldn't have sold herself to that double-crossing, no-good Graham Cunningham. All his plans for her had been just empty promises, and then he had set out to use Caroline in the same way. Once he had had his way with her, he had ditched her for some other star-struck young thing.

Bella kicked at the coffee table in her anger and slumped back in t
armchair. Caroline had not been in touch since she left the house ir
huff, and that was three weeks ago. Or was it four? No matter. S
would see the error of her ways pretty soon.

A strong coffee, that's what's needed, Bella told herself. She wou
take a shower, do her hair, then clean the house up. Better rest for
while though, there was plenty of time. Frank would not be home f
hours, if he bothered to come home at all.

The day wore on slowly for Bella and gradually she began to recove
The fresh bottle of gin remained unopened, although she had a fight n
to take her first drink of the day. She showered and tried to
something with her hair, then she made up her face and changed into
different dress. The housework was a chore that she did not relish, a
after hiding the magazines and papers behind a cushion and emptyi
the ashtrays she had had enough. The remains of last night's meal we
still caked to the plates and she almost heaved as she scraped them cle
and dropped them in the hot suds. The curtains looked ready for a cle
and the carpet was stained in places but they would have to wait. S
couldn't be expected to do it all in one go, whatever Frank thought

In the bedroom both their clothes were scattered messily around, a
as Bella set to work putting Frank's suit on a hanger, a small dia
slipped from a pocket onto the bed. She picked it up and went into t
lounge. She'd earned a drink now, she decided, and as soon as she h
made herself comfortable in the armchair with a large gin and tonic
her elbow, she opened the diary and looked through it. There were a l
of entries which made little sense to her, but the initials P.H. ke
appearing among the pages. It could mean public house, she though
No, it must mean something else. Bella sat trying to think of anyo
Frank had mentioned who had those initials but no one came to min
She sipped her drink and then went to the telephone diary on t
sideboard and scanned the list. Suddenly she saw the name The
Harrison. That was the one-time friend of Frank's who had gone insa
and accused him of seeing his wife, Bella recalled. Frank had told h
about it and she remembered him laughing it off. She had believed hi
and paid little attention to it, since she was heavily involved with h
agent, Myer, at the time. Theo's wife was named Peggy.

The sun was slipping down in the west as Bella poured hersc
another stiff gin and tonic. She remembered clearly Frank telling h
that Theo had died in the asylum towards the end of last year. Fran
had started seeing Theo's widow, she felt sure. The first entry of t
initials was against 5 January and they continued throughout the boo
until the last entry on 2 May. That was two weeks ago. Bella sipped h
drink thoughtfully. Frank was often out in the evenings. There were h
masonic functions and the boxing tournaments, apart from his drinki
nights with clients. Besides, he could have been seeing the Harriso

328

woman during the day. Maybe she was being too hasty, though. The initials could stand for anything. She would need more to go on.

Bella felt apprehensive as she glanced up at the ornate clock over the fireplace. It was nearing seven o' clock and Frank had still not come home. The diary had been put back in his coat pocket and the room looked neat and tidy. There was nothing he could find fault with this evening, she thought. The casserole was doing nicely, and she had found some tinned fruit in the larder which she intended to serve with cream.

She drew the curtains and straightened the sideboard, moving the telephone diary away from the trailing phone lead. It was then that a thought struck her. She opened the diary and found what she was looking for. Then she hurried into the bedroom, took out the diary from Frank's coat pocket and thumbed through it. She scurried back into the lounge and checked the dates against those in the telephone diary. That was it. The initials P.H. were listed against Frank's masonic evenings, and on those nights he always came in late, sometimes in the early hours. He had noted the masonic dates in the diary long ago, she remembered him doing it. The next date was on the Wednesday of next week.

Bella glanced at the gin bottle on top of the drinks cabinet. Maybe just one more, she thought. She would need to be steady if she was going to confront that double-dealing husband of hers.

Carrie hummed happily to herself as she cleaned the house. The letter had arrived that very morning but she had been too nervous to open it. Joe had taken it from her and she had waited with bated breath while he opened it and read it in silence. His face dropped and he looked up at her without speaking. Suddenly he beamed and grabbed her in his arms. 'Yer've got it, Carrie!' he cried.

'We've got it,' she remembered correcting him.

It was the big one. The long-term, lucrative contract with the brewers which would set her up for the future, won against the competition of the Galloway tender. Carrie saw it as another step towards her avowed goal of seeing her arch rival's business crumble. The next stage would be a country-wide permit, which would allow her transport firm to deal with the big local traders and their depots in the provinces. If she was successful in getting it, then the sky would be the limit. She had already bought another secondhand Albion lorry in good condition from a local firm that was selling up, and her letter to the labour exchange, asking for two more drivers, was ready to be sent.

Carrie had another good reason to be happy. There had been a letter from Rachel that morning too. Tony O'Reilly was finally coming home and he had been promoted to sergeant in the field. Rachel told her that she had leave outstanding and was going to save it until her man got his

329

leave. She went on to say that the letter she had received from Tony was nearly two months old, which meant he could already be on his way.

The morning's news put all the household in a happy frame of mind. Joe decided it was time he rebuilt the roof of the vehicle shed, which had been badly damaged in the last air raid, and Nellie put on her best hat and coat to pay an overdue visit to her old friends in Page Street. And when Tom Armfield drove into the yard, Carrie called him into the office and put her proposition about promotion to him, which he promptly accepted.

The clandestine movement of troops and supplies to the south coast was now taking place on such a large scale that it ceased to remain secret. Everyone was talking about the endless trains and lorries which were heading south, and in large areas of southern England the streets and lanes were becoming snarled up with military transport of all kinds. From bases around England the loud roar of bombers heading out on their missions was heard night and day and it was apparent to everyone that the invasion was at hand.

In the control tower on a bomber base in Lincoln the personnel were anxiously awaiting the return of the squadron stragglers. Since early dawn the first of the Lancasters had touched down, some riddled with cannon fire and flak, others with engines smoking. Now it was quiet and the losses were being reckoned. Four planes were missing, and the news spread through the base. Personnel not on duty stood around, scanning the clear morning sky. Rachel stood beside her friend Connie and the two looked away into the far horizon. News suddenly came through and a cheer went up. C for Charlie had ditched in the Channel and the crew had been picked up unharmed.

The senior duty officer was about to log the three remaining planes as lost when a crackling sound started to come through on the loudspeaker. O for Oliver was limping home with two engines out and wounded aboard. Word spread fast and everyone stood scanning the sky for the stricken plane's arrival. In the control room the faces of the controllers were set firm. The pilot sounded calm but everyone was aware of the dangers involved. The plane's undercarriage had been damaged and it would have to be a belly landing. Fire tenders and an ambulance took up their places on the edge of the runway. The waiting seemed to last for ever.

Rachel scanned the sky, a silent prayer in her heart. Aboard O for Oliver was young Matt Williams, not yet twenty years old. He was just a boy, a lonely, brave lad who had seemed to have an insight into life far beyond his tender years. Rachel bit her lip as she waited. Experience told her that if the plane did not make an appearance very soon, it would have gone down.

Her heart leapt as a cry went up. 'There it is!'

She could see the Lancaster clearly now. It was coming in very low, a trail of black smoke spreading out behind it. It seemed to stand still in the sky for a long time and then suddenly it banked and came down in the final approach, inching lower and lower with its undercarriage still raised. It bounced once then skidded along the tarmac towards them. Black smoke billowed out, covering it, then it skidded completely round. The fire tender started to move towards it when the whole plane erupted in flames. A deafening explosion ripped it apart, reducing it to a blazing mass of twisted metal in seconds. There was nothing anyone could do. The crew of O for Oliver had perished.

The tragedy weighed heavily on everyone in the air force base. Rachel lay on her bed that night, her red-rimmed eyes staring up unseeing at the dusty rafters. Matt was gone. How many more young men like Matt would perish before this war was over?

Footsteps sounded in the corridor and Connie came into the dormitory. She sat down on her bed next to Rachel and stared down at the floor without saying anything for a time. When she finally spoke her voice was gravelly. 'I've just come from the canteen. Did you know it was Matt Williams' twentieth birthday today?' she asked.

Rachel eased herself up onto her arm and looked at her best friend. 'It was Matt's twentieth mission,' she replied.

Billy Sullivan went to see Father Kerrigan one evening but he was unsuccessful in persuading the priest that something more had to be done about the memorial stone in the ruined gymnasium. Father Kerrigan was his usual sedate self and he tried to assure his agitated parishioner that everything had been done to get the stone removed into safe keeping.

'But the demolition men might cart it away,' Billy said anxiously.

'Be sure it won't happen, Billy,' the priest told him blithely. 'I've been on to the firm concerned and they say that all care will be taken to preserve the stone in pristine condition.'

Billy came away from the church feeling very concerned, and he said as much to Danny when he called into the Bargee for a pint.

'Look, Danny, yer know yerself that there's a lot o' labour battalions workin' on the bombed places,' he said with misgiving. 'You've seen 'em, we all 'ave. They're a right mix from 'ere, there an' everywhere. 'Alf of 'em can't speak English. I bet some of 'em ain't even Christians. What does a stone wiv foreign writin' on mean ter the likes o' them?'

Danny agreed with his old friend but he tried to placate him. 'Some o' the firms use their own labour. It's best ter wait an' see,' he replied.

Billy went home and spoke to Annie about it. 'I'm sorry, luv, but that stone means a lot ter me.'

Annie put her arms on his wide shoulders and looked up into his troubled eyes. 'Now listen,' she said. 'I understand, but it's no good you getting yourself upset. Wait and see what happens. You've got to trust Father Kerrigan. He wouldn't lie to you.'

'I know that,' Billy replied, 'but I don't trust the demolition men,'

Annie sighed and shook her head, knowing her husband's tenacity. 'Well, they would have to be heathens to disregard a sacred stone,' she said emphatically. 'After all, it's a war memorial and it's been blessed by the church.'

There was no doubt in Billy's mind that some of the workers in the labour battalions were heathens, but he tried his best to be calm. 'All right, I'll wait an' see,' he told her. 'But I can see trouble.'

Annie slipped her arms round his neck and kissed him gently on the mouth. 'Now sit down and take those filthy boots off,' she told him. 'I've got your supper in the oven.'

Saturday afternoon was an ideal time to go visiting, Nellie knew. The shopping was over and one of her friends would always have a hot filled teapot under the cosy. Sadie would be her first stop, she thought. Sadie always had a nice clean parlour and her chairs were spotless. After all, she was wearing her best coat and she had to be careful.

'You ain't seen Sadie in yer travels, 'ave yer?' she asked Mrs Green a while later. 'I've knocked twice an' can't get any answer.'

'I expect she's at Maisie's,' Mrs Green replied.

Maisie's front door was opened by Fred, who greeted Nellie with a smile. 'She's bin gorn fer ages,' she told her. 'I should look in at Sadie's. That's where she'll be.'

'She ain't at Sadie's,' Nellie told him. 'I jus' knocked there.'

'Well, I can't 'elp yer, luv. Sorry,' Fred said with a shrug.

Nellie decided it must be Maudie's turn to supply the tea this week so she went round to her place. After the second knock brought no response, she was puzzled.

The Dawsons' front door was opened by Wallace, who stood grinning at Nellie's new hat.

'I said is yer muvver in?' Nellie asked for the second time.

Wallace's grin became even larger as he stared at Nellie's hat and she gave him a wicked look as she walked away. Sometimes the women gathered at the Haggerty house, but not very often. Mrs Haggerty usually tried to monopolise the conversation and Nellie knew that Sadie could not abide the woman. Still, it was worth a try.

' 'Ello, Mrs Tanner. I ain't seen yer around 'ere fer weeks. Are yer all right? 'Ow's the children? I saw Carrie the ovver day, ain't she a picture. Yer 'eard about 'im in Bacon Street, didn't yer? That bloke who sells the cockles on the corner o' Jamaica Road. Sorry, what was it yer asked me?'

Nellie drew a deep breath. ' 'Ave yer seen Sadie about?' she repeated slowly and deliberately.

'Sadie? No, I ain't,' Mrs Haggerty replied. ' 'E got done, yer know.'

'Who did?'

'Why, 'im out o' Bacon Street.'

'Bacon Street?'

' 'Im who sells the cockles in Jamaica Road.'

'Oh 'im.'

'Takin' bettin' slips, it was.'

'Yeah?'

'Arfur got six months.'

'What, fer takin' bettin' slips?'

'No, that was 'im out o' Bacon Street.'

Nellie had had enough. The conversation was beginning to make her head buzz. 'Well, I must be orf. Take care o' yerself,' she said with a forced smile.

'By the way, I should try Maurice Salter's place,' Mrs Haggerty called out.

'Maurice Salter?' Nellie said disbelievingly.

'That's right. They've bin goin' in an' out o' the Salters' place like a fiddler's elbow fer the past few days,' Mrs Haggerty assured her.

Nellie was beginning to feel jaded. All she wanted right now was to sit down with a nice cup of tea. The thought of having to deal with Maurice Salter made her feel ready to turn for home. Suddenly she spotted Mrs Watson hurrying along the turning towards her.

' 'Ello, Nellie. 'Ow yer keepin', luv?' she asked.

'Well, I was feelin' fine when I left 'ome,' Nellie told her.

'I'm just orf ter Maurice Salter's,' Mrs Watson said. 'Fancy comin' along?'

Nellie began to wonder whether she was going mad. 'What for?' she asked.

'Ain't you 'eard? Maurice Salter's sellin' loads o' stuff dirt cheap,' Mrs Watson told her. 'My Carol bought a silk camisole fer two an' a tanner, an' I got a smashin' pair o' silk stockin's fer four an' six. Why don't yer come wiv me?'

Nellie decided that what she needed right then was to lie down and rest her tired head. 'No fanks, luv,' she replied as she turned for home. 'I'll stick ter me flannel drawers.'

Chapter Thirty-Eight

On Monday, 5 June 1944, a troop train from Southampton steamed into Waterloo Station. Aboard were men of the Eighth Army on leave after three years in the Western Desert. 'Welcome Home' banners and flags had been strung up on the station concourse and a military band was playing. It was a very emotional moment for the hundreds of loved ones and friends who waited by the platform barrier, and the hum of conversation turned into cheering and loud shouts as the train shuddered to a halt at the buffers.

The veterans of Al Alamein and the Sicilian landings stepped down and hurried towards the waiting throng, their faces tanned leathery, their hair bleached by a fierce sun. They looked lean and appeared apprehensive as they faced the welcome-home festivities. Flashbulbs lit their startled faces and the newspaper reporters vied for stories as the men sought out their families and children. Station officials, policemen and military police tried in vain to intervene but they were all but brushed aside.

Rachel stood among the crowd, dressed in uniform, holding her cap in her hand and desperately searching for Tony. She almost allowed him to pass her by before she saw his wide grin and then she was in his arms.

'It's bin so long,' she sobbed, unable to contain herself any longer.

Tony ran his hand over her fair hair and kissed her smooth white neck. 'I've dreamed about this moment,' he whispered into her ear. 'Two whole weeks. It feels wonderful.'

They turned with arms round each other and found themselves suddenly surrounded by newspapermen and a photographer. One little fat man jostled his colleagues and looked up at Tony. 'That's the Military Medal ribbon, son. Did yer win it in the desert?'

Tony looked embarrassed as he nodded.

'Where was it?' the newsman pressed him.

The two young lovers were blinded momentarily by an exploding flashbulb and Tony's hand went up to the knot of his tie. 'Mersah Matruh,' he said quietly.

'That was one o' the big battles. What was it like?' another newsman cut in.

'*South London Press*,' the photographer announced, pushing the little reporter aside. 'Give me yer names an' where yer from, folks,' he shouted above the general din.

The pressmen finally moved away and Tony took Rachel by the hand as they hurried from the station. During the tram ride to Bermondsey, Rachel kept glancing at her young man, intrigued by his tan and bleached hair. Tony was looking out of the window, as though still not able to believe he was back home at last.

'Yer never mentioned the medal in yer letters,' Rachel said presently.

Tony shrugged his shoulders. 'I didn't want yer ter worry. Yer might 'ave thought I was takin' chances.'

Rachel squeezed his hand in hers. 'I never stopped finkin' about yer,' she said, touching the tiny locket round her neck. 'I kissed this every night an' said a prayer for yer,' she whispered.

Tony was holding coppers for the fare but the conductor ignored him, and when they finally alighted at Dockhead, the conductor turned to him and said, 'Congratulations, son, an' good luck ter the pair o' yer.'

Tony nodded his thanks and Rachel saw he was blushing with embarrassment.

'I fink I'll 'ave ter leave this off,' he mumbled, nodding down at the tiny ribbon on his chest.

'You'll do no such fing,' Rachel said firmly. 'I want ter show you off to everybody.'

They walked arm in arm along the wide Jamaica Road in the warm sunshine, laughing with each other and totally oblivious of the friendly glances and smiles of passers-by. How different this time together would be to their last one, Rachel vowed. Three years ago Tony had been in a state of shock. He had only the clothes he stood up in and they found very little time to be alone. The tragic loss of his mother and her friend Lola had cast a dark shadow over everything and she recalled how they had spent a lot of their leave in Tony's neighbourhood, trying to find the person whose name was on Lola's lips the instant she died. They had been unsuccessful in discovering who Gloria was and they finally had to give up the quest. Now they would make up for those lost years, and as they neared Salmon Lane Rachel looked up into Tony's dark eyes and felt ecstatically happy.

On Monday morning a lorry pulled up in Wilson Street and a motley group of men in plain uniforms jumped down. They were unkempt and of varying ages: persons with no identity, displaced persons and men from internment camps who had been recruited to clear away war damage. Their sergeant was a huge, rough-looking individual, with black wavy hair and thick eyebrows. He shouted obscenities as he ordered them around and the men jumped to his commands.

Sergei was a Georgian, who had fought on both sides as the fortunes of war changed around him. Eventually he had joined the long, straggling lines of refugees and finally found himself in an Italian prisoner-of-war camp. He managed to convince the British that he was a stateless person and was brought over to work on the harvests. He had not been happy with the few shillings he got for toiling in the fields and so he volunteered for the labour battalions that were being formed. His large frame and frightening manner, and an adequate knowledge of English, fitted him for the part and he became works sergeant. The men working under him enjoyed extra rations and a few shillings for their labours, and the sergeant took advantage of it, supplementing his own income by extorting money from them with dire threats. The gang were terrified of Sergei and he liked to be reminded of it.

On that Monday morning the sergeant was barking loudly at them as usual and it was not long before the wooden fencing round Murphy's Gymnasium came down. One man began kindling a fire in a brazier from the waste timbers and others set up a tarpaulin-covered contraption that passed for a tent. The rest went to work manhandling the slabs of brick and splintered timbers into separate piles ready for the demolition lorry. All the serviceable wood was to be used again but Sergei was keen to make a little money on some of the large timbers, though he had to be careful not to arouse the suspicions of the civilian supervisor who was due to call shortly.

At midday on Monday the work was well under way and when Billy passed Wilson Street on his way home to lunch he was horrified. He stood staring at the men sitting in the tent drinking mugs of tea and munching on thick hunks of bread and cheese. Sergei could not pass up a chance to make a few coppers and he came out of the tent and sauntered over to him.

'You wish buy wood? We got plenty wood,' he said, grinning to expose his gold teeth.

Billy gave the sergeant a malevolent glare. 'No, I don't wanna buy wood,' he growled. 'Who's in charge 'ere?'

'In charge? Me the boss. Sergei. What can I help you?' the huge man said, prodding himself in the chest with his forefinger.

Billy decided that he would have to be careful how he handled the strange character. He motioned with his finger. 'See that wall over there?' he said. 'That's a memorial stone. Men who died in war. Got it?'

Sergei laughed and plunged his thumbs into his khaki belt. 'Many men die in war. So?'

Billy felt the blood rush to his face but he struggled to stay calm. 'When that wall comes down, that stone goes ter me, understand?' he said in a firm voice.

Sergei bellowed with laughter. 'Wall come down next day, not today. Motor come take rubbish away. You want buy stone?'

Billy finally lost his self-control and he grabbed the sergeant's tunic

336

collar. 'I don't buy. That stone belongs ter the church, yer bloody eathen,' he snarled.

Sergei's face darkened as his huge fist closed over Billy's and he squeezed hard, pulling downwards to make him let go. 'You want trouble. I make bad trouble,' he growled. 'Go, before I make bad trouble.'

Billy stood facing the large man for a few moments, then he turned on his heel and walked angrily away.

Sadie kicked her shoes off in Maisie's parlour and rubbed her feet. 'Those bleedin' shoes are murderin' my corns,' she groaned.

Maisie was pouring the tea and she nodded. 'Never mind, luv, we've done our bit,' she said with a satisfied look on her wide round face.

The two old friends had been busy for the past two hours visiting their neighbours and now they were looking forward to a strong cup of tea.

'I 'ope Lily Salter passes the message on,' Sadie said. 'They'll need all the 'elp they can get.'

'I should fink so,' Maisie replied. 'She seems a nice gel.'

'What about ole Bert Jolly? I'm a bit worried about 'im,' Sadie remarked. ' 'E's a bit too old fer that sort o' fing.'

'Well, yer can't stop 'im, luv,' Maisie said, handing over a cup of tea. 'Same as my Fred. 'E'll be there, yer couldn't stop 'im.'

'I know my Daniel would, if it wasn't fer that chest of 'is,' Sadie said, rubbing her sore foot.

There was a knock at the door and Maisie hurried out to answer it. She came back into the room with Maudie and Dolly, who sat themselves down with satisfied looks on their faces. 'Nellie Tanner's 'avin' a word wiv young Carrie,' Maudie announced. 'She said not ter worry.'

Sadie sat back and sipped her tea. 'Well, ladies, it looks like the Page Street women 'ave done their bit. Now we'll see 'ow the blokes get on.'

The Bargee was usually busy on that Monday evening. Danny Tanner sat talking to Billy Sullivan and Fred Dougall, and Ernest Mycroft was there with Bert Jolly, Josiah Dawson and Tom Casey. Suddenly the door opened and Maurice Salter came in. 'I got the message,' he said to Billy. 'What's it all about?'

Billy nodded to the counter. 'Go an' order a drink, then we'll get started,' he told him.

Maurice looked at Billy curiously but did as he was told, and when he was seated Billy held up his hands for silence.

'Now listen,' he began. 'The reason me an' Danny asked yer all ter come 'ere ternight is 'cos we're bein' stamped on, and when I say we, I mean all of us.'

'What's 'appened?' Maurice asked.

Danny got up from his chair and stood alongside Billy. 'Now you all know the 'istory o' Murphy's Gym,' he said in a loud voice, looking round at the gathering. 'You all know that Murphy's is very special to us all. It wasn't just a buildin', it was a memorial to all our bruvvers an' friends who fell in the last war. All right, it's only a ruin now, but one day, when this war's over, it's gonna be built again, make no mistake. In the meantime they've started clearin' the site. They started terday.'

Blank faces greeted Danny's words. 'What's that got ter do wiv us, Danny?' Bert Jolly asked.

'I tell yer what it's got ter do wiv us,' Danny replied in an angry tone. 'The memorial stone.'

'They'll leave that, won't they?' Bert queried.

'Well, yer better ask Billy about that,' Danny said, nodding to his old friend to go on.

Billy slipped his thumbs into his braces and looked from one to another of them. 'They've sent one o' those labour battalions ter clear the site,' he told them. 'Now the sergeant in charge is a bullyin' no-good whoreson who ain't the slightest bit interested in what 'appens ter that stone. In fact 'e offered ter sell it ter me when I asked 'im what they were gonna do wiv it.'

A roar of anger erupted and Bert Jolly stood up gesticulating. 'The bloody man must be evil. Fancy wantin' ter make money on such a fing,' he cried.

'What did yer tell 'im, Billy?' Tom Casey asked.

'What d'you fink?' Billy growled. 'Now listen. As far as me an' Danny's concerned, that memorial stone is ours. It belongs to everybody round 'ere, an' we ain't gonna stand by an' see some bloody foreigner try ter put a price on it.'

'Too right,' Maurice cut in. 'I reckon we should take the law into our own 'ands an' take that stone down ourselves, an' if the bugger gets in the way, we'll lynch 'im.'

Danny held up his hands as the angry voices grew. 'That's the reason we've asked yer ter come 'ere ternight. Me an' Billy are gonna go round Wilson Street an' remove that stone ourselves. Any of yer that wanna give us some 'elp are welcome.'

Bert raised his arm. 'Count me in,' he said with a determined look on his face.

Every one of the assembly followed his lead. 'We're wiv yer,' the cry went up.

Josiah stood up. 'We've gotta do this right or there'll be injuries,' he remarked.

'Josiah's right,' Danny shouted above the din. ' 'Im an' Billy are both in the buildin' game, so we'll be guided by them, all right?'

The men began to make for the door and Danny banged an empty glass down loudly on the table to attract their attention. 'We'll see yer at the gym in 'alf an hour,' he shouted.

The women of Page Street stood at their front doors on that warm June evening and watched the men leave in a group. Maurice was wearing his dungarees and he had lent a spare pair to Bert who walked beside him as though he was marching off to war. Tom wore his painting overalls and Fred had sorted out a pair of his old trousers from the rag bag. Ernest followed behind them, along with Josiah. All their faces were set firm.

'Mind 'ow yer go,' Maudie said anxiously.

'Keep yer eye on 'em,' Maisie shouted out to Josiah as they passed by.

The whole street seemed to have turned out to watch the men leave and Sadie nodded sadly. 'I 'ad ter practically 'old my Daniel back,' she told Maisie.

At Wilson Street the men gathered round Josiah and he took control. 'Now listen,' he said authoritatively. 'That wall's rickety. What we've got ter do is ter stand clear an' push it over wiv poles. There's plenty o' wood we can use fer 'em. We'll rock the wall down away from us, an' then chip the stone loose. What we gotta make sure is that we don't shatter the stone, so pay attention.'

A few bystanders and two small boys watched intently as the strange crowd of men leaned on their lengths of timber. Josiah was urging them on but the wall proved stronger than he had thought. It rocked precariously, but would not fall. He appealed for more effort and Bert Jolly in particular was grunting loudly as he strained against his pole. Billy and Danny shared a length of timber and they suddenly became aware of two people standing over them.

'Yer wanna push a bit 'arder,' one of them said.

Billy turned to Danny. 'Well, if it ain't Wally Walburton an' Tubby Abrahms,' he said grinning. 'These two are like a couple o' bad pennies.' He looked at Wally. 'Well, don't just stand there, let's 'ave the benefit o' yer muscle.'

'We 'elped yer when this place went up so we thought we might as well 'elp yer pull it down,' Wally said grinning.

The extra weight proved decisive and the wall finally toppled. Josiah had designed a crude casing behind the wall where he estimated the stone would fall, and his calculations were correct. As the wall collapsed in a cloud of dust, the stone tablet fell in the centre of the casing and remained intact. The next task, chipping the remaining bits of bricks away from the stone, was simple, and it was soon accomplished. Josiah looked satisfied as he sorted out the next problem, that of getting the heavy stone from the site. A pathway was cleared and lined with timbers, and then the stone was manhandled into position with the aid of poles. Fred and Ernest looked pleased with themselves as they exchanged grins. Tom was mopping his brow with an exaggerated show

339

of fatigue. Wally Walburton stood back and flexed his muscles. 'C'mon then, lads, what we waitin' for?' he said.

Inch by inch the stone was laboriously levered along the makeshift ramp. Before it had been moved more than a few feet a lorry drove into Wilson Street and pulled up at the site. Paddy Byrne jumped down from the cab carrying a coil of rope.

'This might 'elp,' he said, throwing it at Josiah's feet.

The rope was tied round the large stone and then Paddy secured the other end to the rear of his lorry. Slowly he drove his vehicle away from the ruins, dragging the stone along until it reached the edge of the pavement. Willing hands carried thick lengths of timber from the stack and rested the ends against the tailboard. Wally and Tubby joined Maurice, Danny and Billy on the vehicle and the rest of the men stood back holding poles. It took a lot of effort on everyone's part, but after a great deal of heaving and levering the stone was finally set in place on the lorry.

It was a very satisfied group of men who sat round it as they were driven to St Joseph's Church in Jamaica Road, and it was a very surprised Father Kerrigan who answered the request for sanctuary and threw open the gates to let the lorry back into the churchyard.

The morning of Tuesday, 6 June, was warm and sunny, and when the demolition team arrived in Wilson Street, Sergei was very angry. All day long the men toiled and Sergei hollered and railed wildly as he took his rage out on them. They cursed him silently and bent their backs to the hard work, oblivious of the momentous events of that morning, until one of the men who spoke English exchanged a few pleasantries with a passer-by.

In nearby Page Street folk were spilling out of their houses as the news came over the wireless, and some of the women were near to tears.

'They've gone in!' Bert shouted to Sadie.

'The invasion's on!' Maudie shouted across the street to Mrs Haggerty.

Dolly did a jig outside her front door and Maisie put her hands together as she lifted her head to the sky. 'At last,' she cried out. 'Gawd it's 'appened at last.'

Annie shepherded her children to school, then she went to see Sadie and the two women hurried off to St Joseph's to say a special prayer. Maudie went to church that morning too, while Maisie joined Dolly for a lunchtime drink in celebration. There was a widespread mood of elation, and all day long the latest news bulletins were passed from person to person. Maurice Salter, though, was feeling badly in need of sleep. He had gone straight from his long shift to the Bargee meeting, and then when he got back home late that evening he had been besieged by the latest wave of customers for his range of American silk stockings and underwear. He had long since exhausted his supply, for his daughters' American boy friends were now employed on a more dangerous front in Normandy, but the women of Page Street persisted nevertheless, and Maurice was compelled to paste a notice on his front door. 'Gone to bed, girls. Supply exhausted.'

That evening a very determined Billy Sullivan took a detour on his way home from work. He was not to be disappointed, for he saw the demolition gang still hard at it. As he approached, he saw Sergei throwing his arms about as he bawled out one of his unfortunate workers, and Billy's jaw muscles tightened.

The bullying sergeant suddenly caught sight of Billy and his eyes narrowed. 'You! You come on my place. Take stone. Who say you take stone?'

Billy was well aware that he was dealing with a highly volatile character who was obviously very strong, and he stayed just out of arm's reach as he smiled mirthlessly at him. 'The stone's wiv us, pal. Now why don't yer finish the job an' piss orf out of it. We don't like your sort round 'ere.'

Sergei's command of the English language was sufficient to know when he was being insulted and his face flushed a dull red. 'I teach you manners,' he snarled as he reached a huge hand out for Billy's throat.

Billy had expected it and he moved his head sideways and down, at the same time throwing a hard punch from his shoulder. All the power that Billy could muster was in that punch and it caught Sergei full in the face. He staggered back, his nose beginning to drip blood, and with a roar he rushed forward. Billy hit him again as he came on, this time a left hook on the temple. The huge man dropped to his knees and shook his head. He was not finished, however, and his face was contorted as he climbed to his feet. This time he did not make the mistake of rushing in blindly; instead he opened his arms wide and came forward slowly, crouching slightly like a gorilla. Billy backed away carefully, not wanting to be caught up in those massive arms, and he suddenly feinted to strike with his left fist and threw out a hard right. Sergei ducked it and leapt forward, coiling his arms round Billy's body. His eyes were glaring like a madman and he grinned evilly as he squeezed the life out of his opponent. Billy was fighting to breathe but his arms were pinned to his sides; his face quickly became scarlet and a sea of red mist grew in front of his eyes.

Suddenly his breath came; he fell back and gasped air into his tortured lungs. There was loud noise all around him and he heard Sergei's mad bellowing. The sergeant was having to fight off the demolition men. He went down under a flurry of blows and kicks and suddenly his head was opened as one of the men he had been bullying bashed him with a brick. Still the workers clustered round, aiming kicks and punches at the prone figure. Billy was on his knees and he struggled to regain his feet. 'That's enough lads, you'll kill 'im,' he shouted.

The men backed slowly away to reveal a very gory sight. Sergei had a gaping head wound and his face had been pummelled till it looked like raw meat. His nose was broken and one eye was shut tight. He was lying in a heap not making any sound. Billy staggered over and looked down at him.

Just then one of the workers, a tall dark man, threw a bucket of slops over the huge sergeant and he groaned and stirred.

'I want to thank you for showing us the way,' the worker said in perfect English. 'That animal has been bullying us for too long. This should have been done long ago.'

Billy looked surprised and the tall stranger smiled, showing a set of perfect teeth. 'My name is Antonio Morelli. I am an Italian prisoner-of-war,' he said. 'I am Catholic and would not stand by and see your war memorial be taken from this place. We had already made our plans. You helped us get started.'

Billy shook the Italian warmly by the hand. 'Will 'e cause yer any trouble when 'e comes round?' he asked.

The tall man smiled as he shook his head. 'He's already finished.' He turned to his fellow workers. 'We stay together from now on, is that right?'

Blank faces stared at him and he repeated his question in a foreign tongue. The men suddenly nodded their heads and made threatening gestures to the groaning Sergei.

'You can feel sure that we are now all of the same mind,' the Italian said to Billy, extending his hand once more. 'Maybe when this terrible war is over I will come and see your memorial stone in the new building, eh?'

Billy walked home feeling exhausted but very happy. Just like old times, he thought.

Chapter Thirty-Nine

Rachel sat with Tony on the hilly slope overlooking the River Thames in Greenwich Park. It was a warm Saturday, the first weekend following the invasion of Europe, and the two lovers felt serenely happy as they watched a lone tramper steaming upriver. Rachel moved her arms and stretched out on the cool grass, her eyes following the progress of a wispy cloud high in the blue sky.

'A penny fer yer thoughts,' Tony said as he turned on his side and stared down at her.

Rachel sighed. 'I was just finkin' 'ow lovely an' peaceful it is 'ere, an' across the Channel there's terrible fightin' goin' on,' she said quietly.

Tony nodded and pulled a blade of grass from his mouth. 'It 'as ter be if this war's gonna be ended,' he replied.

Rachel sat up quickly and looked at him. 'Are yer sure yer won't 'ave ter go, Tony?' she asked anxiously. 'I couldn't bear ter know yer was in more fightin'.'

Tony shook his head firmly. 'I already told yer, Rachel, I'm finished wiv fightin',' he answered. 'They reckon we've done our share. That's why the regiment was sent 'ome. Oh, it'll go off out again, but it'll be wiv new recruits. Those of us who saw it out are bein' moved around. I'm goin' ter be involved in trainin' the new lads who are comin' in. They can gain from our experiences.'

Rachel sighed and sprawled out again on the grass. 'I want us ter get married soon as we can, Tony,' she said, looking up into his dark eyes.

'I want that more than I've ever wanted anyfing,' he replied, bending down gently to kiss her slightly parted lips.

'We'll be very 'appy, won't we?' she asked him with a note of anxiety in her voice.

'I never doubt it fer a second,' he reassured her, smiling. 'Not fer one tiny second.'

Rachel sat up again and took his hand in hers. 'When the war's ended, will yer sell that property?' she asked.

'I'll go an' see that firm o' solicitors. They'll advise me,' he replied. 'I'll need ter sell if we're gonna start up in business.'

'Promise me one fing,' Rachel said, looking down at their clasped hands. 'Promise me yer'll not let the money change yer.'

Tony breathed deeply and pulled her to him. 'Look, Rachel. It's only money. There's no terrible curse to it, if that's what's worryin' yer. It won't change me, I promise.'

' 'Ope ter die?'

' 'Ope ter die.'

Rachel moved closer, and, as he slipped his arms round her, she tilted her head to one side, begging a kiss. His answering caress reassured her more than his promise ever could, and when they parted she smiled at him. 'I love yer so much, Tony,' she sighed. 'I want us ter start off right, that's all.'

Tony sat up straight and clasped his hands round his knees. 'Now listen ter me,' he said firmly. 'I care about that inheritance. It means only one fing, as far as I'm concerned. A good start out. We'd be just as 'appy wiv or wivout it.' Besides, we can always go an' see Nora.'

'Nora?'

'Yeah, Nora Flynne. Yer remember me tellin' yer what the old lady said ter me on the day I went ter the readin' o' the will?'

Rachel nodded. 'Yeah, that was strange. I wonder what dark secret she's carryin' around wiv 'er.'

Tony shrugged his shoulders. 'Well, we can always find out, if we need to,' he replied.

Rachel suddenly felt afraid and she turned to the young soldier. 'Hold me tight, Tony,' she said.

The clouds were slowly gathering as the two young lovers walked from the park into the bustling thoroughfare, and when they were seated on the tram for the trip back to Bermondsey, Rachel gripped Tony's hand tightly. 'Everyfing seems so good for us, I just feel frightened that somefing'll come up ter spoil it all,' she said anxiously.

Tony smiled as he looked at her frowning face. 'Listen. I'm wiv yer fer two 'ole weeks. Then I'll be gettin' plenty o' leave. I can always slip over ter Lincoln ter see yer,' he said cheerfully. 'We don't 'ave ter be parted fer very long. I wouldn't let nuffink come between us an' spoil what we've got. Now take that worried look off yer face.'

Rachel leaned her body against his, and he rubbed her arm fondly. 'Feeling better now?' he asked.

She nodded, but at the back of her mind she still felt afraid.

Across London, the sorry figure of Bella Galloway sat huddled in her untidy sitting room. It was in darkness, the curtains drawn to shut out the bright sunlight as she rocked to and fro in her chair. That very morning she had finally summoned the courage to confront her husband with her suspicions and he had reacted very violently. He had not been able to deny his involvement with Peggy Harrison after what she had discovered, but Bella had paid a hard price for it.

The previous evening, Frank's lodge had had their regular meeting, and after Frank had left, supposedly to attend the function, Bella had dialled the lodge's number to say that she needed to talk to him as an emergency had come up. The answer she got did not unduly surprise her. Frank was not there; he had resigned from the order six months previously.

Bella removed the damp flannel from her bruised and swollen face and got up painfully from the chair. Her ribs were hurting and she decided there and then to phone Alan Wichello, the bookmaker. He would know what to do, she thought to herself.

One hour later she answered a knock at the door and let in a heavily built man in a smart pinstripe suit. He was shocked to see the bruising on her face.

'Frank?' he asked.

Bella nodded and motioned towards the drinks cabinet. 'Help yourself, Alan, and you can do one for me while you're there.'

'You should see a doctor,' he advised as he poured himself a large Scotch.

'I'll be all right presently, Alan,' she replied, holding her midriff as she sat down painfully in her chair.

'Presently nothing,' he said sharply. 'You could have broken ribs.'

'Frank was like an animal,' she said, starting to sob. 'I've never seen him so incensed.'

Alan passed over her drink and sat down facing her. 'Tell me about it,' he urged her as he sipped his Scotch.

Bella dabbed at her eyes with a lace handkerchief. 'Frank's having an affair,' she began. 'Last night he told me he was going to a masonic meeting but I found out he'd resigned months ago.'

'So you checked up on him?' Alan queried, a ghost of a smile on his lips.

Bella looked up sharply. 'And why not? I gave up my career for that man and that's how he's treated me,' she sobbed.

Alan smiled cynically. 'So you confronted him and he turned nasty. Well, let's face it, Bella, you've hardly been a model wife yourself,' he said, staring down at his drink. 'No one could accuse you of being a paragon of virtue.'

Bella looked up at him, her eye-liner smeared and her bruised face reddening with anger. 'I've not been in the habit of sharing my bed with every man I've known,' she said sharply. 'You were different. What you and I had was special.'

Alan raised his hand to stop her. 'All right, I'm sorry,' he said quietly. 'Frank's gone over the top this time, and I'm foreclosing on his debt. It was only because of you I held back, but he's never understood that I'm answerable too. I can't go on making excuses for the man.'

'You can do what you want as far as I'm concerned,' Bella replied. 'I've had enough. He was like a madman this morning. I thought he was going to kill me.'

Alan twirled the drink round in his glass. 'He's not been violent before, has he?' he asked.

Bella shook her head. 'It's all been building up,' she told him. 'That will his father left was the start of it all and now there's this.'

Alan took the copy of the *South London Press* from her and looked at the picture of two smiling young people in uniform. 'So that's the grandson, and his fiancée. I can see why Frank got upset. The amalgamation wouldn't sit easy with him, would it?'

'He threw that in my face this morning,' Bella said.

Alan Wichello's expression hardened. 'I'm out of patience, Bella,' he said, a resolute edge to his voice. 'Frank's got to pay his debts. I can't stall any longer. I'm going to the yard to collect, and my associates won't stand for any more excuses. It's a lot of money owing, and there's the interest as well.'

'After what he did to me this morning, you're welcome to him,' Bella replied, her eyes filling with tears. 'I'm going to leave this house before he gets home tonight. That's if he does come home.'

The bookmaker got up and put down his empty glass on the coffee table. 'I'll be in touch later, Bella. Send me your new address,' he said as he buttoned up his coat.

As soon as he had left, Bella began to pack, and one hour later she was stepping into a taxi. Her swollen eyes were hidden behind dark glasses and she felt breathless as she hauled her light travelling bag in with her. It had been a mistake leaving the tour, she thought regretfully. She had lost touch with all her old friends and colleagues. New faces were on the scene now, younger, pretty faces who were carving their own niches. Well, she was not done for, not by a long chalk, she vowed. They would once again sit up and take notice of Bella Ford. She would have the audiences eating out of her hand, once she got the break she needed. To hell with Frank Galloway. He could rot in that tatty little business, if he managed to keep hold of it after Alan Wichello and his cronies took their pound of flesh.

'Where to, lady?' the taxi driver asked.

'Shaftesbury Avenue, and hurry,' Bella told him. 'I'm late already. I'm auditioning for a West End show.'

The taxi driver hid a smile. Another suburban housewife with visions of grandeur, he said to himself.

Frank Galloway was feeling ill as he discussed business problems with his yard manager. His head was pounding and he felt dizzy. It was hard to concentrate his mind on matters in hand, and the manager was waiting for a reply.

'I suppose we could subcontract,' Thomas Marks suggested, 'but it'd be costly.'

'No. Certainly not,' Frank said quickly with irritation. 'We'll switch the journeys. Put Baker on the machinery and Peters can do the rum load.'

'Peters?' the manager queried.

Frank stroked his forehead. 'Sorry, I mean Taylor,' he said quickly.

The manager looked at his boss with concern. The man's heading for a nervous breakdown, he thought. Peters left more than six months ago, and Baker's vehicle was not suitable for the heavy machinery contract. 'All right, I'll see what I can do, Mr Galloway,' he said helpfully. 'If you pardon me saying, I think you should go home for the day. You look rather tired.'

Frank shook his head vigorously. 'No, no. There's work to be done. Now let's get on to that garage again. They can't expect us to have two vehicles off the road for three weeks. A cylinder head, you say?'

'No, a stripped flywheel,' the manager corrected him.

'What's wrong with the other vehicle?' Frank asked for the third time.

'A cracked block,' Marks replied. 'That's the three-week job.'

'Well, we'll see about that,' Frank said, suddenly holding the top of his head as a searing pain caught him.

The manager went about his task of rearranging the contract schedules, trying to appear calm despite the volatile atmosphere in the transport office, and when he glanced through the window and saw the well-dressed figure walking into the yard, he got up quickly from his seat and went outside, glad of the chance for a breath of fresh air.

'Can I help you, sir?' he said pleasantly.

Alan Wichello shook his head slowly and turned to face the two heavyweight figures who sauntered up behind him. 'Remember now, we must be civilised,' he told them with a smile.

'Can I help you, gentlemen?' Marks repeated himself, suddenly feeling frightened.

Alan nodded to the yard gate. 'Go take a stroll, it's a nice afternoon,' he said in a low voice.

'I beg your pardon?'

'Granted. Now 'oppit,' the bigger of the two men told him in a menacing voice.

Thomas Marks knew when not to press his luck and he hurried for the gate. Alan Wichello strolled into the office and sat down facing a badly surprised Frank Galloway.

'Hello, Frank. How's tricks?' he asked cheerfully.

Frank put down the phone quickly and stared at the bookmaker. 'Look, Alan, I've been doing my best to come up with the money,' he said nervously. 'You've got to give me a little longer.'

'How much longer?' the bookmaker asked.

'Two weeks. Give me just two weeks more and I'll have every penny, that's a promise,' Frank pleaded.

Alan Wichello stroked his square chin for a few moments and then he leaned forward in his chair. 'No deal, Frank,' he said with a cruel grin. 'You've exhausted our patience, and to be perfectly honest I'd say that you've become somewhat of an embarrassment to us. My two colleagues have a say in this, you know, and they're all for enforcing a little respect – physically, you understand. Now me, I'm all for the "let's sit down and talk" approach, but it doesn't seem to have worked in your case. So loath as I am to let my two assistants loose in this office, I'm afraid I have to bow to numbers. Sorry, Frank, but I'm outgunned here.'

Frank looked up and saw the two menacing characters standing together in the yard and he glanced back appealingly at Alan. 'Now wait just a few minutes,' he urged. 'I can get the money. Today. Yes, today. Just let me make a phone call before you let those two loose in here.'

The bookmaker stared at Frank's sweating face for a few moments and then he nodded. 'Go ahead, make the phone call,' he said quietly.

Frank picked the phone up in his shaking hand and dialled a number quickly. 'Hello, is that you, Peggy? Peggy, look, I'm sorry to trouble you, but I'm in a bit of a fix. No, it's nothing serious. I've got a bit of a financial problem. I can't talk over the phone. Yes, I will. No, I can't wait until this evening. I need to see you now. All right, in one hour. 'Bye, Peggy.'

Alan got up and stretched leisurely. 'That sounds encouraging. Now listen, Frank,' he said with emphasis. 'I'll be back in this office at five sharp, and you'd better be here, with the money. I prefer not to spell out the alternative. I'm inclined to have a weak stomach where such matters are concerned. Anyway, I know you won't let me down, because if you do, your yard, office and transport will be burned, and you'll be in no fit state to travel far, certainly not to that lovely wife of yours. By the way, how is Bella? Keeping fit and well, I hope.'

Frank looked down at the floor. 'She's well,' he mumbled.

Alan Wichello turned on his heel and walked to the door. 'See you at five sharp,' he said with a smile.

Maurice Salter got dressed hurriedly while his three daughters stood together on the landing, and when he came out of his bedroom tucking his collarless shirt into his trousers, they berated him.

'Yer wouldn't listen, would yer?' Brenda hissed at him.

'We said yer shouldn't 'ave broadcast it,' Barbara growled.

'Yer'd better get yer finkin' cap on, or you'll be in trouble this time,' Lily warned him.

Maurice looked serious as he hurried down the stairs and walked into the parlour. 'Morning, gents. Nice day,' he said with as much gusto as he could muster.

The two American military men stood up and nodded to him. 'We've been entertained by your cute daughters,' the shorter of the two said. 'You're a lucky man.'

Maurice grinned. 'They keep me on me toes, that's fer sure,' he replied, glaring briefly at Brenda.

'Mr Salter, I understand from talking to your daughters that they were walking out with Army Air Force personnel from Uxbridge, is that correct?'

'If they say so,' Maurice replied.

'Don't you know?' the taller man asked.

Maurice plunged his hands into his trouser pockets and rocked forward on his toes. 'Fer a start, I don't allow no boy friends in this 'ouse while I'm workin', pal,' he said. 'Now, I work awkward hours, like two ter ten an' ten ter two. Sometimes I do a split shift an' ovver times I do a double shift. I do roll-over shifts an' early shifts on a spread-over, so yer see I ain't at 'ome much, unless I do a two-week roller. D'yer get me meanin'?'

The two officers looked at each other with puzzled frowns on their faces.

'I think we understand,' the shorter of the two replied hesitantly. 'But to come to the point. There's been a spate of filching going on at the base and we're the appointed investigative officers.'

'Go on,' Maurice said, taking his hands out of his pockets and folding his arms.

The tall officer took out a notepad from his breast pocket and consulted it for a few moments. 'Corporal Hiram T. Doppelheimer, Private first class James McKinny, and Master Sergeant Thomas Kanetsky. Do those names mean anything to you?' he asked.

'Don't ask me, I didn't go out wiv 'em,' Maurice said sharply.

'No, but your daughters did,' the officer said quickly.

'Gels, come in 'ere,' Maurice ordered. 'You 'eard those names. Was those the fellas yer went out wiv?'

The three nodded sheepishly and Lily pushed her way to the front.

' 'Ave they bin wounded?' she asked anxiously.

'They'll most likely be shot when we catch up with them,' the tall officer replied. 'They've been running a very lucrative business in silk stockings and other items. Did they ever offer you ladies silk stockings or lingerie in large quantities?'

Lily looked at her sisters and then at the two American officers. 'James offered me a pair o' silk stockin's once, but I wouldn't accept 'em,' she replied.

'Oh, and why not?'

' 'Cos 'e wanted ter put 'em on me,' Lily said indignantly.

'No mention of sales?' the officer asked.

'Certainly not,' Brenda cut in.

' 'Ere, wait a minute,' Maurice butted in. 'Why 'ave yer come ter see us? Yer don't fink we'd get involved in anyfing dodgy, do yer?'

'Well, we got your address from the post room,' the shorter officer said. 'There are letters from your daughters addressed to those three sons of bitches waiting to be re-routed to the front. We have to follow up any leads, you understand.'

' 'Ere, as a matter of interest, 'ow much did they get away wiv?' Maurice asked.

'It must run into thousands of dollars,' the short one replied.

'Good Gawd!' Maurice exclaimed. 'Well, I 'ope yer catch 'em soon, or they'll end up drainin' yer dry. I'm sorry I can't ask yer ter stay fer a bite, I'm just goin' on me spread-over shift an' it starts at nine most evenin's, unless it comes on a short month, then we get what they call a doubler, that's except Christmas Day and Good Friday. Yer know what I mean.'

The two officers stepped out into the fresh air with a sigh of relief, and as they started off along the street with their heads buzzing, Mrs Haggerty came up, ' 'Ere, 'ave you brought the silk stockin's?' she asked them.

Maurice pulled terrible faces at her behind the officers' backs, trying to attract her attention, and when he finally caught her eye he drew his finger across his throat.

'Who's been selling silk stockings around here then, lady?' the tall officer asked her.

Mrs Haggerty had been married to a chancer for years and she had learned to be quick with an answer whenever the police called at her door. Maurice's frantic signalling was more than sufficient to put her on guard.

'Well, as a matter o' fact I see the pips on yer shoulders,' she began tactfully. 'So I ses ter meself, Ginny, I ses, them blokes are American officers. Now, we don't get many officers round these parts, yer understand. Anyway, I ses ter meself, Ginny, I ses, I bet them blokes is givin' stockin's away.'

'And what makes you think we'd be giving silk stockings away?' the short officer asked.

'Well, that's what the ovver American soldiers said,' Ginny Haggerty replied.

'What soldiers?'

'Those ones who've bin walkin' out wiv the Salter gels.'

'What exactly did they say?'

'They said that only the officers get silk stockin's an' they 'ad ter put up wiv sticks o' chewin' gum,' Ginny replied. 'I don't fink it's fair. After all, yer all in the war tergevver, same as our fellas are. 'Ere, by the way, are yer goin' over ter France like the rest of 'em?'

The two officers exchanged sharp looks and hurried off along the

350

street. When they reached their Jeep in Jamaica Road, the taller of the two jumped in and leaned over the shoulder of the driver. 'Let's get the hell outta here,' he said urgently. 'The whole street's suffering from battle fatigue.'

Chapter Forty

Peggy Harrison felt no pity or warmth of any kind as she sat listening to Frank Galloway's pleadings, only a cold anger welling up inside her. There was nothing left, only contempt for the man who had used her, and she shook her head firmly. 'No, Frank. I won't. I've come to your aid more than once, but enough's enough,' she told him.

'But, Peggy, there's no one else I can turn to. You're my last chance,' he begged. 'Those men will do for me, as sure as I'm sitting here.'

Peggy would not be moved. 'You should have thought of that before now,' she countered. 'I begged you to give up that gambling. I told you it would be the finish of you, of us, but you wouldn't listen. No, Frank, I won't lend you another penny.'

Frank got up from his chair and went over to her as she stood by the fireplace, putting his arms out to her.

'No, Frank, I'm adamant,' she said firmly, backing away from his grasp. 'You'll get no more help from me. I couldn't help you even if I wanted to. Theo's money's all gone. There's just my monthly income, and it's barely enough as it is.'

Frank lurched forward, beads of perspiration standing out on his flushed face. He took her roughly by the shoulders and shook her. 'You must help me or I'm dead. Can't you understand?' he cried, his voice rising hysterically.

'And can't you understand? I've no money to give you,' Peggy shouted at him, turning her head away from his sour breath.

'What about that jewellery?' he said, his voice pleading. 'There's that necklace I gave you, and the ring. I'm desperate, Peggy, can't you see?'

He held her tightly against him in his helplessness, and she felt nothing but a faint disgust. He had been so romantic once, so good to be with, but there was nothing left now. He had slowly killed all the love she had for him by his treatment of her, his cheating and lying. All the promises of going away together, all the oaths swearing undying love for her and her alone were just empty words, spoken on the wind and now blown away for ever. He had changed so much; his hysterical behaviour left her feeling dead inside.

'Take the necklace,' she said angrily as she ripped it from round her neck. 'Take the ring,' throwing it at him as he backed away from her.

Frank went down on his hands and knees, mumbling to himself as he fumbled for the small gold band.

'Now get out!' she cried, fighting back angry tears. 'I never want to see you again, not ever.'

Frank climbed to his feet, his eyes narrowing, and for a moment he stood staring at her, then he turned and hurried out of the house, staggering down the front steps and wincing as the constant pounding in his head increased in intensity. He collided with a young woman in the street, bundling her against the railings as he dashed past without a word of apology. They were all deserting him, like rats leaving a sinking ship. Well, he would not founder. He'd show the lot of them, he told himself as he stopped and leaned against the railings to catch his breath.

'Are you all right?' a voice called out to him.

He released his grip on the cold iron and glared at the old man who stood looking at him with concern. 'Of course I'm all right,' he said quickly. 'They want me to go under, but I won't, you'll see. I saw the picture in the paper and I could tell they were mocking me.'

The old man turned away, feeling sad for the wild-eyed stranger who was evidently yet another uncounted victim of the war.

Frank hurried on, his tortured brain aware that time was fast running out for him. They would be waiting back at the office, but not for long. They were sure to come looking for him and exact their revenge. He must hide. He must find some secure place where he would be safe from them, with someone who would watch out for him and tend his needs. But where, with whom?

The clattering tram gave him the answer as it passed by and he happened to see its rear destination sign: Rotherhithe.

Sammy McCarthy was whistling happily to himself as he applied the white paint to the rotting windowframe. He had been glad to see the back of that warring family at long last and the ten-shilling note sat comfortably in his trouser pocket as he worked. The new tenants seemed a nice sort of family, and the man had enough spare pennies to pay for a few extra services.

Sammy put down his brush and wiped his sticky hands on a rag that he took from his back pocket. Time for a break, he thought, grunting as he sat himself down on the front steps of the block and took out his tobacco tin. As he was rolling himself a cigarette, he looked up to see a well-dressed man approaching him.

'I wonder if you can help me,' Frank Galloway said as he reached the caretaker.

'That depends,' Sammy replied, drawing on his cigarette and thinking that the man looked vaguely familiar.

'I'm looking for Gloria Simpson,' Frank said, trying to appear casual despite his anxiety.

'D'yer know 'er?' Sammy asked suspiciously.

'She's an old friend, as a matter of fact,' Frank replied, forcing a smile. 'I've been away on business and I wanted to look her up.'

'I thought I knew the face,' Sammy said, studying the end of his cigarette.

'I beg your pardon?' Frank said, becoming more anxious as the pain in his head started up again.

'You was a client o' Gloria's. I remember yer face,' Sammy said, stroking his chin. 'Never ferget a face, I don't. I 'ave ter look out fer the gels, yer know. There's bin some very funny geezers 'angin' round 'ere lately.'

'Well, I can assure you Gloria will be glad to see me,' Frank said, fishing into his trouser pocket and handing the man a ten-shilling note.

Sammy's eyes lit up. Business was booming, he thought. Two ten-shilling notes in one day wasn't bad. 'Well, in that case yer better go up,' he said, jerking his thumb towards the block entrance. ' 'Er flat's on the top floor. It's all right, she ain't got a client wiv 'er right now.'

Frank nodded his thanks and climbed the steep stairs. It was good to get off the street, he thought. It would be good, too, to sit down out of the heat and let the headache pass. Gloria would take care of him, she always did. She wouldn't hold it against him that he had sent her away from his house rather quickly. After all, it would have been disastrous to let Bella catch her there. She was a good girl, was Gloria. She'd take care of him.

Frank was puffing hard as he reached the top floor and knocked on the door. His head was pounding again and for a moment he swayed, putting his hand out to steady himself. At that moment the door opened and Gloria stood framed in the opening. Her eyes widened as she saw who it was and she made to close the door on him.

'Don't, Gloria. I must talk to you,' he said pleadingly. 'It's a matter of life and death.'

She hesitated, then stood back to let him in.

'Can I sit down for a few minutes?' he asked her.

Gloria motioned to the settee without speaking, her eyes fixed intently on him as she noted the fear on his face. For an instant she felt pity, but the incident at his house came flooding back into her mind and she realised that she could be in grave peril.

'What's wrong?' she asked as he slumped down into the cushions and dropped his head in his hands.

'My life's in danger,' he said flatly. 'There's a couple of men after me and when they catch up with me they're going to kill me.'

'What've yer done?' Gloria asked.

'They're bookmakers and I owe them money.' Frank told her. 'I only need a few more days then I can raise the necessary cash. I need a place where I can stay. Somewhere they won't find me.'

'Well, yer can't say 'ere,' Gloria said quickly. 'I've got a livin' ter get, an' besides, I well remember the last time we shared an' 'ouse.'

'Look, I'm sorry I got angry with you then, Gloria, but I was desperate,' he said. 'Bella was due home at any time and I had to let you go. Surely you understood?'

Gloria sat down in the chair opposite and glared at him. 'I came away wiv more than a few bruises. Yer wounded me pride,' she told him. 'I've never let a man do that ter me before, an' I can assure yer I'd never stand it again.'

'I wouldn't lay a finger on you, believe me,' Frank implored her.

'Well, yer can't stay 'ere, unless yer can pay the goin' rate, an' I don't fink yer can,' she said coldly.

'Don't send me away, Gloria. Those men'll kill me for sure, and it'll be on your head.'

'Oh no. You can't put that one on me,' Gloria said angrily. 'I'm not responsible fer what yer've got up to. I didn't ask yer ter get in the bookies' clutches. Now yer'd better go. I've got a client comin' soon.'

Frank looked at her with wide, glassy eyes and she felt a cold fear run down the length of her spine. She had seen that maniacal look once before, when he attacked her at his house. 'There's a caretaker lookin' after these flats,' she said quickly. ' 'E watches out fer us gels. Any trouble an' Sammy sorts it out.'

'I won't make trouble for you, I promise,' Frank said, holding his hands up in front of him. 'Just a few days, that's all I ask.'

'The answer's still no,' Gloria said firmly.

Frank got up slowly from the settee. He could feel the pain in his head getting worse and he ran his fingers through his hair. Sweat lay in beads along his hairline and he was beginning to tremble. A red mist was forming at the edges of his vision and he mouthed a curse. 'You're all the same. Take, take, take. Never give, only take. It was mine, do you hear? It was mine, and now they're laughing at me. I saw them in the paper. Laughing at me, they were. She laughed too, but I stopped her laughing. She won't laugh any more.'

Gloria had backed away from him and was inching towards the door. He was mad, she thought, stark raving mad. 'Who yer talkin' about?' she asked as calmly as she could, hoping she would reach the door before he got to her.

'Why, that woman who was looking after Mary O'Reilly, that's who,' he snarled at her.

Gloria felt her heart miss a beat and suddenly she was terrified of what he was going to tell her. 'That was my friend Lola,' she said, shaking her head. 'You didn't 'arm 'er. She died in the air raid. Lola was burnt ter death.'

Frank laughed aloud, a wild, frightening laugh, like a prowling animal crying out as it cornered its prey. 'She saw me, so she had to die,' he growled.

'Saw yer?' Gloria said, hardly recognising her own voice.

'Yes, she saw me. I was getting ready to burn the house down but she had to interfere. I told her I was seeking justice, and she laughed at me. She stood back and laughed at me so I hit her. I stopped her laughing,' Frank cried, his voice rising to a crescendo. 'She'll never laugh at me again, do you hear?'

Gloria was sick with anger and fear. She had been shocked to learn of Lola's death after the last bad air raid more than three years ago, but she had not thought for a moment that it was a cold, brutal murder. The memory of her beating at the hands of Frank Galloway flashed into Gloria's mind, and she realised with horror that her fears then had been justified. Frank Galloway was capable of murder – he had just admitted it. He was mad, raving mad, and her life was in mortal danger.

'Come away from that door, Gloria,' Frank said with spite in his voice. 'Come away or I'll have to kill you too.'

Gloria made a sudden dart for the door handle but he was too quick for her. He grabbed her round the waist and quickly clamped his hand over her mouth. 'If you try to scream I'll strangle you, do you hear?' he snarled.

Gloria was paralysed with fear and he could see by her eyes that she understood. He slowly released the pressure on her mouth. 'Right then, we'll sit you down,' he said, his voice becoming calm again as he forced her down into an upright chair. 'Just remember. One sound and I'll throttle you.'

Gloria's mouth and throat were dry and she sat rigid as he pulled her arms tightly behind the chair, holding them together with one hand as he leaned sideways and reached for the curtain cord. She was soon trussed up rightly, and Frank then went into her bedroom and came out with a couple of her silk slips.

'Why are yer tyin' me up?' she asked fearfully.

'Because I've got to go out,' he replied. 'There's a little matter I've got to take care of. They won't laugh at me any more after this night, you can be sure of that.'

Gloria saw the mad look in his eyes and she flinched as he came towards her. He bent down and used the slips to bind her feet to the legs of the chair, and when he was finished he studied his handiwork. 'Now for the gag,' he said aloud.

Sammy McCarthy was putting the finishing touches to the windowframe when Frank came down the steps. 'Was Gloria pleased ter see yer?' he called out.

Frank drew a deep breath and ambled up to him. 'She wants me to stay a few days but there's a problem,' he said casually.

'Oh, an' what's that then?' Sammy asked.

'Well, Gloria was expecting another client,' Frank replied smiling. 'I wonder if you'd be so kind as to tell him when he turns up that Gloria's indisposed for the time being?'

'I can't be lookin' out fer Gloria all the time,' Sammy said, gazing down at his paint-smeared palm.

Frank took out a one-pound note from his wallet and held it out. 'We'd like a bit of privacy, if you know what I mean,' he said, smiling slyly. 'I'm just away to make a phone call, then I'll be back.'

Sammy nodded and watched his benefactor walk quickly along the turning, then he pocketed the pound note and picked up his paintbrush once more.

Carrie was listening to the early news broadcast when Nellie called out. She hurried to her mother's room and found her trying to get out of bed. 'Now yer must stay there, Mum,' she said firmly.

Nellie winced as her daughter helped her back beneath the bedclothes. 'I don't want ter be a burden,' she groaned. 'I only wanted ter come downstairs fer a while. Besides, I don't want yer fetchin' an' carryin' all the time.'

'Look, I've got Joe to 'elp, an' there's Rachel. I'm not doin' it all,' Carrie said quietly but firmly.

Nellie sighed as she leaned back on the pillow. 'I feel so weak,' she said.

'Mum, it's pleurisy, an' yer know what the doctor said. Yer gotta stay in bed an' rest,' Carrie reminded her. 'Give it a few days an' you'll be as right as rain, but if yer start gettin' up an' sittin' in the draught, yer could get pneumonia easy as anyfing.'

' 'Ark at little Nurse Nightingale,' Nellie chuckled.

'Well, do as yer told then,' Carrie said smiling, patting her hand fondly.

The phone rang and Joe picked it up. As Carrie came down the stairs, he slipped his hand over the mouthpiece. 'It's the *South London Press*,' he whispered. 'They wanna to do a piece on our Rachel an' Tony.'

'She's slipped round ter one of 'er friends,' Carrie told him. 'She'll be back soon 'cos Tony's callin' for 'er.'

A few minutes later Rachel walked in and flopped down in the chair. 'I've picked up all the gossip,' she laughed. 'Mary Wilshaw's got 'erself a new young man an' Josie Phillips is pregnant again.'

'Well, I've got a bit o' news fer you,' Carried said. 'The *South London Press* wanna do a follow-up story about you an' Tony. They're gonna ring back shortly.'

Rachel's eyes opened wide. 'Well, well,' she replied, grinning. 'We're gonna be famous.'

Carrie stood over her, arms akimbo. 'Just remember ter tell 'em yer're

357

a backstreet child, an' proud of it,' she said with feigned seriousness.

Rachel laughed aloud and stood up stretching. 'Oh well, I'd better get me 'air washed,' she said. 'We're goin' ter the flicks ternight.'

Ten minutes later the phone rang again and when Carrie answered it she passed it over to Rachel. 'It's them again,' she whispered.

Nellie called out just then and Carrie hurried up the stairs once more. When she came back down into the parlour, Rachel was putting on her coat.

'They wanna see me right away,' she said excitedly.

'Just you?' Carrie asked, looking quickly at Joe as he walked into the room.

'Yeah. They wanna see me about arrangin' a proper meetin' wiv the two of us termorrer. They're sendin' a taxi right away,' Rachel told her. ' 'E said it won't take long an' 'e'll drop me back 'ere afterwards.'

'It seems a funny way ter do business. Couldn't they wait until termorrer?' Carrie said, pulling a face.

' 'E said 'e was sorry about the rush but they want ter get it in this Friday's edition,' Rachel explained, adjusting the collar of her coat.

'Well, don't be too long,' Carrie replied. 'Remember Tony'll be 'ere early.'

Frank Galloway had been cursing his luck after the first phone call, but ten minutes later he was smiling as he climbed back up to the top-floor flat in Rotherhithe. Gloria was sitting with her head bowed as he let himself in, and she looked up and stared balefully at him. Frank checked the gag round her mouth and then took a piece of clothesline that was hanging over the gas stove. He proceeded to tie one end round Gloria's neck and then pulled it rigid, fastening the other end to the cross-rail under the chair.

'Now listen to me,' he said, waving his finger at the trussed woman. 'That's a lorry knot I've just tied round your neck, which means that if you struggle, the rope will get tighter. Try to get free and you'll slowly choke, so for your sake you'd better sit very still until I get back. If all goes well, I won't be long. Then we'll get a little more civilised.'

With a last quick glance at his prisoner, Frank let himself out of the flat and hurried down the stairs.

It was only a short walk to Rotherhithe Tunnel, where he hailed a passing taxi. Two minutes later the cab turned into Salmon Lane and Frank sighed with relief as he saw that Rachel was waiting by the yard gate and she was alone. As the taxi drew up, he opened the door and she stepped in smiling. He pulled her down quickly into the seat and her face blanched as she saw the large carving knife in his hand. 'Don't scream or try to attract the driver's attention, or I'll put this in you,' he whispered.

Rachel looked into his face and saw the terrible wild look in his eyes.

'It was you on the phone,' she said. 'You tricked me.'

He nodded. 'We're taking a little trip and I want you to do exactly as you're told. I'm desperate and I won't hesitate to run this knife right into you if I have to.'

Rachel fought to stay calm as she felt the pressure of the knife in her side. There was nothing she could do to attract attention without getting hurt, and Frank Galloway looked capable of anything. She knew both father and son by sight, had heard her mother talk endlessly about the Galloway family and about Frank Galloway's misdeeds, but she had never considered for a minute that the man would be so stupid as to threaten her, or do her any harm. What was he trying to achieve?

The taxi driver had already been told where to go and he turned into Jamaica Road and then left into Rotherhithe Tunnel. Necessity and sheer desperation had set Frank to thinking hard and he had laid his plans well. Their destination was a derelict riverside warehouse in Wapping. It had once stored dried fruit and canned goods from the Orient, but now the bomb-blasted building was abandoned to the rats that searched the deserted floors for rotting titbits.

Frank had been shown over the building some time ago by a businessman he had befriended at a masonic dinner. They had discussed buying the derelict property and renovating it for furniture-making after the war was over, and for a time Frank had been excited about the project. He had planned on investing as a partner, once he gained his inheritance but his dreams had been shattered.

The taxi reached the end of the tunnel and turned sharply left into a narrow lane. On each side, high gloomy warehouses shut out the light and the taxi rattled over the rough cobbles.

'This will do, driver,' Frank ordered, and then he turned to Rachel with a stern look on his flushed face. 'Now don't try anything as we get out. Just keep close to me,' he warned her.

Rachel felt his grip on her arm tighten as he paid the driver, and then he pulled her roughly towards the debris-strewn warehouse yard. They entered the derelict building through an opening in the brickwork at the end of the yard. The air inside was foul-smelling. Rachel felt her blood run cold as she heard a scurry. The place is rat-infested, she thought with horror.

'Why are yer bringin' me 'ere?' she said suddenly.

'Just keep quiet,' Frank hissed. 'I warned you once. Don't talk.'

She was hustled along inside the filthy warehouse, then pulled roughly towards an iron door. Frank held her tightly with one hand and reached for the door handle with the other. The next instant Rachel was violently shoved into the dark interior and before she had time to think the door was slammed shut.

Chapter Forty-One

Tony O'Reilly had had a busy day. In the morning he had been to see an army friend who was recovering from his wounds at the Woolwich Military Hospital, and then afterwards he had gone to the Bermondsey baths, where he soaked luxuriously for almost an hour before going to get his hair trimmed. His next visit was to a jewellery shop in Whitechapel, where he bought a gold ring which had five tiny diamonds set in a raised shoulder. He had it in the inside pocket of his coat and he occasionally reassured himself that it was still there as he strolled along Jamacia Road in the warm evening air.

He was feeling happy. He had read the early edition of the evening paper on his way back from Whitechapel and it appeared that the invasion was going well. Tonight he would give Rachel the ring he had bought and hold her close in the darkness of the cinema. Life felt good for him as he turned into Salmon Lane, blissfully unaware that his happiness was about to be shattered.

Joe met him at the gate, his face dark. 'We've 'ad a phone call, Tony,' he said urgently. 'Somebody's 'oldin' Rachel.'

'What?' Tony exclaimed. ' 'Oldin' 'er? What d'yer mean, 'oldin' 'er?'

Joe led the anxious young man into the house and he was immediately confronted by Carrie in tears.

'Rachel went out before five this evenin',' she said, fighting to compose herself. 'Somebody phoned ter say they wanted ter meet 'er. They said they were from the *South London Press* an' they wanted to arrange a meetin' ter fix up an interview wiv the two o' yer. Whoever it was said they'd send 'er back by taxi an' it wouldn't take long. Then not long after, we got anuvver call. They said if we wanted ter see Rachel again we'd 'ave ter pay a ransom. Oh God, why didn't I stop 'er goin'?' Carrie sobbed.

Joe went to her and put his arms round her. 'Yer mustn't blame yerself,' he said, patting her back gently. 'We wasn't ter know it was a set-up. 'Ow could we know?'

Tony's face was ashen as he looked from one to the other. ' 'Ave yer any idea who it could be?' he asked.

Joe and Carrie both shook their heads and Tony gripped his fists tightly in anger.

'They said they'd ring later to arrange payment, and if we went ter the police they'd kill Rachel fer sure,' Joe told him.

'Did they say what time they'll ring back?' Tony asked.

'No, they rang off before I could say anyfing,' Joe replied.

Just then Nellie called out and Carrie hastily dabbed at her face. 'I daren't tell Mum, it'll kill 'er,' she groaned.

As soon as Carrie left the room, Joe turned to Tony. 'I don't know much about such fings, but by the way 'e sounded, I reckon 'e'll carry out 'is threat if we do go ter the police,' he said quietly. 'I just feel so 'elpless. What can we do?'

Tony shook his head. 'I didn't want ter say anyfing in front o' Rachel's mum, but we can't be sure 'e won't 'arm 'er, even if the ransom is paid. We've got ter find 'er, Joe,' he said.

Suddenly the phone rang and Joe went quickly to answer it. Tony felt his heart pounding as he watched Joe's face darken with anger. Then he put the receiver down.

' 'E told me jus' ter listen carefully an' that if I spoke 'e'd put the phone down right away,' Joe said, his voice shaking. ' 'E's askin' fer two thousand pounds. We've got ter 'ave it ready by midday termorrer.'

' 'Ow's it ter be paid?' Tony asked.

' 'E said 'e'd give us instructions later. 'E's gonna call sometime termorrer mornin',' Joe replied, slumping down in a chair.

When Carrie came down into the room she was white-faced. 'What's 'appened?' she asked anxiously. 'I 'eard the phone go but I couldn't leave Mum. I'm sure she suspects there's somefing wrong.'

Joe told her the message and she held her hand to her mouth.

'There's nuffink we can do till the mornin', luv. We can only wait,' Joe said, running a hand over his forehead.

Carrie shook her head. 'There's nearly a thousand in the bank, an' I can raise the rest in the mornin', but I feel so 'elpless. I wonder where they've got 'er, Joe? Will she be all right?' she asked tearfully.

'She's gonna be all right, believe me,' Joe said, taking her by the shoulders. 'We've jus' gotta try ter stay calm.'

Carrie shook her head. 'I can't sit still. I'll make us a cuppa. It's gonna be a long wait.'

Nellie walked slowly into the room with a blanket covering her shoulders. 'What the bloody 'ell's goin' on 'ere?' she asked.

Gloria Simpson sat arched backward in her chair. The knot pressing against the back of her neck had tightened when her head slumped earlier and she knew that to relax her back would be fatal. The gag in her mouth was hurting and she realised that she had lost the circulation in both feet. Frank Galloway was a maniac, she thought with hatred in her heart. He had openly admitted to killing Lola and it was quite probable that she would be his next victim now that she knew his dark

361

secret. She must get loose somehow. Her life depended on it.

Gloria looked round the room in desperation. Her chair was faci
the window; a tall vase sat on the windowsill. She could feel the bon
beginning to bite into her swollen hands and she tried to move h
fingers. The rope from her neck to the back of the chair had been pass
over her tethered hands and she started to search for it by spreading h
fingers, at the same time arching her back still further in an attempt
loosen the rope. Suddenly she felt it and managed to curl her thun
round it. If she could hold it and stop it tightening any more, she mig
be able to jerk the chair towards the window.

Gloria took a deep breath and moved her hips forward in a quick jer
The chair moved an inch or so and she gasped with the effort. The ro
had not tightened any further and Gloria took heart. It was going to be
painful task, she realised, but it was the only way.

Sammy McCarthy chuckled to himself as he sat drinking Guinne
from a pint bottle. It had been a good day and there had been very lit
work involved. That businessman would have been a little upset had I
known that Gloria wasn't going to receive any clients that eveni
anyway, but he was well able to afford the pound note he had pass
over, Sammy decided.

The soft music coming from the wireless was lulling the caretaker
sleep and the sound of smashing glass and something shattering in t
street outside jerked him up sharply.

'Not anuvver bloody warrin' family,' he said aloud as he hurried o
of his ground-floor flat into the street. 'Oh my good Gawd!' he gasp
as he saw the smashed vase at his feet and Gloria's head hangi
through the broken window above him.

Sammy dashed up the flights of stairs, scared that Gloria would c
her throat on the broken glass before he could get to her, and he w
gasping for breath as he charged his way into her flat.

A little later Gloria sat recovering as Sammy rubbed her lifeless han
and feet.

'Yer was lucky yer didn't get more than a scratch from that glass. I
personally take that evil git apart limb from limb,' he growled. 'Just yc
wait. I'll 'ave 'im screamin' fer mercy.'

Gloria suddenly looked at him, her deathly white face full of fea
'Sammy, there's two young kids in deadly danger from that evil git.
must warn 'em.'

Nellie had seen the worry on everyone's face and Carrie had been force
to tell her everything that had happened. Now the old woman s
sipping a cup of tea, her face white and drawn. 'Who would 'ave do
such a terrible fing?' she said. 'It was that photo in the paper, that
what done it. I never 'eld wiv 'avin' yer photograph in the newspapers.

362

ink it asks fer trouble of one sort or anuvver.'

'Now, don't upset yerself, Mum,' Carrie implored her. 'We've got ter stay calm fer Rachel's sake.'

At six o' clock the gate bell sounded and Joe hurried out to answer it. When he returned, Gloria and Sammy were with him, and his face was red with anger. 'This is Gloria Simpson, an' yer better listen ter what she's got ter say, Carrie,' he told her, his hands squeezed into tight fists. 'It's Frank Galloway who's got Rachel.'

'Frank Galloway!' Carrie gasped, hardly believing her ears.

'Yer fella told me yer daugher's bin taken,' Gloria blurted out. 'That's what I come ter warn yer about but I'm too late.'

Carrie motioned Gloria and Sammy to sit down, and everyone listened in horror as the Rotherhithe street woman told them what had happened.

' 'E kept 'oldin' 'is 'ead like 'e was in agony,' she told them. 'But it was 'is eyes that terrified me. I can still see 'em.' She turned to Tony. 'I'm sorry about yer muvver, Tony. That evil Galloway's got a lot to answer for.'

Tony was sitting numb with shock at what he had just heard and he merely nodded. Carrie hurried to Gloria's side as the distraught woman lowered her head and burst into tears, while Sammy sat upright in his chair, feeling partly responsible for everything by allowing the madman to get to Gloria. Suddenly he looked up at Joe. 'I'm wiv yer in this,' he growled.

Joe was already putting on his coat. ' 'E might be 'oldin' Rachel at 'is yard, though I doubt it,' he said quickly. 'We'll 'ave ter try there though, we don't know where else ter look.'

Joe and Tony hurried out of the house with Sammy McCarthy, Gloria's warning ringing in their ears. 'Be careful, remember 'e's off 'is 'ead.'

The three hurried out onto Jamaica Road and it was not long before they reached Wilson Street. They walked down to the padlocked yard. Joe peered through a gap in the wicket gate and then turned to Tony and Sammy. 'It looks all quiet inside, but Galloway could be in there,' he said. 'The wicket gate's not fastened from the outside.'

'Gis a leg-up an' I'll go over,' Sammy volunteered.

Tony was burning with hatred for the man who had wanted to kill his mother, and with a sudden cry he took a running jump and his hands found the top of the gate. With little effort he pulled himself up and rolled over, dropping out of sight of the two older men. His heart was pumping fast as he crossed the yard and reached for the handle of the office door. Suddenly the door opened quickly and he was grabbed by his coat lapels, a hand going round his throat. He barely saw his assailant before he was spun round with brute force and wrestled to the floor. The man's heavy bulk was bearing down on him painfully. 'Who

363

are yer an' what yer doin' 'ere?' the man growled at him.

Tony looked up into the huge flat face staring down at him. 'I'm lookin' fer that bastard Galloway,' he gasped defiantly.

'Well, Galloway ain't 'ere,' the man replied, easing his weight from the young soldier.

'Who are you?' Tony asked, gingerly rubbing his bruised throat.

'Let's say I'm someone who's lookin' fer Galloway too. I've bin waitin' fer 'im ter come back 'ere wiv the dosh 'e owes me an' my pals,' the big man replied, getting up from the floor.

Tony got to his feet and stared at the man. 'I've gotta find 'im quick,' he said urgently. ' 'E's gone off 'is 'ead, an' 'e's kidnapped my fiancée.'

The man turned towards the door as the sound of Joe's voice carried into the yard. 'Who's wiv yer?' he asked quickly.

'It's me gel's stepfarvver an' a friend,' Tony told him.

The man crossed the yard, with Tony following on his heels. He slid the bolt of the wicket gate and ducked out into the street.

'Let's go find Alan Wichello,' he said simply.

Rachel had stumbled onto her knees as she was pushed into the filthy storeroom and she screamed out to Frank Galloway as the door was slammed shut on her. She clambered to her feet and rubbed her grazed knee. In the dim light that came down from a high barred window she looked around at the room. It was empty apart from a wooden bench on one side and a row of bare shelves on the other. A naked wire hung from the ceiling and the light switch was hanging down off the wall. The floor was littered with cardboard and scraps of paper and the place reeked of decay.

Rachel had realised very soon after getting into the taxi that Frank Galloway was mad, and that she would have to remain calm and not agitate him in any way if she were to have any chance of survival. Help would come, she knew, but they would have to find her first, she thought with sudden panic. It could take days. She tried the door but she could tell that it was securely bolted from the outside. The window was too high to reach and it was barred. Rachel involuntarily brought a hand up to her mouth as she looked down at the paper and cardboard strewn around the floor, suddenly realising that there could be rats nesting there. She crept over to the empty shelves and found a loose length of wood which she wielded like a club as she very gingerly moved the litter with her foot. When she found nothing, she leaned against the bench, trembling with the very thought of having to kill the things.

For what seemed an age, Rachel stayed pressed against the wooden workbench, trying to stay calm. They would all be looking for her now, she told herself. She would have to help them locate her somehow. What could she do, though?

Suddenly she stood up straight and went over to the empty shelves, picking up another length of wood. Working slowly and as quietly as she could, she began prising the shelving loose, and after several minutes she had succeeded in removing two long battens. She pulled up her skirt and tore a strip from her cotton slip, using it to bind the two lengths of wood end to end. Very carefully she lifted the long pole to the window and prodded at the glass. She tried again and again until her arms were exhausted, but it was thick factory glass and resisted all her efforts to break it.

Rachel sat down on the filthy floor and rested her head in her hands, willing herself not to give way to her fear. Tony would find her. He would find her somehow, she told herself.

Alan Wichello had been phoned and he joined the small group who were waiting in a little pub off Jamaica Road. After he had introduced himself, he sat down and opened his wallet. 'Get us all a Scotch, Jim. I think we could all do with one,' he told his associate. 'I want to get the drift.'

By the time Jim returned with the drinks, Alan Wichello had been briefed and he was stroking his chin thoughtfully. 'Now let's think this thing out,' he said, toying with his glass. 'We know that Rachel was taken by taxi from your yard, and we know that she wasn't taken to the Galloway yard. Now from what this prosser told you, Galloway was desperate for somewhere to hole up in. Would he take the girl back to the prosser's flat?'

Sammy shook his head. 'I'm sure 'e wouldn't go there. 'E knows I keep me eye open fer the women an' I'd wanna know what 'e was doin' wiv the gel,' he replied.

Alan looked at Sammy with distaste. 'Pity you didn't do your job properly in the first place,' he said quickly, turning to his helper. 'Jim, go with Sammy here and check out the prosser's flat. Hang around there in case he shows up, but keep out of sight. Remember, the man's crazy and we don't know how he's thinking. He could be out to silence her.' The two men left and Alan looked slowly from Joe to Tony. 'We've also got to remember that Rachel knows who he is, so we've got to find her quick,' he added, voicing the fear that was already eating into Joe and Tony.

'There's a lot o' derelict ware'ouses an' wharves on the riverside,' Joe said, sighing with frustration. 'Rachel could be in any one o' those.'

Alan Wichello suddenly gulped his drink and put the glass down with a bang. 'You've just given me an idea. I won't be a minute,' he said, getting up and taking some coppers from his trouser pocket.

Joe and Tony watched as the bookmaker went to the bar and exchanged a few words with the publican, then they saw him disappear behind the counter. A few minutes later he was back. 'C'mon, chaps, I think we're on a winner. I'll explain in the car,' he said urgently.

Joe and Tony followed him out of the pub and within moments the were being driven towards Rotherhithe Tunnel. Alan sat back behind the wheel, staring straight ahead as he steered the Bentley along the quiet Jamaica Road.

'You got me thinking when you mentioned the derelict warehouses' he said, glancing briefly at Joe. 'There was mention of forming a loc consortium at our lodge some time ago. Certain members were talking about raising capital to renovate a riverside warehouse and turn it into furniture factory. Galloway was a member of the lodge at the time though he's since resigned. He was one of the people interested in the project. I couldn't remember exactly where the property was, so phoned a pal of mine who was involved. He told me it's in Wapping an I've got the directions. Now you realise that this is a long shot,' he sai with emphasis. 'But I remember Galloway being enthusiastic about th property at the time, and I remember him saying that he had looked over, so we could be on the right track, fingers crossed.'

Joe turned to Tony as the car drove through the Rotherhithe Tunne 'I owe young Rachel,' he said. 'I want the first chance with Galloway

Tony smiled bitterly. 'After I've finished wiv Frank Galloway, yo can 'ave 'im,' he said in a gruff voice. 'I've got two good reasons ter b first, Joe. I'm gonna marry Rachel, an' remember it was Galloway wh set my 'ouse alight. Galloway's mine.'

Alan lifted one hand from the wheel and wagged his finger. 'You tw had better not forget that Frank Galloway's crazy, and that makes hi very dangerous,' he reminded them. 'Besides, he might have gone bac to the prosser's flat. If so, you can rest assured Jim'll get him.'

The car came out of the tunnel and swung down into the narro riverside lane. 'Here we are,' Alan said, pulling up at the kerb. 'No let's watch each other's backs and keep our wits about us. If he's her we'll have him.'

The three men walked cautiously into the litter-strewn yard and Jo spotted the opening in the brickwork. 'This looks like a way in,' he said

Frank had started to feel more at ease after crossing the river, for h knew that Wichello did not have any influence in east London, but h had to go back. He had been stupid to tell Gloria about killing he friend Lola. She, too, would now have to be silenced for good.

He took a taxi back to Rotherhithe and was pleased to see that ther was no sign of Sammy as he arrived at the buildings. When he le himself into Gloria's flat, panic seized him – she had someho managed to get free. Everything was starting to go wrong again, h groaned to himself, squeezing his temples to ease the pain that cam back to torture him.

As he hurried out of the buildings, he saw a taxi turning into th street and he rushed across into an alley opposite which led towards the tunnel. It was them, he thought. They were coming for him. He must get back to Wapping right away. He ran along to the tunnel steps and dashed down the footpath. There was no more money for taxis.

He hurried along the smoky tunnel, trying to focus his mind on what he had to do. They would pay the money for the girl and then he would get right away, from the ailing business, from Bella, from everyone, and he would start afresh someplace where nobody knew him. Once this was over, he would be able to rest and the pain would leave him, he felt sure. It was blinding him, making it difficult to think clearly, but he knew instinctively that he had to cover his tracks. They would get the girl back but, like Gloria, she would have to be silenced first. Frank stopped in his tracks, suddenly remembering that he had not killed the prostitute. But he hadn't been able to. He remembered now. She had gone when he got back. If only this headache would stop pounding, he groaned as he hurried on once more.

At the end of the tunnel he turned down the path towards the warehouse and as he ran towards it he saw the Bentley parked at the kerb. His heart missed a beat as he recognised the car. Wichello was in the warehouse waiting for him, he realised. Well, he would deal with him as well as the rest. They were all the same. Everyone was against him but he had to survive somehow. He felt the knife in his belt as he crept silently across the yard and into the building, reckoning that as he was familiar with the layout, he had the edge.

As he tiptoed into the dim interior he saw the three figures in front of him and moved quickly into an alcove. He watched them turning round and coming back towards him. He knew they were looking for the stairs and would have to pass him. He slunk deeper into the shadows and waited. He could see that Wichello was leading the way, followed by Joe Maitland and Tony O'Reilly who was bringing up the rear. Frank drew his knife and as the young soldier came abreast of him, he suddenly lunged out. Tony uttered a startled cry and staggered to his knees holding his side. His two companions turned to see Frank running away into the shadows. Joe bent down to Tony, but he waved him away. 'I'm all right. Get 'im!' he groaned.

Joe hesitated as he saw the blood oozing from between Tony's fingers, but the young man was insistent. 'Don't let 'im get away!' he shouted.

Alan was already in pursuit and Joe hurried after him. They ran up the long flight of stairs and as they reached the next landing, they heard the sound of bolts being slid and then a scream. They could see Frank clearly now. He was standing in the middle of the warehouse floor, holding Rachel with one arm round her waist and the carving knife pressed against her chin.

'Come any closer and I'll cut her throat,' he shouted.

'Yer finished, Galloway,' Joe shouted back. 'Let 'er go.'

The bookmaker laid his hand on Joe's arm. 'Careful. Let me talk to him,' he said quietly.

'Go home and wait for my call, like I told you,' Frank called out.

'All right, let the girl go and you and I can have a talk,' Alan said calmly. 'You must see the sense in it.'

'Sense nothing. I'm done with the lot of you. You're all against me,' Frank shouted.

'He's really cracked up,' Alan hissed to Joe.

Through her fear Rachel saw Tony staggering out of the shadows, holding his side, soaked in blood. He walked slowly towards them, bent almost double, and Rachel screamed, 'Tony! Tony!'

Frank moved the knife against her throat. 'Keep away, do you hear?' he shouted.

Suddenly Tony fell headlong onto his face and Frank started.

Rachel saw her chance. She reached up, grabbing the hand holding the knife and sinking her teeth into the thumb. Joe immediately sprang at Frank and his fist landed full in his face. Alan dashed forward and between them the two men managed to wrestle the knife away from the madman. Rachel rushed to Tony, her blonde hair hanging over his face as she bent down and cuddled him to her. 'Yer mustn't die, d'yer 'ear me?' she cried.

Suddenly Frank broke free and he backed away, his eyes staring wildly at his adversaries. He looked from right to left, like a cornered animal, then with a maniacal scream he dashed to a crane door and stood balancing precariously on the footboard above the yard.

'I fooled you, I fooled the lot of you,' he laughed, a wild, desperate laugh. Then he turned and dived head first into the yard.

Alan Wichello and Joe came out into the quiet lane supporting Tony between them, while Rachel held a handkerchief pressed against his side. They sat him down gently on the kerb. The bookmaker had already rushed up the road to phone for an ambulance, and Joe had covered the body of Frank Galloway with a piece of tarpaulin that he found in the yard.

Rachel crouched down beside Tony and stroked his hair. ' 'E'll be all right, won't 'e, Joe?' she asked fearfully.

Joe nodded and smiled at her. 'Tony's gonna be fine, ain't yer, son?'

Tony smiled briefly. 'Bet yer life. we've got a weddin' ter fix up,' he replied.

Rachel kissed his cheek. 'Soon as we can,' she said smiling. Then she turned to Joe. 'I knew yer'd come fer me, Joebo.'

'I 'ad to, luv,' Joe told her. 'I owed yer. Yer came fer me once, remember?'

Chapter Forty-Two

All day long family and friends had called to see Nellie Tanner as she lay very ill in her little back bedroom. Danny and Iris came and returned later with their children at Nellie's behest, and Billy came round with Annie. Carrie had spent most of the time sitting with her mother as the pneumonia raged, and during her periods of wakefulness Nellie had much to say. Tony had been an early visitor that day, along with Rachel, and Nellie was quick to advise them on their forthcoming marriage.

'Yer the last o' the Galloways, son,' she said. 'What's past is gone ferever. Yer'll carry the name on an' yer'll no doubt sire children. Teach 'em well. Make sure that the ghosts o' the past don't visit 'em. As fer you, me gel, yer need look no furvver than yer muvver fer guidance. Keep a good table an' make yerself presentable an' yer won't go far wrong.'

Rachel and Tony exchanged smiles and Rachel kissed her grandmother's feverish brow before she left. Nellie went to sleep. Later she roused herself enough to greet her old friends. Sadie came and sat chatting for a while and was joined by Maisie. The three old ladies recalled fond memories until Nellie became tired and drifted off to sleep once more. Maudie and Dolly called and stayed a while, then the three inseparables came round. Mrs Green led her two friends to the bedside and Mrs Haggerty and Mrs Watson looked very serious as they gazed down at Nellie.

All night long Nellie's fever raged and the next morning when the doctor called he shook his head. 'She's very weak, and her age is against her,' he said. 'She could drift off at any time, you understand.'

Carrie nodded sadly. She cared for her ailing mother, got on with the task of running the business, and at the same time helped Rachel to arrange her coming wedding. Joe worked hard and eased Carrie's burden as much as he could, but after days and nights of tending, fetching and carrying, Carrie felt exhausted.

Late one afternoon she looked in on her mother, and seeing that the old lady was sleeping peacefully she went down to the parlour and put her feet up for a short nap. She had been asleep for less than an hour when voices in the yard roused her. She sat up abruptly as Joe showed a young soldier into the room. He was tall and fair, with a tanned skin and the deepest blue eyes. His smile seemed to light up his face and as he leaned forward to shake Carrie's hand, he nodded knowingly.

'Yes, you're exactly as my father described you. I'm William Tanner,' he said.

Carrie was suddenly on her feet and she threw her arms round him, hugging him tightly. 'Charlie's boy! I can't believe it,' she blurted out. 'Joe, just look at 'im, ain't 'e the spittin' image?'

Joe exchanged grins with the young man and Carrie began to fuss over him. 'Take a seat. Make yerself comfortable. Would yer like a cuppa?'

As William eased his large frame into the chair, Carrie stood gazing down at him. ' 'Ow's yer dad, an' yer mum of course?' she asked.

William's face became serious and he looked at Carrie kindly. 'I'm afraid they're both dead,' he said quietly.

Carrie felt her tears rising for the brother she had not seen for so many years. ' 'Ow? When?' she asked him.

'They were interned by the Japanese,' William replied. 'They both died in the prison camp. Lawrence and I were away at school in Delhi when the Japs overran the area where my parents were staying. Dad was still attached to the military as an adviser, you see.'

Carrie shook her head sadly. 'And Lawrence?' she asked.

'Oh, he's fine,' William said smiling. 'He's staying with Mother's family in India at the moment.'

'And what brings you all this way?' Carrie asked him.

'I'm going on an officer training course at Sandhurst,' he replied. 'I'm very excited about it and it's what father would have wanted for me.'

'I'm sure 'e'd be very proud of yer,' Carrie told him.

'I had to look you up,' William said, his disarming smile beaming again. 'Dad told me so much about his family, it's as though we've always been living with you. He never forgot you all.'

'We never fergot 'im,' Carrie said with a lump in her throat.

'Is Grandma around?' he asked suddenly.

Carrie's face dropped. 'She's very ill. In fact the doctor says she could pass away at any time.'

'I'm so sorry,' William said quietly, sitting back in his chair.

'Would yer like to see her?' Carrie asked him. 'She's upstairs.'

William nodded and got up quickly.

Carrie led the way up the steep flight of stairs and as the two of them stepped into the tiny bedroom, Nellie opened her eyes.

'Are yer awake, Mum?' Carrie whispered. 'I've brought someone ter see yer.'

William bent over the bed and clasped the old lady's hand gently in his. 'How are you, Grandma?' he asked almost reverently.

Nellie's eyes flickered and then she stared at him for a few moments.

Suddenly her pale face was wreathed in a smile. 'It's me Charlie,' she whispered, closing her eyes. 'The good Lord's answered me prayer. I knew yer'd come back ter me one day, Charlie.'

William turned to Carrie, still clasping the old lady's hand.

'Yer was right all along, Mum,' Carrie said, silent tears beginning to fall down her face.

'Course I was right,' Nellie whispered. 'Now give yer ole mum a kiss, Charlie boy.'

William bent over the bed and very gently laid his lips on his grandmother's hot forehead.

'That's better,' she said, and she closed her eyes.

Carrie and the young soldier backed quietly out of the room and crept down the stairs.

'She'll sleep peaceful now,' Carrie said to the young man. 'She's got all yer dad's letters under 'er bed. She still reads 'em when she's feelin' well enough. I fink we all knew the worst when the letters stopped three years ago.'

William nodded sadly. 'I would have written to you but I didn't have your address,' he replied. 'Everything was destroyed when the Japs came in. As luck would have it my father took a few bits and pieces into the internment camp and I got them when the Japs were pushed back. Among the effects was a notebook with your address in, and when I got my posting to England I swore I'd look you up. But actually it wouldn't have mattered if I hadn't had it. Father used to say that everyone knew the Tanners. All I had to do was get to Bermondsey.'

Carrie smiled sadly. 'Yeah, an' everyone loved yer dad. We all did.'

William took out an envelope and from it he removed a small notebook. 'I wonder if you would like this as a keepsake,' he said, putting it down on the table.

Carrie picked the book up and held it to her for a few moments. 'This was Charlie's, yer dad's?' she asked.

William nodded. 'You'll notice that the writing is very very small. You can understand why. There were virtually no writing materials available and that book was precious. There are things in there that I don't understand. Perhaps you'll be able to make some sense of them.'

Carrie put the book in the cupboard drawer and smiled at him. 'You must stay for tea,' she said.

He shook his head. 'I'm sorry but this has to be a flying visit. I've a train to catch, you see,' he replied. 'I'll definitely call again very soon and then we'll have more time to talk.'

When William had left, Carrie took the book from the drawer and sat down in her favourite armchair to look at it. It was tattered and stained and the writing was very cramped, but she was able to make out the words. Many times that evening she sat back and pored over her brother's innermost thoughts. One piece of writing had caught her eye.

Again the dream. Dark waters, full moon. When will it leave me? Not until the whole family sleeps. Sleep well, my love. You were too close. I chose to go in ignorance and to their comfort. We chose the path. Dark waters and another land. The knowledge gained is sent. In tiny pieces on the wind.

Carrie hugged the tiny book to her breast, tears filling her eyes. Those words would not have made any sense to Charlie's son, but they told her everything. Charlie shared the terrible secret that had sent Josephine to her chosen death. She had written him a suicide note, knowledge gained, and he feigned ignorance to protect the family – to their comfort, he had written. Charlie had torn the letter up and scattered it on the wind. He had found happiness with a wife and two children, but his words said what was still in his heart. He would never forget the tragedy of his first love until his dying day.

Joe walked into the room, his face set firm. 'I've just looked in on yer mum, Carrie. Yer'd better come up,' he said quietly.

The two stood looking down on the serene features of Nellie Tanner. 'I'm 'appy for 'er, Joe,' Carrie said. 'She got 'er dyin' wish.'

Epilogue

The church bells were silent no more, and as the peels rang out from St James's Church people thronged the streets. In the little backwater by the river, Maurice Salter set up a table and served beer and sandwiches to all his neighbours. Sadie Sullivan danced a jig with Maisie Dougall and Maudie Mycroft dared to dance with Ernest in full view of everybody. Dolly and Josiah held hands and Wallace clapped and giggled at the crazy antics. All the children were allowed to stay up late and people stood around together, their happiness overflowing. Danny and Billy hugged each other and Annie hugged Iris. Carrie and Joe stood holding hands like young lovers, while the Salter girls flirted outrageously. Daniel Sullivan sat at his front door chatting to Fred Dougall, and Bert Jolly asked Mrs Haggerty to give him the pleasure of the next dance. Tom Casey played his harmonica and Mrs Green shared a quart bottle of stout with her friend Mrs Watson.

Tony slipped his arm round his wife Rachel and nuzzled her ear. She smiled happily at him and rubbed a hand down her side as the baby kicked.

'Yer'd better sit down,' he said with concern.

'Sit down nuffink. I want ter dance,' she said firmly.

Neighbours from Bacon Street joined the Page Street folk and together they celebrated. Old animosities were forgotten, and the festivities became noisier as the night wore on. River tugs and freighters sounded their klaxons and fireworks traced patterns across the summer night sky. Public houses stayed open late and the supply of beer was all but exhausted. Children were carried to bed already asleep. Lovers planned, and old folk reminisced. At long last the war was over and in the early hours of the morning Maurice Salter was carried to bed in a state of total inebriation.

The euphoria lasted into the next few days as folk tired themselves out, slowly coming to terms and beginning to think about the future without the shadow of war hanging over them.

Rachel was sitting with Tony in their newly decorated house in Bacon Street and she looked ill at ease. 'I know it secures our future, but I just can't 'elp finkin', an' it worries me sick,' she said.

Tony tried to dispel her fears. 'It all depends 'ow yer look at it,' he replied. 'Money is just a means to an end. Some people try ter make it their god.'

Rachel was not convinced. 'I can't 'elp finkin' that money can be tainted.'

'The Galloway money, yer mean,' Tony said.

'Yeah, the Galloway money,' Rachel replied quickly. 'No one in the family died a natural death. It frightens me.'

'Well, I can't 'ave yer worried, not while yer carryin' our baby inside yer,' Tony said quietly.

'Yer mean yer gonna fink about it?' Rachel asked brightly.

'I'm gonna do more than that,' Tony said smiling fondly at her. 'Yer remember me tellin' yer what that old lady said ter me at the readin' o' the will? Well, I'm gonna go an' see 'er.'

'When?'

'First fing termorrer.'

Rachel stood up and held out her arms to him. 'Tony, I'm so pleased,' she said as he went to her and held her close.

The day was warm and sunny as the two young people walked hand in hand into the church home for the elderly in Camberwell and were shown into a small office. The sister in charge came into the room and smiled briefly as she sat down at her desk.

'You asked to see a Mrs Nora Flynne?' she asked.

'Yes, that's right,' Tony replied.

The sister folded her hands on the desk top and leaned forward in her chair. 'Mrs Flynne died two years ago this September,' she said quietly.

Tony and Rachel exchanged glances and the young man frowned as he looked at the sister. 'I'm sorry. I wish I'd 'ad the opportunity o' seein' Mrs Flynne earlier but I was in the services,' he said.

The sister smiled kindly. 'Yes, I know. Mrs Flynne half expected you to come and see her before she died but the war was on. She understood. In fact she left you something.'

'Left me somefing?' Tony repeated.

'Yes, she left you a letter,' the sister told him. 'Nora Flynne asked me to keep this letter in a safe place and give it to you should you call here after her death. If after five years you had not called, then I was instructed to destroy it. One thing I can assure you, though. Mrs Flynne was in sound mind when she died. I know the content of this letter because the lady dictated it to me. I typed it and sealed it in her presence after she had checked it through.'

Tony and Rachel glanced at each other with puzzled looks as the sister reached down into a drawer and took out a large white envelope.

'I can make a room available to you if you would care to read it here,' she said smiling.

'That would be very nice, thank you,' Tony replied.